Little Wolf and the Witch

Published by Winterbourne Publishing, Western Australia.

ISBN: 978-1-7637115-3-2 (ebook) / 978-1-7637115-4-9 (print)

Little Wolf and the Witch

Wendy Palmer

Winterbourne
Publishing

THE SEASON HAD TURNED. NORTHWARDS, THE telltale smoke trails of the Vaer raiding camp's fires were rising into the bright afternoon, grey smudges against the high blue.

Feilan turned from contemplating this to contemplate his other problem, closer to hand.

Two people were crossing the north field, eschewing the roads, of which there were plenty to choose from, since the Siftar trading post was positioned, sensibly enough, at a crossroads convenient to both the dense settlements of the Riverlands and the safe routes elsewhere.

One of the travellers was either very petite or a child, the other of adult dimensions. They were swathed in heavy woollen cloaks though the afternoon was hardly chilly, and struggling with the uneven divots of the field, which Feilan supposed indicated shoes not fit for trekking in and feet not used to the vagaries of grazed pasture.

They could only be avoiding the roads because they were concerned either about being robbed, which meant they were carrying valuables, or about pursuit on horseback, which perhaps meant they *were* valuable, though not so valuable they'd effected their hypothetical escape with horses of their own.

That was none of the business of anyone in Siftar. But their trajectory was taking them due north, between the river and the northeastern road. The river, one of the larger waterways in an area justifiably called the Riverlands, would guide them all the way to the north coast over the course of a long few days' walk.

But they wouldn't get that far, because, if they did not divert, they'd run into the raiders' camp.

Freyja had been severe when the bear-warriors had sailed upriver to make that camp seven summers ago: they were welcome to their staging post and she'd happily provision them, if supplied with appropriate amounts of coin, silver or goods. However, they were not to overwinter, no matter how common that practice was becoming along the northern and eastern coasts, and they were absolutely not to touch a single Riverlands town. She hadn't spent years building her prosperous northwestern trading base to have her countrymen front up and destroy every skerrick of hard-won trust by raiding locally.

The hersir grumbled, but the provisions she could deny his men on a whim could not be risked, and, more to the point, Freyja Anjasdottir was not to be crossed, not by breaking their pledge and definitely never by trying to raid *her*.

But if two Riverlanders wandered into reach of this season's newly arrived raiders, their mettle already up in anticipation of blood-and-flame service to the bear-god, their legitimate targets still far south along the river... Their self-control could not be relied upon.

Feilan turned to Gytha, the sentry on duty at the overlander gate, who'd fetched him when she'd spotted the travellers and correctly anticipated the problem. 'We better bring them in. Send me some men and then go warn Freyja.'

The strangers saw the Siftar men coming at them, and at least didn't try to run: it was too open here by the crossroads for any such attempt. The taller one stepped in front of the shorter one. They were both short, when surrounded by men of Vaeringa, the icy heartland of a raiding people. Well-dressed in dyed linen breeches, their good leather shoes and lower legs splattered by the dirt of the field, and traces of mud. They'd come by the river, then, though that didn't mean they'd crossed it. They might merely have kept low along its banks to avoid roads and inquisitive eyes.

Feilan signalled for his people to keep a fair distance, and came closer himself.

'Heilsa,' he said, choosing to be friendly with his advantage. He was Freyja's left hand, her information-gatherer – her spymaster, to some people's more suspicious minds. It had made him a certain flavour of personable.

He went on in Riverlander, the local language. 'What brings you by, travellers?'

The taller of the pair was a man somewhat younger than Feilan, but not a youth. He was clean-shaven, as was the Riverlands custom, and had his hair covered with a stone-grey knitted cowl, like a southern maiden. He was dark-eyed, and slender, and elegant, a man who might have been a skaldr, a poet or storyteller, back in the heartland, for he was too scrawny for raiding.

He raised a stubborn chin to meet Feilan's curious gaze without flinching, which put him already on the admirable, or foolish, end of bold. Feilan was not only built to the general mould, if not quite the same scale, of a proper Vaer warrior, but he also bore his grandmother's witchy eyes, the pale blue-green of polished jasper. He'd not met many who could meet those eerie eyes and not at least blink.

With disarming directness, the stranger demanded, 'Are we being taken hostage?'

Feilan raised his brows. 'This is Siftar. We're a trading post.' That local name was a mangling of the Vaer name of Sif-Torg, Cursed Market.

'You're barbarians.'

Feilan's eyebrows inched higher. He was well used to prejudice, aimed either at his own self or, less acutely personal, the entirety of his people. That was not to say Vaeringans didn't earn a goodly dose of it. The grey smoke from the campfires was scenting the air northwards. The black smoke from their raids would soon be polluting the air southwards, though not as thickly as in years gone by.

It was just that people both outnumbered and outweighed by armed Vaer did not usually have the front to call them barbarians to their faces.

The other, shorter, traveller was a youth somewhere in the nebulous age between childhood and adolescence. Despite the breeches and simple tunic and cap, Feilan came down on the side of girl, mostly because he could see the inky plait rolled and clipped with silver at her nape, almost hidden under the folds of her cloak. She had similar eyes to the man, though their hue was more brown and warm than black and snapping. She stared at Feilan, mien clear and sweet, wearing the slightest of smiles.

He managed to stay pleasant, for the sake of the child and that tremulous smile. 'We're traders, friend. Come on in and have a little chat with the boss.'

'If we're not captives—'

This one didn't know when to shut his mouth. That was enough like Feilan's own permanent flaw that he discovered another half-ell of patience. 'You're not our captives, but you're not free to continue on your current path.'

'Then we're captives,' the Riverlander said obstinately.

Feilan gave up. 'Then you're captives,' he agreed. 'Step this way. Freyja Anjasdottir will want a word.'

Upon the news he'd made himself and his young companion into prisoners instead of guests, the man raised his hand, causing Feilan's silent guard contingent to shift their weight in unison. But he was merely running fingers along the edge of his cowl, elegant face pensive, not trying for a weapon. He might not even be armed, under the thick cloak.

A lot of wool had gone into that cloak, both cloaks, Feilan the trader adjudged as he escorted the pair in. Not as much as went in to the striped sails of the clinkers, the Vaer river boats, but they were of a quality that puzzled him. Why were two people of quality wandering these fields on foot?

Through the overlander gate, escort dismissed back to their usual duties, the strangers looked around, the girl with innocent interest, the man ready to be scornful, if his haughty expression was any indication. Feilan revised his assessment – not a skaldr, though the most successful of those had a good dose of arrogance. This man had the taste of the pampered scion of a rich or powerful man, all privilege, no responsibilities.

Siftar was laid out on Vaer lines. He and Freyja had spent twelve years travelling all the lands of Enea, from the little duchies of the Jodian Sea down to the isolationist caliphates spread along the southern coast, and seen all manner of architectural styles. But when Freyja had decided it was time to finally settle, when she had only a few summers on Feilan's age now, it had turned out that the most important thing, aside from time and money, was knowledge. They knew how to build longhouses, so they'd built longhouses, though they'd used thatch for the roofs instead of turf.

Four longhouses formed the central axis. The meeting hall was by the main gate to the river. The warehouse lay to the rear, chickens scratching in the dirt nearby. These days, Freyja was more the facilitator and protector of an immense trade network than an actual trader, but she reserved the right to the bounty the Vaer brought along with their summer raiding. They arrived with ivory and amber and soapstone, furs and wool, as well as more goods from their wide-flung trade routes, beads and gemstones of every colour, rich damasks and silks, glass and ceramics, spices and wines, and metal coins, and they departed having traded Freyja southern plunder, jewels and gold, all for their preferred silver, bearing her mark. Every last scrap of that wealth filtered via the warehouse.

Twin longhouses mirrored each other across the open yard in the centre, one accommodation for the travelling merchants who arrived by river and road at all times of the year, the other the barracks for the hired guards who protected Siftar's walls and accompanied the merchant trains bearing Freyja's colours and her golden reputation. The stables lay beyond.

A toddler, sturdy legs moving fast, dashed across the yard, scattering chickens in noisy protest. One of the older children, designated child-minder, ran after her, calling her name.

Feilan picked up the little one as she tried to dodge past. The kid instantly set up a wail right in his ear. The stranger flashed a look that implied he might be thinking of trying to wrest her from his arms and Feilan felt his brows go up again. The older child arrived then, red-faced and cross, and delivered a stinging slap across the girl's bare leg.

'None of that,' Feilan said mildly, hoisting the screaming child over to his other hip to protect her from both potential assailants.

'Feilan, she ran away!' The boy, himself only six or so, stamped his foot. 'She won't listen and she keeps running off!'

'Hitting her won't make that any better.' Feilan dropped his free hand, and the boy took it, bottom lip pouted out. Feilan's father would have backhanded him for that sort of sulky look, but Freyja ran a different camp, simultaneously gentler but with paradoxically higher expectations for managing one's own behaviour. 'Let's get her settled back with the others.'

He walked off, bouncing the little girl until her wounded sobs turned to hiccups, and then to smiles. The visitors perforce trailed him. He could feel the man's eyes boring a hole in the back of his head as he went, and indulged himself with a smirk. He supposed he was currently being judged not only for being a barbarian, but for being weak as well, coddling the warring pair instead of dealing out a few clips around the ear and sending them running to their mother.

He wasn't either child's father, actually, and had only the smallest inkling of their names, but Siftar had the same village approach to child-rearing as the heartland did, if not so intent on policing the slightest deviance from strict norms, and far less of leaving the work to the women.

He took the children back around to the rest of the young ones, some still about their chores, taking scraps to the chickens or pigs, carting water and hay for the horses, digging over the vegetable beds, carefully stacking cords of wood, scraping hides and grinding grain, those minor tasks small hands could manage with each other to help. Others were already done with their fair share and played nearby, tossing a roughly stuffed cloth ball back and forth or gathered about some serious doll business.

Setting his giggling bundle down, Feilan squatted to talk to the combatants at their level. Only once both children were mollified and an agreement of sorts negotiated did he rise, dusting off his palms, and nod to the strangers to follow him towards the river gate.

Directly by the gate sat the largest of the longhouses, the meeting hall. It was the most impressive structure in the trading post, and even then, it was small for a magnate's hall, its clay-daubed planks smooth and grey with age, except the fresher patches where they'd made repairs over winter. It had been the first one they'd built, he and Freyja and their small collection of other Cursed, when they'd decided to make a permanent home here.

Freyja kept talking of replacing it with stone, the local yellow-hued riverstone, to blend in better with the wealthier homes among the closest settlements. They hadn't done it yet.

Feilan touched the carving on the lintel, heartlander protection runes, the lines of the sigil softened, blurred, since he'd etched them thirteen years ago. Soon, in just a few more summers, he would have spent longer in this one place than he had the village of his birth.

The hall was warm, though summer had not yet begun to bite. When they'd crisscrossed the breadth of Enea, establishing Freyja's reputation and trade networks, the summer heat in the southern caliphates had made a brutal contrast to their far northern homeland across the Vithisa Sea. Their Riverlands trading post was a compromise in more ways than one.

Freyja's domain was kept from stuffiness and murk by ventilation holes and reed-wicked oil-lamps. It was richly decorated with tapestries on the walls and rugs on the packed-dirt floor, regularly removed to have the ash beaten from them. By the door, Feilan had their problem guests hang up their cloaks and headwear. The girl doffed her cap without demur, but the man seemed strangely reluctant to remove his cowl. Only when Feilan made it clear it was a gesture of respect to the boss did he deign to slip it off, revealing shoulder-length hair, longer than Feilan kept his own, loose and gleaming true red in the sunshine falling through the open door, as dark and bright as pure prized carnelian.

He paused as if expecting a compliment, or at least a comment. When it was not forthcoming – though Feilan was instantly enthralled by the unusual shade and had to work to keep it from his face – he hung the cowl on the hook by the girl's cap. They followed Feilan down the central aisle, delineated by the two rows of carved wooden columns, to where Freyja waited for them on the far side of the unlit firepit, attended mostly by Siftar women industriously working distaffs, the scent of the wool grease a warm grey haze over their heads. A few guards stood attentively by.

Freyja was dressed plainly but well, in a rich overgown mimicking the traditional smock, dyed deep blue over a paler underdress. Her honey-blonde hair was tidied into twin braids, left lying over her shoulders since she did not consider herself a married woman. Her manner was lordly, her bearing regal. She did not quite sit a throne, but her high-backed chair was large and ornately carved, with broad arms for her to rest her own bare arms on, showing off armlets, bracelets and rings, and with legs tall enough that the bench set before it perforce seated visitors lower than her.

Feilan waved the guests down on to the bench; he took up position between it and Freyja's seat, hands loosely clasped behind his back. The girl sat, with an odd little flick at her breeches that Feilan recognised meant she was more used to skirts, likely the kirtle bodice and skirt arrangement popular locally. The man hesitated, then made the deep bow accorded to Riverlander elders. Fair: Feilan was contentedly strolling into his forty-second summer, which meant Freyja was grazing her sixtieth despite only a few threads of silver in her hair, and she didn't just sit like a queen, she bore the expensive garments and jewels befitting one; she lacked only a circlet of gold.

The man sat very neatly, set his hands on his knees, and looked expectantly at Freyja. The bench at this time of day was illuminated by a shaft of light from an overhead smoke hole, and the thin sunshine set off amber glints in the carnelian.

Standing loosely to attention, Feilan was increasingly fascinated. The locals here and southwards tended to be wide variations on dark-haired, like the girl. His own people came from the land of the pale-haired, ranging from near-white to the poet-blessed golden colour of ripened wheat, to a darker sandy colour like his own hair and short beard. There were some with a tinge of copper, usually a sign of western heritage, but he'd not ever seen anything quite like this carnelian shade.

'Rufran,' he said to himself, which meant Little Fox, but which could have a decidedly less innocent interpretation, something along the lines of Foxy.

Freyja quelled him with a glance, and he shut his mouth, suitably chastened. She then presented the older of the pair with an imperious look; really, the woman needed a literal crown to accompany her metaphorical one. 'Well?'

Either unaware of Feilan's interest and Freyja's dismissal of it, or valiantly ignoring it, the man said, 'My name is Renart Nivardus. This is Adeline.' He paused, but neither Vaer said anything, so he continued, 'You may be aware that King Geroald of Seven Hills recently died.'

'We are,' Freyja said, and they were, because keeping abreast of developments that might impact the trade networks was Feilan's job, and he was good at it.

The whole of the Riverlands was rife with little realms governed by little rulers, of which Seven Hills was a particularly minor example. While it wasn't unusual for the multitudinous lands of Enea to bear litters of kings in snapping distance of each other, Riverlands allegiances were woven together not by the perceived strength of the powerful man, or occasionally woman, on the throne and the depth of his or her purse, but by close-knit bonds of kinship and intermarriage. It made for a tapestry of the finest of weaves, tight and strong, and thus a peaceful and stable region.

That stability of allegiances was both a boon to Siftar, and a difficulty, which was why the change of power at Seven Hills was of particular interest. King Geroald had steadfastly refused to allow passage for Freyja's traders. Inconsequential little kingdom it may have been, but Seven Hills bottlenecked them from myriad little kingdoms beyond.

'Adeline is his daughter. His only child.'

Freyja and Feilan looked at the girl. She offered a dip of her chin in acknowledgement, more rueful than regal.

'You...' Freyja paused, giving a flick of a look towards Feilan: was she addressing a princess, then?

Feilan murmured in rapid Vaer, 'They let women rule, but she wouldn't necessarily inherit as a matter of course. Looks like a leadership dispute, if she's out here with such a paltry escort.'

Freyja grimaced. She liked to take advantage of local politics; she did not like to get involved in them.

'The heir, yes,' Nivardus said, glancing uncertainly between the two of them. He was following something of the Vaer, then; many Riverlanders did have some grasp of it, given how long Vaeringans had been visiting the region, peaceably or otherwise. 'But her age, it's a problem.'

'Who are you to her?' Freyja asked. 'Brother?'

'Uncle,' he said. 'I am, I *was* King Geroald's youngest brother.' He added hastily, 'I'm not in line to inherit.'

'You are,' the girl piped up. '*Everyone* is. That's the problem.'

Nivardus held up his hand as if they'd tried to interrupt. 'I will try to explain. Please tell me if I go too fast.'

'Can't expect us barbarians to keep up,' Feilan muttered, and got another dark look from Freyja.

Nivardus once again chose to ignore the byplay. 'If Adeline were a grown woman, the inheritance would be clear. If she were a boy, an inheritance under guardianship until the age of majority would be clear. But she is a girl.'

Freyja looked to Feilan, but his knowledge of Riverlands customs failed him. 'This matters because…?'

'Her guardian may marry her.' He saw the looks on their faces, amid the murmur of surprise among the attendants. 'To someone of his choosing, I mean. Who will then be king.'

Freyja addressed the girl. 'How old are you, then? Older than you look.'

'I've twelve winters,' Adeline said, and Feilan felt the ripple of shock as everyone recoiled; she was not at all older than she looked.

Freyja said, diplomatically, 'Child-brides are not something our people engage in.'

'And they call *us* barbarians,' Feilan said, less diplomatically.

'You barbarians take children for slaves,' Nivardus snapped.

'At least we don't rape them and call it marriage.'

'What do you think happens to slaves, you ignorant—'

'Stop,' Freyja said, softly but with a crisp snap that quietened both men instantly. 'Be aware we are traders of mid-Vaeringa, our people have not taken slaves for over one hundred years, and I do *not* appreciate the implication.'

Nivardus managed to wrestle his expression from a scowl into something approaching contrition. 'I apologise,' he said stiffly. 'I meant only— Never mind. Just to know that the inheritance is being questioned because there is some concern among our allies that Adeline's guardian will marry her off to his own advantage, making his position too strong for their liking.'

'You could pledge not to, surely,' Feilan pointed out.

'I am not her guardian,' Nivardus said with flat dislike and the cadence of explaining something to a particularly dense child. 'She would not be at risk if I were.'

'You think the possibility of such a marriage is high, then?' Freyja said, since Feilan was too busy indulging in a minor seethe to fill in the gap for her.

'Very much so. And remains so, because of the proposed solution.' He paused, but neither spoke. He nodded. 'You have not heard this yet, I see.' Before Freyja could give Feilan a stern look, he said, 'It is not a failure of your intelligence network, as limited as that may be—'

'Ooh, you whining little shit,' Feilan said under his breath. Freyja's eyes gleamed in amusement at his expense.

'—as this was only decided last night. There is to be a contest, open to all acknowledged claimants – anyone in the bloodline who desires to partake.'

'A feat of arms? The current guardian's champion against the contenders'?' Freyja asked.

'A monster hunt. King Geroald was killed by a monster that stalks our lands. He who wins its head wins a regency. Perhaps hand in marriage, too. Mostly, though, a regency, to overrule the guardianship.'

Feilan was still back at the beginning of this explanation. 'The king was killed by a monster,' he repeated.

'As I said.'

'A bear,' Feilan said.

'A monster.'

'Did you see it?' Feilan said. 'Because in the mist, among trees—'

'I saw the wounds on the body.' Nivardus spoke very coldly, eyeing Feilan with overt hostility, but his voice trembled.

Feilan opened his mouth to point out that a mauling death, no matter how gruesome the injuries, was more readily attributable to the crushing bites and gashing claw marks of a wild and angry bear than to a mythical monster, too rare in this age to be probable. At the slight downturn of the little girl's mouth, he remembered he was speaking to the dead man's brother, in front of the dead man's daughter. He desisted. It was almost certainly a bear, perhaps even an old and wily boar, but he did not press further.

Freyja, at least, was managing to follow the salient point. 'You hope to take part?'

She managed to not give Nivardus and his slender, if not scrawny, limbs an insulting once-over, but Feilan didn't. Nivardus caught it, and glared at him. 'We may compete by proxy. A contender may enter a champion pledged to them by mercenary or marriage contract. We are here to hire champions.'

'Champions?' Feilan repeated, heavy on the plural. 'Both of you?'

'Yes. If Adeline's champion wins, she proves she has the blessing of our goddess and the mettle to rule in her own right, with advisers of her own choice.'

Here Adeline gave her uncle such a warm smile that Feilan had to draw the conclusion that Nivardus had managed to slide this provision across the table during whatever negotiations had occurred to come up with this archaic dispute settlement.

A quick glance Freyja's way told him her opinion was in concordance with his: a win for Adeline was both an unlikely outcome, and unlikely to be honoured in full by whoever actually held the reins of power back in Seven Hills. But the weave of alliances holding Adeline's throne safe for her would at least allow her some leeway with this clever condition in place.

If Nivardus noted their doubt, he had enough sense to ignore it. 'If my champion wins, I assume the regency, and can keep her safe till she is of age. We double our chances if we both submit champions to the hunt.'

'And you planned to obtain your champions from the bersverdar camp?' Feilan didn't hide his opinion of the stupidity of that course of action; he even used the Vaer word to underscore it.

'If I've not been clear, we require the win,' Nivardus said, also not hiding *his* opinion of Feilan's stupidity. 'A Vaer warrior is our only hope of that.'

'Your niece would have been safe enough, but you would have been fair game,' Feilan told him bluntly. 'Thank your lucky stars we intercepted you.'

'We go with good silver to make a fair deal!'

'That works here,' Freyja told him, more gently than he deserved. 'Not among the raiders. They would simply take your silver and then demand ransom from your people as well.'

'If they're thinking ahead,' Feilan said. 'If not, they'd've just murdered you for the fun of it, right in front of your niece.'

The girl flinched. Freyja gave a single nod, mouth set in a grim line. 'You've forgotten what our countrymen are like.'

'Believe me, I have not,' Nivardus said, looking daggers at Feilan, who held up his palms in mock innocence, though it was also actual innocence, because he had no notion what he'd done to earn it, aside from childishly matching the obnoxious tone of their obnoxious guest.

He raised his brows at Freyja with some amusement. She sighed.

'Stay here tonight,' she said. 'We will step in to broker the deal tomorrow. I hope you have a great deal of silver, however. Vaer warriors are not, generally, sellswords. They're here for plunder, not to hang about inheritance disputes.'

Instead of showing an appropriate level of gratitude for the unprecedented favour of Freyja Anjasdottir offering to interfere in local politics, Nivardus said, 'Can it not be today?'

'They won't come today. They only just came in from the sea, they're still making camp.'

'It doesn't have to be from the raiding camp,' Nivardus said, a touch desperately. 'Perhaps two of your sentries will take a contract?'

'My men are contracted already, to me,' Freyja said in her driest tones. 'I don't reward disloyalty.'

Nivardus grimaced. The desire for haste, together with the troublesome but hidden route over the fields, on foot, told Feilan something. 'The princess's actual guardian doesn't know you're doing this.'

He knew he was right when Nivardus shot him a filthy look. 'He does not wish her to enter her own champion,' he reluctantly admitted.

'And Great-Uncle Bertrand wants Uncle Remy to also not have his own champion,' Adeline said. 'I think he doesn't realise Remy would die if he entered the monster hunt himself.'

'I wouldn't die, Lina,' Nivardus told her crossly. 'But I wouldn't win the head for you, either.'

'You would *die*,' his niece said.

'Thank you.'

'Welcome.' She smiled cheekily.

Despite himself, Feilan's heart panged for this very young girl who'd just lost her father and was now attempting to avoid both her legal guardian and her own marriage with only her ineffectual uncle for help.

Freyja hid her own smile. 'The bear-warriors will be visiting tomorrow for their provisions. We can try for your contract then.'

'You just have to hope your guardian assumes approaching bersverdar for a contract is far too jolterheaded a move, and searches for you elsewhere in the meantime,' Feilan added.

He smirked to Nivardus's scowl; he felt he'd scored a point there. He got another severe look from Freyja. She was being remarkably protective of their visitors. He rather thought she liked the girl, who was quiet and serious, and then teased her uncle with that cheeky grin.

It made the pretty, obnoxious, uncle slightly more palatable, too. Uncle Remy, indeed.

'I should warn you,' Freyja said, which only strengthened Feilan's supposition that she'd warmed to their guests, or to one of them, 'the bear-warriors are here in service to their god, and for their own glory and enrichment. They will likely be highly reluctant to turn from taking the river-road south. You will need to offer plentiful silver to even tempt them.'

'We have silver and gold,' Nivardus said, absently reaching under his tunic, presumably to pat a fat purse tied at his belt.

Freyja looked at him through half-lidded eyes, but said no more. Feilan knew she greatly doubted the man truly understood how much he would have to offer to secure the twin mercenary contracts he desired.

'We shall feast,' she said instead, with a nod to Feilan.

He went off to arrange that. It was one of the oldest customs of the heartland, displaying wealth through the copious provision of food and ale, especially ale, and one of the few customs Freyja hadn't shaken off. It wasn't a bad tactic, all round, for securing good trade connections.

He did wonder why she'd bother, for such minor royal figures who likely wouldn't have any political influence going forwards.

2

THE GUESTS STAYED OUT OF THE way on one of the benches lining the meeting hall until evening fell and the fire was lit in the pit. The tables were brought down from the lofts and laden with platters of sliced roasted pork and parsnips on beds of sharp bitter greens, grilled river fish, white cheese drizzled with honey, and bowls brimming with berries and the last of the winter nuts. The lull before summer harvest could be lean, but not in the wealthy, fertile Riverlands. The rich scents of the food left a haze of mingling colours at the edges of Feilan's vision, not quite strong enough to be annoying, soon fading away.

Freyja had bid not just ale but mead and fruit wine served, copiously. By about halfway through the small feast, the Siftar residents were merry enough that when Gytha tripped and dumped a brimming jug of ale over Feilan, the drenching was greeted with uproarious laughter and friendly jibes aimed at both of them.

Feilan shook his head to clear his vision of the hazy amber washing across it, set off by the strong smell of his ale bath. Gytha had covered her face in mortified amusement, and he gave her a friendly nudge and a sly, 'Did you want my clothes off for any *particular* reason?'

She scoffed and swatted him, retrieving the jug.

His soaked tunic was clammily sticking to his skin, and he pinched it away with some minor fastidiousness. He was promptly waylaid by a couple of women eager to help him peel it off so they could ostentatiously whistle at his bared chest, which was blatant teasing: he helped enough with Siftar's physical work that he still sported solid muscle across shoulders and chest and thighs, but he was softer in the belly these days. There were plenty of bare-chested younger men about to admire, not to mention the anticipation of the incoming bersverdar, *real*

Vaer men. But, given he was generally good-humoured yet uninterested, the women enjoyed pretending to swoon over him to tease.

He played along, obligingly preening and flexing. Wiping his hair and beard off with the dryish back of the tunic and tossing it aside, he caught Nivardus staring at him. His cheerful smile dimmed. Adeline was laughing at the raucous antics, but her uncle, arm protectively about her shoulders, looked – not contemptuous, exactly, but certainly unimpressed, eyeing Feilan's bared form as if appalled by the indiscretion at the feasting table.

High spirits slightly dashed, Feilan turned back to his plate and his cup of ale, refilled with showy care by Gytha.

It wasn't long after Adeline had finished her own plate that she began to droop. 'Uncle Remy,' she said sleepily, leaning against her uncle. The corners of her mouth turned down. 'I want to go home.'

She wasn't a composed young woman vying for her own crown anymore. She was a little girl, far from her own bed, and possibly trying not to give way to overtired weeping.

Nivardus gently stroked her dark hair as her head came to rest on his shoulder. 'I know, sweetheart. We will, as soon as we can. Safe and sound. Ready to win you your crown.'

'Promise?'

Nivardus frowned. He looked around the table, accidentally meeting Feilan's eyes as he shamelessly eavesdropped, sipping his ale. Uncle Remy didn't want to make a promise he wasn't entirely sure he could keep, it seemed.

But he said, heavily, 'Yes. Promise,' and looked over at Feilan again.

His strikingly dark eyes were ink-black in the dim light of the hall, and Feilan felt a frisson down his spine. He was almost glad to break eye contact when Freyja leaned over to direct Nivardus to where he could put his half-asleep niece to bed, pointing him to the spare sleeping niche beside her own.

That surprised Feilan, a little, but then, he had already suspected Freyja liked the girl. She wanted to keep an eye on her. Doting Uncle Remy, presumably, would bed down on the floor beside his niece's bench, wrapped in his thick cloak.

Feilan thus didn't expect him to return once he'd settled his niece, but he did, without the cloak – he must have given it to Adeline, extra padding for a princess habituated to soft beds and layers and layers of linens.

He took a seat by Feilan, and accepted another cup of ale. By now, Feilan's fascination with the carnelian hair and those dark, sharp eyes outweighed his awareness that neither of them liked the other.

'Why are you staring at me?' Nivardus asked, on the very edge of leaning into Feilan's personal space and demanding it.

He was drunk, or at least not sober. Vaer ale was stronger than the local brews, though from the face Nivardus had pulled when he'd first sipped it, it didn't taste as good to local tongues. And he'd tried both mead and wine before circling back to the ale, too. Definitely not sober. Still a bit of an arse.

But that pretty hair was probably long enough to wrap around Feilan's hand a turn or two.

Feilan lowered his cup. He'd grown up marinated in the disdain of his countrymen, and lived all his adult life as the dishonourable nothing that was a Cursed, sifr, known to willingly take the woman's part during the only kind of fucking considered obscene, so much so it was a profanity – serth and all its variants – in their language. He'd wrestled with shame and bigotry, and grown, perforce, a thick skin. He could even, without so much as a blush at the hypocrisy, insult other men by calling them serthar.

He shrugged and said it. 'Here's the thing, Uncle Remy. I'm wondering if you ever fuck men.'

Riverlanders were a good deal more relaxed about buggery than the Vaer were; it was part of the reason Freyja had settled here, having collected both a wide network of trading connections and a goodly number of loyal Cursed. He still readied himself to hear revulsion in response.

'I...don't,' Nivardus said, without any particular distaste, or rather, with a rather nuanced tone that suggested any distaste came not from the notion of lying with a man, but of lying with a man he thought of as a barbarian.

Feilan shrugged again and turned to refill his cup. It was no loss to him. He had several casual bedmates in the trading post – one of them, Meik, was lingering nearby even now, waiting to see if he'd be looking for solace – and was anticipating the bersverdar's visit just as much as half of Siftar.

'I...might,' Nivardus said, and Feilan glanced back with renewed interest.

The man looked at him, head on one side, gaze travelling over his bare shoulders and chest and stomach and arms, a slow evaluation that made that little shiver go down his spine again.

'For Njorda's sake, don't leave me in suspense, Rufran,' he said.

'That's not my name.'

Laughing at the querulous tone, Feilan hooked a friendly arm around his slender shoulders, making it heavy, letting him feel the press of the muscles he'd been appraising.

'It means Little Fox,' he said. 'Like Feilan means Little Wolf. That's all.'

'I don't prefer men, as a rule.' Again, he eyed Feilan off in that unintentionally provocative way, now close enough, ensconced under Feilan's arm, that he felt his ale-touched breath on his lips. 'But...'

'But you're going to make an exception.' Feilan was no longer surprised by how many men did.

'I need another drink, first,' Nivardus mumbled.

But he had three more drinks, fast, to Feilan's one, and by the time Feilan got his arm around his shoulders again to take him to bed, he was wobbly on his feet. Feilan took a soapstone light-pot and lit its waxed rush wick from a glowing coal on the edge of the firepit, then guided Nivardus out into the night air, exchanging a rueful smile with the disappointed Meik as he left.

The stars overhead swathed the velvet sky, and the moon was just past the glare – full, to Riverlanders. Nivardus curled in close to his side as they walked. Under the ale on his breath, he smelled herbal, almost perfumed, a whiff of scent that gave Feilan a lightning flash of green as bright and new as spring grass. He turned his face up to Feilan as if for a kiss, but if he didn't usually countenance men, he wouldn't want kissing, not on the mouth. Feilan didn't want to misconstrue an invitation, especially if it lost him the invitation he did have. He already had doubts on that front, if he was going to be scrupulous about it.

Vaeringans traditionally lived in large extended family groups, all within the same longhouse; Freyja was set enough in the old ways to have kept to her curtained-off niche within the meeting hall. But they did have private quarters, too, since Siftar wasn't entirely Vaer. Besides, Feilan and some of his fellows had travelled foreign lands long enough to appreciate separate living spaces and some modicum of privacy.

The simple huts ran in a row between the warehouse and the overlander gate, the bathing pond beyond and the garden plots and latrine trench opposite. They were simple one-room structures, wattle and daub, thatched like the longhouses, with a hide to block the doorway.

Their interiors were dark, hence the little oil-filled pot of light Feilan carried with him, though some had square windows cut, their hide curtains pulled aside to let in air or light. In mild weather, small iron braziers adequately heated them, and the residents simply relocated to the warmth of the longhouses in the bitterest of the long nights. Tonight was temperate enough, though the morning would be cold.

Inside was bare, his furniture only his heavy wooden trunk and a bench along the back wall, both carved with runes and iconography. He had thick layers of fur for his sleeping mat, a spare cloak on a hook, and a few personal belongings atop the trunk, a comb carved from an antler for his hair and beard, a whetted steel knife with a handle of bone, copper nailbinders of varying thicknesses, a scatter of glass beads, a clay ewer of water, a rounded cup of smoothed shaped leather, a copper bowl. He spent most of his time outside, and only came here to sleep, and even then not always.

Feilan set the light-pot on his trunk. In its low glow, Nivardus was heavy-lidded, swaying. Feilan smiled and touched his face, feeling the rasp of incipient stubble under the rub of his thumb. He didn't often meet men who went to the trouble of keeping their cheeks clean of hair, though he was aware Riverlanders preferred it. His own people found it unmanly, which had made him scrape his cheeks out of spite until he matured beyond allowing shadows from his past to dictate his behaviour in any way whatsoever.

The last truly beardless man he'd met had been a eunuch of the caliphates, an Incised, caught up in a raid by Vaer slavers – not Feilan's people, as Freyja had been at pains to tell their guests – traded east, castrated, and sold south. He'd been the majordomo for a wealthy southern merchant household, icy with affront at the idea of linking trade networks. Some prejudices were too lodged in personal history to be argued with, and Feilan hadn't tried.

Nivardus had his own prejudice towards the Vaer, but it appeared more generalised, the same suspicion that saw Feilan and Freyja escorted under guard into towns during their first years of trading, before Freyja's name became a golden promise of exotic goods and scrupulously fair dealing.

It wasn't deep-seated enough to stop him, anyway. Shifting restlessly, nudging against Feilan's solid body, he turned his face into the touch, so that Feilan's thumb brushed over his lips, which parted under the slight pressure.

'You want...' Nivardus said muzzily, lips tickling Feilan's skin. 'I suppose you want...' And then, almost to himself, 'It will take away the vile taste of the ale, at least.'

Feilan started laughing; he couldn't help it. Renart made a noise, half-complaint, half-moan, and pressed closer to him, trying, if Feilan was any judge, to keep his balance.

'Here,' he said. He hoisted the ewer, held the spout to the man's lips. 'Drink some water, you sotty jolterhead.'

Nivardus reached up a hand, but took hold, not of the ewer's handle, but Feilan's wrist, in a surprisingly strong grip, fingers wrapping tight. Sucking the short lip of the spout into his mouth, he turned Feilan's wrist to tip the jug enough that the water flowed into his mouth. Holding Feilan's eye, he swallowed heartily and with some facility. Feilan watched the muscles of his throat flex and felt a bolt of lust shoot through him.

Still. He'd never consider a bed partner who wasn't an active and willing participant, both aware of what they were doing and capable of enjoying it. So when Nivardus sank dazedly to the furs, he didn't follow him down despite the persistent drag on his wrist.

Nivardus mumbled something fretful and irritated, on the edge of incoherence and too soft to hear anyway, and Feilan wasn't surprised to see his eyes droop closed almost immediately, his grip finally loosening. He made one last mutter when Feilan rolled him onto his side and threw another fur over him so that only the flame-lick of his soft hair was visible.

Feilan strolled back to the meeting hall in the vague hope that Meik or some other regular bedfellow would be lingering, but found only Freyja, enjoying a cold herbal tea by the last embers of the firepit.

She handed him a cup. 'You tuck our princeling in?'

He grunted a confirmation. She didn't query further; aside from the brevity of his absence, she knew him too well to assume the worst of him. Though no longer a Vaer man, he'd been raised as one, and Vaer men had a strong taboo about that sort of thing. Forcing a woman was known to be unmanly: a real man never need stoop to it. Of course, Vaer men also tended to confuse fear with respect, silence with consent, and provocation with permission. Putting aside those rather large caveats, the absolute height of unmanliness would be to inflict oneself on someone too drunk or drugged to even wake up for it.

Feilan, Cursed, was the Vaer epitome of unmanly, but the taboo ran deep, even if he hadn't had a strong preference for activities both parties would enjoy.

'He's a pretty one,' Freyja commented, because, yes, she knew him too well.

'Only in the face,' he said. 'Plenty about who're pretty inside and out and don't call us barbarians in the same breath as demanding our help.'

'True enough.' She took a slow sip. 'Such good sense from my clever Little Wolf today. Will we see good sense tomorrow if and when Tryggvi Jansson comes strutting about?'

Feilan sniggered into his cup and said, 'Doubt it,' with enough charm in his smile that he earned a mere sigh instead of the censure he sorely deserved.

THE RIVER MIST WAS STILL LINGERING when the Vaer clinkers nudged up to the dock below the trading post, passing under the arched bridge that connected the eastern roads to two westerly paths.

If the low-riding boats hadn't been able to slide under that bridge, coming and going, the Vaer raiders would have destroyed it every summer.

Freyja must have sent a message over to her countrymen's camp, for the clinkers were full of not only the usual trading goods and the two reithar, foremen, who accompanied the load to tick off their provisions lists and attempt the haggle, but also a double-handful of bersverdar.

They swaggered up the beaten path to the river gate, leaving the Siftar traders to port the goods. Emptied, two of the clinkers put out downriver, the third holding at the dock to lade with provisions.

Freyja established the outpost right by the dock when they'd first settled here. It only took the first winter to realise the mistake. The locals could have warned them about the tendency for flood but Feilan couldn't really blame anyone for not spreading their arms wide to welcome in Vaeringans of any stripe in those days, not even Freyja Anjasdottir of the golden reputation.

There was no more than a tolftar, a dozen, of the bear-warriors, but that was already more than would truly be interested in taking a piddling Riverlands mercenary contract when the summer raiding season lay ahead. Most would merely be taking the opportunity for an innocuous, perfectly reasonable, perfectly explainable excuse to visit the Cursed trading post. More of them might have come along, if they didn't all know Freyja's feelings on too many bersverdar inside her palisade, even disarmed.

There weren't any women in the raiders' camp. Women couldn't be true bear-warriors, and barely even warrior-like, not without risking exile from the light of their homeland and the blessings of their gods – in a word, Cursed. Siftar, however, was full of Cursed women; some of them even had women's bodies. A few of the men had women's bodies too. Others of the men, like Feilan, had become Cursed for getting caught taking a woman's part.

Siftar also held a strong contingent of Vaer men and women who had never been Cursed, who could still live within their communities and be traders or warriors or farmers or fisherfolk or artisans, or village wives, and chose not to. Living among their Cursed compatriots was safer than the alternatives, given the generalised distaste for the northern barbarians, and Freyja paid fairly and on time.

It meant the congenial outpost was of perennial interest to the sex-starved men of the seasonal raiding camp. It wasn't even hypocritical. As long as the warriors could point to the shortage of women, had their perfectly reasonable excuse to visit Siftar, made sure to never do anything so unmanly as kiss, and always took the man's part, they were not at risk of getting cursed themselves. It was even, to a certain way of thinking, a moral choice: the Cursed couldn't be cursed again, after all.

It'd be a wild night tonight, after the completion of the trade exchange and the contract negotiations.

Torben was among the visiting bear-warriors, as Feilan had assumed, or hoped, or prayed to deaf gods, that he would be; his old friend had survived another raiding season, another overwinter back home.

His pulse picked up. The nice thing about Torben was that he knew Feilan would keep his mouth sewn shut even under the most extreme threat, and so, in private, he *would* kiss, though not on the mouth, and he *would* play more than the man's part, and he was only a little rougher than Feilan liked men to be.

Feilan knew better than to greet him, however. Given they'd grown up together in the same village, it was probably more of a clue to their periodic liaisons than a coldly formal salutation would have been, but there it was: by the skin of mere moments in a storehouse some twenty-five summers ago, he was a Cursed and Torben was a hero of the bear-god, and so they did not acknowledge each other.

He glimpsed Renart Nivardus fidgeting beside his niece, until the pair were lost in the crowd of residents who'd come out to greet the new arrivals and help unpack the goods. Nivardus wanted the negotiations done with, plainly, the contracts signed, before the mysterious true guardian, Great-Uncle Bertrand, showed up. But he couldn't divert Siftar's mercantile purpose. There was business to be conducted.

The bersverdar lounged in the sunshine, as befitted their status, while the reithar and Freyja's delegates opened up crates and bales and argued over the contents. Feilan wasn't overly involved in the true meat of Siftar, the fingering of cloth, the weighing of metals, the exaggerated exclaiming over exotic semi-precious stones from the east, the grit of the haggling. Freyja had better people than him for that.

He looked around to check on their uninvited guests. Adeline was peeking over the shoulders of the children around her age – they were grinding seeds, a light job they made a game of, but a job nonetheless, which the young princess, after a moment of careful observation and an exchange of a few words, joined in on.

Her Uncle Remy was twitchier, pacing to the river gate to peer out over the westerly ways, and back again, chewing on a nail and fiddling with the edge of his cowl. Feilan strolled over to the increasingly jittery River-lander, who glanced up at him, and immediately looked away, a flush staining his cheeks.

It occurred to Feilan that Renart might not remember what had happened the night before. Or perhaps, remembered only Feilan's teasing touch at the outset, and not the subsequent chaste tucking into the furs.

'You might as well try to relax,' he said bluntly. 'Nothing will happen this morning.'

'But—' He waved a hand to where the warriors were at an obvious loose end.

'Freyja's busy.' Even vaguely disliking Renart, he didn't wish upon him an attempt to make the contract without her severe oversight. 'It'll be this until well after highday.' He added, to Renart's blank look, 'Midday,' in a sop to local cadence.

Renart's concern had been in a different direction. 'That long? But aren't they almost done?'

'They've barely started. And right now, we're just buying. We'll be selling next.'

'Provisioning them for their raiding.'

There was a distinct note of disgust there, dislodging the previous dismay. Feilan shook his head and started to walk away.

'Can you not hurry them along?' Renart demanded. 'Didn't I perhaps...' His voice dropped. '...earn a small favour from you last night?'

Feilan snorted. 'No, Rufran, you did not. If you had, I promise you'd know about it today.'

That telltale flush spread over Renart's pale face. 'Did I not perform as you wished?'

'You were drunk.'

This did not appease the Riverlander. He snapped, 'I know,' sounding, if anything, even more indignant. 'That was the only way I was going to get through it.'

'Yeah, thanks,' Feilan said, with something of Freyja's famously dry tones. 'I enjoy it when men have to drink themselves into oblivion to stomach me.'

'That's not—' Renart swallowed. 'I meant because I was nervous. I did...want to. Try it.'

Feilan shrugged, hiding that he was charmed by this frank admission. 'Why are you so desperate to get this contract done before Adeline's guardian finds you, anyway? If she can't sign a contract without his say-so, then anything she signs today is void.'

Renart hissed irritably. 'This guardianship... If she weren't here, he could sign the contract on her behalf without even asking her opinion. Since *he's* not here, she can't sign it on her own behalf – unless she has the permission of an older male relative instead.'

'Ah. Uncle Remy.'

'Indeed.'

Feilan thought about again warning him how expensive hiring a bersverdr as a mercenary would be. The truth was that even if the guardian failed to find them before the contract negotiations began, they were unlikely to be carrying enough silver to tempt two Vaer away from the raiding. They'd have to have a chest of silver ingots for that, which they plainly were not carrying about their dual personages.

But prickly Renart Nivardus wasn't proving overly receptive to advice, and Feilan's mother had often told him he pushed too much, too proud of being the smartest one in any given hall. Insisting the supposed monster was a bear last night, cramming his opinion into the teeth of two grieving people, was a case in point.

Feilan tried to sow the seed instead. 'At least if he does show up, you can still make your own contract. You'll still have one champion acting in her favour.'

'I'd rather she win,' Renart said disarmingly. 'I want her to rule in her own right, not subject to any regent, even me.'

'An untrammelled twelve-year-old queen?' Feilan asked, notwithstanding he had his valid doubts that that would ever happen.

'With advisers.' Feilan must have still looked too sceptical. Renart
swept him with his black-eyed scowl. 'If she may marry at twelve, she
may rule at twelve.'

Feilan held up his palms placatingly. 'I don't doubt your little queen,
Uncle Remy.'

Renart folded his arms, turning to watch Adeline as she laughed with
the other children, cheerily wielding the pestle and mortar in time to the
staccato clap of their hands, accompanied by a singsong rhyme. The set
of his shoulders eased, and he smiled, which made him look quite a bit
more like his niece, and even prettier than he'd looked in the firelight last
night. Feilan wished he wouldn't wear the cowl; he wanted to see the
hair glinting in sunlight.

'It is good that she can spend some time being a child, however,'
Renart murmured.

Feilan cleared his throat, and when Renart looked at him cautiously,
said, 'Thank you, Feilan. I appreciate you not letting us walk into the
raider camp, Feilan.'

Renart's smile was still lingering, but it slipped in the face of Feilan's
pointed teasing. He said nothing, merely glared sullenly. Feilan's dislike
of the man was becoming distinctly less vague. He was still in enough
good humour to laugh at the display of ill-temper as he reprised his
shake of the head from his first attempt to walk away, and this time did
effect a retreat.

He collected the reports from his contacts across the heartland, etched
on runesticks and carried to Siftar by the reithar as one of the conditions
of trade, and spent the morning sorting through them at his small table
in the meeting hall, set in the corner behind Freya's rosewood chair, out
of the way of the usual daytime bustle in and out.

The news was old, gathered during the overwinter, but fresh to their
part of the world. Feilan made notes, and he and his two clerks spent
some concentration of time connecting the snippets to the wide-flung
news brought in by their merchants networked across Enea.

He'd put the work aside and was breaking bread with Gytha and Meik
some time after highday when Freyja entered and gave two sharp claps.
The effect was instant. The guards about the walls stood to attention.
Every unessential person in the hall, including Feilan's clerks and his
dining companions, rose to leave, the clerks abandoning their inkpots

and knives, Gytha swallowing her last mouthful of cheese and bread and hastily brushing her hands clean, Meik taking a last dark rye slice with him, dripping honey in his wake.

Freyja was followed in by the Riverlanders, who this time were quicker to strip off their cloaks and head coverings. They'd taken some time to brush and straighten their clothes and tidy their hair. They sat at the table Freyja pointed them to, positioned in the best light, Adeline straight-backed on the hard wooden bench with a youthful grace Feilan envied, her high-strung uncle beside her, narrowly elegant face tense. As when he'd met with Freyja the day before, he sat neatly and unnaturally still, all his restless fidgeting under tight control. The bright sunshine falling from the smoke hole kindled fiery highlights in his hair.

Helpers carrying trays of food came next. Freyja earned her generous reputation: as guests, the men from the camp would all receive bread and cheese and ale at no cost. But inside the hall, platters of cold roast pork and bowls of berries were added to the bounty, tempting in a greater subset of bersverdar prepared to hear out the terms of the River-lander contract than Feilan had expected.

Torben ducked his head as he came in, unnecessary but only just. Like all bersverdar, he towered, and his shoulders were square and broad. Feilan admired those shoulders, and thought entirely too long about seeing them bare later, and perhaps even from behind.

He was inappropriately amused to see him pause, take in the sight of Renart's hair gleaming in the beam of light, and then murmur, 'Rufran,' in the exact same tone Feilan had said it the day before. Freyja, sitting by Adeline, huffed in annoyance, making Feilan grin as he settled by Torben with the bronze scales. The other warriors filled the benches about the table, scooping slices of meat onto the dark bread.

Freyja had already made the general offer clear to the potential mer-cenaries. Now she indicated with a nod for Renart to make his opening bid, which he did by untying his purse from his waist and upending the contents, a mix of silver and gold coinage, locally minted, onto the table. Feilan, exchanging a glance with Freyja, wanted to smack his own forehead, especially when Adeline, devotedly copying her uncle, also spilled her entire wealth onto the table from her own little purse.

The warriors, entirely unimpressed by the pitiful hoard, continued picking over the platters. Feilan nudged Torben, who elbowed him back but did turn his attention to the negotiations.

'This is all you offer?' he asked in rough Midlands, which wasn't anybody's first tongue, but, having arisen in the great Chalcadean ports where the peoples of Enea freely mingled, had spread to become everybody's second tongue. He flicked a finger across the coins dismissively, scattering the pile. He saw no need to bother with the scales before he pronounced, 'Too little.'

Feilan was prepared to translate, but Midlands was usefully widespread enough that even the Riverlanders from an isolated little kingdom knew it. Remy touched his niece's arm, giving her a small nod, encouragement to answer on her own behalf.

'It's all we have,' Adeline said in her piping voice, spreading her hands. 'This isn't a negotiation tactic, sir. It's the very upper edge of what I can offer.'

The honest naivety of a sweet-faced child was, in fact, a fairly decent negotiation tactic in some rare circles, but Torben merely shrugged those broad shoulders. 'We can each make at least thrice this as our fair share of raiding.'

'There is less risk of death with this contract,' Renart said, just as disarmingly frank in Midlands as in his native Riverlander.

The men muttered at that. Most were already rising, piling pork high on the chunks of bread and grabbing handfuls of berries on their way out of the hall, eager to move on to their real reason for visiting the Cursed.

Torben was easy-going, ready to relax and be argued with. He chewed a piece of pork crackle and watched Renart with half-lidded eyes. Renart turned from the sight of the great proportion of his potential pot of warrior-stock strolling out the door and ran straight into Torben's best smile, looking briefly flummoxed to be subjected to it.

Torben leaned in and said confidentially, 'We like the risk of death, Rufran.' He said the byname like he meant Foxy, too. 'Can *you* offer anything else?'

Feilan couldn't tell if Renart understood he was being propositioned. Tone remaining cool and even, he said, 'The hunt is at the dark of the moon. The coming new moon, and perhaps the next. You won't miss the whole raiding season.'

'My party will have already sailed south. I won't catch them in time to claim full share.'

'If you're competent enough, you'll get the job done the first moon. You'd only be a half-month behind them.'

'If I'm competent enough?' Torben repeated, amused but with a hint that he was prepared to not continue so.

'Do you fear to travel alone to catch up with your party?' Renart asked, which may well have been an innocent question or may well have been as barbed as the comment about competence. Renart might not have realised quite how barbed such an accusation was, to a Vaer man.

Torben's eyes narrowed. 'I fear nothing.'

Feilan didn't need Freyja's quick glance to know to press a hand down on Torben's right hand. A bersverdr did not tolerate accusations of cowardice.

'Add on two good cloaks,' he said. 'Top-quality wool, silver clasps. And the little girl's silver hair-clasp, too.'

Adeline blanched and her hand flew to the ornamentation at the nape of her neck. Renart said, 'That was a gift from her mother.'

'Worthy of a queen, then,' Feilan said, merciless. 'Enough for one contract?' When Renart opened his mouth again, he knocked his knuckles lightly on the table. 'Is its sentimental value worth a crown, Adeline?'

Renart, finally remembering his own determination to let his niece rule, subsided, not without snapping a resentful look Feilan's way, which Feilan merely smiled at. Adeline bowed her head. She loosened the silver clasp from the dark plaits nested at her nape, and laid it on the table amid the coins. The well-polished silver gleamed in the stream of light from overhead, swirls and curls of flowery scrolls trellised across its surface, studded with filigree rosettes. She gave one of the rosette studs a last lingering stroke before raising her gaze to look earnestly at Torben.

Torben and the last few of his companions conferred in low voices. The others shook their heads and made their way out. Torben dropped the hair-clasp on one of the pans of the scale. The pan sank substantially; without bothering to put the matching polyhedral lead weights on the other pan, and certainly keeping the cloak-clasps in mind as well, Torben gave a satisfied nod.

'But I can't take a token of the little girl's mother,' he said then, which deep-buried softness was exactly why Feilan had referred to Adeline like that. 'Let's hack it in half.'

Feilan winced. He'd been a trader too long; he'd added value in his rote appraisal of the hair-clasp for its function and beauty. Vaer raiders cared solely about purity and weight. But Torben was trying, in his crude way, to be kind: he'd hack half for the silver, and she'd keep a portion as her token. That it would be forever ruined didn't cross his mind.

Renart abruptly stood. His niece was almost in tears, trying very hard to not let them fall, and he had no way to recognise the kind intent. He could therefore only take it as an insult to his liege; even a less ill-tempered man might have.

Bristling with offence, he snatched the clasp from the pan. 'And that is the end of the contract negotiations.'

He swept the clasp into Adeline's hands, and swept the coins back into his purse, and swept himself and his niece out of the hall, without taking their cloaks or remembering to thank the boss. Freyja, looking sour, departed after them.

'Foxy has a temper, does he?' Torben said in Vaer, rising smoothly. He'd gaped at the display of spleen, but had already shrugged it off, smiling down at Feilan, wide enough to crinkle his eyes at the edges.

'Do stay for our hospitality tonight, naturally,' Feilan said, in thrall to that smile, as he had been the moment Torben had first strolled in through Siftar's gates seven summers ago; as he had been twenty-five summers ago, for that matter.

'I am ever fond of your hospitality,' Torben murmured, which was actually quite a clever quip from a man who was normally nothing but straightforwardly blunt.

Feilan was too wise to broach the subject again until much later, when Torben was loose and magnanimous with rich food and plentiful drink – though the feast tonight was somewhat the opposite of the previous night's, less merry, less ale, more food – and pressing his fingers to the inside of Feilan's wrist with a meaningful look. He evidently wanted to move the evening onwards to its inevitable conclusion.

Feilan glanced around. Both Riverlanders had joined the feast to eat but were absent from the hall now, or perhaps already wrapped in their cloaks in one of the curtained niches, trying to sleep amid the noise of the crowded tables, the shouts and flirts of the bersverdar. That was good. There were things going on not suitable for a child's eyes.

Careful to maintain distance from his friend, he said, 'You won't consider the contract at their best price? It's a monster hunt, after all.' He added enticingly, 'It could be the making of your saga-song.'

'It's a bear,' Torben said. 'You know it's a bear, Little Wolf.'

'A big, old, canny bear. That must hold some interest, surely.'

Torben grunted. *He* wasn't being careful to maintain distance. He was practically leaning on Feilan, hand about his hip. But then, he'd come on this expedition with a tolftar of hungry men who'd all tacitly decided to turn a blind eye to what they each did tonight.

By the time Feilan rose to circumspectly slip out first, most of the other warriors had already vanished with their accommodating partners for the night, except one who was sitting on the rug by Freyja's knee wearing a blissful expression while she petted his hair.

Feilan wrinkled his nose at her – the man was more than half her age – she scowled at him – she was none too fond of Torben – and they silently but mutually agreed to ignore each other's lack of good sense.

He went out of the hall. Torben didn't bother to make his own exit anything other than right on his heels.

Outside, the air was crisp, the stars and moon brilliant overhead, and the yard was quiet, though laughter and voices raised in song could be heard from the far side where the most cheerful revellers had spilled out to enjoy the soft night air. Beneath the open revelry were the sounds of sex, whispers and moans, grunts and sharp imprecations.

'You could...' Feilan faltered as Torben pressed harder into him from behind, his mouth hovering over his bare neck. He didn't let his lips touch Feilan's skin, but Feilan could feel the ghost of them and it raised goosebumps. '...demand a gratuity if you win the contest for her.'

'What kind of gratuity?' He'd got both hands around Feilan now, holding him tight, pulling him in close, letting him feel his muscular breadth, his want. 'Take me somewhere private.'

'I *was*,' Feilan said acerbically. Squirming loose, he reached for Torben's hand, but quickly desisted, jerking his chin towards his hut instead. 'She'll be a queen,' he said. 'She could throw open her brand-new treasure house.'

Feilan didn't know why he was insisting on this. But Renart had been desperate enough to offer up his body last night in exchange for merely putting in a word towards the contract. He'd likely be off seething at himself for not controlling his mouth. Feilan would have to find him, tell him it had been the price, not the mouthiness, and now he'd be able to say he tried and he wasn't even expecting Renart to make good.

On that thought, he added, 'They're desperate enough to offer you anything, if you win.'

'I'm desperate enough to put you on your knees right here if you don't hurry it up,' Torben said, hand on the nape of his neck.

'Yes, yes, all right,' Feilan said with a mock show of irritation, swatting his hand off and zagging abruptly into his hut, Torben right there with him. 'As if you would.'

That was said with less mock irritation and more actual annoyance than he'd intended. It wasn't Torben's fault their entire culture reviled the Cursed. A man in Torben's position could follow a Cursed with the transparent intention of a fuck, but he would never do anything in the open that couldn't be denied, if only facetiously.

Especially not when he'd come within a heartbeat of getting caught in his youth, gleefully fucking the mouth of his childhood friend.

Stark-naked, he'd bolted from the old storehouse when a watchman flung the main door open and raised his lamp, shining unwelcome light on unwholesome activity. He'd gone out the rear door into the chill night without looking back, leaving Feilan on his knees to face the elders' wrath.

The watchman had seen only blond hair and the muscular physique of a big man's backside. Ironically enough, Torben's back side was well enough known among the girls that they might have been able to point to the scar on his thigh or the constellation of freckles under his left shoulder blade to identify him. But to the watchman standing over Feilan, he could have been anyone.

It was the one and only time Tryggvi Jansson, byname Magni Torben, had ever run from anything.

Feilan had steadfastly refused to salvage his honour by accusing his fellow transgressor, let alone hint that if the watchman had opened the door even a thumb's width of time earlier, it would have been Torben caught taking cock, and not in the mouth, either. Only his stubborn silence had saved Torben and left him free to be the great warrior he indubitably was – not many devotees of the bear-god made it to his age, after all – to the glorification of his name and all that saga draf.

Feilan didn't begrudge his friend. Permanent exile eventually lost its sting, and he stopped missing the mountains. He'd never missed the bitter cold. Comfortable, safe Siftar made for neither a hard life, nor a lonely one. And it was by far the better alternative, for he'd been facing execution for his silence until Freyja had precipitously intervened.

The room was in pitch blackness. The rush wick of the little light-pot Feilan had left lit must have guttered. The moment the doorway curtain fell behind them, Torben was pushing him down onto the furs, pulling at his clothes.

'Been too long,' he said against Feilan's collarbone, letting his mouth taste his skin in a kiss now they were off the thoroughfare, in the dark.

He still wouldn't kiss Feilan's mouth. He never had, not even before his close brush with dishonour and exile.

'The summer's barely started,' Feilan protested. 'I know it's near a week's crossing but surely you can manage yourself for longer than—'

'Too long since I've had *you*.'

Torben's fingers scrambled urgently over the knots of Feilan's shirt ties, couldn't decipher them by touch alone, and shoved his shirt up and over his head with scant regard for ears or hair, all while Feilan was still thinking about that.

Torben was not affectionate. They fucked during the summers, for the brief interludes when Torben was at the nearby camp between raiding forays. Feilan never knew if he'd come back from those, or if he would come back from the overwinter in the heartland. Even if Torben could read and write like Feilan could, he wouldn't be sending missives between these rare visits. He'd never before intimated that he might miss Feilan, or at least his cock, in the between-times. He'd more a *you'll-do* sort of attitude.

Having successfully bared both himself and Feilan to the waist, Torben pushed Feilan back down and knelt over him, kissing and nipping along his clavicle and down his chest. He found a nipple, grazing his teeth along it. Feilan clutched both hands into Torben's thick locks, biting back a whimper.

'Serth, I'm going to make you squeal *loud* tonight,' Torben muttered in between tonguing his other nipple intently, hand heavy on his stomach.

His fingers traced the thick scar seaming Feilan's side, earned in his first and only summer of raiding. Torben always touched that ridge during these seasonal trysts, running fingertips along it like he was reading a map that led him into the past. He never said anything about it, and didn't this time either, too intent on sucking and licking both Feilan's nipples into hard nubs that he could close his teeth on and tug at, making Feilan yelp appreciatively.

'There you are.' Torben's hand trailed lower. 'Let's get louder.'

Feilan jerked his hips in anticipation of the touch, wondering if he had oil to hand. From Torben's intensity, he thought he'd be playing the woman's part tonight and it would be a teeth-rattler. He had linseed oil, he remembered, tucked in his trunk.

He hissed as Torben palmed his painfully hard cock through his trousers. Even as close as they were, he couldn't see Torben's face or his muscular, scarred body, but he could hear the self-satisfied smirk in his voice as he said, 'You like that? Beg for more.'

'I'm,' Feilan said, gasping as Torben rolled his hand over him again, and again. 'I'm not the one deprived of sex.'

Over him, Torben chuckled complacently; Feilan had sounded far too desperate to be convincing, even though it was true enough; he was surrounded by men who liked to fuck men in Siftar, one of the various reasons his exile had not been such an irrevocable blow.

But none of those men was Torben.

Torben's hand slipped through the loosened ties of his trousers and under his braes, and his fingers, calloused and firm, took hold. 'Yes? And who do you fuck when I'm not around, Little Wolf?'

This was when Renart chose to sit up and uncover the light-pot.

'H VAT UM SERTH?' FEILAN AND TORBEN said in unison.

They were half-naked, and Torben was over Feilan with his hand still shoved in his trousers. Renart stared at them with wide eyes. In the low light, his pale bare chest and one lithe leg gleamed where the furs were askew.

'I didn't,' he said, and cleared his throat. 'Know where I should sleep.'

'Not here, obviously!' Feilan snapped.

He squirmed, but Torben didn't take the hint. His hand tightened again, and he began to slowly, showily, pump it up and down, watching Renart with half-lidded eyes.

'Foxy,' he murmured.

To Feilan's discomfit, his cock was taking as little hint as to the change of circumstances as his friend was, hardening rapidly under Torben's rhythmic ministrations. To his further discomfit, Torben wasn't taking his rapt gaze off their unexpected voyeur, who, to be fair, also wasn't quite tearing his own gaze from the sight sprawled before him.

'Looks good enough to eat,' Torben growled. Hand still working, he leaned close over Feilan, nibbling his ear, making him muffle a gasp. 'Plenty for both of us.'

He was still speaking Vaer, but now their very local, village-specific, dialect, the literal mother-tongue they'd both had been enjoined against, Feilan because he was the son of an elder, Torben because he was destined for warriorhood.

Feilan was sure Renart wouldn't understand the words, but his eyes widened regardless. It was the purring, predatory tone, and the way Torben was looking at him.

The way Feilan was looking at him, too.

That slim, smooth body nestled in Feilan's furs, as if he'd claimed him like a raider of the previous generation might have. That loose, silky hair glinting copper highlights amid the darker red, long enough to knot a fist into. Those full lips, slightly parted, ripe to be pushed wider, plundered.

That growing fear.

Feilan wriggled free of Torben, not the easiest of tasks when the big man was both intent and over him. He adjusted his trousers to cover himself, and propped himself on an elbow, casual, lazy…and between Torben and Renart.

'You don't want this one,' he said. 'He's like a flea, once you get him in your furs, you'll never get rid of him.'

Torben, equally casual and lazy, reached out and gripped his jaw in one strong hand. His gaze flickered over Feilan's shoulder, and back to his face, incredulous. 'You're not sharing, Little Wolf?'

Feilan, against the strong, pointed grip, shook his head. 'You don't want this one.'

Torben's fingers tightened, though he was still restraining his full strength. The only thing saving Feilan right now from sporting rounded bruises across his cheek and jawline tomorrow was Freyja. Notwithstanding accepting he'd be the most reliable warrior for Adeline to contract with, Freyja despised Torben, bone-deep. She'd tear him apart like a she-bear if Feilan emerged from this liaison with visible bruises.

Torben let go and thumped back against the furs, making a muffled whomp like a bushel of wool landing dockside during unlading. He looked from Feilan to the princeling and back again. Then he shrugged.

It was the *you'll-do* shrug, and Feilan relaxed, though he knew what was coming even before Torben undid his laces. Still staring, the thwarted warrior growled, 'Best suck me, then.'

Feilan knew not to hesitate. Men and women in the communal longhouses couldn't be fastidious about privacy for the act, and here in Siftar, absolute discretion was not required either. Even within the huts, the walls were thin, the door a mere hide, and locations other than one's furs remained popular as well. Tonight, the bathing pond would be put to good use, and bystanders could turn their eyes away or watch as they so desired. These days Feilan preferred his own furs but he could profess to neither innocence nor shame in the matter.

He moved to kneel between Torben's sprawled legs. Torben smiled and reclined, arms behind his head so his massive biceps flexed. He thought Renart might cover the light again, but he didn't. He was, perhaps, shocked, or he was watching. Feilan didn't know the local customs, in this regard, though privacy was a rare resource almost everywhere he'd ever travelled. He did know Riverlanders had a more relaxed attitude about sertha, but he'd never sought out a local before last night. He had his easy compatriots in the outpost, and he had Torben.

He had Torben now, baring his thick cock from his trousers and swallowing it down almost in the same motion, hands set on those muscular thighs. Torben grunted in complacent pleasure as Feilan's mouth plunged his full length, and bucked his hips to take himself deeper. Feilan withdrew slightly at the sudden pressure. Torben immediately locked both fists into his hair and thrust, forcing himself deep down Feilan's throat. Feilan struggled a little and choked a little, mostly because he knew Torben liked it when he did that, and partly because he couldn't help but do so. Torben felt his helplessness and jerked his hips faster, harder, grunting with the effort, hands clamping Feilan's head in place. He froze, murmured, 'Aleifr,' with a familiar little hitch in the middle, and then spent in a great gush, thrusting his way through a stuttering climax with a long, pained groan, pinning Feilan there the whole time.

The saving grace – aside from the broken way he always whispered Feilan's birth name – was that it was fast, and that afterwards, he would drag Feilan up to kneel on his chest and hoarsely command, 'Return the favour, Little Wolf,' letting Feilan fuck his face as wildly as he'd just done to him. Depending on his mood, he might even roll onto his stomach and spread his legs with a languid, 'You know what to do.'

Except, this time, he pushed Feilan off, said, 'You can sate yourself on Foxy,' and departed before Feilan had even caught his breath.

Feilan swallowed a couple of times, coughed, and then swallowed again. Even for Torben, that had been intense. It was difficult to call it unwanted, but he'd expected his payment in kind, and was aching with the denial of that expectation. He wasn't sure what had put Torben in such a vicious mood, unless having a witness to unmanly activities had done it, which was ever possible.

He shot a glance at Renart, not sure what expression the other man would be wearing.

He was wearing a very blank expression. He silently poured water from the ewer into the leather cup, and held it out. Feilan took it and drank, swishing his mouth out and soothing his throat.

'Are you all right?' When Feilan didn't immediately reply, he added, 'That seemed quite rough.'

'I like rough.'

Renart didn't know what to do with that. After a moment, Feilan abruptly leaned towards him, provoking a sharp intake of breath. He smiled mockingly as he reached past to return the cup to its spot and cover the light-pot. He stretched out, and heard the soft rustle as Renart followed suit.

Sleep eluded him, however. It was early enough that the noises of revelry and sex were still penetrating the thin walls from nearby huts, quiet and yet awkwardly omnipresent with the judgemental stranger lying right beside him. And he remained stubbornly aroused, his cock alive to both the denied opportunity and the naked body a handspan away.

He's not *naked,* Feilan told himself, *he must be wearing braes at least,* but the memory of the gleam of Renart's skin in the rushlight, bare chest and bare leg, was insistent, as was the memory of him last night, eyes glittering, body slackening against him. He fidgeted, wanting to toss and turn, but conscious of his sleeping guest.

Eventually he pushed himself up to sitting, and paused there, thinking. He was going to have to take himself in hand before he could sleep, and he pondered whether he should do it right here, go out and duck behind the huts, or visit the bathing pond and see who of interest might still be there. He couldn't quite be bothered with the last.

He felt, then, the cool trace of fingers across his bare back. Renart was still awake, and must be wondering what the barbarian was doing in the dark. He smiled with a touch of malice, as he imagined the reaction should he pleasure himself right here beside the Riverlander. Maybe kneel up and frig himself until he spent all over that slender, gleaming chest, that elegant face, see those black eyes widen with—

With *fear,* he reminded himself and his throbbing cock.

He expected the hand to jerk away once Renart realised he was touching skin, but it didn't. Instead Renart curled fingers over his hip, where his loosened trousers had slid down.

'Do you...' The voice out of the dark was almost dreamy. 'Do you also like gentle, at all?'

Feilan's lustful thoughts, slightly resentful and slightly ashamed, spiralled wildly. He said, 'Yes,' and rolled towards the voice.

It almost made him laugh, though he quashed the impulse: one of the euphemisms for sex in the sagas was that, turning towards one another in the dark, and they were playing it out exactly. He supposed Renart had been aroused by watching him suck Torben, and wanted it too. But Feilan wouldn't make the same mistake: he'd get his pleasure first this time.

Renart had kept his hand on Feilan's hip as he'd moved. He pressed his fingers in, finely balanced between tugging Feilan closer and pushing him away. 'Can you do gentle?'

'Yes.' He was too lust-addled to even resent the implication behind the question. At this point in the trajectory of his urgent need, Renart could make any sort of assumption and call him any sort of name, as long as he was riding his cock while he did it.

'Will you... *Will* you do gentle?'

Feilan said, 'Yes,' and leaned across to uncover the light again, arm brushing the smooth muscle of Renart's bare chest, the hairs on his forearm rising in tingling response.

Renart blinked in the dull shine, bright only by dint of competing with near-absolute darkness. Feilan half-expected the Riverlander would lose his bravado in the light, but his gaze was knowing, aware. He couldn't meet Feilan's eyes for long, though, looking away with a lick of his lips which was all nerves but still sent another spike of arousal through Feilan.

'What do you need me to do?' Renart asked.

'It depends on what you want.'

He frowned. He said, 'All of it?'

Feilan shrugged with pleased surprise. 'I can do that.'

He peeled back the furs and discovered Renart was as fully bare as his cock and his imagination had pulled together like an ox team to picture for him. He made a low, appreciative noise, stroking fingers through Renart's hair. It felt as lovely as it'd looked in the sunlight, caressing his skin like finest silk. He took a fistful and tugged, pulling Renart's head back and baring his throat.

Renart's breath caught. Feilan pressed a kiss to the hollow between his collar bones in silent reassurance before spanning his hands over his ribs and running his palms across the satiny skin, leaving a trail of goosebumps. Like touching his hair, it felt better than he'd expected.

He stroked Renart again, from his throat to his groin, where he was only half-hard. Feilan rectified that, working him with one hand while his other hand massaged the tightness of the muscles of his inner thighs. His shy cock, nestled in coppery hair that would be as red as his head in stronger light, began to respond. Like the man himself, it was slimmer than Feilan was used to, but of pleasing length and responsive hardness.

Renart was tense with nerves, but he began to slowly relax as Feilan proved he could indeed be gentle.

'All right, there,' he said soothingly, shifting closer against the pale, naked body in his furs, letting Renart feel his arousal pressing into his hip through the confinement of trousers and braes. 'That's a good lad.'

Renart huffed. With some of the ill-advised spirit he'd shown earlier, he complained, 'You're talking to me like I talk to a flighty horse.'

Feilan laughed against his shoulder. 'You were so nervous last night, you drank enough to pass out.'

'I didn't mean to.' Renart sounded exasperated. 'Better tonight, anyway.'

'Why so?'

After a pause, Renart said, 'Because now I know you won't hurt me.'

'Yeah,' Feilan said. 'Yeah, Rufran, I won't hurt you.'

Renart turned his face towards him as if expecting a kiss, but Feilan knew better than to respond to that; most men didn't kiss on the mouth, and he'd still taste of the lingering flavour of another man's seed, regardless. He did not want to spook this flighty horse before he had a chance to mount.

Still gently stroking and rubbing, he soothed Renart over onto his stomach, and found the oil. Renart, head pillowed on his folded arms, tensed again as Feilan's slicked fingers explored between his legs, beginning to nudge against his hole.

'I haven't done this before,' he blurted into his elbow.

'You what?' Feilan said, with a sinking sensation that was really more of a complete serthing plummet.

'I haven't... I've never...'

'*Never?*' He was appalled, before recovering himself. Renart had said he didn't fuck men, as a rule, and Feilan had promptly assumed that meant he had a long list of exceptions, as so many men did, and had pushed. But apparently his rule was stricter. No wonder he'd drunk himself insensible. 'You mean with men. You did say that, yes.'

'Never, with anyone.'

Feilan, kneeling over him, looked down at the lithe body laid out before him, the sleek lines of his shoulders and back, the curve of his waist and his arse. 'But why not? You are bonny enough.'

'I don't want to talk about that.'

Feilan crooked an eyebrow at the sharp response.

'Or anything, right now.' Renart's tone had become slightly conciliatory, as if he'd read the rebuke in Feilan's silence without having to look around.

He was tempted to demand answers anyway. He came from a superstitious people and a beautiful maiden left unaccountably untouched raised whispers of curses and tricks in the back of his mind, even if the maiden happened to be male.

But his blood had rushed away to his cock and it was doing all the thinking now. That was a problem in another sense. It took him a moment, but he managed to make himself say it: 'We don't have to fuck.'

'I want to,' Renart said, very much belied by the fact he was still hiding his face from view.

Feilan put his hands on that tempting mound of arse, and ran them all the way up Renart's spine, thumbs dragging over tight muscles, the tension confirming his suspicion. He followed his hands with the rest of his body, so that he straddled Renart in a crouch, and said in his ear, 'How about you avail yourself of my mouth, and let me rut between your thighs, and you can work your way up to the advanced fucking later, good?'

'No,' Renart said stubbornly. 'Do it.'

Feilan had to admire his own valour when he found his next words. 'Not all that interested in a trembling little virgin, myself.'

Renart abruptly rolled under Feilan's all-fours crouch over him. Feilan was amused to be met with indignation and an interestingly assertive grip on his achingly hard cock. 'I think you might be.'

Once again, he was tempted to kiss that luscious mouth, set in its stubborn lines; once again, he resisted. That was about as far as his resistance went.

'And that's how you want it?' he asked. 'Me to fuck you?'

Renart looked up at him, pupils dilated in the low light. 'I need your cock in me, Feilan.'

There wasn't much Feilan's better self could do against that except remind him to take it as slowly and gently as he could manage and try not to begrudge the delay too strenuously. He thus set to it, using his mouth and hands all over Renart, relaxing him, steadying him, tasting that smooth skin, breathing in the remnants of the clean herbal scent he'd noticed the night before, too faint now to set off the corresponding flash of colour in the corners of his eyes.

Despite the edge of impatience he was having to blunt, he discovered a great deal of pleasure in feeling Renart's spine melt from rigid to pliant, his fingers unlock from white-knuckled fists in the fur into rhythmic helpless clutching, his breathing transform from short, harsh pants into bitten-off gasps and moans. It was something like soothing a timid wild creature into eating from his hand.

Unbidden, he remembered the feral kitten he'd tamed as a youth. It had taken a full moon-turn of patience to earn the little cat's trust, but eventually she'd sit in his lap and take scraps of dried fish from his fingers. He'd been so proud of himself.

His father had drowned her in a bucket, because it was unmanly to dote on a pet.

That had been when— Well. The incident had proven Aleifr Ulfrsson had the blessing of the bear-god, because he'd never felt rage like it, not even all the times he'd had to watch Ulfr beat his mother. It was an unnatural fury, bulwark against guilt and grief and helplessness, but since punching his father would have gotten him, and perhaps his mother, killed, he'd taken the only revenge open to him, driven by reckless spite intertwined with a good dose of unacknowledged want.

He knew the most popular, the strongest, of the other boys sometimes looked at him in a recognisable way. He knew sometimes Tryggvi Jansson's hand brushed across a hip, lingered over a knee, in a not entirely accidental touch. He knew the petty delight the bigger boys took in wrestling him roughly to the ground sometimes had a different flavour when Tryggvi did it.

He'd pushed Tryggvi into the woods, where the boys took their girls, for the scarce privacy the white trunks afforded them. He'd said, 'I want to do for you what the girls do for you,' and he'd thrown himself to his knees and torn free the laces of Tryggvi's trousers. It had been a messy, slobbery affair, and he'd seized his fingers about Tryggvi's hips so hard he'd left bruises.

When Tryggvi, swearing and tugging on his hair, had spent mightily into his mouth, he'd felt such bitter triumph, he could have marched back into the village and spat the mouthful at his father's feet in the exact contemptuous manner Ulfr had thrown down the sodden body of his kitten.

But Tryggvi had slid down the trunk he'd shoved him against to sprawl companionably next to him, trying ineffectually to do up his ruined laces. 'Yeah, the girls only use their hands,' he'd said cheerily. 'You can do *that* anytime.'

It had left young Aleifr laughing, and relieved despite his fatalistic fury, because he'd known then, and only then, that Tryggvi wasn't going to play at disgust and deliver him to the magnate for a pat on the head. He'd known – Gods, and how it had ended – he'd known he could trust his friend.

Still, aside from a few opportunistic gropes in the dark, and one delicious interlude up in the shieling at the high pasture, when Tryggvi had taken both their cocks in his big hand and frigged until they'd shouted into each other's shoulders, their seed intermingled over his fist, they'd tried very hard to pay more attention to the risk than to the temptation. It hadn't been until after their first summer raiding and the winning of their bynames that Torben had pulled Feilan into the dusty storehouse at the outskirts of the village and they'd worked out how to fuck properly.

Speaking of. He'd come to a stop, unfairly and unusually accosted by memory, one hand splayed over Renart's chest. Renart's cool fingers traced over his shoulders, curled against his pectoral. 'Are you....'

'You good?' Feilan said, giving himself a mental slap. He had himself a willing partner right now, and no cause to be wasting yet more time in pointless reminiscing. He started to push Renart onto his stomach. 'I'm going to lick you open, good?'

'I don't think so,' Renart said, sounding appalled.

Feilan immediately stopped pushing, but he explained, 'You still want it gentle? Right, then you see the practicalities here, you'll want me to start with something smaller than my cock, yes?'

Renart shut his eyes and muttered under his breath before saying, 'All right, yes. I suppose people must enjoy it?'

'Don't take what you don't want,' Feilan admonished him. He traced an oiled finger between Renart's thighs, feeling the skin quiver under the light touch. 'Fingers better?'

'Oh, yes, thank you.'

'And where were these lovely manners earlier, Rufran?' Feilan said, smiling, and Renart sighed and spread under him.

Feilan was still smiling as he leaned over him, and Renart raised his dark eyes to gaze at him, eyelids fluttering as Feilan stroked the sensitive passage behind his balls and then eased a finger in. He took his time working in another, and then a third, as the Riverlander arched and gasped, hands bunching and releasing against Feilan's chest, the counterpoint to the involuntary jerk of his hips in response to the gentle vee and crook of Feilan's fingers.

He murmured against Feilan's skin, lips tickling his shoulder. He wasn't speaking endearments or even appreciation, but rather, low words of encouragement that, once Feilan deciphered them, appeared aimed at himself. But when Feilan paused, qualms trying to rear up, Renart gave him such an imploring look that he was helpless not to continue, curling his fingers and shivering waves and waves of pleasure through his trembling little virgin until he cried out loud.

At last, Feilan stripped and readied himself, fisting his own engorged cock, its length catching murky glimmers of light in the oil he was thickly applying. Renart watched, sprawled on his back in languorous anticipation, eyes wide and unwavering. Feilan put his free hand to his shoulder, nudging him to turn over with another murmured, 'Good?'

'There's just one thing,' Renart said, *again* not shifting to go along with the nudge. 'It's a small thing, really. I'd feel bad if I didn't do it.'

'Not looking to make you feel bad,' Feilan said, obligingly enough; at this point, he would have obliged Renart in absolutely any request so long as he then got on his hands and knees and took Feilan's cock like an eager little wanton.

'There's some words we say, when we surrender our virginity,' Renart said. He trailed his hand down his body and over his cock, his breathing hitching for a telling moment. He wrapped loose fingers around his length, making a small sound in the back of his throat.

Feilan couldn't look away. He was going to spend before he even got inside the Riverlander if this nonsense went on much longer.

'Go on, then,' he said, trying to keep the impatience from his voice. He'd promised to be gentle, and he would be, but he wanted to be gentle for longer than the shamefully few thrusts it was going to take to get off once Renart finally stopped talking and bent over for him.

Renart began to recite, still stroking himself and watching Feilan with that wide-eyed, irresistible longing. The ritual words must have been very formal, or even archaic, because Feilan couldn't make out anything of them, except that it included Renart's name, and he heard his own byname in there too.

When Renart finished, Feilan tried, with somewhat more insistence, to roll him over again, but Renart said, 'You have to say it back to me, please.'

He didn't bother to argue. He didn't even think. He simply stumbled his way through the foreign words that Renart, touching himself all the while, intoned for him to repeat, phrase by agonising phrase. He rattled out Renart's name in the middle of a garble of only faintly familiar syllables, and didn't at all countenance delaying long enough to explain his own birth name so he could use it instead of his byname.

And then finally the strange old ritual was over with, and Renart was nodding with the sort of relief that came with completing an onerous task and turning to all fours in front of him.

With no capacity for further ado, Feilan gripped Renart's hips and breached him. He'd prepared him well, and he took him in with just a few throttled gasps and squirms of discomfort. Feilan thrust with short, spaced jerks, slowly sliding further into the tight heat with each sortie.

'Serth, you feel good,' he groaned as he sank all the way home at last, his entire length engulfed in warm silk.

Renart made a noncommittal noise which implied he might be having a somewhat different experience.

Feilan chuckled. 'I'll do you right, Rufran. Bear with me.'

He pressed Renart down, from his hands onto his elbows, and leaned his weight over that slender, tautly arched back, seating ever deeper.

He thrust, still moving slowly, gauging the reactions, and Renart whimpered, and then he moaned, and then he flung his head up with a startled cry, and then he was pushing back into Feilan's thrusts, with a hard gasp that sounded very much like, 'More.'

There wasn't going to be much more, after that long lead-up, but Feilan did his best to make it last, counting the bales in the store in his head and concentrating intently on Renart's responsive carnality as he arched and writhed under him. He wondered how those sharp, dark eyes looked, gone soft as sable in pleasure.

It made him wish he'd taken him on his back so he could watch his face, see his eyes fly wide open as Feilan's cock slid deep inside him, see him bite his lip against helpless moans.

Feilan had intended to suck Renart afterwards, but now he put a hand under and found his cock, hard and leaking, and pumped him in time with his own urgent thrusts. Almost immediately, Renart shouted, bucking like a wild horse under Feilan, hot seed spilling over his hand.

That was good enough. Feilan tightened his hold on Renart's hip and buried his wet hand into the carnelian hair, pulling back enough to make his spine arch like a bow, listening with the tiniest quarter of his mind for the demands for more to become demands to stop. They didn't, and he lost his last hold on the reins, and fucked away in a frenzy, Renart wailing and writhing under him.

His climax thundered out of him and he fell forwards hard enough that Renart's arms gave way and they ended up collapsed on the furs in a sticky mess.

They lay like that for a time, Feilan too shaky-limbed to even muster a roll off the smaller man, who must be at least a little bit crushed. Feilan wasn't overly big for a Vaeringan, but he was for a Riverlander. Finally he found the wherewithal to withdraw, not missing the wince that ran over the shoulders and down the spine of the body under him.

'Less gentle than I intended, at the end there, sorry,' he muttered, petting Renart's back, all awkwardness now the sex was done and he remembered that merciless grip at hip and hair. 'You'll feel it tomorrow.'

Renart rolled over and stretched bare limbs out in all directions. 'I think I was going to feel it tomorrow, regardless. I see what you meant this morning, about knowing about it.'

He looked a little stunned, but also pleased with himself. He gave Feilan what may have been the first genuine smile of their acquaintance. Feilan couldn't have done so poorly by the man, then.

He shifted away. He was growing heavy with sleep in the aftermath of slaking his intense lust, and didn't want to risk putting his arms around Renart during the night by lying too close to him. Men didn't kiss, and they didn't cuddle. Other bedmates would have left for their own hut, or the trader quarters or guard barracks.

Renart had been bundling back into the furs, but he paused and looked askance at the distance Feilan had placed between them. 'Oh. Should I go?'

'No.' As Renart settled back down, a worm wiggled at the edges of Feilan's drowsy drift. 'I thought you didn't have anywhere else to sleep.'

'I can ask about.'

Part of Feilan worried at the very thought, this soft, lovely, provocative creature wandering about a trading post full of drunken, lusty bersverdar, smelling of sex and looking well-fucked, asking for a bed.

Another part of him said, 'You could have done that earlier.'

Renart looked at him for a long time. 'Yes.'

Feilan sat up, alert now and swearing at himself. He was smarter than this. 'Why, exactly, were you waiting for me bare-naked in my furs?'

Without answering, Renart covered the light, but Feilan wasn't deterred that easily. 'Why, after holding on to your precious chastity for however many years—'

'I've seen thirty-three winters.'

'And you, what, suddenly conceived a mad notion to give yourself away to a barbarian, did you? Determined enough to try it twice in a row, too.'

'Do your people not have some sort of saying about not looking bald luck in the eye?' Renart inquired of the darkness. 'Because my people do.'

'We do, and we also have an awful lot of stories about when luck is too good to be true. What do you want so very badly that you spread your thighs for me?' *Drop the other boot, Foxy, let's get it over with.*

'I wanted the fuck,' Renart said, voice very flat.

'With me. A person you clearly dislike.'

'You dislike me too, it obviously isn't a reason not to!' He made a softly startled noise that suggested he'd tried to run a fretful hand through his hair and discovered the matted state Feilan had left it in. Quieter, he said, 'You seemed the safest option.'

Feilan paused at that. He could see the logic, actually. If Renart really had abruptly decided to avail himself of sex for the first time – and it could have been as simple as fearing death during a monster hunt he seemed determined to join just so there'd be one less champion working against his niece, or even merely being out from under the eye of a watchful family, which Feilan could sympathise with – then Feilan could well imagine him deciding on a *you'll-do*. He'd even said it: *I know you won't hurt me.*

His irritated suspicion subsided. 'Thanks, that's flattering,' he said wryly. 'You got what you wanted, then.'

It was a long time before Renart's voice floated out into the dark, long enough that Feilan had almost fallen asleep on his side of the furs. 'I got what I needed, yes.'

5

The uninvited guest was gone from the hut in the morning. Slightly disappointed – he'd hoped to make good on the exchange of suck for rut he'd offered last night – Feilan crawled out of the warm nest of his furs and made his way to the bathing pond. It was deep, lined with rocks, refreshed by the same underground flow that filled Siftar's well upstream, and sheltered by the palisade wall and the traditional ash tree.

None of that made it any warmer. His breath frosted as he washed, exchanging greetings with a few sandy-eyed fellow Siftar residents.

He was, however, shortly summoned to the meeting hall by a whistle from one of Freyja's message-runners. He took a moment to peek out the river gate. The clinker was still at the dock, and lading was underway. Their visiting bear-warriors were still about, then, but were most likely sleeping late, sprawled in whichever hut they'd been beckoned into last night, or relegated to the guard barracks' bunks.

Clean and dressed, hair combed and still damp, beard freshly trimmed, Feilan entered the meeting hall and took a seat alongside Freyja at the negotiation table she'd set up yesterday. She looked thoughtfully across at Renart, fidgeting in a clean shirt too large for him. He was scrubbed, hair combed free of knots, and seemed ready to depart.

Perhaps this was a formal farewell then, though Feilan couldn't imagine why his presence had been demanded for it, or why the princess's presence had not been.

Renart glanced at Feilan as he sat, but looked away before Feilan could read his expression. He stopped tapping his fingers against the loose shirt, and set his hands on the table, cutting off his fidgeting with the same exquisite discipline as yesterday.

'Feilan, did you have sex with this man last night?' Freyja asked, without the single word of warning he would have *greatly* appreciated.

He raised both brows. The last thing he wanted was to discuss anything of the sort with Freyja, but she had the tone of merely confirming what she already knew. They hadn't been quiet, after all, and he'd mused on the thinness of the walls himself. But no one who'd overheard them would have had any reason to report it to Freyja, unless—

'Is he making a complaint?'

'The very opposite, I'd say. You said some words in his language? A rite of some sort?'

Feilan glanced at Renart, who stared straight ahead. '...Yes?'

'Voluntarily? You knew what they were for?'

'Yes,' he repeated. 'A ritual spoken before taking a virgin. He said it was necessary.'

Freyja slapped her forehead. She said, 'Feilan, you married him.'

Feilan frowned. He'd misheard. 'I...?'

'You married him, my boy.'

He contemplated this statement from all directions, attempting to find a way to interpret it to mean something other than what he thought it meant. Weakly, he asked, 'Is marriage between men customary in the Riverlands?'

Renart was as conspicuously still as a prey animal trying not to be noticed. 'It's...not specifically disallowed.'

Freyja tilted her chin. 'You willingly completed an ancient and binding marriage ritual, and then you willingly consummated it. Willingly, and, by all reports, enthusiastically. You married him.'

Feilan was still watching Renart, who shrunk under his steady, accusatory regard. 'You said it was a local custom for when you give up your virginity.'

Renart, addressing his own hands, said, 'Also known as a wedding.'

Feilan thought about how much Renart appeared to dislike him, before getting drunk and considering the notion of sleeping with him for the sake of a minor favour. Before showing up naked in his furs, running cool fingers over his back. How he'd insisted on an all-the-way fuck, despite being tense to the touch, despite it being his first time in bed with anyone. How he'd performed under Feilan's gaze, washing away his unease with the bloodrush of lust, skating casually over the need to say a few ritual words first while Feilan was well and truly distracted by the sight of him fisting his own red-swollen cock.

Wonderingly, he said, 'I *knew* you were up to something.'

'If you knew it,' Freyja said, 'why did you go along with it?'

Feilan stared at her, and then lifted both hands towards Renart, because that was plainly the only explanation required.

'Thinking with your cock like every other Vaer man,' she said. 'I expected better from you. We'll have to change your byname to Amleth.'

Feilan hadn't much liked his byname when he'd first been gifted it – the sarcastic intent, the diminutive aspect, and the play on his father's name all rankled – and had once hoped to earn a new one, but he was attached to it now. It had greatly helped to realise that it came from a dialectal word folded into Old Vaer from the western peoples they had constantly raided a few hundred years before. He had maternal ancestors there: his byname thus became an insult to his father and a compliment to his mother, both very backhanded.

Being renamed Fool wasn't in his plans, and he gave Freyja a speaking look which said so.

Freyja returned him a smile. 'Yes, all right, dear.'

At this evidence that her sense of humour remained intact, the tension ebbed from Feilan's shoulders. Freyja wasn't too alarmed, and wasn't more than passingly annoyed. That must mean she knew such trickery wouldn't stand. He'd been, if not quite coerced, at the very least badly misled. There weren't many contracts made under such deceptive circumstances that would be honoured, anywhere else in Enea. It would be the same here in the well-regulated Riverlands.

Renart cleared his throat. 'He confirms he said the words and consummated it.'

'I heard,' Freyja said dryly. 'Not knowingly, but yes, he did do that. And what is it you're after, Rufran?'

Renart narrowed his eyes at the name, but from her it wasn't Foxy, more along the lines of You Crafty Little Shit. 'I want the marriage honoured.'

'No, you don't,' she said. 'Come along, we don't have all day. You want, what, a payment of silver for your sullied purity? You're pretty enough, I suppose, but you're not a woman who's given up any chance of making a high marriage, and you're certainly not a Vaer man waving his violated honour about. Did you really think you could bargain your arse for enough silver to make that contract after all? Advice from a trader: make the bargain *first* next time.'

He flushed; Freyja had as good as called him a whore. Feilan judged her a touch more than passingly annoyed. His alarm rose accordingly.

'I don't need to make a mercenary contract, because I have a marriage contract.' Renart spoke with great deliberation. 'He said the words, he knew what they were for, he is my husband.' He finally looked at Feilan. 'You're my champion in the monster hunt.'

'I'll be properly buggered before I do a cursed thing on your behalf ever,' Feilan informed him.

He was not, by nature or by upbringing, a shouter, another thing that differentiated him from the bersverdar. His tone was almost pleasant. Renart took a moment to hear the hostility in the words.

His mouth tightened. Apparently finding Feilan unreasonable, he addressed Freyja. 'It's two new moons, at the very most, and then I'll free him from any further obligation. And Queen Adeline will pay him.'

'She won't, because her regent won't let her, because her regent won't be you, because I'm not winning the serthing monster hunt for you.'

'I will make it worth your while to win.'

Feilan said, strangled, 'Do I look like I can win, Rufran?'

'That is not my name, and you are Vaeringan, so *yes*.'

'Oh, Njorda's tits.' Amusement was surging in his chest, drowning out his anger and, yes, his sheer embarrassment for unthinkingly walking – rutting – into such an obvious trap. 'Oh, no, come on, did you not notice the difference between me and the bear-warriors? Between me and even the Siftar sentries?'

Freyja chuckled too. 'I love this man like a son—'

'Mother!' Feilan said, throwing adolescent pet into his tone. 'You're not funny.'

'*Mother*?' Renart said, looking aghast, as well he might, since he was the one who'd decided to drag their sexual exploits into the light of maternal judgement.

'You might have guessed,' Feilan said, further delighted by his discomfit. 'We have the same eyes.'

Catching Feilan around the shoulders, Freyja roughly tousled his hair before he could duck. 'My boy has many sterling qualities,' she said. 'But he's not a warrior. You've caught yourself the wrong fish, Nivardus.'

Recovering his composure, Renart lifted his chin. 'He'll have to do.'

'I'll have to do,' Feilan echoed, amusement winking out under a good dollop of bitterness, which surprised him as much as it appeared to surprise Freyja and Renart.

He was pissed off at Renart, and annoyed with himself for being fooled, yet still found a moment to be hurt that he was once again a *you'll do*, even under such outlandish circumstances. The ridiculousness of that reaction spurred him to make the point he didn't understand why Freyja hadn't made yet.

'I've seen contracts made from one end of Enea to the other, and I don't believe they're made any differently in the Riverlands than anywhere else, and I don't think trade contracts are so different to marital ones, either,' he said. 'If Adeline's guardian is the one who established the terms of this monster hunt contest, I'm sure he'll have some things to say about the validity of the appointment of your champion. Trickery annuls contracts.'

He'd hit his mark: Renart was as bad at hiding chagrin as he was every other emotion, except, apparently, the triumph he must have kept under wraps last night – or perhaps that had been what had inspired those genuine-seeming sounds of pleasure as his unsuspectingly newlywed husband had taken him.

And he'd felt bad about the frantic end to their fuck, too – he wished now he'd ridden the sneaky little drit harder.

'I did suppose you might go that route,' Renart said carefully. 'It would have to go to hustings.' That was a royal gathering of the Riverlands rulers or their delegates; the Vaer had a similar thing. 'The next assembly's three moons away. You might as well play along until then.'

Feilan opened his mouth to decry any inclination at all towards such good will, and Renart said, still carefully, but in a rush, 'And I will play along in return.'

He promptly turned red, his whole face flushing rather than just his cheeks. Head lowered, he stared at his trembling hands while Feilan stared at him. 'Play along with *what*?'

'Play along with…the marriage.'

'He's embarrassed to be offering you sex in front of your mother,' Freyja translated helpfully.

'Can I be the arsehole you tried very hard to raise me not to be for a moment?' Feilan asked her in Vaer.

'Go ahead, you're a grown man.' Truly, she had no call to be this amused by his predicament.

He said, 'Rufran, I've had you. I had you very thoroughly last night, I'm not upturning my entire *very pleasant* life to take part in a monster hunt I can't win just so I can get more sex from an unwilling man when I've plenty of willing partners about. You're attractive, but you're not that attractive.'

'Feilan, I'd like to speak to you alone for a moment,' Freyja said.

'This better not be going where I think it's going,' he said, closing his eyes.

Once a still-red, very chastened Renart scurried from the hall, Freyja said, thoughtfully, 'He *is* attractive, isn't he?'

'You think I should take him up on his offer?' Feilan asked her dryly.

'That part's your business,' she said, but then added, 'I did raise you better.'

'I wasn't planning on indulging in marital rape, Mother.'

'Decent of you.'

'Thanks, I appreciate a low bar.'

Freyja sighed. Abruptly, she said, 'I like the little girl.' He kept his mouth shut until she waved a hand irritably and admitted, 'I want her to win.'

'We don't involve ourselves in local politics,' he reminded her. 'We merely watch, and take advantage.'

'I know that, Little Wolf,' she said, with the maternal note that warned him to shut his cursed – Cursed, even – mouth again.

He didn't. 'Though...we *are* talking about a realm that's been steadfastly against making trade with us, blocking the further valleys. Her future gratitude might open up that whole region.'

He raised his brows at her invitingly.

Freyja drummed her fingers on the arm of her chair. 'I don't deny it'd be useful to have been the new queen's supporter in the unlikely chance she *did* win – but it's far too dangerous to be seen to be her supporter when she inevitably loses and whoever has rule over her looks about to consolidate his power. And stupid not to back the strongest contender, if we *are* going to interfere.' She shook her head, face set in a contemplative frown. 'And yet. I want the little girl to win.'

He simpered. 'Does she remind you of me when I was her age?'

'Not everything's about you, dear,' she said. '...Of me, actually. She reminds me of me.'

Freyja had married – been married off – young, to Ulfr Njallsson, a brutal man, a bersverdr of the hardest sort. It'd been an unhappy union, Feilan the only surviving issue, to his father's vocal disgust. And perhaps Freyja's quieter dismay: he'd been too weak to defend his mother against his father, after all, and the same obvious, shameful, weakness provoked the man's rage against them both too often.

Perhaps that was all to Feilan's eventual luck. If she'd been content with her husband – or content *enough*, the near-inevitable state of Vaer wives – and had plentiful other children, she might have allowed Feilan's execution to go ahead for the sake of holding on to the little life she did have.

As it was, he was likely a *you'll-do* to her, too, just enough of an impetus for her to leave her marriage and the village, towing a Cursed son behind her and earning a cursing of her own for her trouble.

No. He wasn't being fair, carrying Torben's indifferent shrug and Renart's grim *He'll have to do* too far. She'd always protected him, for his own sake. She'd taken beatings throughout her marriage; it was a Vaer man's right to discipline a disobedient wife, and Ulfr took that right very much to the heart he didn't have, even though most men were more controlled.

But those beatings were nothing compared to the thrashing her husband gave her when she'd pushed too hard, too insistently, for Feilan to forgo the summer raiding.

'Not every boy goes,' she'd pleaded, again, keeping her voice low in the scant privacy of the alcove they shared in a longhouse filled with extended family, Feilan's cousins and half-siblings, and all the drudges and sworn men and servants of the farm. 'Boys who won't be devotees don't have to go.'

'My son goes,' Ulfr had said. 'Any son of mine is meant for the bear-god.'

'He'll die.'

In his own alcove nearby, young Aleifr Ulfrsson, no byname yet, had squeezed his eyes shut, knowing she was right. Wishing she would stop, before his father started hitting her. Hoping she wouldn't.

'Better that than shame,' Ulfr said.

'Please, Ulfr. Please. I am begging you, husband. If you *ever* cared for our boy—'

Her next words were cut off by the sound of the first blow. In a house filled with people, no one stopped him. No one ever did. It was his right.

If there was any sort of good to be wrung from the night Feilan had been caught on his knees sucking cock and dragged before the elders, it was that his father had been one of them. The look on his face when he realised his son's secret shame was laid bare, the look on his face as the other old, hard warriors, his peers, had turned to stare in silent, self-satisfied disgust *at him*, mighty Ulfr Njallson, had warmed Feilan on many a cold night since.

The other good, the good that made him never regret it at all, was that it had given his mother the chance to claw her way to her second life, where she was practically a queen, and knew it, and knew she'd done it all on her own merit, her own hard-earned reputation, now worth solid gold.

And now she was looking at another young girl, even younger than she had been, with the potential to be a queen, whose agency was going to be shackled to men so her own light would never shine, and might even be extinguished, if she was given over to the local equivalent of a brutal Vaer husband.

Feilan said, 'I'll do it,' so she didn't have to ask him to. She'd never asked him to stop his father, either.

'Dearest,' she said, soft.

'But I'm going to be a right bitch to him while I'm at it.'

She sighed. 'As I say, you're a grown man.'

'Don't try to guilt me out of my fun, Mother.' He paused. 'I can't promise the win. I'll try.'

'*That* part, I'm working on,' Freyja said. 'Send the little queen in, would you?' She smiled a wicked smile. 'And your beloved, of course.'

Feilan made a cheerily offensive gesture, and went out to do that.

ORD WAS BEGINNING TO SPREAD. CLEVER Little Wolf had been outsmarted. Lingering outside the hall while Freyja laid plans with Renart and Adeline, Feilan got good-natured teasing, claps on the shoulder, and even sincere congratulations, including from Meik.

'You'll make a good husband,' Meik told him, before wiping away an honest-to-goodness tear and wandering off.

Feilan was still looking after him bemusedly when Torben, arriving from the other direction, stuck his head in the meeting hall and was snarled at by Freyja. He ignominiously retreated, and spotted Feilan beckoning him from his relaxed sit on a grass tuft beyond the hall.

He'd been all ready to mock Feilan without mercy, Feilan was sure, but Freyja's loud rebuke had knocked the wind from his sails. Throwing himself down on the mild slope of goat-trimmed grass by Feilan, he managed a bare, 'Bet you feel a right jolterhead.'

'Bet I do.'

'I was jealous last night,' Torben offered, which might have been an apology, if Feilan squinted.

'Yeah? He's pretty, fair enough. Not pretty enough to *marry*, mind, and he's got a bit of a temper on him. Jealous now?'

Torben was staring at the hall. 'Wasn't jealous of *you*.'

'Of him?' Feilan asked in surprise. This notion was about the closest Torben had ever skated to admitting Feilan was anything but convenient.

'Didn't like the idea of Foxy having you,' Torben muttered, plucking blades of grass between thick fingers. 'Don't know why.'

'Now he has me for half the season,' Feilan said, poking him. 'Walking out on me rebounded on both of us, didn't it? You'll be gone raiding by the time I come back, and I won't see you again until next summer.'

Torben turned onto his back so he could stare up at the cloud-streaked sky. 'If I survive this summer.'

It was Feilan's seasonal fear. He said, 'Morbid.'

'I feel the cold wind blowing, Little Wolf.'

'Is that saga-talk for telling me you feel old?'

'I *am* old, for a raider.'

'That means you're good, for a raider.'

Torben brightened considerably at this; bersverdar loved a tug on their battle-pride. But after a moment, he said, 'It's not how it was when we were young.'

'You sound like every old man ever.'

'Do you know we don't even actually raid now, half the time? We extort, instead. We knock on the gates, and *threaten* to raid, and they hand over their silver. Not even *all* their silver! A politely negotiated amount! And do you know what we do then?'

'Yes,' Feilan said, smiling. 'You give them a receipt.'

'We give them a receipt, Little Wolf!'

The receipts were stamped clay tokens. The citizens of the raided-by-proxy towns would carry them, to prove they'd already paid up that season. It was safer, all round, more peaceable. Better for trade, certainly. Freyja had been quietly encouraging the trend for years. So had someone else.

Torben was well into his fulminating now. 'And do you know what happened last summer? We went down to Aldhelm and demanded silver, and the king came down to us at the gate, and it was, I don't know, some buggering Snorri Snorrisson' – this was the Vaer equivalent of an Old-What's-His-Face – 'and he said, you can't raid here, it's my town, this whole region's mine. He'd settled there, Little Wolf! Brought along his whole family, too. And you know what else?'

'If you're referring to Olvar Korisson, I think I can guess.'

'He told us the other three closest towns were his, too!'

'Uh huh. He's got his own baby empire. It's six towns, by the way, across four former provinces that all belong to him now. You can let your commander know to take Elfurt and Trither off his plans.'

Feilan had good reason to closely monitor Olvar's progress, more than simply weighing its impact on their trade network. Torben was right: Olvar had brought his whole family, grown-up sons and daughters all ripe for parcelling into alliances. But he hadn't brought his wife. Whether he was widowed, or still had a winter-wife back in the heartland, Feilan didn't know, but he did know the budding emperor had made overtures to Freyja, and Freyja was considering it.

That was, he was sure, part of the reason she was breaking her own rules about staying out of local politics to help Adeline. The chance to widen their trade network was only the first benefit. The flow-on was substantial: she would bring that trade network to the imperial negotiation table.

Torben groaned. 'The young ones think this is *normal*,' he said. 'We're bear-warriors. Fire and blood, in the service of our god. Proper worship isn't performed by handing out *receipts*.'

Feilan looked down at his friend from his lofty perch on the tuft. An ant was traversing the grass; he flicked it away before it could reach Torben and bite. 'At least your cold wind is more of a temperate breeze, then.'

A complicated expression passed over Torben's face. He said, 'I don't fear to find my death.'

'Gods forfend I accuse Mighty Thunder Bear of any such thing.'

Torben heaved a decidedly long-suffering breath and swatted Feilan's leg, a lazy rebuke. 'In battle, Little Wolf. I don't fear to die in battle. The fact that I'm getting less and less opportunity is...'

He didn't seem inclined to finish his thought. His hand came to rest around Feilan's ankle, and squeezed. He gave an experimental tug. Feilan kicked him off before he could exert himself and pull him from his little hummock. Torben glanced around, and then, no fellow bersverdar in sight, snaked his hand over Feilan's calf. His thumb pushed in, rubbing along muscle, deliciously on the edge of too painful.

'Speaking of opportunities,' he said. 'I've got time. You got time?'

Feilan hesitated, looking at the meeting hall. If his mother didn't need him again, he should be about the last of his Siftar business, collating the reports the travelling merchants sent back to him, talking in person to those who had recently arrived to see what else they had observed, briefing those about to depart on the latest news along their trade routes, making sure his competent clerks were well-placed to take on his duties while he was away.

'Come on.' Torben's voice was summer-shallow water across riverbed gravel now. 'I hear tell you're good for unquestioningly sticking your cock in pretty men who ask nicely enough.'

Feilan snorted, and then fell into real laughter, the release burbling up through his chest. Truthfully, he'd been feeling an utter fool, and quietly angry with Renart, and even slightly aggrieved at Freyja despite his best intentions, and that all slid away with the pleasure of having this big, blond jolterhead wrap callused fingers about his calf and tease him.

'They do have to be pretty, though,' he said, casually enough that it was a couple of heartbeats before Torben said 'Hoi!' and swatted him again.

Feilan shoved back, Torben bore down on him with what could only be a featherweight of his full strength. It looked set to turn into a wrestle.

Feilan increased his stubborn resistance to being pushed over. 'I am too old and dignified to roll about with you on the grass.'

The grapple became intimate, a sweep of thumbs over hipbones. 'Come roll about in the furs, then.'

Feilan admitted, 'I don't know how my new husband feels about that, and Freyja will have your balls if you bugger up her plans.'

This made Torben let him go, to his minor regret. Sitting up, the bersverdr waved towards the hall. 'I don't know why your mother dislikes me so much.'

Feilan coughed, a sharp inadvertent sound of surprise. 'Do you mean aside from that minor incident in our youth when you were perfectly prepared to let me be executed rather than speak up?'

It was Torben's turn to be surprised – more than that, shocked. 'She knew it was me? You *told* her?'

'Thunder Bear.' Feilan found himself laughing again, though his amusement had a diamond glitter on it now. '*Everyone* knew it was you. The whole village knew. Why do you think the magnate and his elders went so hard trying to force me to name you? They practically expected it of me, but you? One of their biggest, strongest up-and-coming warriors, a Cursed? They were looking to weed you out if they could, before you brought shame on the village and infected the other warriors with your weakness.'

Torben went pale, and then, rapidly, red. There was a reason they didn't talk about this, Feilan supposed, not once in the seven summers since Torben had sauntered into Siftar and had Feilan flat on his back within a thumb's measure of their reunion. He'd been incautious, lulled by lying and laughing in the warm sun with his sometime lover, his childhood friend.

And – why should he be cautious? He was Cursed. The worst had happened, and he'd ended safe and accepted and valued within Freyja's trading empire. He'd examined his preferences, dragged them into the light, tried them out every which way, and purged the last lingering remnant of dishonour and guilt and shame and self-hatred. If, after all these years, Torben still hadn't found a way, *any* way, to accept the secret, dishonourable part of himself, Feilan couldn't help him with caution.

So he said, 'You know, the next time you were away from girls too long and gave in to the temptation.'

That was the way it had been, their first summer raiding, Feilan's only summer raiding. Before that, in the village, they had those few rare encounters, Feilan pushing Torben into the forest, Torben prodding Feilan up to the high pasture, but Torben had mostly slaked his need with willing girls.

But away from home, death riding close, opportunities to slip away rife, all taboo, all restraint, was gone. And young Torben's outsized reaction when Feilan went down under a sword, side split open like he was a pig gone to slaughter – that had all but given the game away to the other raiders, though Torben had been absolved once he'd proven battle-bold, exceptional with his axe, extraordinary once he stolen a proper sword instead of the cheap one he'd trained on.

Feilan touched the ridge of his scar through his woollen shirt. He'd been lucky, but he'd also had Torben to drag him back to camp and shout at the healers.

'It's normal enough.' Torben had gone wild around the eyes, the way bersverdar sometimes did before a battle. 'They expect a bit of that, when there's not enough women about.'

It was why the handful of raiders was here in Siftar, after all. And yet... 'Not normal to take the cock, though. How the symmetry of it works out, I'll never fathom.'

Torben suddenly lurched and seized Feilan's shirt, fisting his hands into the wool, distorting its fine weave. 'It's your fault,' he snarled, shaking him. 'Bugger you, I never would have done it if you hadn't been mooning over me.'

'Let go.' Feilan grabbed his wrists and tried to wrest him off, without success. 'You came to me. You had plenty of girls mooning over the Mighty Thunder Bear after that summer, and *you* found the storehouse, *you* took me there, *you* knew what you were asking for.'

Torben yanked him off the tuft and slammed him into the ground, hard enough to smart the skin on his back. Feilan bit his tongue and resorted to his best copy of Freyja's coldest stare from witchy sea-ice eyes.

Torben shoved away, threw himself back onto the grass, and ran his hands over his face. 'Your arsefucking mouth.'

It was unclear whether he was referring to Feilan's willing mouth back then, or decrying his current mouthiness now.

'You came to me,' Feilan repeated, softer, 'and you kept coming to me for months, until we got caught and it turned out you'd rather watch my execution than face exile.'

'Your mother saved you before I could act,' Torben said sullenly.

'Oh?' Feilan raised a brow, quelling the tremor in his chest. 'You would have acted? Admitted it? Forsaken the bear-god and gone into exile with me?'

Torben's broad shoulders sank. His gaze dropped.

There had been a telling moment, all those years ago, with the watch-man standing over Feilan, still on his knees, lips red and swollen and wet from hard use, only just beginning to realise the very deep shit he was in. He and the watchman had both turned from watching Torben's broad naked backside flee out the rear door of the rickety little shed into the cold night, and looked at each other.

Feilan had tried to rise, to face his shameful fate on his feet, and the watchman had held him on his knees with a heavy press on his shoulder, and touched the ties of his own trousers, where his arousal already bulged.

Just that, a mute offer of exchange: silence for service. Feilan had just as mutely begun to undo the ties with trembling fingers, already supposing this would not be a one-time extortion but going along with it anyway, because he knew the penalty if he didn't.

Then one of the other watchmen had called out, probably alerted to trouble by the crash of the rear door as Torben had escaped, and the watchman had stepped back briskly, tightening his ties and shouting, 'Cursed. Cursed here! Caught him on his knees with his mouth full of cock.'

Many years had passed since that moment of crisis, the dismal hours that followed. It no longer stung like it once had; shame no longer bit him over his own preferences, the hatred of his own father and most of his people. Years of exposure to the customs of other people had helped greatly, and so had the care of other Cursed, and so had his mother's occasional bracing talk.

But a deeply-buried hurt remained: the knowledge that if he hadn't stripped Torben naked that night, hadn't bared his broad, muscular form so he could delight in the flex and strain of those massive thighs, strong back, and wide, wide shoulders as he took the warrior groaning over the same bale he'd knelt behind afterwards, that if Torben had instead been mostly dressed and thus able to pull his cock from Feilan's mouth when the door opened and shout, 'Cursed here!' as he did up his ties – he would have done it without a moment's hesitation.

Feilan had absolutely no illusions about that, and yet, the way Torben's shoulders bowed now still struck him hard.

'Then shut your mouth,' he said, no jagged humour in it at all. 'And don't you dare ever blame me again.'

It was unwise, both his words, and the savagery of his tone. His friend would take it. But a Vaer warrior wouldn't, *couldn't* bear to stay cowed in the face of that sort of provocation.

Torben decided on the latter, and flared up, rising to his knees to loom over him, growling, 'Ballsy for a man who couldn't hit water if he fell out of a boat.'

'Really?' Feilan said, forcing himself to remain sprawled where Torben had tossed him instead of instinctively lunging to his feet. 'Really, Tryggvi?'

The tension held, and snapped. Torben sagged from affronted warrior into chastened friend. He flopped onto his back again. 'All right, yeah, that was a particularly dick move.'

'You're nothing *but* dick moves.'

Torben chortled. 'And don't you know it.'

Feilan dissolved into a helpless grin, quickly smothered so he could pinch the chuckling Torben with a suitably stern mien. Torben shoved him, Feilan elbowed him in retaliation, Torben rolled towards him; it was about to become a wrestling match, somewhere in the achingly familiar maze between hostile and flirtatious, when a throat cleared nearby.

They both turned to see Renart, looking pink. He probably hadn't understood the Vaer, despite his small facility earlier. He was probably embarrassed by the wrestling. 'Your mother...'

Feilan made an annoyed noise, matched by Torben. As he rose and dusted himself off, Renart finished, '...wants to see Torben.'

'Him?'

'Me?'

Renart's scathing expression demonstrated that he did not find the gape-jawed look appealing on either of them. 'No, one of the many other Torbens here.'

'Sertha af, skroggr.' Torben rose, adding ominously to Feilan, 'Won't wear out his shirt if he keeps that up.'

He stalked into the hall, leaving Feilan with his new and unwanted husband.

'There *are* a few others about,' he said into the awkward silence. 'It's a common byname. It means Thunder Bear. He's Magni Torben, really.' He checked. 'He'd surely have other bynames by now. That's from his first summer. Sixteenth summer. First summer raiding.'

Renart did not seem inclined to indulge the reminiscing. 'I'll need you to be civil,' he said abruptly.

'You first,' Feilan said.

'I am being civil.'

'You're actually very rude.'

'Coming from a barbarian.'

'That!' Feilan said. 'Exactly that sort of snide comment, Rufran.'

'That's not my name!'

Feilan swallowed the childish impulse to follow him around chanting, 'Foxy, Foxy, Foxy!' Not everyone appreciated the Vaer habit of bestowing status sobriquets at every opportunity.

In measured tones, he said, 'I'm literate. I've travelled Enea many times over and seen palaces and artworks you've not dreamed of, and met kings and sultans, warlords and chieftains. I speak nine languages, all of them competently, four of them well. One of them this one, and I bet you couldn't converse with me in many others.'

Renart had folded into himself, shoulders hunched. He made an effort to straighten and meet Feilan's eye. 'I'm sorry,' he said. 'I'm not used to talking to…'

'Barbarians?'

'People,' Renart snapped, contriteness immediately discarded for irritation. 'I'm not much around people, back home.'

Feilan called on the old tales. 'Precious maid confined in the mound?'

'Not quite,' Renart said, looking at the ground, where the ant, or another, was gamely making its way through the grass, hopefully on a mission to bite the sly serthr. He was absently pulling at a lock of his uncovered hair.

'Not quite? Ah, not a virgin after all? Shame, that was my one consolation.' It hadn't been; he was just doing as promised, being a right bitch.

'I was,' Renart said. Feilan figured he was biting his tongue hard, to be responding to the bait with mere monosyllables. 'I don't lie.'

Without intending to, Feilan stopped the needling and asked the question that had been bothering him. 'Do your preferences lie with men?'

'No,' Renart said, looking away. 'As I said.'

'Ah.'

Sex without desire was not an alien concept to Feilan. He felt no preference for women himself, but in their early years, when a trade deal could be closed by a certain exchange, Freyja didn't shy from it, with men or women, and neither did he. Sometimes it was a chore, sometimes an unexpectedly pleasant interlude, and sometimes a short-lived affair that would have happened even without the dangle of the deal.

The first time for Feilan had been in aid of a long-term trade deal with a Chalcadean noblewoman who wanted lusty, strong-lunged grandchildren before marrying her daughters off to what she'd termed milk-weak men for the sake of alliances. She hadn't quite openly demanded Feilan as brood-stock, and Freyja hadn't quite asked her young son to oblige. He knew she'd sealed deals with her own body by then; she hadn't had to ask. Besides, it was nice to discover he could contribute more than a scowl and a hand on a sword grip.

He'd spent his time divided between the three daughters. Two had ridden him with more enthusiasm than he'd expected, legs locked around his hips, nails raking his chest. The third had trembled and flinched, until he'd gently said, 'We can just tell your mother we did,' and she'd glared at him and said, 'I want you to pin me down and ravish me, you great fool.'

That was some game spun from lurid tales of Vaer men from his father's time and earlier, and it wasn't the last time he encountered it, from women and from men. He never could decide if he liked it more or less than the other game, the one where his bedmate wanted to see a mighty Vaer warrior on his knees, subjugated, pleading. It could turn bitter; sometimes those people really had been raided, and wanted true payback. He drew the line at letting them hit him. He'd had too much of that from his father to find any delight in it at all.

It all meant he could hardly be shocked that Renart had gone against his own preferences for practical reasons. But Feilan had only ever engaged in such liaisons both willingly and openly.

It galled him that Renart had been unwilling, and had hidden it, and he said so.

'I wasn't unwilling.' Renart uncrossed his arms, shifted his weight, crossed them again. 'Just...'

'Motivated at cross-purposes to me,' Feilan murmured.

Renart smiled, a curiously innocent, open smile, utterly at odds with his stiff and awkward demeanour. 'One way to put it.' He hesitated, then said, 'I *am* sorry. I am...quite frightened, actually, and it makes me unpleasant, I know.'

Feilan lifted his brows. Men didn't admit to fear, not where he came from. He didn't think he'd ever heard a man anywhere in Enea do so quite this readily. It was almost brave.

'Not of you,' Renart assured him, misreading his surprise. 'The children weren't scared of you, you see. And your friend, the big woman. She spilled that ale all over you, and wasn't scared. Women and children aren't scared of you. So I don't think I need to be.'

It was almost a question, which Feilan failed to respond to. He was too distracted by fighting off another unsuspected latent cultural bias, this time the instinctive reaction to being casually informed that he did not inspire fear in women and children. A Vaer man might parse it as an insult, because of the Vaer commingling of fear and respect.

After a moment, Renart finished, 'And you are being quite mature about this situation, all told.'

Feilan caught the echo of Freyja's *You're a grown man* there, and paused again. He understood she wanted the trade deal, and wanted the best for Adeline; so did he. But he could not understand why she was being so helpful to this obnoxious creature to the extent of handing him extra strings to marionette her own son about.

'It's a Vaer thing,' he said slowly. 'We appreciate a trickster. *Not*—' He held up a finger for emphasis. '—that I much appreciate being the target of it, but I do appreciate the game.'

'I see,' Renart said, like he didn't.

'Well played, Uncle Remy,' Feilan added, belatedly realising Renart had been seeking reassurance that he'd guessed right regarding his new husband's proclivity towards inspiring fear.

He was starting to laugh at the look of astonishment the praise provoked when a whistle sounded; Torben had poked his head out to summon them inside.

Adeline was looking very excited. If she weren't trying to sit up straight in a queenly fashion, Feilan thought she'd be skipping about the meeting hall like the little girl she'd been this morning until he'd summoned her into the hall and back to her duty.

On the table lay a small roll of parchment, held open with lead weights on each corner.

'Adeline and Torben will make contract,' Freyja said, tapping the parchment.

Feilan's brows shot up. 'Why?'

'He's to keep an eye on you, and you're to make sure he gets the head of the monster so Adeline wins the right to her own rule.'

'No, I know that, I mean...' He turned to Torben. '*Why?*'

'The little princess will pay me silver if she's queen, your mother will make good on the payment if she's not.'

That took Feilan aback enough to look questioningly at Freyja. Promising silver, marked with her own stamp, was another step along from merely taking a strong interest in local politics with the ready excuse of her only son's marriage. He read her minute grimace. She thought she was making a good bet, and the payment would come from Riverlander coffers, not hers.

It still didn't seem enough of a reason for Torben to give up his annual pilgrimage in service to his bear-god, especially not when he'd been moping about feeling too old. He *was* old, for a bersverdr, he was right about that. He knew he was approaching the end. Someday soon, maybe this very summer, despite his plaintive rant about the dearth of opportunity, he'd run headlong into battle as he always had, and he'd be just a little slower, or a little weaker, and he'd fail to block a sword or dodge a spear or duck an arrow.

Many would think this looming fate would be a good reason to take a different path. Feilan knew it was Torben's main reason not to. If he did not find his glorious death in battle, what would be the alternative? Eventually he'd be faced with the ignominious fate he dreaded: he'd have to hang his sword on the wall and spend his summers at home, waving off the younger raiders, being ignored by his wife and avoided by his grandchildren.

Some veterans took to village life as elders, advisers to the magnate. Torben wouldn't be one of them. He'd earned enough respect for it, after marrying well, after years of superlative service, after earning his own longsword, after avoiding any hint of dishonour for a solid twenty-five turns of a year since the summer of Feilan's disgrace, but he did not possess, in any measure at all, the interest for it. The magnate had been his father-in-law, and then his brother-in-law, and was now one of his wife's cousins. He in turn served, through a series of lesser overlords, the vik-konungr, the king-on-the-bay. The composition of the hierarchy changed regularly, usually amid piles of bloodied corpses to sate the hungry ravens. Meanwhile, Torben honed his blades and anticipated the next fight, to honour, not some allvaldr on a distant throne, but his god.

Torben coughed. 'I owe you,' he muttered.

'What?'

'Your mother reminded me that I owe you,' he said, louder. 'For your silence.'

Feilan touched his side. 'I owe you for this. You saved me then.'

'As you saved me, when I risked us both.'

It hadn't all been Torben, and, caught together in minor serth, they would only have been at risk of exile, which, yes, could mean death in the hostile environs of the icebound heartland. The fact remained, he supposed: because he wouldn't name Torben, he'd been slated for hanging, usually reserved for men caught enjoying cock in a worse place than their mouths, whereas Torben, because he had not been named, had gone on to live an exalted warrior's life, instead of the Cursed life that might have killed him from the shame of it.

Renart, fidgeting at Adeline's shoulder, sniffed. 'If the mutual con-gratulations are done—'

Horns sounded and he shut his mouth, looking around with wide eyes. 'That's my uncle, he's found us.' He hurried to the hooks by the door, pulling his cowl down. 'Adeline's guardian.'

'It might not be,' Feilan said, watching him anxiously twitching the cowl up to thoroughly cover his hair.

Freyja's merchant corps, if coming in from their far-flung trading routes by river and road, tended to ride or sail in towards evening, but Riverlands merchants came and went all day. It was early, admittedly, but the clinkers, distinctive striped sails now visible on the river, advert-ised fresh goods, particularly prized when they came from the Vaer's exotic eastern trade networks.

Renart made a gesture which managed to be both impatient and dis-missive as he slid onto the bench beside Adeline. 'Can we sign this contract?'

'Feilan, read it to me,' Torben said. 'This one's too crafty to trust.'

Gytha put her head around the door to say, 'Riders crossing the bridge.'

'There is no time!'

'Trying to rush me just makes me more suspicious,' Torben said.

Feilan bent over the document on the table. 'It's not written in Vaer runes.'

'You can't read it?'

'I can,' Feilan said, with a mild glare, 'but you have to give me a moment to translate.'

He tugged the parchment closer. He didn't recognise the letter shapes – he knew the major ones used across Enea as well as the standard Vaer runes they themselves wrote their contracts in, but this was a minor script, a local alphabet he didn't know.

'We don't *have* a moment,' Renart said.

'Read it out,' Torben commanded him, 'and Feilan, you translate.'

'If I'm as crafty as you think I am, I'd change any problematic clauses as I read them out.'

Torben folded his massive arms. 'I'm not signing.'

'I meant...' Renart faltered. '*If*. As in, I'm *not*.' He looked helplessly at Feilan.

He really was extremely bad at people, Feilan decided, with something that might almost have been affection underneath the consistent mild aggravation.

Adeline came to her uncle's rescue. 'But the contract is with me,' she said sweetly, not quite pouting but certainly sounding younger than she usually did. 'Will you not trust me, Sir Torben?'

'Are you going to be mean to the little girl, Tryggvi?' Freyja asked.

Torben's chiselled face wore a stymied expression. Insisting on having the contract terms translated now meant not only being mean to the little girl, but crossing Freyja. Still, he didn't move to dip his thumb in ink.

The sounds from outside were growing louder, distinctly suggestive of horses arriving at the overlander gate, hails and hurrying footsteps underpinned by the jingle of metal.

Feilan said, 'It's a standard seasonal mercenary contract, Torben. As long as they give you all their coins before we leave, they'll have held up their half of the bargain. And they'll not dare cheat you of your bonus if you win. The contract protects *them* from *you*, if anything.'

Torben, scowling, dipped his thumb in the pot of ink and pressed his mark at the bottom of the page. 'I, Tryggvi Jansson, he who is known first by Magni Torben, abide.'

Renart frowned at him. 'By the bear-god,' Feilan murmured in Vaer.

Torben gave him a flat look, but said, 'I swear it by Berguthi. May I fear Him if I renege.'

Adeline took up the quill, and dipped it. She signed with a childish flourish. 'Do I say... I, Adeline Nivardus, Queen of Seven Hills, abide. I swear it by Spenwan, She Who Spins, by Her distaff, by Her spindle.'

She handed the quill to her uncle. 'I, Renart Nivardus, paternal uncle of Adeline Nivardus, authorise *in absentia* of her guardian.' He looked over his shoulder at the doorway as he said the ritual words.

Feilan plucked the quill from his fingers and signed his own true name. 'I, Aleifr Freyjasson, known first and last by Feilan, witness.'

Ignoring the sharp look Renart was directing at him now, he leaned over to blow on the ink, to dry it enough to stamp the wax seal without smearing their marks. Torben was still wiping his thumb off when an entourage of new guests arrived, Gytha walking them in.

Renart Nivardus had got the contract signed *in absentia* by the barest skin of his teeth. Well played, Uncle Remy, with just a little assistance on the side from the barbarians he despised.

Feilan didn't know what he'd been expecting of the mysterious guardian with the outsized shadow: not the small, round, smiling man, somewhere about Freyja's age, who self-importantly toddled into the hall. He had attendants, disarmed, as everyone disarmed before passing through the gate.

Two women followed, both taller than him, though that was not to say much. They were black-haired, like the little queen, and had enough family resemblance about the nose and mouth that Feilan pegged them both as close relatives even before Adeline said happily, 'Aunt Odila! Aunt Rosa!'

And, less happily, hands wringing together, 'Good morning, Great-Uncle Bertrand.'

None of them took off their cloaks or caps. One of the aunts, the younger of the two, hurried straight to her niece to hug her.

The other one marched up to the still-seated Renart and backhanded him.

The worst thing about *that* was that Renart barely blinked. He didn't raise his hand to his cheek, which reddened under the blow. He merely bowed his head as she began to shout at him, holding as still as he did when facing Freyja, his nervy energy utterly contained.

'You *dare*,' she snarled. 'Two days, we've searched for you. *Two days.* And you brought her into a barbarian camp, of all places.'

'It was the last place you would look.' Apparently Renart approached every situation with the same unwise forthrightness.

The woman moved to hit him again, pulling her arm right back to get her shoulder into it, and Feilan caught her wrist.

'Don't touch him,' he growled.

Bertrand's men moved at him, but then Torben was looming by his side wearing the scarily flat look of a bear-god-touched warrior, and Freyja's guards, the only visibly armed people in the room, put their hands on their sword hilts.

Freyja lifted a finger, and everyone froze. Feilan spared a glance about. He'd surprised them, not so much with a display of incipient violence, but because he'd defended Renart. And he hadn't just astonished the newcomers, he saw, but Torben and the other Vaer, and Renart himself.

But not Freyja. She knew exactly the depths those three words had been dredged from, a reach back through time, with all the hard-won knowledge and boldness and confidence of a grown man, to catch and twist the wrist of a violent mean-eyed drunkard standing over a little boy, a defiant wife.

He did manage to stop himself before he actually twisted Lady Slaphappy's wrist, though, letting go and stepping back, drawing a bristling Torben with him. The opposed attendants breathed out, and the air settled.

The older man cleared his throat. The fracas had given him time to orient himself and he bowed to Freyja instead of making the mistake some green traders used to do, of addressing Feilan, or, Gods help them all, the tallest man in the room, who happened to be Torben.

Speaking clearly, he said, 'My name is Bertrand Nivardus, guardian of Queen Adeline, and regent of Seven Hills.'

'Freyja Anjasdottir.' She touched her chest, nodding in lieu of a full bow. She didn't give a title. She didn't have one. She hadn't needed anything more than her golden name for years.

'Thank you for taking care of my nephew and great-niece,' he said.

'A pleasure.'

He smiled affably. Feilan knew this type of man, friendly, reasonable, open-handed, right up until they pulled the knife, usually shortly after they had their signed contract secured.

Or before. 'And we owe you...' He raised his bushy white eyebrows as he delicately trailed off.

Freyja made a thoughtful noise and picked up the embroidery from the basket by her chair. Vaer women kept their hands busy. Most of Siftar had taken up their boss's example, women or not, trained to it from birth or not. Feilan wielded his nailbinders to make small dolls, good enough to sell. Most people made such playthings themselves, but there were always travellers taken by a fancy to surprise their children with some pretty memento.

Bertrand looked around at the other Vaer in plain confusion. Feilan remained blank-faced, though Torben shifted before Feilan gave him a subtle nudge that settled him into a stolid guarding-the-longboat stance.

Freyja made the man wait through a record ten precise stitches before deigning to address him again. 'Were you asking if we have taken our guests hostage?'

He said, 'No, of course not,' very heartily. Fast learner.

He glanced about, saw the contract on the table, and looked over at Torben sharply.

'Queen Adeline has made contract with my pet bear-warrior here,' Freyja confirmed. 'Champion for a monster hunt, it seems.'

Torben didn't twitch. He *wasn't* a fast learner, but he'd had years to learn to bow to Freyja's command, as had all the old warriors who used the staging post and the river-road. If she was calling him her pet now, he'd bark for her.

Bertrand huffed fussily, brushing at his rich velvet tunic. 'She is not of age, I am afraid. As her guardian, I would have to authorise it, and I do not. *Very* sorry to have wasted your time.'

'I did,' Renart said, head still bowed. He'd laid his hands flat on the table in front of him, fingers spread. His nails were bitten to the quick.

'You did, yes,' his uncle said, a note of sternness entering his voice. 'Perhaps you might also apologise, Renart. You are used to having to, after all.'

Renart tapped both thumbs, a light jagged rhythm. His other fingers clenched against the rough wood of the old oaken table, hard enough to garner splinters. He shuddered and his thumbs went still.

He said, 'I authorised the contract.'

'You did what?'

'I am her uncle, I am of age, I may grant permission *in absentia*, in matters of minor contracts.'

Lady Slaphappy paced in a tight line. 'Excuse me? You snuck away from home without a word, made the *queen* of Seven Hills walk about like a drudge—'

'If we'd gone to the stables, the servants would have reported—'

She raised her voice '—you walked into a barbarian camp with our *niece,* and helped her make contract with them?'

'Point of clarification,' Feilan said. 'Not barbarians. Traders.'

'Who are you?' she demanded, ostentatiously rubbing her wrist. 'Who is this, Renart?'

Feilan shifted his gaze to Renart, who pressed his hands even harder into the table. He muttered, 'My husband.'

Silence.

'Speak up, I don't think they heard you,' Feilan said. 'I'm his husband.'

'We heard him,' Lady Slaphappy snapped.

The other aunt – behaviour and apparent age suggested both were older sisters to Renart – had been standing alertly, her hands resting comfortingly on Adeline's shoulders, all this time. Now she came to Renart's side, and, with a sideways look Feilan's way, gently touched the cheek where the hand print was only just fading.

'Felicitations, brother,' she said, laying her hand over one of his. 'I wish you the full joy of my own recent happy event and more.'

Feilan, who had heard but immediately disregarded their names, mentally labelled her Lady Not-Yet-Proven-As-Nasty-As-The-Other-One.

Her words seemed to stoke Renart's courage. Taking a breath, he began, 'Sisters, uncle, this is Feilan, the—'

Torben snorted, and Freyja smiled. Renart stopped in confusion, arrested halfway through the introduction.

'Aleifr Freyjasson, byname Feilan, to do it properly,' Feilan said.

Renart looked decidedly wan in response to his mocking tone. He really did not like the teasing, Feilan surmised, and resolved to do it incessantly.

The uncle had been quiet. Now he said, 'This marriage has been done correctly?'

'Some rituals words were exchanged, I presume correctly.' Freyja shrugged carelessly. 'Renart seemed to think so. Family blessing granted, on this side.'

'Consummated, also,' Feilan said, looking again at Renart's pallid face and thinking about *correctly*.

Renart pressed his hands into the table again. The nicer sister hurried back to Adeline, looking like she might have wanted to cover her ears, though the girl seemed oblivious, or at least too intent on watching her family silently argue via meaningful looks to pay too much attention.

'Family blessing, yes.' The uncle made a show of tapping his full lower lip. 'I'm really not sure,' he said thoughtfully, 'I'm just very unsure, as the head of the family, whether I'm going to allow this marriage.'

So that was the game. Renart had snared Feilan, used that to manipulate Freyja into snaring Torben for Adeline, and was now going to let his uncle save him from Feilan. Feilan, confusingly, was more annoyed than relieved. He shot a hard look Renart's way.

But Renart said, 'It will have to go to hustings, and that is three moons away. He is my husband in the meantime. My champion.'

'No,' the uncle said, tapping away. 'No, *that*, at least, I think I should weigh in on. I don't need the authority of hustings to refuse to solemnise nonsense.'

'Uncle, didn't you give Renart permission to marry for love?' Renart's sister, the one who still hadn't slapped him, said. 'You said, since he's the youngest, and...the rest of it...and we six elder siblings had already made good alliances, if he happened to find love, he could choose who he married.'

The uncle laughed, very jolly, very amiable, eyes narrowing at his niece. 'I did say that, didn't I? I suppose I didn't quite expect anything to *ever* come of it.'

Feilan looked from him, to Renart, whose gaze was fixed on his hands, tendons standing out sharp as blades. His cheeks were turning pink. Was he a scuttling hobgoblin among his own people, despite verging on beautiful to Vaer eyes? Feilan had encountered similar, in his travels, though never so starkly.

'It's the hair, you see,' the uncle confided, spotting his confusion.

'I like the hair,' Feilan said. 'Pure carnelian.'

The uncle made an amused noise. 'If I had known Vaeringans don't even fear *that*, I might have tried for an alliance for him after all.'

Both his nieces and Renart shuddered at the very idea. *Well, bugger you, too, Foxy and sisters*, Feilan thought, shooting a look at Torben and Freyja and seeing from their expressions that they were in rare agreement with both him and each other. It was especially hypocritical of Renart to express distaste for a marriage alliance with a Vaer, for extremely obvious reasons.

He folded his arms. 'Lucky he fell into one anyway, then.'

He hadn't controlled his tone well. The uncle turned a piercing look on him. 'You claim this alliance is the fortuitous outcome of a love match, do you?'

Renart bit his lip, hard. He raised his gaze and met Feilan's, and swallowed at whatever he read in Feilan's face.

A moment ago, Feilan had been irate to think that Renart was going to extricate himself from a game of his own making, irate enough to want to drag him back into a cage he himself should have been thrilled to escape from – and perhaps a little smug to leave Torben in, a minor reprisal for Torben's escape all those years ago.

Now he'd been handed the key himself. All he had to do was say no, and the uncle had the authority, familial if not legal, to override a major contract, where he didn't have enough to override the minor one.

Torben would go alone to hunt the so-called monster, which, since probability said it was a bear, he was perfectly able to manage for himself – if he hadn't been competing with other champions, who would likely be sellswords from all over Enea. Torben could hold his own in a straightforward contest, but he was Vaer, used to fighting alongside other Vaer, loyal fellow devotees of the bear-god. He would be taken utterly by surprise the first time one of his supposed comrades sliced his hamstrings to stop him from beating them to the head of the monster, or because they'd been paid to do it, or both.

He'd lose, or die, and brave little Adeline wouldn't be a queen in her own right, and Freyja wouldn't get the extra trading territories she wanted to bolster her bargaining position when the baby emperor came knocking.

And Renart would return in disgrace to his family home, where it was common enough for at least one of his siblings to strike him in anger that none of them turned a hair to see it, and where it also appeared to be well accepted that not only would no one ever love him, but he wasn't even worth bargaining off for an alliance.

Renart wasn't bad with people. His serthing family was.

'Yes,' Feilan said. 'A true love match.' He'd astonished them all again. 'Cannot...' He cleared his throat and hid a sigh. 'Cannot get enough of him.'

After another beat of silence, he went around the table, conscious of every eye watching his every step. He bent, tugged back the cowl, and kissed Renart's hair, then nuzzled under his ear. 'I will make you pay for this, Rufran,' he murmured.

'Yes,' Renart said, high-pitched but playing along valiantly, reaching up to briefly cup the side of Feilan's head, clumsily cuffing his ear in the process. 'I know. Darling.'

Feilan, summoning every last modicum of talent he had for dissemb-lance – being Vaer, his natural ability was low, but helping Freyja establish her trading network had forced him to practise – draped himself over the back of Renart's chair, leaning an elbow, loitering possessively, letting his fingers brush the nape of Renart's neck above the heavy cowl.

'Very well,' the uncle said, making a heavy meal of those two words.

Lady Slaphappy was more than ready to throw out the words the uncle wasn't saying. 'You expect us to believe you fell in love overnight with a barbarian? Swarf!'

Renart said, 'He speaks nine languages. He has promised to take care of me. He...'

He slowly reached up and touched Feilan's bare forearm, which, if the varied expressions from his adult family members were anything to go by, was enough to signify enormous attraction.

'On your head be it,' the uncle said. 'We'll revisit at hustings. And I suppose we must bring these two barbarians home with us, then.'

'Traders,' Feilan said. He looked at Torben, who grinned back, entirely unoffended. 'Mostly.'

7

THERE WAS NOUGHT FOR IT NOW, but for Feilan and Torben to say their farewells, pack their necessities, and depart with the Riverlanders. Feilan at first thought he had the simpler job there, until he realised that he was meant to be vacating Siftar as a besotted, or at least cock-happy, newlywed man who did not expect to return. He'd have to pack up entirely, and say proper farewells. At least stony Vaer impassivity would bear him in good stead there.

Torben had to return on the laden clinker to his own camp, explain to his hersir that he'd been stolen by Freyja, and come back with a pack and an assortment of weapons, including, snug in its fur-lined leather scabbard, the treasured longsword he hadn't brought with him to a trading post that wouldn't allow armed men past the gate. He'd never leave it in the care of lowly Siftar sentries; it had a name: Hardcleave.

'Oh, right,' Feilan said. 'Do you think you can lend me a sword?'

He, Renart his nervous shadow, was standing by Torben as the visiting bersverdar gathered by the river gate. They'd been rounded up from their beds, and were still yawning and wincing from their debaucheries of the night before. All of them turned and stared at him.

'For the bear?' he said.

'Monster,' Renart corrected him, once again demonstrating he had some grasp of Vaer. Feilan would have lovingly ignored him, if he hadn't added, 'We would hardly approach Vaer men merely for assistance with a bear.'

'Ah, you appear to be saying you'd rather deal with a wild bear than a Vaer man.'

'Not exactly a difficult choice.'

Feilan would have been moved to exchange a speaking look with

Torben, if the big man hadn't been ensconced back with his boys. Instead, he grimaced to himself, and said to Torben, 'I'm also a champion in this venture. I need a sword.'

'I know.' Torben twirled a finger inclusively. 'We're all wondering what happened to your father's sword, that Freyja stole?'

'*Are* we?' Feilan gave a tight smile. 'Sold it off, first chance we got.'

Some of the warriors actually gasped. Vaer men did *not* treat their swords so cavalierly, especially not famed ones like the legendary Skyfire of the pattern-welded blade that danced like the very aurora itself. What's more, Feilan was privileged, whether he liked it or not, to have been trained in swordcraft, and to have gone into his first and only raiding summer armed with a proper steel blade, rather than inferior iron, or even just the usual spear and battle-axe. They expected basic respect, even from him.

His smile twisted. 'I think Ulfr Njallsson would have preferred that, than having it wielded by a cock-craving arsefucked like me, no?'

The small crowd of very large men eyed him in distaste as he blandly aimed the worst word at himself, rassragr, so dishonourable an insult that it justified outright retaliatory murder without fear of retribution. They'd taken their pleasure last night. Now sated and oriented back towards their own camp, their bigotry was reasserting itself. Serthar like him sapped the strength of bersverdar like them, and were reviled.

Torben clapped him on the back, hard enough to make him wobble. 'I'll fetch you a kiddie sword, shall I?'

He'd done this in the village, too, when they'd been adolescents eagerly – or not – anticipating their first raiding season. It had always been kindly meant, casual mocking to turn aside less casual fists, diverting boys who were itching to beat on their weedy agemate as proof of their manliness into merely laughing cruelly at him instead.

And after that first summer, all the way through the long twilight of winter and into early spring, when they'd crept more and more often to the cold and decrepit shed on the edge of the village, the increasingly brutal mocking had added a *distinct* edge to the fucking.

'The sizing's about right,' Feilan said, refusing to give the men the satisfaction of even a flicker of embarrassment.

Torben thumped him again, that half-friendly, half-warning gesture, and tromped off with his comrades. He'd be hours yet, but they'd still leave today. Renart and Adeline might have spent more than half a day walking this way, but on horseback along a good road, it would only be a few hours back to their home, and the daylight hours grew longer.

In the meantime, Feilan had his own round of tasks. He nodded for Renart to come with him, if only because he spotted the sisters, now waiting outside the meeting hall with Adeline while Uncle Bertrand and Freyja hashed out some last details. They were having a rather depressive effect on Adeline, between the scolding and the fussing, and he suspected Renart would receive more of the same, if not worse.

Around the side of the meeting hall, however, Renart pulled him to a stop, or at least tugged at his shirt until he deigned to stop and give him an impatient look.

'My uncle will be watching us closely,' he said. 'He'll be trying to prove we lied about it being a love match. We'll have to play pretend whenever we're in public from now on. He has spies.'

'All right.'

'He'll jump on the chance to refuse to accept you as my champion, if he can claim to my brothers that the marriage is an alliance he didn't authorise, rather than a spontaneous love match,' Renart spelled out.

'Yes, I gathered.'

'You.' Renart took a breath which tried to be deep, and caught uselessly somewhere in his upper chest, making his shoulders hitch. 'You should probably call me Remy. For verisimilitude. It's what people who are fond of me call me.'

'None of your family except Adeline call you that.'

'Yes.' He now tried for a careless smile. 'Her mother used to, too. Queen Margalita. She died.'

'I'm trying to work out why your family don't much like you.'

'*You* don't much like me,' Remy said. 'Surely it's easy enough to extrapolate.'

'But, Remy, I *adore* you,' Feilan said with a sudden grin, flinging an arm around his shoulders. Remy stiffened. 'Your sisters are watching.'

He'd seen them come around the corner, Adeline having somehow wriggled out from their loving attentions. They were staring in their brother's direction, heads together in a suspiciously conspiratorial way.

Feilan lowered his voice even further, stooping to murmur, like a lover cooing, 'Act like you're enjoying this, before they go telling tales to your uncle. Or let them, and take the chance to escape. Which is it?'

In answer, Remy tilted his head, baring his neck for Feilan, which Feilan took advantage of, kissing the warm, herbal-scented skin under

Remy's ear and grazing his teeth downwards until he was muffling his face in the loop of the cowl. Remy shivered, and pressed into him.

'Oh, that's nice,' Feilan said in a guttural tone, hooking an arm around Remy's back. 'I can't wait to put you on your hands and knees again.'

He was experienced enough at putting on performances in his mercantile dealings that he didn't project his voice into an unrealistic shout, but he did let it carry, as if too wrapped up in his husband to heed any onlookers to their increasingly explicit embrace. He was, he realised, becoming hard, because Remy was squirming against him quite convincingly. The sisters, looking mortified, were retreating.

'Can we,' Remy gasped, 'go—'

'Yep,' Feilan said, and hustled him over to his hut.

Once inside and out of sight of the familial spies, they broke apart. Remy was out of breath. He looked at Feilan with wide eyes, and Feilan wanted to shove him down onto the furs.

'Will they go so far as to follow and listen in?' When Remy didn't reply, Feilan added, sharper, 'Remy, pay attention, this is *your* game. Serthing play it. Do we need to make sex noises?'

'Oh! Oh, no, I wouldn't think that's necessary.'

'You sure? You had a fine repertoire last night you might like to trot out again.'

'That was,' Remy said, '...elicited.'

Feilan bit down on a request to elicit it again. He understood that Remy, as transparent as he appeared with his scowls and blushes, was better at hiding his thoughts than Feilan had initially assumed. Nonetheless, he clearly didn't like Feilan, and had clearly said his preference didn't lie with men. That was the end to that.

He therefore turned away and rapidly swept his belongings into his trunk. He already had a good stash of loose gemstones and coins, Freyja's and others, concealed under a panel in the bottom. He eyed off the furs he slept on, before deciding he didn't need to roll those up. They were thick enough to make a bulky bundle, and he wasn't yet sure what sort of transport he and Torben would have.

From among his handful of gold and silver trinkets – he'd watched trifles pass through his mother's hands for so long that he felt little avarice to own any unless their prettiness struck him in a particular way – he found a gold ring and pressed it on a fidgeting Remy.

'We're supposed to exchange ancestral swords, but rings can stand in for it,' he said. 'Do you have a token you can gift me in return?'

Remy touched his waist absently, but his purse was flaccid. 'I gave everything of value to Adeline to strike the deal with Torben.'

'I'll provide my *own*, then, shall I,' Feilan said in mock-offence.

Remy twitched. 'I didn't think to bring... I didn't actually come here with the intention of doing this.'

Since he'd initially been leading Adeline towards the raiding camp, Feilan would very well hope not. Sliding a second, thicker ring onto his own finger, he murmured, 'Lucky me, I suppose.'

Lastly, he slipped on a bracelet of beads, a protective talisman. He hadn't worn it for years, but it meant far more to him than a brusque exchange of rings. He rubbed the cool, smooth beads as he turned back to Remy.

'I'm packed, then, but we best linger.' Remy once again seemed bemused, so Feilan added, 'We don't want anyone thinking your new husband doesn't do right by you in bed, do we?'

Remy's cheeks tinged pink. 'Very well.' He hesitated. 'And what should I call you? For verisimilitude?'

'Feilan is fine.'

'It's not your true name.'

'Obviously not.'

'There's no obviously about it. *Everyone* calls you Feilan, and nothing else. Even your own mother.'

She was hardly going to regularly call him by a name inflicted on him as a squalling babe by his father on the presumption he'd match the feats of a legendary ancestor. Agreeably, he explained, 'Whether they're fond of me or not, yes. Because it's not really a nickname or a diminutive. It's a byname. It means wolfling. Little wolf. I could hardly have had that bestowed on me at birth.'

For some reason, this put Remy into high dudgeon. 'That's how names *work*.'

'I didn't come out of my mother and everyone looked at me and said, well, the peaky bairn looks on the runty side but we reckon he'll be a smart one, let's call him Little Wolf. I saw sixteen summers before I earned that name.'

Earned was putting a nicer light on it than he strictly liked; it had been mocking, in the first instance, because of the way he, blinded by blue, had walked into the sword that almost killed him.

'Why d'you care?' he added, mostly to see what Remy would say; he'd already guessed why he cared.

Remy chewed his lip and avoided the question with one of his own. 'But what do people who are *very* fond of you call you?'

'I promise they still call me Feilan.'

'Torben calls you Feilan?'

Feilan swallowed a laugh and said, 'Torben calls me lots of things, not many of them particularly fond. Look, it won't be suspicious if Feilan's what you call me. And I answer to it. I might not turn around to Aleifr or what-have-you. Good?'

He got a small nod. Remy looked about. 'Can we... Has it been long enough?'

'I don't know, do you feel you've had long enough to be satisfactorily fucked?'

'I don't know,' Remy repeated back to him, with a tremor that might have been a stab at a tease. 'How long does it generally take to be satisfactorily fucked?'

Feilan raised his brows. 'Are you trying to insult me, or is it a happy accident?'

Once again, it took Remy a beat or two to understand, and it punctured his attempt to sally back. 'I didn't mean— Last night was— It was all very...' He ran out of words and stood twisting his hands together very much like his niece.

'Satisfactory?'

'Yes,' Remy said as if he wished he didn't have to. He pulled the cowl up over his hair again.

'Why does your family want your hair covered?'

'I don't want to talk about that.'

Feilan kept his voice perfectly even and friendly, as it had been all along. 'Let's get it straight, you don't get a "don't want" anymore. You are at my every serthing whim for the favour I'm doing you. What is the problem with your hair?'

Remy's stubborn look dipped; it plainly confused him when Feilan's tone and expression were pleasant but his words were hostile. It had been effective when he'd been by Freyja's side while they established the trading network, too.

That, and being a large Vaer. Unless he was standing next to a real bersverdr, who made it clear he was positively short in stature and falling short in Vaer manhood, it was enough to make people cautious of him.

Still, Renart Nivardus hadn't walked the heir to the throne out of Seven Hills seeking the champions his jolly uncle didn't want them to have because he didn't possess an iron core of defiance hidden behind the pink blushes and nervy jitters.

'I know this is a mutual favour,' he said, lifting his chin. 'I know your mother wants access to the west Riverlands through Seven Hills.'

Feilan smiled. He stepped closer to Remy, so he was looming over him, and hooked a finger into the neck of his borrowed shirt. 'We've got at least until the next moon-gloam together.'

Remy slowly licked his lips, but, to Feilan's mild admiration, he held his ground. Of course, he could hardly do anything else, with Feilan's grip on his collar. He kept his gaze straight ahead, boring into Feilan's chest. 'Yes.'

'And then you're going to send me and Torben out to kill a bear for you—'

Not even that would provoke the man to look up at him. 'A monster.'

'A bear. And you'll want us to do our best to win for you and Adeline, yes?'

'*You* will want to do your best to win, for your mother.'

'Uncle Remy,' Feilan said. 'How are you planning to persuade the husband you acquired by trickery to do his *very* best to win a crown for your beloved niece?'

Remy's dark eyes finally snapped to his, flashing pure rebellion even as he spat, 'I am at your every whim.'

Meeting that impudent, wilful gaze, Feilan had to take a moment to allow the desire to push him to his knees and indulge a very specific whim to dissipate. He untwisted his fingers and stepped back.

'We got there,' he said lightly. 'So tell me about the hair.'

Remy still had enough fight in him to delay to straighten the shirt before he said, 'It's red.'

'Since I'm not blind, I remain unenlightened.'

'It's the mark of a witch,' Remy blurted. Feilan made a respectful gesture, two fingers tapped in the air, quick and casual, which Remy seemed to misinterpret, because he said, 'Yes, witches are reviled. In league with demons. Evil spirits. And the unsettled dead.'

'Not ours,' Feilan said. 'They're conduits to the spirit world, sure enough, but they're useful. They tell the future, and drive away illness, and watch over women in childbirth.'

'Our witches...' Remy trailed off, and looked thoughtful. 'I suppose those are things they do, too, but people fear them because they consort with evil, and they can bring down curses, and blights, and afflictions.

Feilan shrugged. 'So can ours. That's why you don't piss them off by not respecting them.'

'*Respect* them? They're hideous, and terrifying.'

Feilan tried to look outraged. 'Are you trying to insult my mother now?'

Remy once again did not take well to the teasing. '*What*? Freyja… Swarf, no! I didn't— She's a *witch*?'

'No,' Feilan said. 'Just *her* mother.'

He laughed, both at Remy's horror and at the memory of Freyja wielding her mother's staff as they'd fled the village, beginning the reputation that kept Siftar safe from raiders to this day.

'Spare me from men who think they're amusing,' Remy said with an irritated roll of his eyes, notwithstanding that he also looked decidedly relieved.

'Spare me from men with ulterior motives,' Feilan shot back, still smiling. 'It's—' He waved a hand to the sudden language barrier. '— seithr. Untranslatable. But nothing to do with red hair. Your family are jolterheads. Fools.'

'I should be clear,' Remy said. 'They know I'm not actually a witch. But they know many superstitious people will suspect that I am and will treat me accordingly.'

'I know about that.' Feilan raised a challenging eyebrow. 'Prejudged on appearance.'

Remy had the good grace to look embarrassed. He mumbled, 'My family try to protect me from it.'

Feilan knew about that, too. 'They force you to hide, cover a vital part of yourself, and act like you'll never marry for love. I repeat, jolterheads.' It was a nicer word than the Vaer invective he wanted to employ. He reached out and pushed the cowl back. 'Keep it uncovered. I like it. Husband's prerogative.'

Remy touched his freed hair, looking at Feilan with his wide, dark eyes. Something flickered in his expression, indecipherable.

Feilan turned from that. 'Come on, Rufran, I've got work to do.'

He left Remy with Adeline, and suspected it wouldn't be long before the uncle and sisters were in his ear again. Remy didn't seem to have much fight left in him to resist, after pulling off the two contracts. Feilan supposed if he did truly believe they were acting in his best interests, he would be feeling guilty about his subterfuge, ripe to take a haranguing.

After briefing his clerks, mostly to reassure himself that they'd manage the information network, running like a vein through the trade network, in his absence, and saying some mellow goodbyes to his closest companions, Feilan made his way back to the meeting hall, and Freyja.

He smiled as he sat opposite her in her private alcove, superficially curtained off from the single-roomed meeting hall. He gestured to her mother's staff propped, somewhat disrespectfully, in the corner, its white wood heavily inscribed with runes and inset with ruby and jasper.

'I was just thinking of that,' he said. 'Renart's red hair means he's a witch, apparently. It reminded me of the day we left.'

Freyja smiled. She straightened her already-straight back to try to make her small frame loom, and raised both hands. 'By Njorda and Heidr, by the ash, by the well, by the raven's eye, I call the flames upon thee!'

She cackled wickedly, sending Feilan into open laughter that had years of gratitude to it. That was what she had cried the night she'd rescued him, a desperate bluff in a desperate moment.

He'd been locked into the same storehouse he'd been caught in, guards on the main door, the rear door jammed and bolted shut. The Vaer didn't usually keep prisoners; banishment or execution happened immediately. But the elders were alternately threatening him and cajoling him, beating him and berating him, trying to force out the name of the other man.

Torben would have been the natural suspect, but when the uproar had spread, he'd emerged, nude and sheepish, in the company of Ingunn, the magnate's daughter, the girl he'd soon marry – mostly because he'd been caught naked with her that night, scuppering the match her father had been negotiating with a fellow magnate.

She must, Feilan had thought when Torben had told him of it years and years later, have been lurking very close by the rear side of that lonely little shed, to have been in a position to offer shelter to the fleeing and naked pride of the village.

He'd heard a commotion outside his makeshift prison, and a moment later, his nose, and the briefest flash of dirty scarlet in the corner of his eye, confirmed what his guards were saying: smoke, rising thicker and thicker from the turf roof of Ulfr's longhouse.

Very shortly after the guards had run to help, Freyja opened the door they'd abandoned. Feilan had already been on his feet, waiting. Hoping for Torben. Expecting his mother.

She'd popped lit light-pots into the turf roof in multiple places, and waited until the damp turf began to smoke. Under cover of the distraction, she, Feilan, the famed Skyfire, a satchel of silver, a few provisions, and an ass were most of the way up the slope towards the pass before the warriors had realised there was no true threat and come storming after them.

If caught, they were both dead, painfully so. Feilan had raised his father's sword, turning to stand between the men and his mother, telling her to keep running, determined that this one time, he would turn aside a blow aimed at her.

That was when Freyja had uncovered both breasts and her mother's staff. She'd never been accounted a witch, but she looked it now, wild eyes the same pale colour as her mother's unearthly sea-ice green, her body bared to the perennial cold wind of the valley.

She raised high the staff with its arcane carvings, and sang that wild incantation, calling on her mother's spirits, the sea witch and the first volva, and the mythical emblems associated with seithr.

And the longhouse roof had burst into flame along its entire length.

Freyja had not intended her distraction to turn into real danger – there were the young and the sickly and the old inside – but nor did she hesitate to take advantage of the coincidental timing, seizing Feilan's arm and dragging him onwards as the warriors ran back to pull people to safety. They fled into the night, leaving leaping flames behind them, and made it onto a ship the very next morning, exchanging the ass and the first handful of silver for passage.

The story spread fast; Freyja was Cursed for the violation against her husband's honour – and was a witch, feared and respected, untouchable by any Vaeringan ever. That she'd never shown the slightest sign of craft before or since didn't seem to matter.

Although...

Feilan wasn't truly superstitious; he'd travelled too widely, and something about being sundered from one's own gods made it far easier to see the illogic and contradictions inherent in the huge patchwork of Enean beliefs.

But it had been one vaett of a coincidence that had saved him and Freyja that day, and they'd had a few since then, too, enough that when he swore to Njorda as one of the few Vaer beings, disir, who hadn't been taken from him, he wasn't entirely spouting an empty sentiment.

He loosened his bracelet, and held it out to his mother.

Freyja gave him a reproving look, but retrieved her old leather pouch and poured its contents out on to a tray. He watched with interest as her nimble fingers sorted rapidly through beads of every shape and hue and material: etched silver, opaque glass formed from melted tesserae prised from the floor of ancient temples, heartland amber and western jet and eastern coral and southern gold-foil, jasper and carnelian and agate in all their varieties, ivory and bone and polished wood.

Feilan's talisman already held red jasper for protection and blue jasper for tranquillity and also pure whimsy; untying the leather knots, Freyja threaded coral for health and heart-strength, golden striped tiger-eye for luck, and carnelian, technically for more protection but which was more likely just Freyja mocking him; she'd even paired it with black agate, ostensibly for warding off evil. She finished her modifications with more blue jasper beads and tied the talisman off, then muttered over it in archaic Vaer, an incantation passed to her by Anja in her youth.

She handed back the newly blessed talisman, and quickly threaded two more, much simpler and quite striking, the stripey tiger-eye alternating with red jasper. 'For our Riverlanders. Luck and protection.'

He tightened the leather loop about his wrist and scooped up the new pair. 'Not one for Torben?'

'He'll have his own,' Freyja said, a distinct note of frost entering her voice.

'It wasn't his fault,' he said. 'I got on my knees for him willingly enough.'

She gave him a particularly maternal look. *You can't shock me*, that look said. 'I'll blame who I like.'

'I've had a better life than I was set to have.' He paused. 'So've you.'

Freyja swept her beads back into their leather bag and tied the strings. 'My dearest, I have always admired your capacity for forgiveness, and yet I have to wonder where in the three worlds it came from, for neither Ulfr nor I taught it to you.'

'You're being suspiciously nice to Renart, in that case. Nicer than you need to be, just to win access to the western Riverlands.'

To this, Freyja merely smiled. 'Rufran,' she said, again with that crafty-little-shit inflection, this time underlain with admiration, because Feilan hadn't been exaggerating when he'd told Remy the Vaer liked a trickster. 'You're being nicer than you need to be, too.'

He shrugged; he wasn't, not really. He was more enjoying provoking his ill-tempered husband, though that had turned – those snapping black eyes, meeting his gaze with wilful defiance – into provoking himself, and he should probably stop.

Freyja made a thoughtful hum. 'You're comfortable, in Siftar.'

'Why am I hearing a note of motherly disapproval about the very notion your son might be happy?'

'I want you happy,' she said. 'I'm not sure comfortable substitutes for it.'

'I don't...' Feilan shook his head. 'No, I don't understand.'

'Vaer men never do,' she said, sighing.

'Not a Vaer man, Mother.'

'A few words shouted at you by malignant old men twenty-five summers ago—'

'I know,' Feilan said, holding up his hands. It was an old argument. 'Let's not. Can we at least agree I'm somewhat higher in your estimation than the vast majority of Vaer men.'

'You *were*,' she said, deploying her driest tones, 'until you followed your cock right into a blatant trap.'

Feilan held up an admonishing finger like an officious southern bishop. 'Uh uh, right into a coveted trade opportunity.'

That made her laugh, at least. She ruffled his hair, and then seized him into a hug, and surprised him by kissing his forehead and murmuring an old Vaer prayer over him like both of them weren't Cursed, invisible to the gods of their heartland. But Njorda, sea witch, might listen, even far from the briny shore.

Rueful, he kissed her cheek in silent thanks, and went out. He then had to politely sit through a formal highday meal with the Riverlanders, offered, like yesterday, in adherence to the heartland tradition of feeding guests; Siftar residents usually ate only lightly between the early daymeal and the late nightmeal.

He lounged with a performative arm around his husband although it made it harder to pick at the cheese and berries and skyr. Remy, for his part, rested a free hand on Feilan's clothed thigh, again a simple enough gesture which seemed to appal his family.

Feilan was wondering if they would even manage to get away today when Torben finally arrived back through the river gate. He'd returned with an assortment of blades in addition to his own dramatic longsword, an axe, his shield, and a large leather bag with straps for his back.

He handed Feilan a sword and scabbard without a word; Feilan accepted it, and tested out its grip and weight. Siftar, as it happened, had plenty of spare swords, but this one was of the best quality, despite being a mere bastard sword plundered from the south rather than a real Vaer longsword. Its steel would still hold its edge. Feilan nodded his thanks.

Torben was, indeed, wearing a talisman of his own, an amulet of silver, inscribed with his god's hammer surrounded by runes, and hung from a leather cord about his neck, further strung with coloured glass beads. He'd also trimmed his golden hair, and had his beard combed and plaited with coins and more beads.

'Did you make us wait just so you could make yourself pretty?' Feilan said, to which he received merely one of Torben's wide grins.

Feilan, shaking his head, turned to where the visitors had gathered with their short-legged horses by the overlander gate as soon as they'd seen the clinker nosing up to the dock. They'd brought spare horses for Adeline and Remy, not anticipating the acquisition of two Vaer. There had been some discussion regarding Adeline sharing with an aunt, and Remy sharing with his husband, before Freyja, pointing out the luggage, agreed to loan two horses and a pack donkey.

Feilan had been, partially, looking forward to having Remy squirming in his lap all the way back to his disputed little kingdom, revenge for the lingering touch on his thigh all through the meal. He reminded himself, more firmly this time, that his husband wasn't attracted to men, wasn't willing, and seemed underprepared to be teased. He took the reins of the loaned horse.

He raised a hand to Freyja, a stoically silent farewell. They'd parted before, of course, in their travelling years, and when Feilan had maintained the networks in the first years of establishing Siftar. This time, though it was only for two moons at most, felt momentous somehow, perhaps because it was forced.

The little kingdom of Seven Hills lay westwards, and slightly south, so they shortly crossed the bridge. The road took them through typical Riverlands countryside, low, mazed by waterways that they crossed by ford and by bridge, before beginning to rise into the hills. As was usual among the little provinces of the region, there was no indication that they'd passed from one territory to another. Feilan looked around with a niggling sense of unease.

Torben brought his horse up to Remy, who had greeted his small brown mare with more fondness than he'd treated anyone except Adeline, but who was looking exquisitely uncomfortable in his horned leather saddle, adjusting his seat every few moments.

'Hoi, kastanrazi,' Torben hailed him. 'The rule is the hunt's during gloam-moon, ja? What if someone goes out and gets it early?' His tone made it clear he meant himself. 'There's only one head, once it's delivered, it's delivered.'

'What?' Remy said. 'No! If you break the rules, they'll make a new contest with different rules. And, anyway, the monster doesn't come out unless it's the new moon.'

Feilan privately disagreed. It was just easier for human fears to turn a bear into a monster when the nights were darkest. That didn't mean it didn't skulk around on other nights. If it had come at full moon, they'd've readily spotted it for what it truly was.

'Guess we're waiting around,' Torben said glumly. Like Vaer warriors since time immemorial, he hated waiting.

Feilan finally realised what had been bothering him. While the copious water and flocks of smelly, noisy sheep might lure in a migratory bear, the land, turned over to pasture, was growing increasingly bare of trees and other cover.

High and sparse, it did not seem like favoured countryside for bears.

8

THE SUN WAS SINKING AS THE small group wound its way up the well-maintained but narrow road towards the palace on the hilltop.

It wasn't really a palace. Feilan had been in the caliphates, he had visited palaces, all red-veined marble and tesseral tiles of pure white or gold or obsidian. He'd visited stone castles too, high-walled and heavily fortified, mostly existing because Vaeringa did.

This place was more organic. It was built of stone, certainly, but of the local pinkish variety rather than the heavy grey that dominated further south. The setting sun cast the pink to a deeper red, and Feilan had carnelian on his mind, apparently, because this place was nothing but a string of beads draped across the small peaks of a green-carpeted hill chain. Seven flat-fronted, peak-roofed buildings sat proudly atop seven summits, with a colonnaded walkway – Feilan had to dredge his memory deeply to come up with 'arcade' as the correct local terminology – crossing the undulating dips of the long ridge's saddles to link them all.

'Pretty,' he said, in a halfhearted attempt to lure his reluctant husband from a miserable hours-long silence.

'Ripe for raiding,' Torben said. 'Not even a token wall.'

Remy scowled.

Feilan leaned over to flick Torben on the ear. He told Remy, 'You're too far from the coast and too far from a major river or a main thoroughfare. And too high.'

'We don't like having to run uphill,' Torben confirmed. 'More effort than it's worth.'

The riverport they'd just ridden through before the rise to Seven Hills, however, had some flat approaches. Admittedly, Vaer raiders would have to row along fairly narrow ways, and even the shallow-keeled clinkers would have to be ported across fords several times, but it wasn't impassable. They might even leave the ships, and follow the meandering roads, deeper and deeper into the rich lands of these patchwork kingdoms, rolling hills and hidden valleys, fat sheep and hops and wheat and salt mines and lime kilns, all of which translated, through hands like Freyja's, into portable wealth.

That supposed that Freyja, eyeing off this exact little riverport for the access it would provide to the towns west and south of here, wouldn't put a stop to it the moment Torben tried putting any bright ideas into his hersir's head.

The road gave out onto a broad paved forecourt before the central building, larger than the others, its pink stone crisscrossed with a decorative pattern of wooden beams ending in whimsical curls at the eaves. It had huge double doors, arched, and matching arches extending along its frontage to meet the arches of the hilltop arcades, one heading eastwards, one westwards, as if the building opened arms wide to its guests.

Two richly-clad men met them in the forecourt. They almost immediately engaged in the family pastime of browbeating Remy, particularly once Lady Slaphappy had hurried from horseback to brief them. The other sister hastened Adeline inside, and Bertrand, after a murmured exchange with the men, bustled after her.

One of the men, mid-harangue, tugged the cowl up, covering Remy's hair, obscuring his face from Feilan's view. Remy was holding himself very still, like he had in Siftar every time he'd had to brace himself for unpleasantness.

Feilan stood by his horse, slowly flexing sore muscles – it had been a while since he'd needed to ride – and wondering when to intervene. Torben casually tossed his reins off to a Riverlander who may or may not have been a stable hand, and plucked the reins from Feilan's hand to palm them off as well.

He smiled around as the horses were led away. 'Welcoming place.'

Feilan thought this was sarcasm before he, too, took in the other people milling about. They were murmuring to each other in a local dialect, not the familiar Riverlander, and openly admiring Torben's form. In fact, it appeared they were milling about, not so much because they were required to attend the new arrivals, but because they wanted to ogle.

Torben waved at a pair of giggling women. 'This'll be delightful.'

'Why aren't they scared of you?' Feilan asked.

'It may shock you to learn,' Torben said, 'that women find very tall, broad-shouldered men with wealth' – he touched the silver arm-ring wound four times about his bulging bicep – 'golden tresses, and trimmed nails to be irresistibly attractive.'

Feilan punched him lightly on his musclebound arm, where, inevitably, Torben didn't feel it but Feilan's knuckle did. 'I meant, the royal family is scared of us, why aren't their people?'

'The royal family isn't scared, they just hate us,' Torben said. 'Don't argue, Little Wolf, I know hate.'

'All right, but why them and not them?' He gestured towards some of Torben's staring admirers.

'That's newfangled educations for you. The peasants don't know any better. Good for them.'

He caught the eye of another young lady, and smiled winningly. There was an equally transfixed man behind her, long-lashed and willowy. Torben glanced around, realised there was not another Vaer man within his extended vicinity, and smiled at him too.

Remy managed to extricate himself from his trifecta of harassment on the excuse of seeing to their barbarian guests. His mouth tightened as he took in the small crowd of lingering retainers and servants.

'Fidelity within marriage is expected here,' he informed Feilan.

Feilan frowned. 'I don't know that word.'

'I'm sure you don't. It means don't get caught with anyone else, or my uncle will seize the chance to disallow you as my champion.'

'All right,' Feilan said. 'I promise I won't get caught.'

'I am very much not in the mood for this,' Remy muttered to himself, more plaintively than angrily.

Feilan broke into a grin. 'None of them are looking at me, you know,' he said. 'They're looking at Torben.'

'They're looking at both of you.'

Taking pity on him, Feilan raised a solemn hand. 'I promise to fuck no one else until the very moment Torben hands over the monster's head.'

'I don't have to, do I?' Torben asked. 'Fidelity, I mean.'

'Of course not, you're on a mercenary contract,' Remy said, innocently missing that Torben was not confused on the terms of the contract he had agreed to, but rather was rubbing in the terms of the contract Feilan had agreed to.

Torben grinned. 'I think I'll go have sex with lots of different people, then.'

'How do you always manage to have more fun than me?' Feilan lamented.

'Wait, I need to show you your quarters first,' Remy said, then flushed when both Vaer looked at him with open amusement.

'What did he just say?' Feilan said. 'He's not joking, Remy.'

'I meant for...after.'

'I'll find a bed for myself somewhere, I'm sure. Food, too. See you in the morning.' He clapped Feilan on the shoulder, rocking him forwards, and waded into the crowd, greeting women and men with equal enthusiasm.

Remy sighed. 'I need to introduce you to my brothers.' He did that – Feilan heeded the scowls more than the names – and then tucked his arm through Feilan's, resting spread fingers over Feilan's forearm. 'Would you like supper soon, darling?'

'We weren't expecting guests of your calibre,' the eldest surviving brother said, spitting that last word as he eyed Feilan with open disdain. 'Not sure if we can rustle up barbarian food on short notice. What do you even eat? Raw meat?'

It seemed all the siblings were as unpleasant as each other. 'Offering me delicacies?'

Remy's hand tightened on Feilan's forearm. 'Or perhaps I shall take you straight to our chamber and fetch you something later?'

'Only if you promise to lay morsels on my tongue one by one,' Feilan said, low and throaty, which made Remy dig his nails in, but also slightly undid the tightness across his shoulders he'd worn since dismounting.

The brother pursed his lips. 'Take your husband to your chambers, and then come back. We're not done talking.'

'We're done.' Feilan smiled at him and then tugged at Remy's cowl, this time pulling it all the way off instead of merely pushing it down. 'And don't wear that,' he said, tossing it to the ground. 'I want to see your pretty hair. I told you. Don't make me tell you again. Take me to our bed.' He lazily twitched his fingers. 'Send my things, would you.'

Remy about-turned and led him, not into the main building before them, but onto the eastwards arcade. They quickly dipped out of sight of the forecourt as the arcade descended into the shallow saddle between the first hill and the next.

'Please don't *try* to antagonise Hughard,' Remy said shortly.

Feilan caught his wrist, forcing him to slow. 'Why not? He's our enemy in this.'

'He's my brother.'

'Remy...' They reached the flat peak of the next hill, but passed that building, a reprise of the first at a smaller scale, and went on into the next dip. 'All your siblings count as contenders, correct?'

'Yes.'

'They'll all be entering champions into the contest. Or will your brothers enter themselves?'

'No, they'll enter champions.'

Feilan had been thinking about the conditions of the contest, how strangely wide the net was cast by rules allowing anyone with a claim, no matter how distant, to enter. He thought he knew why. 'Some of them have children old enough to act as regent, and therefore count as contenders?'

They crested the third hill, Feilan somewhat out of breath thanks to harking from a very flat plain where the only gradient was the mild slope up to Siftar from the riverbank. Another of the pink halls sat there, smaller again. Here, Remy turned down a stub of walkway and led Feilan through a wide doorway into a high-ceilinged foyer with open arches set waist-height in every wall. The foyer floor and minimal walls were starkly bare, but the ceiling was painted with clouds innocuously fluffy.

'Three of my nephews, one of my nieces,' he answered distractedly, walking along a corridor with more of the full arches on each side, a short echo of the main arcade, before they finally entered what Feilan thought of as a proper building, with actual walls and a ceiling of normal height.

'Right. So that's a champion for your uncle, two for your brothers, two for your sisters—'

'I have a third sister. You haven't met her yet.'

'—five for the siblings, then, and another four as well. Ten. If any of them gets the head of the monster, who wins? Who'll be designated regent?'

Remy was quiet so long that Feilan knew he'd worked it out, even before he doubtfully said, 'Hugo might... No, no. It'll be Uncle Bertrand, you're quite right.'

Feilan nodded. Bertrand was just as subtly scheming as he'd suspected: as counter-intuitive as it seemed, the wide net gave him a strong coalition of monster-killers against a loose assortment of independent champions unlikely to take the head alone, while making it look like he was being scrupulously fair.

'Those ten warriors make a formidable bloc,' he explained. 'We'll need allies, certainly, but your family are not among them. We have to treat them as the enemy.'

Having passed several closed doors, Remy finally paused at one, as plain and nondescript as the rest. He toed off his shoes, saying, 'This is why they call you the clever one, isn't it.' He didn't sound happy.

Feilan followed custom with his boots, and Remy ushered him into the room, generously sized but stuffy. While Remy went about twisting chains to raise stiff linen covers off narrow gaps along the top of the outer wall, letting in fresh air and the last wane of the light, Feilan assessed his new sleeping space with the habitually mercantile eye of a longtime trader, digging toes into the thick rug underfoot.

There was a bed, raised off the floor on thick legs, with a mattress, probably not stuffed with straw, and quality linens, and a thick gilt rope hanging over the head, which Feilan tracked to a loop over a hook before it vanished through a hole drilled through the plastered stone wall. He'd seen its like before, and knew it connected to a bell to alert servants to their masters' needs. A heavy sideboard sat against the wall under the window slits, holding a lamp, an assortment of bottles and jars and other bits and pieces, a bowl, and a fancy imported aquamanile, wrought into the shape of a lion's head, aroar. That would be for washing, Feilan again knew from previous forays into the beds of wealthy men. A wardrobe and a trunk completed the furnishings.

'Plain for a prince's bedchamber,' he said, and received the gift of watching Remy open his mouth to superciliously enquire how he knew what a prince's bedchamber should look like, before realising what the answer would be and blushing.

He said instead, 'It suits my needs well enough.'

He paced from one side of the room to the other, breath coming short. He'd been self-contained in front of his brothers, cool-eyed but docile, and was now uncoiling his tension through his restless feet, his tapping fingers.

Feilan took another slow measuring look around. It really was as bare as his own little hut, comparatively speaking, without even the simplest of icons on the wall. He didn't know the goddess-oriented Riverlands belief system, except for a few rote phrases uttered by local merchants, and no idea what form it would take in the specific locale of a seven-summit hill chain, beyond Remy's occasional endearingly pallid swearing, and Adeline's invocation of She Who Spins when she signed the contract.

The lack of iconography reminded him, however. He slid the two extra talisman bracelets from his wrist and held them out. 'For you and Adeline.'

Remy, turning from lighting an elegant glass lamp, swept him with a hostile look. 'We'll wear no Vaer superstition.'

'Look,' Feilan said, dropping his hand. 'I know it's not nice to be told your closest family is your enemy, but that's the game you've chosen to play, and that's why you dragged me into it, isn't it? To tell you these things? Torben for the strength, me for the tactics?'

'No,' Remy said, after a moment. 'I wanted the best warriors I could manage to get hold of.'

Feilan had a blank moment of his own. 'Then why did you trick *me* into fucking you, instead of an actual Vaer man?'

'You *are* a Vaer man,' Remy said. Then, uncertainly, probably because of his two evenings in Siftar, '...Aren't you?'

Feilan was a Vaer and a man, but not a Vaer man: that was what being Cursed meant. He shook his head and made it less confusing for his husband. 'Why'd you fuck me and not one of the warriors?'

'I told you,' Remy said. 'You were the compromise. It was my first time,' he added, to whatever Feilan's expression was giving away. 'I was scared and chose someone who looked strong but who I thought probably wouldn't hurt me. I told you that. I had no idea you were considered clever among your people.'

'*Considered* clever, is it?' Feilan sat on the bed, dropping the two talismans beside him. He bounced up and down. 'Too soft.'

The compromise, he thought. *The you'll-do*. He wanted to spit.

A knock came – that would be Feilan's trunk arriving. The trunk he hadn't bothered to fill with furs, because he'd forgotten other people had these horrid smothering beds.

'The bed's too soft,' he snapped at Remy as he moved to answer the knock. 'Tell them to bring furs.'

Quietly, hand on the latch, Remy said, 'We're meant to be in love. How will I explain you wanting to sleep on the floor to my family?'

Feilan's irritation reached an unfortunate peak, provoked to the roil after simmering all day. 'Tell them it's so I can fuck you on the floor like the little bitch you are without hurting my knees.'

Remy paled, and then nodded and opened the door. Feilan, intuiting that the cursed jolterhead might actually announce the reason right there and then, swooped in and took possession of his belongings from the two young men who'd carried them over, closing the door in their faces with a grunt of thanks that he knew was pure Vaer.

He set the trunk in a corner, dumped his borrowed sword atop it, and sat back on the bed. 'It is no fun to tease you,' he informed Remy, 'if you're just going to believe every word out of my mouth.'

Remy sat on the other edge of the bed, strain evident in the taut line of his body. 'Husband's prerogative,' he said, repeating Feilan's phrase out of nowhere.

Feilan raised his eyebrows in a question.

'You said it. You're aware of the husband's right to claim sex.'

'Draf you will!' Feilan said, mostly from surprise. 'Try that one on, I dare you.' Remy watched him with increasing tension until he abruptly realised. '*I'm* the husband. Ah. Also the husband.'

'Yes,' Remy said, sounding almost relieved that he'd finally understood. 'And I'm at your every whim. So if you tell me you're going to fuck me on the floor, I really have no choice *but* to believe you, do I?'

Feilan huffed his air out in one noisy exhale. The worst of it was, he wanted to do it. Remy had practically given him permission. He wanted to drag him down onto this stupid soft bed and fuck him every way he could think of and make him wail like he had the night before.

'Remy, come sit here by me.' He patted the bed beside him.

His husband eyed off the expanse between them as if it were an impassable eastern steppe. 'No.'

'Promise I won't bite,' Feilan said with a grin that he was sure completely belied his words.

Remy stood, edged his way around the bed, and sat down again near Feilan. Feilan flung a long arm over his shoulders and pulled him closer, until he could feel his heat through his shirt. From his unnatural stillness, Remy was trying very hard not to squirm away.

Feilan said, 'I was not aware of the meaning of a prerogative in this particular context. You said you don't prefer men, as a rule, and I believe you. We never agreed sex is part of our bargain, so it's not. Except for whatever show we have to put on in public. Good?'

'You won't demand sex from me?'

Feilan smothered his smile. Remy didn't sound entirely pleased. There was that *as a rule* coming into play, possibly. 'Not unless there's a dramatic renegotiation of our agreement for all the prerogative you can handle.'

'Our *marital* agreement.'

'Go ahead, keep trying to talk me into it.'

Remy huddled under his arm. 'I don't believe you're taking all this with as much good grace as you're pretending you are.'

'You're right, I'm not. But I'm also not inclined to punish you for it.'

'You're a *barbarian*.'

Feilan squeezed tighter. 'Unless you keep giving me bright ideas like that, Rufran.'

'Sorry. Sorry I keep calling you a barbarian. You've been...not awful.'

'Thanks,' Feilan said. 'Not awful. I'll have it engraved on my runestone.'

He got a snap from those black eyes, before, making the apology somewhat more authentic, Remy picked up one of the talismans and wrapped the leather thong around his wrist. He tried to tie it off himself, before offering his wrist to Feilan, veins stark under his pale skin. He bore callouses on his palm, Feilan noted, though not those of a swordsman.

Feilan shifted the talisman about Remy's wrist until the beads were positioned right, then tugged on the loop to tighten it. He pressed his thumb to the blue vein running down from Remy's thumb, felt his rapid pulse, and let go.

'What do they mean?' Remy asked, as he instantly started to worry at the talisman, sliding the beads back and forth to the limit of the play Feilan had left in it.

'The red jasper for safety. The tiger-eye for luck.'

'You have blue jasper on yours.'

'That's just Freyja amusing herself.'

Remy touched the polished pale blue-green beads and looked at Feilan with the start of a confused query.

'She's reminding me she's watching over me.' They were also part of his verification, beads he'd seal in with missives to Freyja so she knew he was safe, the messages authentic.

Remy's expression cleared. 'The same colour as your eyes.'

'Freyja's eyes, but, yes, mine, too.'

Remy picked up the second bracelet. 'I'll make sure Lina wears hers.'

'Thank you,' Feilan said, a little gruffly. 'Another matter. Where will Torben sleep?'

'Wherever he likes, apparently,' Remy said waspishly. 'It's not relevant to you, husband.'

'It *is*, because if he's expected to bunk down with all the other champions, I won't have it. He has to have his own quarters.'

Remy fidgeted with his new bracelet again. 'There's an old barracks they're clearing out, behind First Hill,' he said. 'They're calling it the warrior stables. Not to insult the champions, it's just a name.'

Feilan managed to refrain from rolling his eyes – there was no such thing as just a name – but he did so obviously enough that Remy tsked. 'He doesn't get special treatment just because you and he—'

'Careful.'

'—are fond of each other,' Remy finished, not giving any indication as to whether he'd changed direction mid-sentence.

'Fond? You can call it that, I suppose. No, he gets special treatment because he's Adeline's champion and I won't have one of the other champions knifing him in his sleep at the behest of their employer.'

'But that's against the rules.'

Feilan found himself unable to address this utter naivety in any conceivable way. 'Just make sure he gets his own room with a proper latch, no matter how you have to do it.'

Almost forlornly, Remy said, 'Swarf, so I should expect nothing but enemies and cheating in this, even from family?'

Especially from family. 'I'll try to win you some allies,' Feilan said. 'But – yes. That's the game, I'm afraid.'

'And you've played these games before?'

'Trade squabbles. Not quite so violent as this one – don't start.'

'I wasn't going to.' Remy turned his face into Feilan's shoulder. Feilan's partly-mocking , partly-intimidating hold on him had become, in the last few moments, a comforting embrace.

Quietly, the Riverlander asked, 'But I can trust you?'

'Rufran,' Feilan breathed, on the edge of a rebuke – what kind of person went around openly asking if he could trust someone and believing the answer? Not someone remotely capable of playing out what he'd started.

Instead, he gently tucked Remy's hair back. 'Yes. You can trust me.'

Remy stared up at him with those wide, dark eyes, nothing but soft willingness to swallow the reassurance, and Feilan would have offered up an awful lot towards that hypothetical dramatic renegotiation of their agreement. He reminded himself of Remy's spikier side...and also that if he remained patient, Remy might come to the idea, the very bright idea, of renegotiation on his own.

He cleared his throat, and added, 'If only because my mother will be dreadfully disappointed in me if I don't win her little queen her crown.'

Remy demonstrated that he was beginning to grasp the edges of the endeavour before him. 'What if Uncle Bertrand offers you access to the trade network if you help *him* instead?'

'Excellent question,' Feilan said. 'Faulty premise. The trade network's just an excuse. My mother wants Adeline to win because my mother *was* Adeline, a long time ago, and lost. Freyja made you a deal, and her word is golden. Her tool, *me*, is the *one thing* you can take on faith here, Remy. I can't promise to win, only to try. I might yet let you down. I won't betray you.'

'Oh,' Remy said. He was struggling for words. 'I see.'

Unable to stand the sheer emotion Remy was losing control of, Feilan said, 'Right, I'm hungry and I'm sore from that ride, so you're going to do something about it, aren't you, husband?'

'Oh,' Remy said again, startling out of the placid, almost yearning look he'd been directing at Feilan. 'Yes. I'll see to it.'

'I'm inviting you to feed me and rub my arse.'

'I did comprehend, yes,' Remy said. 'You don't need to spell out your vulgarity.'

'Never hurts to be clear about these things,' Feilan said.

He did get food, a thick porridge in a trencher of rye, but not the arse-rub. Remy called for hot water instead, yanking on the bellpull over the bed, and Feilan stripped off. Remy was predictably awkward about it, looking away while Feilan slowly sponged himself down, wishing for the cold water of the bathing pond even over the luxury of hot water there wasn't nearly enough of.

Amused, he eyed off his husband's pink cheeks and averted gaze. 'You've seen me naked.'

'It was a little darker than this,' Remy muttered.

'Take a proper look,' Feilan invited. 'We're a people of long things. Longhouses, longboats, longswords, long...swords.'

He put his hands on his hips and gave a waggle. Remy turned a brighter red but he also clapped both hands over a rather wild giggle, his first capitulation to the crude Vaer sense of humour. Feilan sniggered and went on washing.

When he was done, he put on a clean shirt and braes. The room was warm, despite the slits letting in cooler air, and the blankets on the soft bed looked thick: he would have slept naked, if he hadn't known how uncomfortable that would make his husband.

Remy only quickly took a turn with the last of the clean water, now lukewarm, his back primly turned. Feilan, not without a small qualm, admired his arse anyway. He dressed in a long white shift that begged to be pushed back up over his pale thighs.

Feilan turned his eyes away, qualm at the ascendance. This bed was too soft, and it was far too small.

9

REMY WAS ABSENT WHEN FEILAN AWOKE in the morning. He'd rolled right into the middle of the bed, thanks to the sag of the too-soft mattress, and had a vague recollection of his husband having to crawl out from under his arm. He stretched, feeling an unaccustomed stiffness to his back, in all the opposite places as when he slept on too few furs.

He should get some furs, and sleep on the floor.

He washed with the cold water from the aquamanile, combed his hair and beard with implements he found on the ornate silver tray by the bowl, and left the room, putting his boots back on as he went. Remy's shoes were gone, of course, and Feilan noticed none of the other doors along this single corridor had shoes by them. He tried a few latches, and found vacant chambers identical to Remy's, and a drab backroom with two narrow cots plainly meant for servants – as expected, gilt ropes led to a row of bells here – but nothing that suggested a kitchen or a space to gather around a metaphorical or literal fire. That must be back at what Remy had called First Hill, the metaphorical as well as literal centre of Seven Hills. If servants slept here, as the cots and bells suggested, they'd already attended Remy and gone about their daytime duties.

Feilan returned to the cloud-adorned foyer, and down the short walkway to the main arcade. The air was cool, and the mist was still thick below his vantage point. He was a sailor of the skies, gazing out over a white sea in every direction, the other hilltops green islands in the monotony.

He looked both directions, and then strolled the way they'd come last night. Given the distinct morning chill, this must be a miserable place in winter. He suspected the airiness of arches and unglazed high windows in the chambers would be exchanged for smothering wool hangings and heavy blankets, thick cloaks and leg-wraps, and braziers in every corner.

It'd still be a freezing walk in the dark times. Feilan found himself wondering how often Remy faced it. How often he just stayed away in what seemed like an isolated dormitory for guests, of which there would soon be plenty, as more contenders for the regency began to arrive.

On the next hill along, he went up the walkway to look into the foyer. This ceiling was stars painted onto midnight tiles, and the foyer was in use. Furnished with low chairs, plentiful cushions and soft diaphanous drapes, restless in the light hilltop breeze, the foyer was full of women.

Adeline was bent over a pale collar, painstakingly adding a row of golden stitches. The two aunts who had ridden out to chaperone her home yesterday were there, and a third woman with enough family resemblance to probably be the last of Remy's sisters. There were younger women and girls with the same look, most likely cousins, and then other women who were probably retainers of one sort or another. It was reminiscent of his memories of his mother and her friends at pleasant communal chores while the husbands were off raiding, except it had a somewhat more indolent air. Their children wouldn't starve or freeze if this work wasn't done.

But their hands, to be fair, were all busy: most were at needlecraft as they chatted, adding embellishments in silk thread to fine clothing, though some were making drawings, presumably design work. Here was the communal space he'd expected at Remy's lodgings; he'd overlooked the empty antechamber.

Their hands fell still when they saw Feilan looking in, and so did their tongues.

In the stark silence, Adeline rose, clutching her embroidery piece. 'Sir Feilan! Good morning.'

'Heilsa,' Feilan said, smiling at her.

'Are you looking for Uncle Remy?'

'Yes,' Feilan said, for lack of any other purpose today. 'Is he at—' He pointed up the way. 'First Hill?'

'Oh, no, he doesn't go there much. You need to go back past— You know, I think I'll show you.'

'Adeline,' Lady Slaphappy hissed. 'You don't do errands. Send a servant.'

'This is Uncle Remy's husband, Aunt Odila,' Adeline said. 'He's hardly an errand. He deserves a proper tour of his new home.'

She tossed down her embroidery and came smiling to Feilan, taking his arm and leading him away. She was dressed in fine linen skirts dyed deep red, dark hair braided, her mother's silver clasp again at her nape. She wasn't wearing the protective talisman yet, he noted.

Outside, less self-assured, she said, 'Um. *Would* you like the tour?'

'Not really,' Feilan said. 'I suppose the structure we arrived at last night is the main complex, and the sleeping quarters spread out from there?'

'Yes, well done!' she said, and then blushed like her youngest uncle at her own audacity. 'This is Second Hill East, where I reside, and my aunts and their families, and you and Remy are in Third Hill East. We need to go down past Fourth Hill East to find him. That's for visitors, mostly. Second Hill West and so forth are for my uncles, and Great-Uncle Bertrand.'

'Shouldn't Remy be over that side, then?'

Adeline frowned, plainly confused.

'The siblings seem to have segregated themselves by sex.'

'Oh! Not on purpose. And Remy wants to be near his grotto.'

'His...' Feilan decided to wait on explanations for that one.

'Do you know,' she said happily, as they walked along the undulating covered walkway. 'I'm glad you came along. You saved me so many stitches. I do get very bored with embroidery.'

She devolved into bright chatter, then, partly out of nerves, Feilan suspected, and partly a not particularly subtle attempt to impart the family tree to him. He wasn't sure if this was tactical, necessary knowledge for the upcoming monster hunt, or if Adeline had decided he was now truly part of the family.

Did she, he wondered, think the marriage was real? He didn't know children. For all her evident intelligence and confidence, and somewhat shaky royal self-assurance, she might not have the experience to recognise her uncle's ploy, and it might not have occurred to Remy to tell her. He'd been very intent on completing his machinations before his family caught up with him. And then yesterday, when she and Remy had attended Freyja in the wake of the unexpected marital contract, the plotting had been all about obtaining Torben's agreement to the mercenary contract. Both Freyja and Remy might very well have simply taken the marriage as established without wasting time niggling over its inauspicious engendering, especially in front of the child.

There were more people on the hilltop arcade now, making their way between the crests and dips, and coming up from uncovered paths worn into the grass between the arcade and a scatter of lower buildings, presumably where the real work got done. They seemed a mix of servants, retainers, and perhaps minor family, but all seemed to be fed and clean and comfortable, in the manner of a well-managed fiefdom. They greeted Adeline with genuine fondness, she returning the salutations cheerfully, and presented small bows or nods to Feilan.

'They're all very curious about you,' Adeline confided. 'Remy keeps to himself so much, everyone's very surprised he's come home with a husband.'

'Right,' Feilan said. 'Why does he keep to himself?'

'He prefers it that way,' she said airily, before frowning. 'No, that's not true, is it? That's me not thinking properly. It's his witchy hair. Mother always said it was nonsense. But Father said it was safer if he didn't draw attention to himself. Father wasn't entirely pleased with things as they developed, but it does make people happy, you know.'

Feilan tucked yet another question away.

'When *I* am queen, I shall let Uncle Remy do as he likes,' Adeline said with that curiously innocent confidence.

'You're already queen,' Feilan said. 'Why *were* you doing embroidery?'

She stopped dead. He thought he'd overstepped. But she started walking again, saying, 'Great-Uncle Bertrand is in First Hill. He's managing all that for me, as my guardian. My acting regent.'

Feilan said nothing.

'You're right, I should be there,' Adeline said. 'But – I'm worried if I go over there, he'll pat me on the head and tell me to be a good little girl and run along now back to my sewing, in front of all the liege-men and advisers and petitioners, and that will be an end to any hope of authority in my own right.'

After struggling with himself – he was here to help, and wasn't entirely sure he was about to – Feilan said, 'You have a large Vaer man with a sword at your disposal.'

Adeline seemed nonplussed. 'Oh. I do. Perhaps, once I've shown you where to find Remy, you could come over there, then?'

'Your Majesty,' he said gently. 'I'm not a Vaer man. I meant Torben. He's your champion. Learn to use him. It'll be good practice.'

'He is *rather* large, isn't he?'

It occurred to Feilan that Adeline, aside from the signing of the contract, had been avoiding Torben, the very large Vaer man with the very large sword. 'He's a cuddly bear, Lina,' he said. 'You'll see.'

They'd passed both the cloud-ceilinged Third Hill East and Fourth Hill East, built on the same lines, and were approaching what appeared to be the arcade's eastern terminus, a sort of cantilevered balcony jutting over the end of a promontory that promised a lovely view.

There were no people this far down, except one young man who left the balcony as they approached, very flushed and messy-looking, ducking his head shyly in response to Adeline's unsuspecting wave.

The balcony was a pleasant space, large and round under a cupola. It was more like a stone pavilion than a simple viewing platform. It was framed with more of the Seven Hills arches showing unbroken blue sky beyond, and a picturesque arrangement of skeps, the bees still quiet in the early chill, with the precipitous sheep-grazed slope beyond vanishing into the mist below. The landscape suggested there'd be a river at the bottom of the rolling green hill, but not, if Feilan's sense of direction was holding, the same one they'd travelled along yesterday.

There was a cushioned divan fashioned from stone in the centre, for sitting and admiring the vista, and another of those gauzy curtains hanging at the entrance arch, that could have been pulled across to shield the romantic nook from the view of the arcade – and it would have been helpful if the wrecked young man had done that as he'd left after dressing, because the low back of the divan did not much hide that Torben was sprawled out completely naked there, face down and fast asleep.

Not that Feilan did not appreciate the fine view of finer arse, all clenched hard muscle, but poor Adeline clapped her hands over her eyes.

'I don't think I'm meant to see this sort of thing!' she squeaked.

'Give me a moment,' he said. He entered the pavilion, whipping the curtain closed behind him, for all the good the sheer fabric would do now.

He shook Torben's shoulder, which was incautious; Torben lurched up roaring and lunging for his seax, the short almost-sword that all Vaer men carried even when leaving their real weapons at home. Luckily, it was enough out of reach that he'd woken up by the time he got his hand on the hilt.

'Little Wolf,' he grumbled.

'Get dressed, the queen is here,' Feilan said.

'Good morning, Adeline,' Torben bellowed, strolling about the pavilion to collect his scattered clothing with scant regard for his nudity and even less for Feilan's peace of mind.

'Good morning, Sir Torben,' she warbled.

Torben, having flung on his clothes, looped his seax at his waist, and shoved his feet into his boots, scrubbed at his eyes, finger-combed his hair, adjusted the plaits in his beard, and then stepped out to offer the girl a remarkably polite, near-chivalrous bow.

'At your service, Majesty,' he said gravely, though not without a wink Feilan's way.

'We're just going to visit Uncle Remy,' she said, 'and then I need you to escort me back to First Hill, please. Oh, and you'll both need to break fast, too, won't you?'

As she spoke, she was leading them through the northern most arch, where, now Feilan knew to look for it, he could see the marks of a worn path curving down the shoulder of the promontory. It was slippery underfoot, but Adeline managed it agilely, so the two Vaer naturally had to follow without complaint.

'Couldn't find a room last night, after all?' Feilan murmured to his friend.

'Merely a lovely place to watch the sunrise, Little Wolf,' Torben said, and Feilan snorted.

The narrow path divided, one path towards the skeps lower on the slope, the other snaking under the overhang, petering out at a cave of sorts, though really it was a broad-mouthed recess set deep into the side of the hill.

The stone-buttressed earthen walls were lined with cupboards and shelves. There were clay pots and metal flagons and ceramic bowls and expensive glass vials and bottles and jars, plugged with cork with labels attached. One long workbench was covered with bundles of various herbs, with more hanging to dry above. Remy stood there, hair still obediently uncovered, currently occupied with quill and ink over a collection of paper, quite the luxury even for a prince, sewn together down one edge to form a raggedly-bound book.

The burst of scent emanating from the sheltered space, fresh and medicinal, was strong enough to be overwhelming, washing bright green with cheerful notes of lemon-yellow across Feilan's vision. He blinked it away.

He'd apprised Torben of the local superstition about red hair on the ride to Seven Hills. 'Bugger me, he *is* a witch,' Torben muttered now.

Remy spun. 'Oh. You're here,' he said, without inflection. He set down the quill.

'Morning, Uncle Remy,' Adeline trilled. She skipped over and threw her arms around him, and then vanished into further recesses, where the space narrowed and darkened into true cave-like proportions, a telltale trickling sound and wash of cooler air suggesting a small spring back there, too.

'That should make you feel better,' Torben said, nudging Feilan. 'You got tricked by a witch, not a normal person. You don't have to feel so stupid now.'

'I didn't, but thanks.'

'I'm not actually a witch,' Remy reminded them crossly. 'I just happen to have red hair.'

'And be born a seventh son,' Feilan said.

'Seventh *child*.'

Torben took a turn. 'And live in a cave.'

'*Work* in the c— It's not even a cave. It's a grotto.'

'Making potions,' Feilan said.

'Herbal remedies!'

'From a spellbook.' Torben eyed the inkpot with illiterate suspicion.

Feilan, meanwhile, examined the pages Remy was filling with crabbed notation. He hadn't seen many books, despite his many years of travel.

Remy slapped it shut. 'A *ledger*—' He stared between the two of them. 'You're just making fun of me now.'

Feilan patted him fondly. 'We were making fun of you the entire time, Rufran.'

'Witches are only ever women,' Torben assured him. 'Unless...' He rubbed his own beard as he gestured towards Remy's beardless face. 'You sure he's got a cock down there?'

'I'm sure,' Feilan said dryly. 'No need to offer to check.'

Torben theatrically shut his mouth, smirking. He then ruined it by talking. 'Still not sharing, then.'

'Very much *mine* and only mine,' Feilan said, putting a casual arm around Remy's waist and drawing him in close. He felt Remy first stiffen under the touch, and then melt into it.

'His loss,' Torben said. He grinned. 'Yours, too.'

Adeline emerged from the dim shadows carrying a basket in one hand and a put-upon cat under the other arm. 'I knew you'd forget to eat!' she told her uncle.

'Give me back my cat,' he said sternly, and it squirmed from her hold to make a frantic leap to his shoulder. It was smaller than the hefty, thick-furred Vaer cats, and balanced there with neat grace.

There was no help for it, then, but to indulge the little girl, and perch on the edge of the so-called grotto, where the view was almost as good as from the promontory over their heads, and enjoy the copious contents of the basket the servants must've habitually provided to Remy in the mornings – fresh-baked fine white bread, hard-boiled eggs that they rolled on the rocks to crack open, drying slices of cheese and small, sweet apples.

The cat settled on Remy's lap, purring. He absently stroked it until its eyes slit half-closed in pleasure, the same abstracted fondness he'd shown his little horse. Feilan told himself he was not jealous of a scrawny orange cat.

He hadn't pet an animal since he'd tamed the half-wild kitten; despite Feilan's deep resentment, drowning the poor creature had indeed stamped out any nascent desire for giving care to anything that could be lost too easily. He carefully held out his hand, and let Remy's cat sniff at his fingers. It put its ears back, tail twitching dangerously. As hostile as its master, it seemed.

Feilan drew back his hand, then held it up pointedly to Remy, display-ing his bracelet-adorned wrist. Remy sighed but evicted the cat from his lap so he could fossick about and return with the talisman Feilan had left in his care last night.

This he handed without ceremony to his niece, though he did stoop to say, 'A gift from Feilan. He'd appreciate it greatly if you wore it.'

Adeline was *delighted*, even more so when she saw that her favourite uncle and her new uncle were wearing the same tokens. She made Remy tie it about her wrist immediately, and they both received hugs.

'Thank you, Uncle Faro,' she said.

Feilan opened his mouth to protest the inappropriate butchering of his byname into nonsense, before checking himself. The nickname carried a meaning in the Riverlands just as much as a byname did in the heartland. It meant affection. He wasn't so much of a mouthy jolterhead as to throw affection back in the face of an earnest young girl.

He slapped Torben across the arm and gave him a firm shake of the head when it looked like his friend wasn't going to show the same restraint, then caught Remy looking moderately stricken.

Remy had just worked out that his beloved niece had somehow failed to glean that the marriage was a sham. Well. That was certainly his problem to deal with. Feilan beamed at Adeline, and over her head at his husband.

Torben looked sour as he chewed through a slice of bread topped with dollops of a boiled quince and honey mix, though Feilan supposed that was more to do with missing out on Freyja Anjasdottir's protective blessing than Adeline's touchingly sincere gratitude.

Afterwards, they helped Adeline pack up the remnant food, the cat winding between their legs, and then Torben took up the basket as solemnly as any holy relic ripe for plunder. He accompanied the queen away, waving dismissively to Feilan's call of 'Be restrained at First Hill!'

'He...didn't find a room last night,' Remy said, as soon as the pair were out of earshot up the path back to the hilltop.

Remy might have even gone past the pavilion early enough for a close-up view of the active portion of Torben's second-favourite pastime. That was probably going to become a regular hazard, if Torben became attached to his sunrises.

'No,' was all Feilan said for now. No need to horrify his husband again so soon.

Tersely, Remy said, 'I've had him assigned to a room by ours. Tell him to use it.'

Feilan eyed him, the strain in his face, the tension in his shoulders, and wondered what the request for special treatment had cost him. Probably the very last of his defiance, at least for the next little while.

Abruptly, he hoped Torben wasn't *too* restrained, when he gained entry for young Queen Adeline to the royal happenings in First Hill.

Movement below caught his eye. Meandering around the hill slopes, from several directions, were more of the worn paths that he'd noticed intersecting the formal hilltop arcade of the interconnected palace. These ones, however, when he followed them with his gaze, led right to the cave. And there were more than a few people on them, labouring upwards.

Remy scrambled up. Feilan gained his feet beside him. 'I don't have my sword.'

He didn't even carry a seax, or an eating knife. His father muttered in his head for a brief, ugly moment. If there was any more proof needed—

'Oh, no, it's not like that,' Remy said. 'Just...keep out of the way, if you must hang about.'

'If I *must* hang about?' Feilan repeated with deep amusement. 'What am I doing, if not at your service, husband?'

Remy flashed him a sharp look, simultaneously annoyed and guilty, but by that time, the first of the visitors had arrived, the cat fleeing into the darkest part of the cave in tandem.

She was a woman of around Feilan's mother's age, very spry, dressed in the bright kirtle and shawl that was usual in the Riverlands, hair covered with a plain cap. She eyed off Feilan with some concern. Remy said something, in what Feilan was fairly sure was the same dialectical or archaic language he'd used for the marriage rite, that made her chuckle throatily. She squeezed Feilan's arm and moved over to the ledger with Remy, where they fell into a discussion while the next arrivals formed a queue, sitting in a row along the ridge where they'd sat with the break-fast basket.

They were, Feilan realised, customers.

Except Remy didn't seem like he charged coin. Some of the visitors left jars of honey, or the cooked fruit and honey mix like Torben had had on his bread, or more herbs, or collections of seeds, and some left fresh rye loaves, or butter, or little savoury grainy cakes. Some left woven cloth or spun and dyed yarn, a particularly clever payment because it'd cut their share of the town's tithe too. Some left nothing, and Remy didn't treat them any differently.

That was what he was doing, treating them, Feilan gradually deciphered from observing the interactions. He was not exactly sympathetic, but he wore a neutral manner which seemed to reassure them. None went away empty-handed, though some, those Remy spoke to longest, looking very frowny and serious, were evidently promised further, custom-made, remedies upon return in one or two days.

Most were women, though some had to be there on behalf of others, presumably including fathers and brothers and sons. Some of the men who did come for themselves turned around when they saw Feilan, now sitting in the sunshine at the head of the row on the ledge. Some were desperate enough, in their specific ailment, to go ahead with the consultation, which usually involved dropping their pants. None of the visitors was ancient; Feilan suspected the hill would have defeated the very old and the very ill, and assumed some younger visitors were fetching medicines. Not all – some of the girls, scared, alone or with their mothers, were there for that oldest, most useful of remedies.

To all, Remy repeated the same phrase he'd said about Feilan to the first woman. Feilan eventually asked for a translation. 'I'm saying, Don't mind him, he's just my husband,' Remy told him.

With that first phrase, and getting his ear in on the typical questions Remy asked of his visitors – he was surprisingly patient as he teased out more information from their stammering reports of symptoms, usually accompanied with unhelpfully vague gestures – Feilan began to find a way into the new language, which was, after all, closely related to Riverlander. He was good with languages, a talent he never would have discovered if his life hadn't been changed by exile.

By mid-morning, he was able to greet the next visitor with, 'Don't mind me, I'm just the husband,' making her chortle and Remy try not to smile.

But when she'd gone, Remy said, 'You shouldn't be speaking that. It's women's dialect.'

Feilan raised his brows. 'You're speaking it.'

'I have to. To help them.'

Feilan thought of Adeline blithely saying, *Father wasn't entirely pleased about things as they developed, but it does make people happy, you know.* A knowledgeable and tame witch – of course the people were happy. Real doctors were expensive, and often ineffectual as well. Remy appeared to be neither.

'Is it taboo for me to speak the women's language?' he asked.

'It's *unmanly* to speak a woman's language.'

Feilan laughed. 'You do understand what it means to be Cursed, yes?'

'Not...as such,' Remy said slowly. 'No.'

Another client was peeking into the cave. 'Tell you later,' Feilan said, taking himself out of the way again.

By the time the next pause in the patchy stream of visitors came, he'd had time to truly take in the situation. Remy hadn't left his hair uncovered in his cave out of obedience to his boorish husband, but as an unspoken herald of his abilities. The witchy youngest son of one king and youngest brother of the next had established what amounted to a free physick clinic and lowered himself to speak a local feminine dialect, just so he could *help*, and in a way that confirmed local superstition about him, no less.

'You said,' Feilan accused him, 'you weren't good with people.'

Remy, surrounded by the gifts of all the people who appeared to both respect and trust him, looked blank. Then he said, 'I said I wasn't much around people. And I'm not.'

Feilan silently pointed down the hill, where the next customer could be seen walking up from the town below, on a path worn through the sheep-nibbled grass by the sheer number of people trekking the same way every day. There was an even more distant figure behind the first.

'Oh. Those people. They merely find me necessary. There's not normally so many, but I've been away for three days. But *my* people. My family. I— The red hair, you see.'

'I think I've made it clear I *don't* see, Remy.'

'My father said I shouldn't be seen about First Hill, lest our enemies accuse us of witchcraft and our friends turn from alliances. And I was...-lonely. After my mother— After she was gone. I used to wander about the hills and I met... Well. I suppose she might have been considered a witch, old enough that *her* hair had faded to silver and she could just be a wise-woman instead. Her name was Achima. She taught me this.' He held out his hands to encompass the contents of his cave, all those witchy brews and potions. 'When she passed, the townsfolk and villagers needed someone else to go to.'

Feilan, from a village, an entire homeland, where the problem was that one was *never* alone, felt something of a pang, a queer combination of both envy and sympathy, for a little boy so entirely and pleasingly left to himself, but so roundly and familiarly rejected by his closest people. At least Feilan had always had his mother, and the other Cursed. It sounded like Remy had lost first his own mother and then his fellow witch and mentor far too young.

'And then my brother, King Geroald...' Remy picked at a splinter on the workbench he was leaning on. 'His wife, the queen, the former queen. Margalita. She was always very kind to me. She didn't like me' – a brief smile, achingly fond, flickered over his face as he spoke – 'moping about in my grotto all day, and made me come to meals with the family. And made *them* stop acting like my mere existence would bring down disaster on their heads. She...protected me.'

He turned away from Feilan for a long moment. When he turned back, he was very matter-of-fact. 'Margalita died, last year. Childbirth. Her newborn son died too. Geroald was furious. He said if I was going to hang about serving peasants witchcraft all day, I should have been able to save the queen and the heir, too. I've not been much welcome at First Hill since.'

Feilan swallowed his initial reaction, which would have involved profaning the name of a dead man. He said, 'Must be hard.'

'I should have been able to save her,' Remy said, face terribly drawn and bleak.

Feilan hesitated, and then said, 'You loved her.'

Remy blinked. 'I— Oh, no. Not like that. She was my brother's wife.'

'It's not stopped better men than you,' Feilan said, deliberately brusque. 'Is Adeline yours? Is that why you're so fond of her? Why you want the regency, to be her father in role if not in name?'

'No!' Remy cried, agape, but at least shocked out of that uncomfortable grief. 'Aside from anything else, I'd never… I do not know why you find it so hard to believe that night with you was truly my first time. I didn't lie. I don't lie.'

'Remy,' Feilan said patiently. 'Do you think every one of the young ladies who visited you today truly have sick grandmothers?'

'Of course they do.'

'What about that man who wanted you to take him into the back to look at that supposed problem with his cock?'

'He wanted privacy!'

'I bet he did,' Feilan said, grinning. 'I don't care what your family has told you. Actually, there's plenty of people who both respect and *admire* witches.'

'Not a witch,' Remy mumbled, cheeks satisfyingly pink. 'I said I don't prefer men, as a rule. I…also don't prefer women, as a rule.'

Feilan drew a blank; he didn't know any other options, aside from— 'Eunuchs, then?' He frowned. 'Sheep? Not the cat, surely.'

Horrified, Remy cried, 'What! No! Oh, you—'

Feilan was fairly sure Remy had bitten back a nasty word just then. And he *was* being a bit of an arse, if only towards Gytha, who, having been born with a cock and the expectation of warriorhood, had departed her village having managed to avoid becoming Cursed, and who Feilan did not recall ever seeing with a man or another woman since arriving in Siftar. He *did* recall spending perfectly chaste nights cuddling with her in the depths of winter, snug by the meeting hall firepit. She was simply not inclined to sex, and found him safe, since he wasn't inclined to sex with her or any woman, nor any unwilling man willing to be honest about it.

He supposed Remy somewhat the same, now, and not deserving of the low Vaer sense of humour in return, even if it had taken his mind completely from dwelling too much on the loss of his brother's wife and the depths of grief he'd probably had to mostly hide, to avoid the exact accusation Feilan had inflicted on him.

A cheerful hail came from behind them, then, the visitor Feilan had pointed out in the distance. She was the sort of lean some women got in their old age, with a face worn gaunt and long grey hair in a thin plait, loose down her straight spine instead of elaborately coiled about her head.

She said, 'Isengrim.'

It was a word he'd been hearing all morning. She howled with laughter when he trotted out his women's dialect just-the-husband trick.

He waited outside on the ledge, using a folded cloth as a makeshift plate piled high with some of the baked goods tithed to the witch of Seven Hills. As she was leaving, tucking a small bottle into her kirtle, Remy already greeting the second woman coming up behind her, he asked her, 'What does isengrim mean?'

'Grey hat,' she said, reaching down to cheekily pat him on the head; women who made it to her age really did not have much to lose. 'Those iron helmets you wear when you raid.'

Ah. The local version of jolterhead, then, that useful Midlands pejorative the Vaer had adopted, made their own, and spread back into the common tongue.

'Right,' he said. 'About that. Why are none of you women scared of me, when the royal family is?'

'Oh, you haven't raided this region since I was a child,' she said. 'The Nivardus, though. You did them some damage. The king's mother, you know. Queen Adeline's grandmother.'

'I do *not* know.'

She tilted her head. 'Ask your pretty husband, then, young man.'

Feilan made a face, which achieved the hoped-for cackle. He said, 'What about this monster that killed the king?'

Sobering, she said, 'We have tales about her, stretching back two hundred years or more. She hunted here long before the Vaer did.'

'Right,' Feilan said, smiling and waving to his makeshift platter of graincakes, 'how about you sit for a spell and tell me about her, good?'

B Y THE TIME FEILAN HAD HEARD the first tale, another client, a young woman, had come up, and she sat to rest on the ledge to tell her own version. She was from a village on the other side of Seven Hills, not the town. The customer who'd come up behind the lean old woman, a middle-aged woman with a bad cough exacerbated by the climb, had yet a third version as she departed clutching medicine that smelled pale pink.

Once they'd all three gone, Feilan paced across bare ground in front of the wide mouth of the cave. One end of his circuit looked out over the joining of the two rivers and, if he craned, Seven Hill's riverport; the other had a sightline the other way, past the skeps into the great bowl of open farmland that lay behind Seven Hills. At his arc's very apogee, upwards and back, he could glimpse the hilltop arcade, its covered length straight as an arrow at a slope back towards Fourth Hill East.

As he paced, he looked out over the view, which he'd been assessing all morning with a creeping sense of his own presumption. The rolling hills, grazed by sheep, almost bare except for the occasional clump of trees at the crests. Narrow valleys dipping in every direction, the occasional glint of water at their bottoms flashing in the sunlight now that the mist had completely lifted.

A bear *could* survive here, Feilan thought, pacing. It *might*.

'What are you doing?' Remy asked from behind him.

Feilan glanced around. Though Remy had a stone mortar and pestle on the workbench, a faint haze still lingering from the initial pungent scent of crushing herbs into oil, he'd stopped work so he could stroke his cat. It bunted his chin, turning under his petting hands. Even apart from the absence of anyone on the paths now, Feilan took its reemergence as a sure sign that the clinic had closed for the day.

'This is a barbarian thinking,' he said. 'I know you're not familiar with the sight.'

Remy grimaced. 'I'm sorry I kept calling you a barbarian.'

With a conciliatory shrug, Feilan admitted, 'And I shouldn't have kept insisting your brother was killed by a bear.'

'You believe me about the monster?'

'Yeah,' Feilan said. 'You said you saw the injuries. You want to tell me about them?'

'Not particularly,' Remy said, 'but I will.'

His voice trembled with the effort to sound dispassionate as he outlined what he had seen when his other brothers and the Nivardus retainers had brought the fatally injured King Geroald to him. Another one he hadn't saved, but it seemed in this case no one could blame him; no one could have saved the king.

He'd been torn open, three rents from collarbone to navel, and died screaming.

Between the stories and Remy's account of the brutal wounds to his brother, Feilan had begun to build up quite a picture of this monster in his head. He was frowning over it, and pacing to his full extent before the cave, when movement snagged his attention. He glimpsed a figure traversing the arcade towards the pavilion, presumably intending to come down the informal path and around to Remy's cave.

Here came the reaction to Torben's incursion into First Hill, then.

Tsking disgustedly, he went back inside. 'Lady Slaphappy's coming.'

'You have to at least try to learn their names,' Remy said, rolling the pestle under one fidgeting hand, other hand still stroking behind the cat's ears. He hadn't fidgeted at all when he'd been helping his visitors. 'I know this is a sham, but if you act like you know it's over as soon as the monster hunt is, you'll—'

Feilan broke in, 'Eldest surviving brother, Hughard, married to Ida, three children all married off. Other brother, Lambert, married away to Irma, only one daughter, also already married and gone, first grandchild on the way. Eldest sister, free with her hands and almost here ready to use them, Odila, married to Ludolph, three surviving children. Middle sister, Hilda, Lambert's twin, married away, to one Landric, four adolescent daughters left unmarried, very much trying to make them best friends with Adeline while the family's in residence for the monster hunt. Adeline despises all but one. Third sister, Rosmunda, married away, now widowed and recently returned and remarried to Conrad, no children yet. Least objectionable of your siblings but unlikely to break ranks with your uncle's plan.'

He'd been advancing on a gaping Remy through this recitation, and now settled his hand on his hips and gave him a small push back against the benchtop. The cat fled.

'What?' Remy said, watching his pet escape like he wanted to follow its lead.

'Don't make me repeat it, it was boring enough the first time.' He nudged in between Remy's legs, and burrowed his head down against Remy's neck so he could run his mouth over the soft skin, taking in that herbal scent, fresh and strong now he'd been working again. 'Hmm, that's good.'

Instead of joining in the game, Remy made a confused noise. Feilan muttered, 'Arms around me, jolterhead, your sister's walking in, any moment now.'

Remy hesitantly put his arms around his back.

'Tighter, make it convincing. No. You know what? I'm going to make your family far too appalled to ever try sneaking up on us again.'

Feilan went to his knees. He looked up at Remy, smiling as he reached for his laces. 'At least *try* to look like you're about to have the time of your life, Rufran,' he said. 'Take a double handful of my hair.'

Remy choked, but his fingers settled onto Feilan's scalp, catching at his hair.

'Grab *hard*,' he ordered, and felt the clench of fists.

Those hands spent their days chopping herbs and grinding seeds and mixing pastes; they were *strong*, and when Remy committed to the game with a yank on Feilan's hair, Feilan felt lust jolt not just from his head to his cock, but all the way to his toes.

He heard an accusing, 'Renart—' behind them, and shoved his face into Remy's crotch.

Remy's gasp was drowned out by Odila's. From the noises of hasty retreat, she'd whirled on the spot and literally fled. Feilan chuckled, holding his position, face pressed into Remy's breeches. Despite his hasty loosening of laces, Remy was still covered, but Feilan could feel the swelling under the linen in his way. It would take the work of a bare moment to free that responsive cock from the cloth and take it in his mouth in truth.

Remy let his hair go and let his own knees go at the same time, slithering to the ground in front of Feilan in a helpless heap.

'Do the Vaer just *immensely* enjoy public sex?' he asked weakly, his head falling back against the bench strut.

Feilan laughed, sitting back on his heels with only a momentary pang of regret. 'We share our longhouses, from birth to death. We can't have inhibitions. We get used to having sex with other people in the room, or hearing other people at it. That's men and women. Two men have to find privacy, and that's usually outdoors somewhere, and quick. Two women...' He paused. He hadn't thought about this before. 'Women can cuddle together in a way men can't. So they can possibly be a little more subtle, under a blanket, if they're just using fingers.' Remy's eyes were widening; Feilan hid his smile. 'Women don't upset the honour of warriors like men acting like women do. Anyway, once we've left the heartland, and are in more accepting places... It's not on purpose, really. It's more of a reaction to having to keep things so secret for so long. And' – he shrugged – 'we really do not have inhibitions.'

Remy said, 'And the Cursed? You said you'd explain it.'

'Men who didn't quite find enough privacy. Men taking the passive role, the female part.' To Remy's blank look, he said, 'Taking cock, Remy. Cock-cravers.'

'Oh! That's...frowned on?'

'It's dishonourable. Immediate cursing and exile. There's not,' he added, 'anything wrong with it in truth, just because my people take against it. They think of it as weak, and infectious, to act the woman. I've think we've both met enough women to know there's nothing weak about them.'

'Yes,' Remy said softly, and Feilan wondered if he was thinking of the iron-cold strength of his sisters, the silky-soft strength of Queen Margalita who wouldn't let him mope alone, or Adeline's bright and underrated courage, clear and pure as diamond.

'And,' he went on, 'should you wish to engage in a dramatic renegotiation of our agreement...'

Remy sucked in a breath. He obviously hadn't expected Feilan to ask, but Feilan wasn't going to ignore that blatant evidence of desire if it let him get his mouth around Remy's cock, or his own cock buried deep in his husband again. Remy might not prefer men, or women, as a rule, but Feilan was evidently breaking the rule.

'It's... It would be my choice.'

'Of course.'

'No, I mean—' Remy bit his lip, and then looked at Feilan, bleakness coming back to his earnest face. 'I mean, I had to let you have me, before, for the marriage. But if I allow it now, it's my choice. I'd be deliberately fucking a Vaeringan.'

'A barbarian,' Feilan said, unable to stop a roll of his eyes. 'Would you—'

'One of the people who sold my mother into slavery.'

Feilan shut his mouth. After an excruciating moment, he asked, 'When?'

'I was seven.'

He counted back; it was his father's generation of raiders. Of course it was. That didn't mean his father was involved. Until the raiders set up camp by Siftar seven summers ago, the bersverdar of his village and the surrounding regions had based themselves further south and east. Either way—

'Would it help if I said it wouldn't have been slavery?'

'No.'

'If she was taken by the mid-Vaer who traditionally raided this region, it would have been a kidnapping for ransom. And if she wasn't safely returned, the ransoming went wrong. But she wouldn't have been sold as a slave.'

Remy pushed himself to his feet. 'I said it doesn't help.'

Feilan rose, too. He couldn't stop himself from saying, 'Mid-Vaer don't take people for the slavers. We had a queen who— It doesn't matter now. They take prisoners, to tend the camps during the raids. But they let them go at the end, with a set of good clothes and a purse of silver.' Remy directed a cold black-eyed look his way. 'It's not much better, I know, but it's not the same as slavery. And your mother... They wouldn't make a servant of a queen. They'd have wanted the ransom.'

'Your people took her, she didn't come back, it doesn't make a difference why not,' Remy said flatly. With jerky motions, he scraped the oily green paste from the mortar into a jar. 'I'm riding down to take this to a sickbed in the town.'

Feilan, just as frustrated, let him change the subject. 'Then I'll come with you.'

'You won't.'

'I have to,' Feilan said, feeling as cruel as his father, but more wretched about it. 'It gives me a chance to reconnoitre the hunting ground.'

'I don't—'

He sliced a hand through the air, chopping off the head of the argument. 'Do you want Adeline to win or not? You put personal feelings aside to make it this far. Play your serthing game, Rufran.'

'Fine.' Remy swept up a satchel and a plain grey cloak and stalked out.

Feilan rubbed a hand over his eyes and followed.

At the stables, he received a clear indication that Remy's uncle, or his personal cabal composed entirely of Remy's siblings, was spying closely upon his newly-married nephew. He didn't notice the retainer who must have watched them make their stiffly silent way down the path behind First Hill, but whoever it was must have scurried fast to report.

The jolly-faced uncle himself, Bertrand, arrived to spoke Feilan's wheel. 'Champions are not allowed to leave Seven Hills once arrived, or they forfeit their right to compete. You know this, Renart.'

'He's my husband,' Remy said, eyes lowered. 'We're going on an outing together.'

'You have plenty of time for him to be your husband,' Bertrand said, smiling. 'But for now, he is also your champion, and the rules apply to him. You've already spent your coin, wrangling Adeline's champion his own quarters. Or will you trade one concession for the other?'

'I'll be right here, Rufran,' Feilan said.

For the sake of the pretence, he pressed Remy's hand, receiving a snapping look from those black eyes before Remy turned away to take the reins of his horse, the same small mare he'd ridden from Siftar.

'Oh, Renart.' Bertrand patted his shoulder, then left his hand, heavy with rings on every finger, firmly in place. 'You don't have to wear yourself out with these pointless rides about the place every afternoon.'

Remy had gone stiff and still under the touch. He kept his gaze lowered, but his voice was firm. 'I go to those who are too sick to come to me.'

'How long will you try to atone for losing Margalita and Geroald? There is no need.'

As far as Feilan could tell, the soft reassurance offered no comfort, but rather conveyed the opposite of his statement's meaning. Since he knew his instinctive dislike was colouring his observations, he couldn't, for now, decide if Bertrand intended that or not.

Bertrand gentled his voice even further into cloyingly cooing tones. 'Adeline doesn't blame you, you know.'

Ah. Now he'd decided. He said, 'Ja, he knows. Queen Adeline is constant in her affections. She doesn't blame him, because no blame is warranted.'

'Of course, of course, as I said.' Bertrand seemed about to say more, but Feilan's expression must have dissuaded him. 'Remember, stay on the grounds.'

Watching Bertrand's back as he scuttled off, Feilan opened his mouth to voice some fairly strident opinions. Remy abruptly mounted and pulled his cloak's hood up, before flashing another glare Feilan's way and pushing it back to ride away with his bright hair catching sunlight.

It left Feilan at rather a loose end, and annoyingly disconsolate. He strolled the arcade past First Hill onto the western side of the hill ridge, putting his head into each of the three foyers that way. Their ceilings were of a red star, a flood, and a fierce but badly drawn beast he decided must be a lion, like the shape of the aquamanile.

He finally realised what he was seeing – all the ceilings were painted in honour of She Who Spins, who had to be one of those complicated agricultural deities incorporating both abundance and dearth, fecundity and barrenness, and thus, eventually, sex and death, and so love and war. The eastern halls were decorated with a peaceful night sky, clouds promising life-giving water, and whatever adorned Fourth Hill East – he'd bet on a lamb, seeing the lion. Those were the ancient motifs of Her first aspect; the west bore the ominous star, the destructive storm, the lion, the opposing motifs of Her second.

He followed the beaten paths beyond the highest curve of Seven Hills, coming across servants' quarters and various outbuildings, and the new barracks, all tucked out of sight of the hilltop arcade. Seven Hills had much of its wealth from sheep – meat, wool, and cheese – and its tithe of the riverport, but the sheltered dip behind the hills was fenced off with stone, the bright green of new leaves showing on old, gnarled vines, and he thought he saw, in the distance, the bright white crust that indicated the low entrance to a salt mine. He didn't go closer; now he had been warned, he did not want to accidentally step beyond the formal and invisible bounds of Seven Hills.

By the time he'd wandered his confines, it was late afternoon, and Remy could have ridden to the town and any of the smaller scatter of villages several times over. He came across Torben, still accompanying Adeline as she left First Hill after a long day of ruling as queen. She greeted him happily – she must not know what his people had done to her grandmother – and waved Torben off to leisure.

Feilan helped Torben shift himself from the still-empty old barracks – the warrior stables – to the room beside the one he shared with Remy.

Since this involved a single leather bag, a couple of wicked seax, and the longsword, shield and spear, it didn't take long.

'Come in for a fuck?' Torben invited him, looming in his doorway while Feilan dispiritedly walked the couple of steps to his own door.

'I'm being watched,' Feilan said.

'Let them watch.'

'So the uncle has an excuse to call the marriage invalid,' Feilan elaborated. 'Rescind his agreement to it.'

'I can take it from here,' Torben said. 'Come on in, we'll make it nice and loud, and then you can toddle on back home to Freyja. I'll win Adeline her throne.'

'Njorda grant me the confidence of a jolterheaded bear-warrior,' Feilan said, though he couldn't help smiling at his friend, who smiled his big, open grin right back.

Remy came in from the open passage from the foyer, then. He looked weary, grey smudges under his eyes, but the moment he saw them – Torben halfway into his room, Feilan only a few steps away – he drew himself up and snapped, 'Fidelity.'

Feilan had been planning how to be nice to Remy all afternoon. 'I serthing know,' he snapped back. 'Do I look like I'm sucking his cock?'

'You look like you're about to.'

'Wonderful.' Torben clapped his hands once with brisk good cheer. 'Get about it, then.'

Feilan threw open the door to his own room, stormed in, and slammed it dramatically behind him. He wasn't used to doors that could slam, and found it quite satisfying. By the time Remy followed, which took long enough that Feilan had to worry if Torben had intercepted him, he was calmer.

'Let's keep it civil,' he reminded his husband.

'I'm not the one who just slammed the door and told my servants and therefore my entire family we're having a quarrel.'

'Married people quarrel.'

He tried to sound indifferent, but he was annoyed at himself for the display. The Vaer temper, properly roused, was surely a sight to behold, but that was his father, not him.

Ulfr had tried to force it into him, turn echoes into a battle-roar. His mother had done better training it out of him, reminding him remorselessly that he was Cursed and so the bear-god would never bless him: any anger he felt was thus merely human and very, very controllable.

Deliberately slowing his breathing, he bent and began to get his boots off, to put them outside their door. Even emotionally heightened, Remy hadn't forgotten to remove his own shoes.

'Don't bother,' Remy said. 'We have to go eat with my family now.'

Tension was thrumming through him. Feilan was moved to try to lay a comforting hand on his shoulder.

Remy practically arched his back and hissed like an angry cat. 'It doesn't escape my attention you lost your temper the moment you realised you're not getting sex from me.'

'I said it already: sex isn't part of the agreement.'

'You thought it would be.' Remy folded his arms, smiling thinly. 'And as soon as you knew I'll never *ever* let you fuck me again, you're slamming doors and cavorting with your barbarian friend.'

Feilan's jaw tightened. Despite his efforts, his breath was quickening. He *had* been smugly anticipating Remy's capitulation to the desire he did seem to feel. He thought he'd been offended by the accusation he was about to suck Torben when he'd been virtuously refusing to betray his pact with his pretend husband. But perhaps he also did resent Remy's rejection, simultaneously unjust and yet faultless.

He reminded himself he did not actually much like Remy, increasing attraction, slight sympathy, and mild admiration aside. It was no loss to him if he couldn't have him again. In a moon-turn or so, he'd have Torben again.

And there was a gods-cursed reason he was stuck in a sexless arrangement with a man who despised him. That reason was standing in front of him being a good deal too self-righteous.

'You trapped me here.' He was trying not to shout. It made his voice come out in a low growl, menacing enough to make Remy retreat a step. 'You tricked me, you're using me, you don't get to dictate the exact shape of my behaviour, not when I'm doing my thrice-cursed *best* by you, Rufran.'

He waited for a snide comment about the abject failure of his best. Remy, however, had taken the rebuke to heart. He'd gone still and lowered his eyes like he did when his uncle or siblings were telling him off, which Feilan was surprised to discover was utterly infuriating, much more so than the spiky obnoxiousness.

'I didn't take your mother,' he growled. 'It was nothing to do with me or mine, and I won't be blamed for it. I'm not a serthing bersverdr, I'm not even a Vaer man, I won't be judged as one.' Silence from Remy, eyes submissively lowered, fingers curled into his palms, body unnaturally still. 'Oh, you have a spine, you mouthy *serthr*, rediscover it!'

Remy's temper bloomed in direct response to the challenge. 'You don't want to be judged for it, but you happily use it! You know people are wary of Vaer raiders, and that lets you frighten them or be nice to them as suits you.'

'Draf! Hogshit! Do you know how many times I've been in a fight because other men thought it'd prove something to take down a lone Vaer? Do you know how many times me and Freyja were turned away from town gates because they took one look at me and refused to let us in? Do you know how it feels to let your own mother walk alone into a hostile town because that's the only way we'll trade enough to eat?'

'Yes, I do!' Remy shouted at him. He checked. In a smaller voice, he said, 'I know what it is to not be allowed to be with my mother in case I endanger her.'

Feilan said, '*Serth*,' with far more force than he'd intended.

He made himself take three slow breaths, counting. Then he was able to say, 'Let's just get this family meal done,' without snarling or throwing things or, horrifying thought, acting like his father and using his fists.

This temper was *not* given unto him divinely. He would control it.

They walked to First Hill in silence, sat at the table full of siblings and marriage partners and children in silence, and endured jibes from Hughard and Odila in silence, while Uncle Bertrand kept Adeline occupied whenever she tried to turn the topic.

'Everyone argues,' the youngest of the sisters, Rosmunda, said at last, evidently taking pity. 'But it's such fun making it up, isn't it?'

'Sure is,' Feilan said, slinging his arm over the back of Remy's chair and managing a smirk. 'Right, Rufran?'

'Yes,' Remy said dreamily, taking Feilan's hand, his talisman brushing against Feilan's own.

Feilan had the sinking feeling they would have to fake sex noises after all, for the benefit of the spies Remy was so very certain were hovering behind every corner.

Luckily, by the time they returned to their room, in silence, Torben was entertaining an evening guest loudly enough that they could wash and sink into bed in yet more, increasingly dismal, silence, trusting that the noise from next door would cover their own icy lack.

Their days fell into the pattern set by the first. They'd fall asleep, each to their own edge of the bed, in a cold silence made strained by the sound of Torben's activities next door. Feilan would inevitably awake alone in the sagging centre of the soft bed.

He'd make his way along the arcade above the mist, as thick as ever as the moon waned and the days crept further into summer. Often he'd pass Torben, dozing on the divan after he'd had his way extravagantly with some willing Seven Hills resident at sunrise. Sometimes it would be a flushed and giggling woman, twitching her kirtle skirts and hurrying off up the arcade. Sometimes a man, lips swollen or gait a touch stiff. Feilan would go on past after giving Torben a shove to get him moving to find Queen Adeline at First Hill.

He'd eat the daymeal, or, as the locals had it, break fast with Remy and the ginger cat. Its name was Breone, which Feilan thought translated as Little Flame. He counted it as a triumph the day it sniffed his fingers and then, instead of laying its ears back, bunted its head against his palm, inviting a stroke of its head. He obliged.

He spent his mornings at the cave, chatting with the visitors coming up the hill. It was never again as busy as that first day, but there were always at least one or two women, and occasionally men, sitting on the ledge outside the wide mouth of the grotto, waiting to see Remy or resting before the walk back down. Adding to their visible fascination with the witch's barbarian husband, he brought along his nailbinder and took yarn from the gifts to the witch, to make stockings or his little dolls, keeping his hands busy. As a bonus, since he tended to hand a finished woolwork to whoever he was talking to at the time, he garnered very many visitors willing to linger beside him. He asked for more tales about the legendary monster, and skirted around the raid that had taken Remy's mother, Queen Leonore, gradually chipping away to collect enough fragments to make a picture of what might have happened.

He found himself watching Remy more and more as he bound yarn and gathered information. Within his own tiny domain, Remy the witch of Seven Hills was a different creature to Renart the badgered and beleaguered prince and Uncle Remy the anxious and outmatched protector of a little girl. Gone were the telltale defensive stillness and the opposing nervy pacing. The Remy that moved about the shallow cave, from workbench to ledger to freshwater spring, was confident, calm, and very skilled.

More than once, Feilan came back to himself with nailbinder and yarn lowered to his lap, the women around him giggling and nudging each other because he'd been so enthralled in watching his slender, elegant husband and his slender, elegant hands. All he could do then was make the same silent explanation he'd made to Freyja, an open tip of both palms to invite the women to just *look* at the man.

'He's pretty,' he'd say, making them laugh in indulgently amused agreement.

It was an understatement. Remy outside was pretty. Remy the witch was, in fact, bewitching.

It was, Feilan decided, a symptom of his lack of sex; he concentrated harder on the task he was here to complete.

Remy escaped every afternoon with the excuse of delivering medicines and visiting his sickest patients, patently vanishing for the rest of the day with his horse, as fond of the small mare as he was of the little cat.

Feilan, meanwhile, found Seven Hills servants willing to talk to him, trailing them through the hidden-away outbuildings where they gathered or prepared food or traipsed back and forth in an endless fetch-and-carry, or scrubbed the linens and draped them over the lavender bushes to dry, the mingled scents of the bruised flowers and damp linen making a silver haze in the corners of his eyes.

He talked to them about many innocuous things, to disguise that it was also about the sheep flocks and goat herds, about the salt mines, about the waterways, about where the hills were loneliest, where the valleys were deepest, where they narrowed to crevices, where they wove and crossed and petered out into dead ends, where the worst of the fens lay.

One old retainer, thrilled for the attention, sketched him out the lie of the land in charcoal on a scraped piece of hide, and added to it every time Feilan brought it back with more questions. He also spent an inordinate amount of time with a goatherd, negotiating.

By habit, he assessed the Seven Hills defences. There were some fifty liveried guardsmen quartered in the large and comfortable new barracks tucked down with the other outbuildings. The guards, divided into three shifts each comprising sixteen men and a captain, patrolled in pairs along the arcades in both directions, or stood at attention in the forecourt and halls of First Hill. Off-duty, they went to and fro from their families in the riverport; that was where the bulk of the militia would be summoned from, too, in the event of a bigger crisis than young men in fancy uniforms could manage.

After a few days, Feilan asked Remy for ink and parchment, to write to Freyja. 'If not, a bit of wood, and I'll carve a runestick. Letters can be sealed, is all.'

Remy proved he was learning to play the game despite his antipathy towards it, and towards Feilan, when he looked thoughtfully in the direction of First Hill, where such supplies were no doubt plentiful, before saying, 'I have to go to the apothecary for the medicinal ingredients I can't source locally. I will buy you parchment there.'

He was still naive enough, however, to delegate delivery of the message to the stable hand tasked with returning the borrowed horses and donkey. Feilan therefore used heartland runes and the beggar's script cipher to write his letter; unlike Remy, he had no reason to trust the sealed message would not be intercepted, but his only recourse bar forcing Remy to ride to Siftar himself was to make it as difficult as possible to read it.

He could not guarantee the message would even reach Freyja, except he'd enclosed a jasper bead off his talisman and told the groom in no uncertain terms that he expected a particular bead — yellowed walrus ivory, though he did not share that information — from Freyja's hand in return, and if it was not forthcoming, he would make sure someone paid for it.

Remy still otherwise avoided him, meeting instead with Queen Adeline as she finished up her duties for the day. This afternoon visit appeared to take the place of their break-fasts, now that Adeline had taken up her proper role at First Hill. Feilan couldn't quite decide if the cessation of the morning visit was more to do with that new early schedule or Adeline's justifiable caution about walking past Torben's favoured fucking den.

Either way, he was glad to see niece and favourite uncle establish their new visiting routine in the once-bare foyer of Third Hill East, reclining on giant cushions Adeline politely requested from the servants, sipping tea and nibbling on snacks, usually fresh gifts to Remy from his town clients. Feilan was careful to keep his distance, because Adeline insisted on sweetly inviting Uncle Faro to join them if she saw him come in, and that was just too awkward with the icy wall between him and Remy.

The moon inexorably waned towards the gloom. Other warriors began to arrive, mercenaries and sellswords coming in the train of contenders for the role of regent, guardian, husband. They were all big men, scarred, muscled, arrayed with blades, cold-eyed, though not all of them were as cold-eyed as the contenders they accompanied.

Seven Hills filled up, until both Third Hill East and the empty Fourth Hill East, its foyer indeed lamb-adorned, were crammed with guests. Adeline regally greeted each new cluster of arrivals, contender, champion, retainers, guards, servants, confidence buoyed by Torben's remarkably steadfast attendance. He seemed to be taking his role as her champion both seriously, and with no little pride.

Feilan raised this with him, late one afternoon, after Torben had escorted Adeline to her afternoon visit with Remy at Third Hill East. They sat on the divan in the pavilion, Feilan uncomfortably aware Torben had fucked half the population there. The patrolling guardsmen turned around at Fourth Hill East these days. His days of abstinence were telling on him, and an incident earlier that day involving a very insistent young man had not helped.

'I'd like her to win,' Torben explained of his unusual dedication above what was required to honour his contract. 'I'll win it for her, if I can. She—' He'd been staring straight ahead, over the view, but now he looked at Feilan. 'She reminds me of my sister.'

It seemed he was seeking a particular response, but Feilan didn't know what it was. He resorted to mocking, their usual grease. 'Wouldn't she remind you of your daughters, old man?'

'I don't know them. I spent their little summers raiding eastwards, and we usually overwintered, too.'

Torben sounded matter-of-fact; it was a normal state of affairs. Feilan had three children from his time at stud in Chalcadea, and, given he'd obligingly fucked their way into a stable trade route, he'd probably met them more often than bersverdar ever met theirs. They were who he'd learned to nailbind his simple yarn dolls for. The dolls were merely modified pouches, with coloured rows for hair, face, clothes and feet, stuffed with waste spinning fibres and sewn closed with a few more stitches to shape the neck and ankles.

He'd never been acknowledged as their father, of course, nor Freyja as anything other than a doting friend of their real grandmother's, and he hadn't seen them since he and Freyja had established Siftar. By now, he'd surely have Chalcadean grandchildren he'd never meet.

He took a breath, reaching for Torben in a surfeit of fellow feeling. His friend batted his hand away and went on gruffly. 'Went home long enough to throw silver at Ingunn and put another baby in her every few years, and that was about it.'

As much sympathy as he was currently feeling for Torben, Feilan didn't extend much to Torben's village wife. He'd always wondered why the watchman had been checking the old storehouse that evening, why Ingunn had been so handy for Torben to find refuge with. The scandal of it had been eclipsed by the bigger scandal, but the fact that she, the magnate's daughter, had been found unchaperoned with the bare- -naked Torben didn't just give him his alibi – it secured her a marriage to a young and glorious warrior instead of a dry man her father's age.

But Vaer wives, in the general... He knew how busy their chores kept them, spinning and weaving, tilling and harvesting, picking and pre- serving. He could imagine how much of relief it would be to wave the warmongers off, and how annoying it must be to have them show up at the end of summer, throw a bit of silver down, wave their cocks about as if the women should be grateful for the ride, and then sit about all winter polishing their swords and expecting to be worshipped.

The parallel struck him. He whacked Torben across his arm, bruising his own knuckles and not affecting his friend at all.

Torben casually retaliated, shoving him even as he added, 'Though I wouldn't want to count back too carefully from the day of their births.'

'You can't expect pity for that, surely. You must have bastards from one end of the known lands to the other. Probably another full clutch from this jaunt alone.'

'I know. I'm not complaining. Just saying. I don't know my daughters, and they've gone off married now and don't care to know me.' He looked up sharply. 'I never raised a hand to them, Little Wolf, nor Ingunn, that's not why they...'

'I know.' For all Torben's more noxious qualities, he'd always lived the true warrior code: strong men never need hurt those weaker than themselves. The code did presuppose who should fall into the category of weak, of course.

'But they're not going to want the likes of me dandling their tots on my knee.' Again, he stopped. 'If that wasn't women's work.' He cleared his throat. 'But, growing up, I did know my little sister.'

Belatedly, Feilan remembered Thora, hair the same wheaten gold as Torben's, blue eyes bright with adoration directed entirely at her big brother. He remembered that she'd died, a sudden fever taking her almost overnight. He remembered that that was when Torben had prodded him up to the high pasture, roughly taking the comfort that, as a Vaer man, he couldn't seek any other way. He remembered that Torben had held still with his forehead pressed to Feilan's shoulder for a long time after their frenetic activity had rushed to its completion.

'Oh,' he said. 'Thunder Bear. That's surprisingly sweet.'

'And you can bugger right off with that,' Torben said, but this time, smiling, he let Feilan curve his hand around his forearm.

'Queen Adeline,' Remy said from behind them, 'is hosting a feast tonight. All champions are expected to attend.'

'I suppose you're going to shout at me for innocently sitting next to my friend,' Feilan said over his shoulder, switching languages seamlessly.

'Copping a feel,' Torben helpfully supplied, raising the heavily muscled forearm Feilan was still clasping. Feilan pinched him, to no effect.

'I am not, no,' Remy said. 'After all, it's not sunrise.'

Torben sniggered. Feilan fought his own smile.

'I am intimately acquainted with *that* habit,' Remy went on, 'since I must walk past it on so many mornings.' With a glimmer of humour that had been absent for days, he added, 'Though, if I am scrupulously fair, your dawn company does appear to be very much enjoying themselves.'

Torben straightened, half-turning to direct his broad grin Remy's way.

'Still not sharing,' Feilan said. His own turn towards his husband was more in the line of an indignant scowl. 'He doesn't need encouraging.'

'I wasn't,' Remy said.

Feilan folded his arms and weighed the likelihood that his innocent husband truly did not know when he was engaging in flirtation. He thought of the way Remy, drunk, had wrapped his fingers around

Feilan's wrist and made him lift the spout of the ewer to his lips so he could swallow, holding unwavering eye contact the entire time. He still couldn't decide how deliberate that had been.

'May I speak with you privately?' Remy went on.

'He's going to ask to be shared, Little Wolf,' Torben said, slapping a hand across Feilan's shoulder, to far more effect than Feilan's own effort.

'Go away,' Feilan replied, also in Vaer, rolling his shoulders and cranky for no particular reason. 'Oh, no, wait.'

Torben, halfway to the arcade, turned around, beaming.

'*I am not sharing*. At this feast, though, we'll be talking to the other warriors, trying to work up alliances. As far as we're concerned, the monster is just a bear, right? We spread that word, no matter what the others are saying.'

'It *is* a bear,' Torben said.

'That'll be easy, then,' Feilan said agreeably, and saved his, 'You poor jolterhead,' for when Torben had swaggered off past Remy and down the arcade.

He was still smiling as he turned his attention to Remy, who ducked his head and ran fingers through his hair, pushing it off his face.

Feilan stopped smiling. 'What happened?'

Remy self-consciously touched his temple, where a cut had been hidden by the fall of his loose hair. It looked small, and freshly washed, but swollen. Remy was perhaps on his way to his cave, to apply one of his own remedies.

'Someone threw a stone at me.' He shrugged. 'My family were not wrong about the general opinion of witches in this region. Only the very poorest must visit the witch on the hill.'

Feilan the trader could have corrected him on the basis of the quality of the women's clothing alone. 'Someone needs a lesson.'

'It was only a little boy,' Remy said.

'Then he only needs a little lesson.'

He was being sharper than he'd normally be towards a child, because he'd made the unspoken connection: Remy had gone down the hill with hair uncovered, at Feilan's boorish command, and this was the result.

'That's not what I came to you for.' He offered a small, somewhat shy, smile. 'I want to apologise,' he said. 'I have been thinking a great deal, and I've realised...' He shifted his weight. 'You were right.'

Feilan was still looking at that cut. Still thinking about a thrown stone. Thinking about it happening regularly enough that Remy seemed neither surprised nor bothered by it. Thinking that Remy had known the risk of going uncovered to the villages, and obeyed him anyway without complaint.

'Often am,' he said absently. *But not this time.*

Again, Remy surprised him with a flash of amusement rather than disdain. 'I don't prefer women, as a rule. But you were right. I see now that Queen Margalita must have been my exception. *Unacted upon.* You pointed it out, and that made me understand what my feelings for her were.' He swallowed. 'And I don't prefer men either, as a rule. And *you* are my exception there.'

That broke Feilan's rumination immediately. He had to battle to keep the gratification from his face, which prevented him from doing anything else alarming, such as leaping up to grab Remy and fling him onto the very divan Torben had so industriously demonstrated the various uses of.

He merely said, 'Also to remain unacted upon?'

Remy gave him a narrow-eyed look, but his smile lingered. 'I thought I was angry at you, and I wasn't. I was angry at myself. Because Vaeringans took my mother, and I should hate you, and all I want you to do is—'

He stopped, expression decidedly alarmed. Feilan raised his brows in his best expression of polite enquiry, *willing* his husband to finish the sentence.

Remy shook his head. 'I just needed you to know. I was angry at *myself*, and that made me unfair to *you*. Because that's another thing you were right about – I trapped you here, and you are being...' His smile this time was sudden, and true, and it lit up his whole face. '*Remarkably* good-natured about it.'

Entirely captivated by that smile, Feilan still managed, 'For a barbarian.'

'For anyone, you jolterhead,' Remy said. 'You've been very kind.'

'Right.' Feilan grimaced; he couldn't let himself dwell in the glow of Remy's change of heart. 'Remy, I'm Vaer. I'm not kind.'

'You won't take the compliment?' Remy asked. 'Have I finally stumbled on the one thing that scares a Vaer man?'

'Not a Vaer man,' Feilan said, 'but – yes. Accusing a Vaer of softness...' He tutted.

'If it helps, you're also quite mean.'

'Thanks, it does.'

Remy shifted again, on the edge of the full nervy fidget. 'Why do you keep saying you're not a Vaer man?'

'I was stripped of manhood when I became Cursed,' Feilan said, keeping his tone cheerful.

'Ah...' Remy tangled his fingers together. 'You certainly applied your manhood well enough on our wedding night.'

'Njorda's tits, Remy!' Feilan said, helpless not to laugh. 'It's not a euphemism, it's a status. I was stripped of the *status* of Vaer manhood.'

'I see,' Remy said. 'No, I don't. You seem very manly to me. And, sorry to have to say it, kind.'

'I'm still *Vaer*. We can't afford to be kind, not in a heartland as harsh as ours. I can't doubt for a moment Vaeringans really did kidnap your mother.'

'Yes, your people did,' Remy said. 'You didn't.' He raised his palms. 'Not kind, then. But honourable.'

Feilan, full of good humour a moment ago, gave a harsh bark. Remy plainly very much still did not understand. Honour was reserved for men like Torben. It had been years since it had been taken from Feilan, and years, he'd thought, since he'd let it bother him. As Freyja had known from the start, a trader's reputation was worth solid gold, far more valuable than a warrior's honour measured in hacksilver.

He said, to explain his inexplicable noise, '*Cursed*. We're defined by dishonour.'

'Stop arguing with me, I'm trying to be nice to you!' Remy was smiling, though. 'And I'm also sorry it took this long to come and tell you I was wrong.'

Torben would have said something along the lines of *better you kept your emotional shit to yourself*. Feilan said, 'I'd rather you quietly work out where the problem lies and then come and tell me what you need than that we argue endlessly over the wrong thing anyway.'

'My family calls it sulking.'

'I call it sorting your own shit out,' Feilan said. 'And. Well. You were also not wrong. Because I do use the Vaer reputation to my own advantage, sometimes. I do like that most people are cautious about crossing me.' He paused. 'I like that you're not.'

Remy looked horrifically pleased about that, the poor lonely creature. Feilan accompanied him down to the cave, already in shadow, the sun setting westwards and the sliver of moon not yet risen to cast the grassy slopes below the promontory into dappled silver. Remy found his way with perfect competence in the darkness to the cupboard with the salve he wanted, while Feilan neglected to let his eyes adjust, and so promptly tripped over the cat and swore about it, not least because the mishap sent it fleeing from him again after all his progress.

He joined Remy at the bench and took the salve. He swiped up a good fingers-end of the gooey paste, which smelled green but came with a burst of blue as pale and bright as a clear winter's sky when he scooped his fingers through it. He gently lifted Remy's face to the starlight to dab it on, leaning in to compensate for the dimness.

Remy seemed disconcerted to be on the receiving end of the same sort of care he doled out to everyone else. Though...he *had* just admitted a degree of attraction. Feilan shifted closer, letting his fingers linger along his cheekbone.

'Why are you bothering with this?' Remy said, somewhat waspishly.

Ah. The first assumption, then. Feilan had to think about it, that instinctive *don't-touch-what's-mine*. 'It's a Vaer thing. We protect our own.'

'Vaer honour?' Remy said, which was quite pointed after the conversation they'd just had in the pavilion.

He was right. It was a Vaer *man*'s honour, as ruler of a holding, no matter its size, no matter his feelings for the people within it; they were his to protect, whether he disliked them, desired them, or a little of both.

Feilan shook his head, surprised at himself, and at the unexpected strength of a conditioning he'd been free of for well over half his life. He still pocketed the rest of the jar, so he could do it again in the morning.

12

FEILAN WALKED SIDE-BY-SIDE WITH his husband towards First Hill. Passing Fourth Hill East, however, Remy abruptly ducked under Feilan's arm, drawing it around him.

Aside from moments ago, when Feilan had applied the salve – he could still feel Remy's skin under his fingers where he'd taken his chin to tilt his injured temple towards the light – it was almost the closest they'd been since that first night at Seven Hills, Remy huddled under Feilan's arm on the bed while Feilan told him he could trust him.

There were figures further up the arcade, servants perhaps. Spies, certainly.

'Ah,' Feilan said, enlightened twice over. 'Moon-gloam tomorrow night. Was your uncle sounding off about refusing to solemnise the marriage because we've not been putting on enough of a performance of being in love?'

That was polite. They'd been frankly frosty, the veritable opposite of newlywed lovers.

Remy worried at his lower lip before saying, 'Yes, but I also truly did want to apologise to you.'

'No bother. And that explains my afternoon, also.' He glanced down at his husband. 'Handsome fellow, servant livery, made a spirited attempt to' – *suck my cock* – 'seduce me. A ploy by your uncle, no doubt.'

'Oh.'

'Told him he was looking for Torben, didn't seem to deter him.'

'I see.'

'He wasn't an ill-tempered redhead with pretty eyes, so I refrained.'

'Thank you,' Remy said, blowing out air in a blatant huff of relief.

'Thanks for assuming otherwise,' Feilan replied, straight-faced.

'I didn't!' Remy protested. 'I just...wasn't *entirely* sure. I realise it must be difficult for you.'

'Yes, there's nothing I find more tempting than men who are contractually obliged to have sex with me.'

'No, I meant...'

Feilan put him out of his misery. 'What, the no-sex?' To Remy's small nod, he said, 'I'll manage, Rufran. I know what I've agreed to.' Since Remy was distracted by scowling at the servants as they walked past, he added, 'Leave the man alone, he was just doing what he'd been ordered to do.'

'I imagine he volunteered,' Remy said. 'If he was even acting under orders at all.' He glanced up at Feilan. 'Oh. But you must surely realise you are comely.'

'Must I?' Feilan said, brows arched. 'People like a bit of barbarian cock occasionally, I suppose, but with Torben strutting about as an extremely available and easy option...'

Remy, cheeks pink, chewed a thumbnail before saying, severely, 'I'm hardly going to argue the point with you.'

'I appreciate the sentiment, regardless.' They walked in what felt enough like a companionable silence that Feilan felt he could ask, 'Do you want to tell me what happened with your mother?'

Remy tensed under his arm. He said, 'There's nothing to tell. She was visiting the market in the town. She often did. It was Vaer, coming upriver from the west. They claimed they were traders, but they took her. And they took the ransom, which Uncle Bertrand delivered to them personally on my father's behalf. They killed his guards, and they beat him.' He waved a hand at his own face. 'I remember he came home with a black eye, and scratches on his cheek. And they didn't give her back. He said they wanted both the ransom and the profit from selling a queen.'

It tallied with the story Feilan had gleaned from the visitors to Remy's cave, the ones who would speak to him about it. They spoke of Queen Leonore's kindness and wisdom in reverent terms. They said she'd visit the market, because this was a little kingdom and she was called a queen but she was more like a mayor's wife, and she visited the shopkeepers to give them her personal custom and let them tell her about taxes and tariffs and trends and traffic. They said she had no guards, because the town wasn't dangerous. They said she was unlucky. They said she'd walked with the Vaeringans to their clinker, so no one else would be taken and no one would be hurt.

He hadn't yet heard back from Freyja, which meant she was taking his request for more information seriously, and had set his clerks on it. He could guess that those Vaer really had been traders, in the early days when Vaer traders were viewed with even more suspicion and dislike than Vaer warriors, because the bersverdar were at least honest about their intentions. Perhaps they'd been bad at trading, and turned back to more familiar ways to stave off starvation. Perhaps they'd grown tired of being treated poorly and turned away from every gate without even being given a chance to show their wares. Perhaps they'd just been unable to resist the temptation of such a wealthy, easy hostage.

The one thing he did know was that they would not have both accepted the ransom *and* refused to return Queen Leonore. You did that once, you never won another ransom. The uncle was lying. He might have failed to pay the ransom, keeping it for himself, and the queen was duly killed. But that wasn't the story. The story was the ransom was paid, and the queen was not returned. The story was that Uncle Bertrand had been beaten, and Queen Leonore had been sold into slavery.

And perhaps those jolterheaded Vaer really had been stupid enough to try a double-deal, and Feilan was just spinning excuses for his people because he didn't want them to have murdered or sold Remy's mother.

He'd wait to hear from Freyja.

Remy said, 'My father never recovered from losing her. Even before he died, mere months later, Uncle Bertrand was acting as his regent. He took care of all of us, and that can't have been easy, when we were all grieving. And he didn't fight at all when Geroald took the throne in his own right.'

That, thought Feilan, *was because King Geroald was too strong to fight, with too many allies in the neighbouring kingships who would have quibbled his overthrow.*

'It makes it hard to think...to think he might not be doing right by Lina. Because he did right by all of us, you see. That's why Gero trusted him with Lina's guardianship, when he...when he was dying.'

As far as Feilan was concerned, Uncle Bertrand had been playing a long game, carefully inching his way through the labyrinthine traditions and alliances that stood in his way, and exercising outside influence on his nephew the king, and all the other Nivardus siblings, in the meantime.

He revised his estimate of the odds that the man would take drastic action if it looked like his faction would not win the head of the monster, finally delivering him a throne he'd been quietly working behind and towards for years.

It must have been a veritable gods' gift when Adeline's father was killed by the monster, leaving his young daughter and sole heir orphaned and vulnerable.

Oh.

'How did your brother run across the monster, anyway?' he asked.

Since this was apparently out of thin air, a confused expression passed across Remy's face. 'It had been attacking sheep.' Feilan knew this; he'd been talking to shepherds during his idle afternoons. 'Uncle said Geroald owed it to his people to kill it or drive it away. It was his royal obligation to do so.'

'Right,' said Feilan, trying not to sigh at this naive little fool. He tightened his arm, bringing Remy in closer to his side. Remy slid his own arm around Feilan's waist.

As they approached First Hill, Feilan said, 'Shall we pause here and make you look ravaged? Sell our reconciliation harder?'

Remy reflexively flinched before straightening and turning to face him. 'How do we do that?'

'Mess up your hair,' Feilan said, giving the loose red locks a tousle. 'Disarray your clothes. Say something too direct about sucking you so you're looking flustered and pink-cheeked.' He considered. 'Yes, just like that.'

'You...pretend to be Torben when you say things like that, don't you?'

Feilan raised his brows. 'I did warn you we have few inhibitions. But yes, I do reference the cruder examples of Vaer manhood at times, you quite correctly accused me of it.'

'There are other ways of...' Remy glanced around, though the pathway in the dusk was empty. '...showing you're in love than inappropriately graphic displays of affection.'

'Oh, yes? Tell me.'

That stymied him. After a moment, less tartly, he said, 'Fond words. Laughing at each other's jokes. Compliments.'

'Right. So I should stop telling everyone you wail like a cat when you climax and start saying how pretty I find your eyes?'

'*You have not been telling ev*— Oh, you're not serious. Oh.' Remy put a hand over his mouth to smother a sound that might have been a laugh, though it was of relief, not amusement.

That didn't stop Feilan from throwing his arm back around his shoulders to say, 'There we are, laughing at my stupid jokes. We're halfway there already.'

'Half...way,' Remy repeated dazedly, and then went very quiet as they walked along the airy facade of arches towards the main doors of First Hill.

Just as Feilan opened his mouth to demand to know his thoughts, he said, 'I'm sorry, that was silly. You don't have to pretend you're in love with me. I will act the besotted fool, but you may continue to act as you are.'

'The lusty barbarian?'

Mouth tightened, Remy said, 'I didn't mean that. I meant... Well, it's more plausible this way, isn't it? We're telling a story.'

'A love story,' Feilan said, conspicuously patient.

'No.' Remy paused, framed by the last arch before the doors, as striking as the ornately symmetrical iconography Feilan had seen in the south. *'I'm* in love, so I'm prepared to overlook my family history to marry a Vaer. But you – you're leaving once the contest is done. Thus, it should be obvious to everyone except poor besotted, foolish Renart that you're merely lust-addled, and the marriage won't last. Then no one will be surprised when you leave, and my uncle cannot accuse me of manipulating his rules while I'm heartbroken.' He cleared his throat. *'Acting* heartbroken.'

When Feilan said nothing, Remy repeated, 'It's more plausible. More believable.' He rubbed his brow, wincing as he accidentally touched the cut. 'Lina will be disappointed, though. She's quite taken with you.'

'I trust the crown will compensate,' Feilan said absently.

As he followed Remy inside, he mused over this notion that Remy's family found it entirely plausible that any love affair their youngest sibling conducted would be one-sided.

First Hill was laid out much the same as the smaller residences across the other hills, a foyer leading to an open-aired passage styled with the same pillars and roof as the arcade, leading into the closed corridor with rooms on either side. First Hill was larger, though, the foyer designed to impress visitors. The ceiling was painted with a representation of Seven Hills itself, overlooked benevolently by the feminine figure Feilan could now recognise as that local goddess of sex and death, Spenwan, She Who Spins, her fingers on the threads of the fates of those who worshipped her. She was called the Lady of the Salt, too, by some of the villagers, at least.

Beyond the open passageway, the rooms off the central corridor were larger too, ornately decorated to their purpose: painted figures, all men, arguing in a fresco in the privy council chamber, Spenwan in her abundance aspect overseeing the audience chamber. There was even a library, with a grand total of twelve hand-inscribed books of science. Feilan had rarely seen more collected in one place in such a minor fiefdom. Side passages led off to less public, more practical areas, though the kitchens and laundry were separate structures tucked below the crest of the hill. He hadn't discovered the treasury, in his wanderings, though he'd discovered several areas that armed guards turned him away from.

The corridor ended in the biggest chamber of them all, the equivalent of a feasting hall in some of the bigger towns of the heartland. This was where the Nivardus family gathered for their nightly meal, which was the only communal meal Remy appeared expected to attend. The massive central table had slowly been filling up, not just with siblings and nieces and nephews returning as contenders for the contest, but many minor relatives with a claim as well. It reinforced Feilan's impression that the Riverlands were an interconnected mess of little realms that anywhere else in Enea would be ripe pickings for a high king, if the rulers here, all cousins of one remove or the other, hadn't tacitly agreed to make a metaphorical shield wall against such encroachment, from outside or from within their own ranks.

Even now, Remy quietly greeted familial representatives of both Queen Leonore and Queen Margalita, here to ensure their matrilineal descendant's rights were not trampled. Feilan had expected that, because of the tight kinship allegiances, that close weave, cloth of the highest quality, that was holding Bertrand back from openly taking the throne.

But Remy also pointed out two men and a woman, independent observers of the contest from the surrounding kingdoms. They were eoldermen, formal appointees of the Seven Hill's neighbours and allies who'd forced Bertram to be subtle in his machinations, perhaps not so much because they supported Adeline's claim, but because they did not support his.

Among the arrivals today had also been three unexpected contenders from further afield. Two had unrolled genealogies to prove their claim; a third had been sent away. Either way, there were so many contenders now that a second trestle table had been hauled into the hall, and a third, long, added tonight for the champions.

It made the room unbearably warm, but Feilan kept Remy pressed close to his side as they sat together at the main table, ignoring Torben's shout from the warrior end of the hall. The tables were noisy with bonhomie, but the Nivardus family were, as ever, restrained and distant, making an almost peaceful lull within chaotic surrounds.

He and Remy were far down from the salt cellar, but it still did not take long for one of the siblings to notice and exclaim over the cut to Remy's temple.

'This is what happens when you uncover your hair,' Hughard told him coldly. He stared at Feilan, supercilious in his inarguable correctness. 'You come blundering in without knowing our ways, and see what happens.'

Feilan had slung an arm across the back of Remy's chair, as was his habit at the family's nightmeal, called supper here, a physical possessiveness standing in for any other token of marital bliss. He felt Remy's shoulders stiffen, felt him go unnaturally still. He had a sudden glimpse of Remy's childhood, surrounded by older siblings hissing *stop fidgeting, stop fidgeting, stop fidgeting* because their parents were dead and they had to control something in their lives.

Remy quietly said, 'It doesn't matter if I cover my head or not. They already know the colour of my hair. They all know who I am already.'

'Then they should know you're a prince.'

'As little as you act it,' Lady Slaphappy, Odila, added snidely.

'I rather thought,' Feilan said, and ignored Remy's intake of breath, 'royalty had an obligation to help their people, in exchange for their privilege.'

Bertrand, monopolising Adeline's attention at the highest end of the table as usual, didn't look away from his smiling conversation, but Feilan, watching closely, did think the older man became a trifle more alert, a dozing dog turning an ear.

Hilda, the married-out middle sister, only back in Seven Hills for the time it took Torben to remove her champion from contention, said, 'Renart could surely do so without casting broad the smear on our poor lost mother's name.'

The siblings and their marital partners and grown children nodded and turned back to the trenchers of stew, apparently satisfied that this had been a mortal blow. It was, for Remy; he touched his neck like he was wishing for the cowl.

'No, not following,' Feilan said.

Remy muttered, 'Because of the red. Please don't.'

Feilan didn't lower his own voice, and didn't heed the plea. 'You know that's not an explanation.'

'It is rank falsehood from foolish superstition, may it slough off and gout,' Hughard announced. 'Uncle Bertrand has been very clear with everyone about that.'

'I believe you,' Feilan said, smiling. 'About what?'

None of them wanted to come right out with it. Eventually Rosmunda, seated on his other side, quietly said, 'For Remy to be born with red hair, when no other in the Nivardus line bears that colour...'

Feilan lifted his gaze and directed a long, slow stare, very Vaer, at Bertrand. The family patriarch had finally been drawn from talking at Adeline, and was watching him in return, wearing a strange little smile.

'...the superstitious might whisper about congress with an evil spirit to give her last son witchy powers.'

It hadn't been what he'd expected to hear; Feilan gave a tiny nod, of acknowledgement, almost of admiration. The jolly man behind the crown had outdone himself in subtlety by reassuring his brother, his nieces and nephews, anyone who would listen, not of Leonore's unquestionable fidelity, but of the ridiculousness of local fables.

No one of any sense or influence would truly suggest the popular and venerated queen had fucked a hobgoblin. But if the well-meaning brother of the king, so dutiful, so supportive, kept bringing up the old legend just so he could dismiss the very thought that she'd had relations *of that kind* outside her marriage, they might start to wonder, eventually, if she'd fucked a redhead.

He'd disliked Bertrand before this, on general principle. But now he knew: even before Remy had lost two queens and thrown every last ounce of his meagre weight behind giving the third her due, he'd been subjected to this campaign, a casualty of his uncle's weaselling for more and more soft power. Had Bertrand even considered that undermining the elder queen would ostracise her child?

Perhaps not, but it had been useful groundwork for trying to force Remy from Adeline's side now, with more of the same technique, those slyly gentle reassurances – *Uncle Remy did everything he could to save your mother, save your father, he has no need to feel guilty, to atone through such selfless service to the peasants* – until Adeline might start to falter.

Except she wasn't faltering at all, Feilan only had to think of their afternoon visits, full of untainted affection for each other, to know it.

Perhaps the technique was too subtle for a child to notice, or perhaps Adeline was simply too pure in her devotion to be influenced by her great-uncle's insinuations. She might even be clever enough to remember Remy had been serving the peasants witchcraft long before her orphaning. Either way, intentionally or not, she was standing as firmly by Remy as he was by her. It must be annoying Bertrand.

Until now, Feilan had been working for Freyja, for her desired trade network, genuine fondness for Adeline and the odd mix of sheer lust and reluctant admiration for Remy notwithstanding. But his new, deeper, understanding changed all that on the instant.

He was working for his husband now.

Feilan let his smile return, gaze still locked to Bertrand's. *I see you, grimr*, he thought, and the challenge fizzed through him. Freyja had been right: he'd been comfortable in Siftar, and it had turned into complacency. He felt awake in a way he hadn't felt for some time.

Bertrand, clearing his throat, turned back to Adeline to say something light and jolly and, without a single doubt, quietly undermining. She fidgeted with her talisman, head bowed.

The siblings apparently noticed him murdering their beloved uncle with dagger-eyes. Odila said icily, 'Shouldn't you be over with the other barbarians?'

On cue, Torben gave the shrill whistle used to summon attention back in the village.

Feilan leaned to murmur in Remy's ear, which was probably ringing like his was from that piercing whistle. 'I do have to go drink with the warriors, and try to form alliances.'

Remy turned his face into his, speaking just as quietly. 'Why look for alliances? There's only one head, only one prize.'

'You'll see. Will you be all right if I leave you here with this nest of vipers?'

'I did manage family suppers before you came along, you know.'

'I think they've been on you like vultures since your Queen Margalita died. I thought Ulfr Njallsson was bad with his fists, but this is words, words, words, peck, peck, peck.'

He abruptly tugged Remy's earlobe between his teeth, making his husband jump. Still speaking throatily but now just loud enough to be overheard by their neighbours – not loud enough to be heard by the tender ears of Adeline – he said, 'Eat your fill. Then go back to our room and ready yourself for me. I won't want to waste any time when I come back.'

He stood, and smiled down at his flushed husband. 'You have *gorgeous* eyes, Remy.'

He went to join Torben at the warrior table, and prepared to get far too drunk, far too quickly.

13

Feilan staggered back to Remy's room late that night, and, by the dimmest combination of starlight and arcade torchlight falling through the uncovered upper slits, managed to navigate to the bed to fall fully dressed thereon. Remy, asleep on his stomach in the middle, jerked, but Feilan somewhat aggressively flung an arm and a leg over him to hold him flat to the mattress.

Muzzily, he explained, 'Don't wake up. Got news but tell you in the morning.'

That was the end of that, as far as he was concerned. He shut his eyes. The darkness immediately began a slow whirl behind his eyelids, murky. He grunted and shifted, opening his eyes to discover his mouth right by Remy's ear.

He muttered, in series, 'Head spinning. Haven't drunk so much in years. Had to. Had to join in. Serthing warriors. And their serthing ale. Traders worse, t'b'fair. Get you stoned, too.'

Remy was making small, obliging noises of agreement to each slow thought, most likely, a part of Feilan recognised, because what else were you meant to do when a large drunk man was lying half atop you breathing ale-tainted fumes all over your face.

He was too heavy to move, head too full of whirl. He buried his nose in Remy's hair. 'You smell good. Green.'

Remy's small humouring sounds stopped.

Feilan took it as surprise at receiving a compliment, and justified himself. 'I compliment you. Eyes. And told your uncle. Hair. I like your hair. And...and told you. You know. How pretty you are. And how good you feel.'

'Yes.'

'You know. With my cock balls-deep in you.'

The aforementioned gave a lazy twitch, but was otherwise too drowned in strong ale to muster itself. But the thought or memory or bright idea was enough to make him notice that Remy was tense, trapped face down under him, and naked.

'Yes, I did see. Ah. Thank you?'

'Sleeping bare.' He should be mustering the energy to roll off. Instead, he let his head lower so his lips could brush a bare shoulder. 'Readying yourself. Just a joke.'

'No, I was restless, I thought I might be hot.' Remy sounded strangled. 'I thought you'd bed down with Torben.'

'I share a bed with Torben, I get fucked one way or t'other. You asked for fidelity, you're getting fidelity.'

All the breath seemed to exit Remy. He tried and failed and the second time managed to say, 'All right.'

And Feilan felt his thigh nudge into his own as he spread his legs under him.

Feilan gave a gusty sigh, tainting the air with more stale fumes. His cock had managed to stiffen after all, the moment those thighs had spread for him, and was pressing insistently against Remy's tight arse. Feilan couldn't possibly find oil in his current state, but all he had to do for quick gratification was slide a little further atop Remy, order him to squeeze those supple thighs shut tight, and rut between them with a bit of spit to ease the way.

He wanted to do it so much. The fingers of the arm he'd slung over Remy were digging, probably painfully, into Remy's side as if already holding him still to be roughly used, slaked upon.

He wondered if Remy would bother with the performance he'd put on the night they'd fucked, or if he'd simply lie still through the whole sordid rut, as quiescent as he was now.

He rolled off him. 'Sorry. Drunk. Wasn't...whatsit. Forgot the River-lands word. Don't use it much.'

'Propositioning.' Now freed, Remy sat up, leaning down the length of the bed.

'Don't get dressed,' Feilan said. He squinted, and concentrated, pushing away lush insobriety so he could string his Riverlander sentences together. 'Sleep bare if you like it. I told you sex isn't part of our bargain, and it's not. You've been clear. I won't lay a hand... I won't lay more than the occasional hand on you.'

'I'm not getting dressed, I'm—' Remy made a huff of effort, and then wriggled out of the covers and crawled partway down the bed, which put his naked arse on view, lovely, rounded thing that it was, toned from all that afternoon riding. '—trying to get your boots off.'

Indeed, Feilan could now feel the jerk on one of his legs as Remy tugged at the ties of his boot. The effort was making Remy's backside jerk in interesting ways, too, a gleam of pale skin in the dim nightlight, his balls a delicious hint of shadow amid shadows. Feilan enjoyed the view while Remy levered off one boot and went to work on the other, leaning over Feilan to reach, one hand on his thigh for balance.

'If you...' Feilan said, watching that bobbing arse fixedly, making fists in the linen to stop himself from seizing Remy's wrist and dragging that supporting hand from thigh over to definitely-wide-awake-now cock, a move that would achieve nothing but planting Remy face-first into— *Serth*. 'If you happen to overcome your strong and perfectly valid objection to barbarians and decide you want sex, though...'

'I did presume so,' Remy said, though without any arrogance that would have made it obnoxious. 'It seems you've decided you haven't had me quite so thoroughly as you initially thought.'

Feilan squinted at the ceiling for some time before saying, plaintively, 'Are you flirting, or not?

'I do not,' Remy said, 'have a single notion of how to flirt. Is that more comfortable?'

'Yes and no,' Feilan murmured.

Remy put the boots by the door in lieu of stepping outside, and returned to bed. 'What's your news? I'm awake, you might as well tell me.'

'It's not good news.' Feilan eased his eyes mostly closed. Even the dim light falling through the high slits was becoming too bright for a head already threatening to ache. 'No alliance for us.'

'I see,' Remy said, in that way that Feilan was beginning to realise was his default response when he didn't know what else to say; he deployed it constantly with his family. 'Why do we need an alliance?'

'Because there's thirty-something champions, and ten of them have formed a strong bloc. If we can persuade even a handful of the others to help Torben get the head, or even to stand back and let him get it without contesting for it, we stand a better chance.'

'Why would they, though, if they're other contenders' champions?'

Feilan smiled; his husband's naivety never failed to amuse him.

'Bribery. They're all on mercenary contracts like Torben. They can take that money, and then quietly accept another sizeable payment for *whoops, missed.* It'd have to outdo their promised bonus for winning, of course. And other bribery bids, too.'

Remy sat up so abruptly that Feilan was forced to open his eyes. 'Will Torben—'

'No,' Feilan said, drawing it nice and long for emphasis. 'Praise the wonders of the inflexible bear-warrior honour code, husband. He made that contract under oath to his god. There's nothing that could make him break faith, nothing.'

Remy slithered back down on the strength of his sigh of relief. Feilan flung an arm over him fondly. Remy turned into the casual touch, so he left the arm there.

'Were the other champions too honourable to take our bribe, then?'

This time Feilan laughed aloud. 'Fine jest,' he said. 'No, it's that we can't pay them upfront and they don't think we'll be able to settle our debts. They think even if Torben wins, Adeline won't really be allowed to rule in her own right, so she won't be able to pay out from her treasury. And, ah—' He gave a little shrug, lying there in bed with his naked husband somehow fully in his arms. 'They don't believe *I* can win, to at least give you a nominal regent's authority to make good. Regretting your choice of husband?'

Remy nestled even closer and said, 'No.'

'The good news is your uncle's bloc isn't looking to add more into their alliance, either. I think your uncle's having to scrimp. Too many contracts, not enough left over for bribes. Torben would be the only one he thinks could be a real threat to the bloc, anyway.' He shrugged again. 'Vaer.'

He felt Remy nod against his side. 'Hence, his own room.'

'Hence.'

He'd deposited a roaring drunk Torben next door; he'd been too drunk to even try to drag Feilan into the bed after him. His snores came faintly through the thin wall between the two rooms.

'Are you concerned for him?'

'Hah! No. He was magnificent when I last saw him fight twenty-five years ago, and I have no doubt he'll be magnificent now, too.'

'May I ask...' When Feilan made an affirmative noise, Remy went on, 'what is between you two?'

Feilan sniggered. 'What do you think? You saw it for yourself.'

'You don't seem at all jealous of his current exploits, though. He doesn't seem to care I married you. He doesn't seem to miss your— You.'

Torben had actually been a touch jealous over Remy, Feilan recalled. Still, he said, 'It's not like that. It's... You know how sometimes you have an itch and you know you shouldn't scratch it or it'll just inflame and make it worse, but then you *do* scratch it and it *does* make it worse, but it just feels so, so, good? That's him.'

With a heavy dose of acerbity, Remy said, 'There are salves for that, you know.'

Feilan, smiling, collected a lock of Remy's carnelian hair, releasing a green-tinged waft of that herbal scent he was beginning to think really was witchcraft.

He gave a gentle tug. 'Ja, I know.'

REMY WOKE FEILAN UNFAIRLY EARLY THE following morning, prodding him until he stopped spouting Vaer profanity and batting his hand away and sat up to glare fearsomely, whereupon Remy forced a cup of hot, steeped and powerfully aromatic herbal tea on him.

It smelled of Remy's usual hazy blue and fresh green remedies, but with a bright note of citrus, a zingy orange haze.

'It'll help with the hangover,' Remy insisted, scowling at Feilan until he rolled his – aching and gummy – eyes and took an obliging sip. It didn't taste awful.

With some wryness, he tilted the clay mug at his husband. 'Need me in fighting form for tonight?'

'Apparently not. Apparently we're relying entirely on Torben.'

Feilan took another sip. It was almost soothing this time. 'It's not a terrible plan,' he said, more defensively than he'd meant to.

'I think it a perfectly sound plan, given what you laid out for me last night.'

'Right.' Feilan paused. 'Was I coherent?'

Remy eased down onto the bed beside him. 'Surprisingly so.'

'Serthing warriors,' Feilan muttered, though his headache was beginning to recede. He was too far along in his life to ascribe it to youthful resilience; his next sip of the tea was thoroughly appreciative, as was his smile to his husband.

It faded somewhat when he took in Remy's hair, however. He had a vague memory of it being loose last night, that he'd played with the carnelian locks briefly, and probably inappropriately, before collapsing into unconsciousness.

This morning, though it was still uncovered, it was also tightly braided back so that the deep red couldn't gleam in the light so eye-catchingly. This was so obviously an attempt to appease both husband and siblings that Feilan inflicted one of his raised-brows looks on Remy.

Remy said, 'Would you do whatever you were cursed for—'

'*Literally* craving cock, Remy.'

'—openly in the middle of your village?'

'Now?' Feilan said. 'Probably.'

Remy made a small frustrated noise. Feilan remembered the undeniable relief he'd felt in the afterwash of the reckless rage that had driven him to drag Torben to the woods that first time.

He conceded, 'Fine, not back then. Not without Torben fully committed to protecting me from the consequences.'

He grimaced without meaning to: Torben had done a fantastic job protecting *himself* from the consequences, certainly.

Remy eyed him, puzzled, but merely said, 'Then allow me leeway in learning to break my own people's taboos, please.' Almost shyly, he added, 'While I have my own large man prepared to stop little boys throwing stones at me.'

Feilan, inordinately pleased by this minimal sop to the Vaer protective instincts he wasn't even meant to have, ran his hand over Remy's scalp, feeling the smooth bumps of the braiding under his fingers. Remy couldn't have done it himself, one of his attendants must have helped him.

On impulse, he said, 'Let me do this for you, next time.'

Remy looked up at him with wide, startled eyes before clearing his throat and changing the subject. 'About last night.'

He winced, dropping both hand and smile. 'Got a little too affectionate there, didn't I? Surprised you didn't run screaming.'

'You weren't going to hurt me,' Remy said. 'You were in no shape to do much of anything.'

Feilan snorted at the inadvertent – at least he thought it was inadvertent; he thought perhaps it almost always was – insult.

Remy licked at his lower lip, and then said, with a tremor to it, 'Besides, I like your affection. It's like swimming in an icy lake.'

After a moment to consider this, Feilan said, 'Dare I hope for invigorating? Breath-taking, even? Or more along the lines of, I'm enjoying the risk but I hope I don't die?'

He received quite a stern look for the jape. 'Bracing, I'm never entirely sure I'm coping at the time, but I do very much appreciate it in retrospect.'

'Once it's over,' Feilan said, laughing.

'Quite,' Remy said, fighting a small smile. 'Now. The oath Torben swore to...ah, the bear-god? Bergoth, is it?'

'No, it's—' Feilan drained his mug in a compulsive gulp, drowning his near-mistake. 'I can't say the bear-god's name, you realise? Cursed. The names of the Vaer gods are forbidden to the likes of me.'

Remy looked taken aback. 'I'm sorry.'

'Cursed,' Feilan repeated cheerfully. 'Not just a status, it's a whole lifestyle.'

'What happens if you say it?'

'Probably, nothing,' Feilan said. 'Possibly, smiting.'

Frowning darkly in direct proportion to the lightness of Feilan's smile, Remy said, 'But...'

'I know it makes no sense, move on.'

He'd kept the smile, barely. Remy gave a small shake of his head. 'The oath Torben swore, to fulfil his contract to Adeline.'

He must need confirmation now Feilan was sober. 'You can rely on it *absolutely*. Nothing can break it.'

'No, I understand.' Remy took the empty mug from him and leaned to set it atop his trunk, then turned back to deploy maximum earnestness. 'You made him.'

'I...'

'You *made* him swear fealty by the bear-god when he signed that contract. I wasn't following the Vaer well enough to work it out then, but...that *is* what you were doing, wasn't it?'

'It's called planning ahead,' Feilan said. 'I know it's a concept unheard of among we barbarians, but—'

Remy put a hand over Feilan's mouth. 'Thank you, Feilan.'

Feilan hooked fingers around his wrist and pried his hand aside so he could say, 'Don't mention it, Rufran.' He added with another merry smile, 'Really, don't. Torben doesn't tolerate manipulation as well as I do.'

He earned a small lick of the lips, pure nerves, before Remy understood he was merely teasing. But instead of making him relax, the realisation seemed to make him tenser. He worried at his bottom lip, watching Feilan intently with dark, serious eyes.

Feilan raised his eyebrows questioningly. Remy swallowed. Slowly, he said, 'I think it's beyond the bounds of our existing arrangement.'

'Ah, so sorry for being too helpful?'

'No, I mean...' Remy took a breath. He lingeringly stroked fingers along the cord of muscle in Feilan's forearm. He was watching himself do it as fixedly as Feilan was. 'I mean, you've earned...more.'

'Right,' Feilan drawled, notwithstanding the lick of heat following in the wake of those trailing fingers. 'More transactional sex, is it?'

'Yes,' he said, 'if you would like it.'

'Do you want me to agree to it? Would you find that comforting?'

'Comforting?' Remy froze. 'Hardly. I'm whoring myself, after all.'

'Nothing wrong with whoring, whether it's professionally or as the occasional gambit,' Feilan said. 'No one castigates a mercenary for hiring out his sword arm, do they, but hire out your genitals instead and you'd think you'd brought about the last nightfall.'

'I'm not complaining. I'm stating a fact. I will be your whore, right now, if you would like it.'

Serth, he *would* like it. He steadied himself, saying reasonably, 'See, the problem here, Rufran, is that *you* would like it just as much as I would.'

Remy withdrew his hand and sat stiffly, face flushing. 'No, I—'

'No, you *would*, you've said as much. But you hate that you'd like it, from a Vaer. So you want me to take control, and take the blame.' He shrugged. 'If you need to tell yourself you had to submit to the barbarian, then fine, that's the way it is, I'll go along with it. You can get whatever you're after off your mind, or your chest, or your cock, and we can move on. Ask for what you want, but be honest about it.'

Remy rose and picked up Feilan's empty cup without looking at him. He took the cup to the sideboard, where a steaming metal pot sat, and refilled it. By the time he returned and presented Feilan with more of the zingy herbal tea, he'd given himself enough time to think it through.

'You're almost right,' he announced.

'*Am I?*' Feilan said, with deep sarcasm. 'Imagine that.'

Remy managed a smile. 'The problem, actually, is that if you let me pretend that you're the only one of us that would enjoy himself, I will likely end up talking myself into hating you for it.'

'And that matters to you?' Feilan asked curiously; he'd supposed Remy would rescind the offer, given a blunt laying out of his unconsidered motives, but he hadn't guessed this would be the justification. 'The occasional hate-fuck never hurt anyone. And you'll never see me again after the monster hunt's done.'

'I would prefer to keep my memories of you...fond. So, if you can wait until I...'

'Sort your own shit out,' Feilan supplied helpfully.

Remy tipped his head ruefully before arriving at, '...resolve my internal reservations, we can possibly...engage in less transactional sex before the end of the hunt. Is that acceptable? Or would you rather...' He made a small gesture, a slight flick of the hand towards himself.

'Fuck you now and to the drit with how you feel about it afterwards?' Feilan lifted his brows in his best *you-judgemental-serthr* expression. 'Yeah, I'll wait on that one, thanks.'

He sipped the cooling herbal brew. If one cup had taken the edge off his hangover, the second should brighten him right up. He took a bigger mouthful.

Remy set his hands on his hips. 'Good,' he said, abruptly brisker. 'We don't have enough transactions left to cover all the sex acts I'll want you to do to me, anyway.'

Feilan sputtered, and wiped helplessly at his dripping beard, staring at Remy in open surprise. After a moment, the corner of Remy's mouth twitched up, and Feilan became *certain* he'd timed the comment just to watch him spit out his tea.

'Did you enjoy that?' he asked, laughing.

Remy took up a silk cloth and dabbed demurely at Feilan's face, murmuring, 'Did you?'

He was coyly pleased with himself; it was sweet. Feilan looked at Remy's mouth, the slight curve to his lips, the self-satisfied little twist at the very corner. He wanted to press his thumb there, his mouth, his tongue, lick that nascent pleasure right up. It took some effort not to move, but they had just agreed that the progression of any relations between them was entirely in Remy's hands, so he merely admired his husband's innocent delight without sullying it.

And so it was Remy whose dark gaze went hooded and intent, Remy who shuffled himself to slip between Feilan's parted knees, Remy who leaned over him, cloth-encumbered fingers slowly curling against Feilan's cheek, Remy who—

Torben opened the door and said, 'Little Wolf, come do some sword work— Oh.' He went on, mostly, in Midlands. 'Chamber work. Moving slow this morning, are we, slokar?'

Remy swiftly retreated, busying himself clearing away the half-empty cup and damp cloth. Feilan suppressed an annoyed huff and merely said, 'Turns out Rufran's got a fine line in flirting.'

He'd thought he would: it was extra nice to be right in this particular case.

Torben grunted. 'Don't see the point of flirting. Get on it, or don't.'

'Torben...' Feilan said. 'You know you flirt with me all the time.'

'You don't count,' his friend said dismissively.

'Right. Of course I don't.'

Torben was giving Remy an almost hostile look, which was odd. He didn't have the attention span to hold a grudge and had no real reason to dislike the witch anyway, except on general principles.

Remy lowered his gaze under the weight of that heavy stare, turning to stir the pot of herbal tea. It couldn't have helped that Torben was armed with his longsword today, carrying it shoulder-slung so the hilt was ready to hand at his waist.

Feilan drew his attention with a wave towards the sword. 'Are you going to the yard by the new barracks?' he asked, and received a short nod. 'I'll be along, then.'

In their dialectal village-Vaer, he added, 'I'm about five heartbeats from a fuck here, so make yourself scarce.'

Torben did not oblige. He smirked at Remy, though Remy was keeping his back to them now and so could not catch the mercurial return to perennial joviality. He switched to village-Vaer too. 'Can I join in?'

'*No.*'

'Can I watch?'

Feilan opened his mouth to announce an even more definite no, and paused. Remy, horrified or not, had watched him and Torben together, which might mean he had a tendency towards voyeurism, which might mean—

'It's no!' Torben exclaimed, throwing up his hands. 'Berguthi's balls, Aleifr, even I know the answer's no and I'm a jolterhead.'

Remy finally turned from minutely cataloguing the contents of his own sideboard. 'I am going to make an offering at my family shrine so that the goddess looks benevolently upon our endeavours.'

Feilan bit his tongue quite hard and controlled his expression; he was either going to swear at Torben or plead with Remy and neither choice would help persuade his husband to come between his thighs and touch his cheek again.

Remy continued, warily, 'Would you... Do either of you wish to attend?'

Torben tapped his sword grip and then thumped his chest. 'I don't need to kneel. I carry Berguthi's protection always.'

'And the gods aren't listening to me, remember?' Feilan raised his wrist in another reminder, the smooth beads on the protective talisman mere dull lumps in the room's dim light. 'We're far from the sea but surrounded by water; Njorda might bless me.'

'Your mother could have given me one,' Torben said in a resentful mutter, thus revealing the source of the hostile look he'd given Remy, who was innocently wearing his own gift from Freyja.

'You could have asked her for one,' Feilan said, and chortled.

Torben stared at him, hostility glimmering again; Feilan was, after all, all but stating outright that Torben had been too afraid to do so, and you didn't accuse a Vaer man of cowardice, you just didn't.

'Grab your sword,' Torben said, voice rumbling low. 'Let's go sweat this hangover out.'

Feilan sighed with a minor curse to it, since he could foresee a near-future of being thoroughly smacked around for his mouthiness, not an outcome entirely unfamiliar to him.

Remy slipped between them, holding the mug, brimful. 'Would you like tea?' he asked Torben. 'It will help with...' It likely occurred to him – finally, the witch was learning good sense – he was about to tangle with Vaer notions of weakness. '...stamina?'

That could have been almost as offensive as implying he couldn't take his ale. Torben, however, chose to shoot him a slow smile. 'Is my stamina on your mind, Rufran?'

'Don't see the point of flirting, Njorda's *arse*,' Feilan said, and hastened Torben out the door before any of those bright ideas took hold on either serthing side.

15

IN ANTICIPATION OF THE FIRST STARS, the champions gathered in the small dip that lay beyond the crest of First Hill, behind their barracks, called the warrior stables. Uncle Bertrand's bloc anchored one end; Feilan had jostled Torben all the way down to the far end.

Bertrand had been sensible: he had known contenders might like to watch the hunt, if only to catch out cheating, but had also recognised that the monster, if on the run, might circle up towards them. The barrack's flat roof had been cleaned off and laid with big cushions for seating, and wooden steps with a railing had been built to safely lead up there. The flames of pitch-torches at the roof corners were dancing in a paltry breeze powerless against the rising mist.

The mist was going to make things interesting, Feilan thought. He'd accounted for it; he wasn't sure how many of the other champions had. It was summer, if an early and very northern summer, and that was not normally a time for mist – except here in the ever-damp Riverlands, where cold and warm air relentlessly mixed and blanketed the world in white.

He'd dressed in thick wool, much the same as he'd done the first time he'd gone raiding, and sported his borrowed sword shoulder-slung like Torben did. When he'd returned, somewhat sore, from his unaccustomed morning sword work and his usual afternoon errand, Remy had given him a leather jerkin to wear as well. Torben was mostly in wool and brown leather, and had his studded wooden shield in addition to his longsword. He looked good, but he always looked good.

'What's that?' Torben asked, gesturing at the small silk sachet tied to Feilan's wrist.

Feilan lifted his wrist to give Torben a better look at it, scenting its aroma of mugwort and cedar oil, earthy and woodsy brown notes. Remy had pressed it on him, a second gift to accompany the jerkin, or perhaps a third, if Feilan counted the herbal tea brew. He felt strong and clear-headed in a way some of the other heavily-drinking warriors perhaps didn't.

'A local luck charm, I believe,' he said. 'Remy made it for me. I think he asked for a blessing for it at his shrine.'

His husband, it occurred to him with mild surprise, was worried about him.

'Didn't make one for me.'

Feilan dropped his arm. 'You didn't marry the little witch, did you?'

'Just like your mother didn't make me a protective amulet.'

'Are you angling for Freyja's talisman, Mighty Thunder Bear?'

'Bugger it, *yes*,' Torben said.

'And bugger off if you think you're getting it.'

They both sniggered, received reproving looks from the rather grim warriors nearby, and sniggered again. Feilan's nerves were jangling; he needed Torben's complacent confidence to help settle him, and Torben seemed to know it.

Feilan whispered, 'Does your commander put you in charge of the first-timers?'

'Every. Single. Time,' Torben agreed, sounding both aggrieved and baffled. He squinted at Feilan, twirling a finger at his face. 'Ah, what is this look you are giving me now?'

'It's fondness, you jolterhead.'

'Well, knock that shit off,' Torben said, and they both snorted. He sternly folded his massive arms. 'Would you *try* to take this seriously, Little Wolf?'

This time Uncle Bertrand, standing at the edge of the roof about to address the cluster of champions below him, glared at their childish chortles and turned a reproving look on Remy, seated in the front row on a cushion by Adeline. Eschewing his usual plain and practical clothes, Remy had dressed as the minor prince he was, softly lovely in green and grey velvet and a thin band of gold about his head, bright against his hair, still tightly bound back.

It also occurred to Feilan, with even more surprise, that his husband had made an effort to dress up for him, the contender representing the champion just as much as the other way around.

He was, however, now looking censorious, angling his eyebrows meaningfully. Feilan and Torben nudged each other into respectful silence.

'Now, in the dark of the moonless night,' Bertrand dramatically began as soon as they'd subsided, 'comes the time when warriors shall be tempered—'

Feilan and Torben started laughing again; that was another Vaer metaphor for sex. Bertrand rubbed between his eyebrows and continued to talk, but Feilan was distracted by then. All the warriors were distracted by then, because a new champion was striding onto the field.

She was immensely tall – Feilan was the shortest on the field – fat and broad, her greying dark hair tightly plaited. She bore the same sorts of scars as Torben, those worn by all blade fighters, but her nose looked like it had been broken several times, and one of her ears was mangled, as if she fought by hand, too. Her legs were slightly bowed, a memento of a childhood on horseback. A large curved sword hung at her waist, and she was fully outfitted in leather armour plating.

'We didn't meet *her* last night,' Torben said.

Feilan took a quick look at his friend. Women warriors, among the Vaer, were rare, and had a complicated relationship with the highly masculine bear-god and His associated cult-like male followers. But Torben sounded more admiring than disapproving. He'd been raiding for too many summers to not have encountered the women warriors of other peoples.

Torben laughed suddenly. 'You know, whenever I see your mother, I'm always surprised by how tiny she is. And now I realise *this* is what I picture when I think of her.'

'She'll find that hilarious,' Feilan said.

'I'm hardly going to tell her.' Torben grimaced, which Feilan took as silent acknowledgement of the justice of his ill-advised comment that morning.

He said, 'I will, though,' and earned a rib-bruising elbow.

The woman's appearance had created some consternation; some of the champions hissed at her as she strode past them, face stony, and on the spectators' rooftop, a minor commotion had arisen. Feilan glanced up there. He could only make out gesturing, but he could guess some of the contenders were arguing about whether a champion was allowed to be a woman.

The woman, magnificently aloof from the hisses and catcalls of the others, paused as she came abreast of Feilan, eyed him up and down, and then took up position beside him. He knew why: he looked safe.

She was older than he'd thought, faint lines about her eyes and mouth the sole indication that she was somewhere between his and Freyja's age. She had high flat cheekbones, a firm wide mouth, and a large brand high on her right cheek, the pattern standing out raised and palest pink against her bronze skin. Although abstract, it made a recognisable eye, staring unblinkingly out disconcertingly close to her real eye. It was the mark of a slave from the eastern markets.

'Evening,' he said in Midlands.

'Why so chatty?' she replied in the same language.

Feilan grinned, and then said, 'Alliance?'

'No chance,' she said. 'My price is the freedom mark.'

That went on over the slave brand, negating and announcing the bearer as manumitted, a freedman – or -woman. It could only be applied by a handful of officials, using a secret technique and a secret ink, which made it unfalsifiable. Slaves who tried were burned alive.

It was a regretfully powerful motivator. 'I probably don't need to ask if your master would be a kindly regent to Queen Adeline?'

She stared at him. 'I wouldn't leave him alone with her.'

Torben leaned until he could see past Feilan, though the two warriors could very well see each other over his head. 'How about I thrust my longsword—'

'Torben.'

Torben smacked the back of Feilan's head and finished, '—through your master's throat and we call it good?'

Her face set in contempt. Feilan explained, 'She'll still be marked as a slave. She'll just go to his heirs, if they don't execute her horribly for colluding in her master's murder. She needs the freedom tattoo.'

'It's not for me.' The woman jerked her chin up at the rooftop, where a feminine figure, curvaceous in the playfully flickering torchlight, knelt lithely on the cushions in the second row, attending an aesthetically thin shape. 'It's for her. Aminah.'

Torben unwisely let out a low whistle, presumably because he assumed the freedom tattoo was in the way of a love-gift, which to be fair, Feilan had been too, slightly disapprovingly – it was too big of a gift to make the girl anything but beholden to her rescuer and thus not much freer than she had been.

But he'd seen the look on the woman's face at Torben's crude admiration. He stepped smartly back as she shot her arm out like a striking snake and grabbed Torben by the throat.

'Aminah's my daughter,' she said, which actually made Torben pause in the middle of jerking his fist up for a retaliatory throat-punch. 'Go near her and I'll rip your stones off.'

'Speaking of,' Feilan said, tapping both her shoulder, and Torben's, settling them both and bringing their attention to where everyone else's was riveted, a second late arrival gliding onto the field of champions.

Feilan remained the shortest: this one was tall to the point of gangling, with long, toned limbs, narrow shoulders and waist, wide hips and strong thighs, contrastingly slender calves, and a beardless face. He was dressed in light silken garments, with a sash cinching his waist, and carried no visible weapons.

Once again, the new arrival assessed the musclebound warriors and decided that the best place to stand was at the end, with the short one and the woman, somehow contriving to lounge there while standing completely upright.

After a moment of silence, broken only by snatches of conversation from the rooftop as the rules of the contest were consulted, Torben leaned in again.

'What are you, friend?' he asked in Midlands.

'My name is Micah Alexei,' the new arrival said, staring straight ahead. His voice was light, but not what Feilan would have thought of as feminine.

The woman placed a hand over her chest where it flattened out oddly. 'I am Noura Alikarmi.'

'I said what, not who.'

'Torben.'

'I am a eunuch,' Micah said wearily.

'What's that?'

'Thunder Bear,' Feilan said in Vaer. 'How can you not know? You spent all those years raiding.'

'Yeah, it's not a cultural exchange, Little Wolf.'

Feilan was perhaps being unfair; Torben might simply not know the Midlands word. 'He's a gelding. One of the Incised.'

'They caught him young and cut his balls off for his singing voice?' He switched back to Midlands, and addressed both newcomers. 'We're mid-Vaer.'

'He means we're not slavers. We had a queen—'

'I am more accurately one of the crushed,' Micah informed them, having parsed the Vaer. 'I was placed naked into a basin of warm water as a baby, and then when my cockles were soft and pliable, they squeezed—'

'That's—' Feilan started.

'You can stop,' Torben rumbled over him.

'And so we will now refrain from asking if we do not wish to hear the details,' Micah said.

The woman warrior snorted and offered him a fist bump, which he accepted with a carefully precise touch of his knuckles to hers without taking his challenging gaze from Torben.

'But does your cock still work?' Torben promptly asked. Feilan nudged him.

'Come to my bunk, darling, find out firsthand.'

'Don't know why you assume I wouldn't.'

'Ignore the jolterhead,' Feilan said. 'Would you be interested in an alliance?'

'No,' Micah said. 'Observe, up there among the spectating contenders. The boy sitting next to yon young queen? He is Prince Afzal.'

Adeline had indeed been joined by another child, with whom she was delightedly conversing while the argument continued around them. Between the distance and the low and uneven light, it was difficult to tell ages, but he seemed her age, perhaps younger.

'The boy's father was my dearest friend. Unfortunately, he did not choose his second wife wisely. Before he died—'

'Was that related to the unwise matrimonial choice?' Feilan asked.

'Unproven, and yet indubitably,' Micah said. 'He called in the life-debt I owed him to pledge me to keep the boy safe. Unfortunately, this means I must win the regency for his stepmother. She intends to wed her wards then, one to the other, and rule over them both. If I fail, she will slit Afzal's throat.'

'Obvious question...'

'I cannot slit her throat first,' Micah said coolly. 'She keeps the boy by her side at all times. He sips from her cup, eats from her plate. If she sees me coming through her phalanx of bodyguards with her death in my eyes, if she *doesn't* see me coming but her men start dropping, if a *snake* comes too close and she decides it was me, she will kill him with her last breath, merely to make me suffer.'

Feilan nodded. 'I take it she put you in as champion rather than one of her guardsmen with similar sadistic reasoning?'

'To watch me risk my life just to keep the boy alive but delivered ever further into her clutches via a marriage alliance with a child-queen she also controls... It is to her great delight.'

'A real treasure,' Noura said.

Feilan nodded, resisting a heartfelt sigh. These two perfectly decent people were his and Torben's enemies. All the other champions only had coin on the line. These two had flesh.

'She's buggered herself, though,' Torben said. 'Look at you, Sveltlar.'

That roughly translated as Skinny Shanks, and was somewhere in the marshes between a compliment and an insult.

Micah bowed to contemplate his own stork-like length. 'Yes?'

'Can't see you winning.' Torben shrugged. 'Sorry for the kid.'

'I will win,' Micah said. 'I am a trained assassin. I know one hundred and six ways to kill a man. I imagine at least one of the techniques is adaptable to taking the head of a monster.'

The argument over the rules ceased then. Noura was not dismissed from the field. Uncle Bertrand, somewhat stilted, finished his little speech, to the great boredom of the warriors it was ostensibly aimed at, and the hunt began.

The champions turned en masse and headed down the hill, vanishing singly and in clusters into the thickening mist, fanning out as they went. Some of them, jolterheads who'd be dead soon, uncovered small horn-paned lamps as they went.

Feilan hooked a few fingers into Torben's leather shoulder-strap, subtly slowing his pace until they were lagging behind the others. Then, hidden by mist, he tugged him westwards, crossing the north face of First Hill low enough to avoid the eyes of the spectators, moving carefully through the dark. He angled him up and over to a sheltered outcrop of rock he'd explored previously, facing northwest over the broad bowl behind Seven Hills. They were above the enveloping white shroud up here, with an open view as far as the starlight allowed, and the rock at their backs.

Torben immediately raised his face to the sky and made a genuflection towards the great wash of the Gods' Way. So thick with stars it made a white bridge overhead, it was the main contributor to the subtle skyglow that let them see anything at all, along with the light reflecting back from the copious lamps and torches lining Seven Hill's arcades and buildings.

All was quiet. The mist was real fog in the dips between hills, thick enough to muffle sounds, though the occasional clink and call carried to Feilan's ear as the warriors moved across the hunting grounds to establish their own positions, or perhaps even to dutifully begin to trace the monster's tracks.

'Little Wolf—'

'Keep your voice down,' Feilan said softly. 'We're hidden by the mist, but we don't want any attention.'

Torben exaggeratedly whispered, 'Why are we cowering here?'

'Calculated risk. You'll see. Shush.'

His friend managed that for all of a handful of heartbeats before saying, 'It's boring out here.'

Feilan translated that as Vaer for eerie. It was, the gloam-moon hiding away until dawn, the skyglow only enough to discern the occasional eddy in the mist below as the cool night breeze began to pick up. Faintly, he could hear something that sounded like a cry for help, which he knew was the distraught bleat of a goat separated from its herd. Otherwise, thanks to knowing who was out there and what could be out there – men and monster, respectively – it was the kind of ominous quiet that raised the hairs on the forearms and made the breath want to catch in the throat.

Torben cleared his throat. 'Can I ask a stupid question?'

'You so often do.'

'Shut it.' Torben flicked him on the ear. 'Does this seem like bear country to you?'

Feilan turned from scanning the mist for signs of movement. 'You noticed.'

'Do you think it's really a monster?'

'I do.'

Torben nodded. He looked satisfied. 'Makes it more interesting. Can we get on after it?'

'Not yet,' Feilan said. 'Probably not tonight.'

Torben paced away, and then back, the mighty warrior righteously stalking. 'I'm restless,' he announced. 'I readied myself for a fight.'

'Poor baby,' Feilan said, smiling to himself.

It only took Torben a single step to be standing too close. He placed a finger on the laces at the neck of Feilan's leather jerkin. The very tip of the finger brushed Feilan's bare skin, and his heart beat faster.

'It occurs to me,' Torben said, 'that I might owe you a suck.'

Feilan, still smiling, said, 'You think? It'll have to wait.' To Torben's sceptical look, he said, 'I'll ruin the game for Remy if I fuck around.'

'We're out here alone, no one will see.'

'Anyone could come out of the mist, and us all unawares. The monster could, if I've miscalculated.'

Torben gave a little ground, eyeing him. 'Are you remembering your marriage is a sham, Little Wolf?'

'Of course.' Reflexively, he added, 'I barely even like him.'

His friend tapped his wrist, whereupon Feilan discovered he was absently stroking the silk of the small sachet Remy had made and blessed for him – stroking it very much as Remy had stroked his face that morning, slowly working his way up to more.

Feilan looked at his own fidgeting with raised brows. 'I don't even like him,' he repeated, thinking, *Shit, I think I like him quite a bit.*

'Then let me have at you,' Torben rasped, once again closing in on Feilan with all of that height and breadth and muscle. His hands slid under the heavy jerkin, thumbs hooking into the band of Feilan's trousers, tugging against the ties.

'I – ah.'

He was saved from a rather urgent decision when the mist swirled below them, a shadow approaching from within its depths. As Feilan nudged Torben's attention to the disturbance, a figure emerged above the white starlit sea, the silhouette distinct enough to be identifiable as the eunuch, Micah Alexei. Like them, he'd been sensible enough to eschew light and wait for his eyes to adjust to the night. He stood with his head angled up towards them, body poised as if he might turn and melt away back under droplet-laden cover.

Instead he chose to stroll closer, until they could make out each other's faces. He watched them with his head to one side, bird-like, but he also looked all about, assessing the outcrop at their backs and their panoramic view over the hunting ground.

'Did I,' he said, 'interrupt something? Carry on.'

'Move your shit along,' Torben said. 'We've staked this position.'

'Hmm, and I do wonder why,' Micah said in his precise tones, sounding more like a particularly officious majordomo than an assassin. 'I do wonder why the one you call clever decided to bring you this way instead of joining the hunt with the rest.'

'Yeah, me too. Doesn't mean he's handing out any answers, the cagey lortr. Sertha af, Sveltlar.'

Micah smiled thinly. 'I think I might hold right here, actually.'

Torben turned so his powerful body was facing off to Micah's long, thin form fully. He didn't otherwise make any threatening moves, but cast a sideways look towards Feilan, questioning.

Feilan weighed it up. Micah and Noura were the biggest threats to

Torben's ability to deliver up the head for Adeline. Most of the other champions, when it came to it, had already been paid, and wouldn't knowingly risk their lives merely for whatever bonus had been promised for success. Some would do it for pride, or because their blood was up and they couldn't resist the challenge. But none had the same sort of urgent motivation as the pair of latecomers.

Noura likely wouldn't be a problem after tonight. Micah was proving smarter. But not so smart that he hadn't put himself in reach of two armed barbarians out of sight of anyone who might accuse them of cheating.

'I remind you,' Micah said, 'I know one hundred and seven ways to kill a man.'

Torben grinned. 'I thought it was one hundred and six.'

'I invented another one just for you, darling,' Micah said. 'It is particularly slow and painful.'

Folding his arms, Torben looked hopefully at Feilan, though it was very difficult to tell, even with the benefit of years of knowing the man, if he wanted permission to attack, or permission to let him live.

'Leave him be for now,' Feilan told him.

'Ah. So you *are* the one giving the orders.'

Feilan was once again saved, this time from Torben's kneejerk reaction to the thought of being ruled by a Cursed, by a disturbance in the mist, the one, finally, he'd been expecting. It was a shout, abruptly cut off, and then an outbreak of less distinct noises, muffled enough that it was difficult to tell if they were cries or the thumps of bodies running or clashes of weapon or claw.

'You buggered it, Little Wolf,' Torben said, smacking him hard in the shoulder. 'They found the m— bear and we're miles off.'

'I have already supposed it is not a bear.' Micah stared down at the mist blanketing the great bowl below them, as if trying to read the indeterminate noise. 'And I do not think your friend has, in fact, buggered it.'

'They're killing each other, Torben.' Feilan spoke Midlands for Micah's sake, though the eunuch seemed to have the usual grasp of Vaer exhibited by any people subject to their piecemeal raids.

'They're...' Torben blinked. 'They're what?'

'Killing each other,' Feilan said. Torben fought side by side with comrades; there was no other way for a Vaer man to fight. He could fully see the logic of knocking off Micah as a competitor and yet still not expect wholesale bloody treachery. 'The uncle's bloc, taking out other champions while the mist hides what's happening. Others will have had the same idea.'

Torben was silent for a long time. Then he said, 'I hate that.'

'I know.'

'But you should have let me down there. If they won't play this game with honour, I'll play it their way. I'd have taken care of a few.' He glanced at Micah, who shifted his weight to his back foot, ready to leap away. Torben smirked. 'More than a few. Didn't you think I could?'

'They would have gone for you exclusively,' Feilan said, surprising him into silence again. 'It was more risk than I wanted to undertake on your behalf.'

Torben's mouth tightened – oh, that bersverdr pride – before he abruptly chose to ignore the insult from Feilan, or accept the compliment from the other warriors. 'Serthing right, they would have tried,' he said loudly, preening.

A little way around the bowl, a figure immediately discernible as Noura emerged out of the mist. She was panting heavily, and, as she came closer, Feilan could see that her leather armour was rent in multiple places. Her great curved sword, bloodied, hung from one big hand, almost dragging.

A gang of men came out after her, five of them moving together in a loping prowl after the exhausted and injured woman. That was an alliance knit together by bribery; Feilan had watched it form at the feast.

'Ah,' Micah said.

Feilan shook his head. 'I thought they'd go for her, too. Not even in with much of a chance alone, but they didn't like a woman on their field.' He paused, then added judiciously, 'Drafdritar.'

Torben muttered, 'Run, die tired,' and charged across the slope towards her.

Feilan shouted his name, and then smartened up and backed away from Micah, watching him narrowly.

'I'm not going to kill you tonight,' Micah said. 'You remain useful.'

'Thanks,' Feilan said, only moderately sarcastically. 'I'm still not turning my back on you.'

Micah gave him a lazy smile and loped off into the mist, cutting towards where Torben had crashed into the fight. The big man hadn't given much indication, thundering down upon them, as to which side he was going to be on, which meant he split two heads with two mighty blows before the other three even responded. By the time they'd moved to try to flank him, Noura had turned and Micah had materialised, and it was quick, if savage, work to dispatch the aggressors, shocking blue flashing across Feilan's vision as the scent of blood and entrails released into the damp air. He didn't expect Noura to survive it, but she was still on her feet when the flurry of fast and brutal activity was over.

Feilan sauntered to meet them, holding up his hands in a peaceable gesture as Noura and Micah raised their blades towards him and Torben, as if sure the truce had been a short one. Noura, in particular, looked wild-eyed, fully prepared to be turned upon in ambush again.

Keeping his palms up and open towards her, Feilan said, 'Alliance? For the night, if no more.'

'I'm wounded,' she grated, not letting her sword drop, though the tip wandered tellingly.

'I can see that,' he said. 'Are you wondering why we don't finish you off?'

'I am wondering that,' Micah said, though he'd obligingly lowered his wicked blade, a needle-thin knife he'd used to slither in close and pierce the vital point under his opponent's armpit.

'I'm not *not* wondering that,' Torben admitted with a shrug.

'I want the alliance,' Feilan said calmly. He pointed to Micah. 'Both of you. You've seen the lie of the land now. None of us have a chance alone.'

'Only one head,' Noura said flatly, to Micah's nod. 'I have to win it for my girl. Any alliance is a cracked lie, the moment the body hits the ground.'

'I'm asking for truce now,' he said, 'and then for you – both of you – to come hear me out tomorrow. That's all.'

'And if we come across the monster before the end of this night?' Micah asked.

'Have at it,' Feilan said.

'You either think your friend can deal with both of us *and* the monster, or you believe we will *not* see the monster tonight.'

Feilan smiled. 'Or, indeed, *both*,' he said, mocking the other man's coolly exacting tones.

Micah narrowed his eyes, but he gave a single nod of agreement, and made his knife disappear about his person in a stealthy fashion befitting his claim to be an assassin.

'Do we want to go hunting?' Torben said, looking into the mist. 'Not the monster. Those cheating dogshits?'

'I know it goes against every fibre of your being,' Feilan said, 'but I'm asking you to play it safe for now, old friend.'

Torben gave a grunt that was both annoyed and acquiescent, and bent to loot the bodies in a desultory fashion born of habit more than greed.

Micah, meanwhile, addressed Noura. 'If we are allied, will you allow me to bind your wounds?'

'You can keep your distance for now, mate,' she said casually.

She kept her face turned towards all three men, and the thicker mist beyond them, while she carefully used ripped linen from her undershirt to pad her injuries – a bad one in the meat of her shoulder that would limit her movement, a cut across her neck where the very tip of a sword must have almost found her jugular, and, once she'd unembarrassedly dropped her leather pants, a couple of gashes across her thighs, surrounded by mottling that would become bruises. The other champions had gone for her hard.

She had to be strong as iron, to still be on her feet. Torben presented her with a salute with his blade and Micah offered up a respectful nod. Feilan, never sure if the warriors of other peoples were as touchy as the bersverdar about taking acknowledgement from weak men, merely silently vowed to do whatever it took to win her into a proper alliance.

They moved in a watchful silence, each alert for dark shapes coming out of the mist in ambush. Their position was good, however, and while other clashes rang out several times, they were not disturbed.

Noura accepted Feilan's shoulder to lean on as they made their way back upslope, jerking her chin for the other two to walk ahead as if they were the only ones who could shove cold steel between her ribs. It was a good sign, that she trusted him enough to accept the assistance; a bad sign, that she needed it.

Once they were almost in sight of the spectators, she pushed herself upright. 'Have to walk in under my own power,' she said. 'Disqualified, otherwise.'

She knew the rules as well as Feilan did. He'd not neglected the terms of the contest itself during his information-gathering, yet had forgotten them in the moment. But she'd have to know them cold – she would have had to know women and slaves weren't expressly disallowed before she bothered negotiating terms with her master.

As they came close enough to be visible in the light of the flaming torches encircling the immediate vicinity of the old barracks, gasps and murmurs arose, and a few of the spectators began to get up. Noura, drenched in blood, was probably the most exciting thing they'd seen all evening, between the mist and the size of the hunting ground.

They weren't really here to watch the hunt, though. They were here to drink and feast and witness for themselves the moment one triumphant champion carried in a great monster head to fling to the ground in the flickering torchlight.

Remy rushed towards them across the sheep-cropped grass from the far side of the building; he must have been one of the people who had leapt up upon spotting Noura, and come flying down the stairs.

But he wasn't looking at the injured warrior at all. 'Are you hurt?' he demanded of Feilan.

Feilan followed his husband's frightened gaze, and realised the sleeve of his tunic and his bare skin were dyed bloody from where Noura had leaned on him. The stain must have looked black and glistening in the chancy torchlight.

'No, but Noura Alikarmi needs your assistance.' He squeezed her shoulder. 'Will you accept? You can trust the little witch.'

'Not a witch,' Remy said. He peered at Noura's visible wounds with a wince. 'I can salve and bandage these, but...'

'I will sew the worst of it up first,' Micah said.

'You?' Noura said, doubt rippling over her stoically stony expression.

'Assassin,' he said. 'It means I know where the arteries lie.' He laid a palm flat to his chest. 'My honour on it, I will do no harm to you, not tonight.'

Noura still hesitated a long moment. At last, she nodded. 'Don't help me,' she snapped when Torben stretched out his hand. 'I walk myself, or I'm out.'

'Take her to my—' Remy stopped; it had obviously occurred to him that Noura would struggle to walk the entire undulating arcade to his cave, or even to Third Hill East. 'Go to the foyer of First Hill and rest there. I will bring what I need. What do you need?'

This last was to Micah, who said, 'Clean water, clean needle, strong spirit, strong silk thread.'

'I'll bring it.'

Noura walked slowly on. Her master, thin and bald, with unpleasantly cold eyes, had come down the stairs, slower than Remy, but she merely looked at him sternly as she made her way with small and pained steps towards the arches of First Hill. Her daughter, Aminah, was in attendance on the man, holding a jewelled goblet of wine. She had the same slave mark as Noura over her high cheekbone, and wore diaphanous layers of clothing that left her arms and legs bare.

No look passed between mother and daughter, but the young woman squeezed her eyes tight shut very briefly before she brought her expression back to the pleasant neutrality required of a slave. When her master snapped his fingers, she was ready with a meekly bowed head and the wine goblet. Feilan didn't know what had happened for Noura to be sundered from her steppe people and sold into slavery, but he was certain her daughter had been born into it.

As Noura's master, apparently satisfied his champion was still in the contest, returned towards the stairs to the rooftop, Remy stepped closer.

'Sorry,' he muttered as he put his arms around Feilan in a full embrace. 'We have a little time before she limps her way to First Hill, so...'

'Worried about me?' Feilan said, patting his back.

'No!'

'Oh.' He'd been amused, in a slightly superior way, and was taken aback by the vehemence of the denial.

Remy pulled back to look at his face. 'Isn't it insulting if I was worried about you?'

'Only for a real Vaer man.'

'But you are a— Oh, this is a Cursed thing, I suppose. All that aside, the other contenders have realised you are both far too clever for comfort and only in the contest on a suspicious-looking marriage contract, and we have to *very much* act like a love match now if we don't want them strongly agitating for your disqualification.'

Feilan looked up at the rooftop. He was certain any talk of disqualification aimed his way would be at the insidious instigation of Uncle Bertrand, slyly spreading gossip as if he didn't know the effect it would have. He didn't need to play innocent with his nieces and nephews, who seemed incapable of doubting their beloved, faithful uncle; those outside observers, and Adeline's maternal relatives, were his audience now.

Remy squeezed against him to hold him tightly again. Feilan, entirely confused as to whether he was being genuinely hugged out of relief or if Remy was merely putting on a show, shrugged. He could enjoy the warmth of the slender body either way, and savour the memory of him stepping between his thighs that morning, fingers trailing along his cheek, intent in his eyes.

Remy added, 'I know you don't kiss, but it'd be very helpful if—'

Feilan said, '*I kiss.*'

He clasped both hands about Remy's scalp, hating the tight braid that stopped him burying his fingers in silky carnelian locks, and lifted Remy's face so he could have his mouth.

Remy gasped under the sudden onslaught and then his lips parted wider and he took Feilan's tongue with a whimper, body sagging into him until Feilan had no choice but to press one hand to his lower back to haul him in even closer, their mouths moving ever more urgently, Feilan tracking every stutter of Remy's breathing as his husband's hands scrabbled at his chest as if trying to claw his clothes off.

When Feilan finally let him go, Remy actually staggered. 'Oh,' he said, touching his mouth with one thumb. He looked astonished. 'I should tell you I know you don't do things more often.'

'Tell me you know I don't suck cock now,' Feilan said helpfully.

Both blushing and looking rather tempted, Remy blurted, 'Thank you, I am sure that was exceedingly convincing for our audience and I must help your friends now.'

He gave Feilan one last, long, look, before hastening off towards the First Hill foyer.

Feilan strolled after him, absently stroking the silk sachet about his wrist.

16

By the next morning, Feilan had had enough of the aquamanile. It was all very fancy for pouring water, certainly, but it wasn't a proper wash, especially not after the exertions of the night before, and the other people's blood he'd ended up partially coated with, the traces stubborn.

'I need somewhere to bathe,' he told his husband. 'I don't know about you, but I'm used to bathing daily.'

'Are you suggesting we don't wash regularly?' Remy folded his arms, no doubt at this slight hint that they might have barbaric practices of their own.

He was peevish this morning. Feilan thought it had something to do with the way his hands had trembled as he'd knelt by Micah last night to hold Noura's gashes closed so the cool-eyed assassin-cum-physician could sew them up as cleanly and neatly as possible, Noura looking deeply unimpressed but not uttering a sound as they worked.

Remy had washed her after, and salved and bandaged the stitched-up wounds, as promised. Then, with Torben delegated to help Noura back to her bunk and Micah agreeing to stand guard over her, the little witch had slunk, blank-faced, back to their room, Feilan trailing behind in puzzlement.

He'd followed Feilan's example enough to thoroughly scrub the blood off his hands at the bowl Feilan was standing before now, and then crawled into bed without a word, still wearing bloodied velvet, hair still bound tight. He'd pulled a pillow over his head and curled up into a ball and gone very still.

He'd been absent early from the room as usual, returning to rouse Feilan from his lazy doze with more of that energising herbal brew. He'd had a servant do his hair again, or the braiding was holding up astonishingly well. There'd been no hope of a reprise of the morning before, nor of that unexpected, and unexpectedly good, kiss.

Remy dealt well with the slowness of sickness, competent and careful without being overwhelmed by the creeping sadness of the waste. He didn't deal well with the quick surprise of bloody death, it seemed.

Feilan thus chose to maintain a brisk, almost careless manner. 'You wash with this business, fine.' He tinked a fingernail off the offending metal of the elaborate aquamanile. 'But I need to *bathe*. Do I walk down to a pond somewhere, or can you provide?'

'I can provide.'

Feilan followed him up the arcade towards First Hill. He looked at his husband as they walked. He had his head down, his face set in the expression he usually wore when going to have supper with his family.

'It was the blood, wasn't it?' Feilan asked. 'It reminded you of childbirth. When you lost Queen Margalita. Right? Or was it your brother? Both? Let's say both.'

Remy stiffened and walked faster, turning towards a side path that curved off the arcade around to the rear of Third Hill East. 'I am aware you are intelligent, you don't need to keep proving it.'

'Remy, svasa.' Feilan caught his elbow, dragging him to a stop. 'I don't know what to say to you to make it better.'

Remy struggled to get loose. 'Then say nothing. And let go!'

This last was in a low hiss, since servants were coming along behind them, arms full of linens. Then, remembering he had to do the opposite, Remy muttered one of his endearing spinning-related curses under his breath – 'Slubs and neps!' – and flung his arms around Feilan's neck in an ostentatious swoon, tight enough to throttle.

'I do not feel like touching you right now,' he snarled, very quietly, in Feilan's ear.

Feilan swallowed his smile and looped his arms around Remy's back. Remy wouldn't be used to seeking comfort, thanks to his shitty family who'd metaphorically banished him for the witchiness of his hair. Even Feilan, literally banished and used to only rough touch from Vaer men, had learned the benefits of a hug from people who weren't Vaer men.

It took the entire length of the servants' traverse up the arcade towards First Hill for the rigid spine under his locked arms to begin to relax.

Eventually, Remy said, sounding less angry but more indignant, 'How can you *possibly* be this good at hugging?'

Mostly thanks to a very patient Ystheran man he'd been sorry to leave on his ridiculously paradisaical island, but he bit his tongue on that. He said, 'You feel like you failed them both. It's why you're so determined to win Adeline her throne, when your siblings who love her just as much will tolerate Bertrand taking the regency. And Bertrand's right, in a way: it *is* a sort of atonement for leaving her an orphan, much more so than your work in your cave. Stop me if I surprise you with something you don't already know.'

Remy fairly well collapsed further into his arms instead, pressing his face hard into Feilan's shirt, muffling what might have been a choked sob. Feilan stroked over his hair and cupped his hand over his nape, under the braid, waiting him out.

At last, Remy stepped back, gaze down, and wiped at his face a few times. 'Sorry. You can make fun of me now.'

'I'm not going to—' Feilan began in indignation of his own, before remembering the crude jokes he'd subjected Remy to in the face of his stark grief previously. 'Oh. We use black humour to cope with this drit. You don't, so I won't.'

'I do know you're trying to help,' Remy said. 'Sorry.'

'You did really well last night,' Feilan told him. 'It was hard for you, and you coped. But I'll try not to ask it of you again.'

Remy turned back to the path, sighing. 'That's a difficult thing to promise, Feilan. Never mind. Play the serthing game, yes?'

'Yes, but...' Feilan shrugged. 'Yes.'

He fell in beside Remy and, almost companionably, they followed the path downhill. After a moment, Feilan touched the small of Remy's back, where he'd firmly set his hand last night during their *exceedingly convincing* performance.

He said, 'Want to guess the *other* way Vaer cope with all this shit?'

Remy was silent long enough that he thought he'd overstepped again, before he finally produced a rather sweet smile and said, 'I could make a fairly solid stab at it.'

'Just so you know it's an option,' Feilan said, smiling back, but letting his hand drop. He was back to making progress; it wouldn't do to push.

Remy stopped before the mouth of an old salt mine, the entrance bulwarked by timber.

Feilan had come across it in his earlier explorations and adjudged it sacrosanct. 'Isn't this the location of your shrine?'

'We're going in past that.'

Remy led him inside to an antechamber, where a stone shrine indeed filled a large alcove. There was a small brass oil lamp there, which devotees, or possibly servants, would have to attend daily to keep lit, and some small votive clay figurines, shaped into exaggerated curves, some with wheat stalks braided around their waists, and a few woven tokens. A symbol Feilan couldn't make out was carved into the back wall of the alcove.

Remy unhooked a lit lamp and started down a very straight, wide tunnel, sloping down into murk. Feilan, who had paused to admire the shrine, was forced to lengthen his stride to catch up.

The tunnel opened into a cavernous space, probably one of the earliest, shallowest salt mines for Seven Hills. The salt dome had long since been dissolved away into brine and pumped out to be transported to the evaporation sheds, and the space carved out had been left to fill with water, its surface still, and very dark except where the gleam of lamplight fell on it and revealed it to be pellucid.

Remy went about lighting more lamps from the one he carried, while Feilan shucked his clothes and boots, and the little scented sachet. His husband turned an interesting shade of pink when he turned from his errand and discovered Feilan naked at the edge of the water.

Feilan, smiling to himself, dipped a finger in, and tasted it. The water was salty, but not as much as a literal salt lake. They'd plumbed the salt to mere traces before abandoning the mine for deeper deposits.

'Am I about to despoil a sacred pool?' he asked.

'No. It's not sacred, it's just traditionally used only by family. And... and you're family, whether my siblings like it or not.'

Glancing over his shoulder at that soft avowal, Feilan bathed his whole hand up to the wrist, so Freyja's talisman was anointed by the briny water. He hung there with something like a prayer on his tongue, but didn't invoke Njorda by name. He had to tread a narrow line in his devotions to his grandmother's guardian witch, so as to not accidentally call on the goddess she was an avatar of.

Done, he slid his feet carefully down slippery stone steps leading into deeper water. It was deep enough to swim, not just wallow. 'Coming in?'

'I don't think I will, no.'

Feilan turned so he could float on his back, looking towards Remy standing at the edge of the steps. 'Remy,' he said patiently. 'Beloved husband. I'm not going to jump on you if you bathe with me.'

'I know that,' Remy said, arms folded close about his chest.

'Do you? You might not have noticed it yet, but I'm a very obedient man,' Feilan said, surprising a scoff of distinct disbelief from Remy. 'No, no, hear me out. Tell me to fuck you, I do. Tell me I have to give fidelity, I do. Tell me to leave you alone, I do.'

'I...haven't told you to leave me alone.'

'You haven't, quite, have you?' Feilan said with his nicest smile. 'But you've certainly warned me off initiating anything. So I won't.'

It wouldn't do to push – and yet that was not a lesson he'd ever learned well. So he added, softly, 'If you want it, Remy, ask for it.'

There was a beat, then another, in which Remy did not seem able to look away. Then he loosened the ties of his tunic and took it off. He reached out a slender arm and dropped the tunic to the ground, gaze never wavering from Feilan's face.

He was slower to take his breeches off. Feilan, not *entirely* pushing his luck, did a few slow laps around the circumference of the pool before he finally returned to the vicinity of the steps and found his husband there, naked but for braes, a scrap of linen about his hips that merely piqued Feilan's interest further.

Remy stood uncertainly on the top step, gazing down at him, eyes very black.

'We agreed I'll not lay a hand on you,' Feilan reminded him. 'You'll have to ask.'

'I heard.' Remy eased a step lower.

Feilan counted back in his head and discovered the sense memory of traversing five steps. Just five, and two were done. He smiled again, and let himself drift away, giving Remy plenty of space to make his way down the final three.

He watched him through half-lidded eyes, though, those lean legs, thighs flexing as he came another step lower. Jutting hips disguised by the scrap of white linen. Pale hollow of belly. Narrow chest, dark nipples standing out. Square shoulders, slender but strong enough to solidly brace Feilan's weight as he'd mounted him on their supposed wedding night.

It had been dark in his little hut that night, and dark the night he'd come in drunk. That didn't mean his body didn't recognise the body that had been under it, arching and writhing, hot and eager, on the first occasion, at least.

He checked. *Not that eager*, he reminded himself, keeping his hands above the water and his body turned away from his nervous husband.

Remy paused and, bending with a lithe flex of stomach muscles, dipped the talisman about his wrist into the briny water in the same way Feilan had. They had come no little way from refusing to abide Vaer superstitions, it seemed.

Then he glided smoothly into the water and stroked straight over to Feilan. Even here in the centre of the pool, Feilan could stand, and did, so that the water lapped his clavicle. Remy had to tread water to keep his mouth above the waterline. After a moment, he rested his hands on Feilan's shoulders, and let his feet stop working. His body drifted and bumped against Feilan's.

Remy made a small noise; he was brushing against Feilan's erection. Feilan stood still. Slowly, very slowly, Remy pulled himself closer, until Feilan could feel his stiffness through his sodden linens.

'Would you mind kissing me again?' Remy asked.

Feilan made a show of looking about. 'Are there spies even here?'

'No,' Remy admitted. 'I just like it.'

'You can kiss me, then.' Feilan angled his face down, and waited.

Remy pressed his lips to Feilan's, soft and careful. He drew back, and Feilan was subjected to an inspection similar to the kind Remy gave his cave's visitors with the strangest symptoms, the sort of close stare that ended with him muttering horrifying things like, 'Oh, but it *can't* be the bloody flux or half the village would be dead already.'

Feilan raised his brows with something of a challenge to it, and Remy abruptly surged into him, clasping both hands about his neck and battening his lips to his like he was starving and Feilan's mouth held the last bite of food in the world. Feilan lost himself in the desperation until Remy came up for air. He tentatively moved his hips to rub their cocks together. Though the intervening fabric dampened the effect, Feilan gave an appreciative response. Remy's pupils dilated wider.

'You can put your legs around me,' Feilan told him.

Remy obeyed, hooking his knees about Feilan's hips. Feilan finally let himself touch, sliding fingers under the braes to cup Remy's arse. He nestled him closer so their lengths were pressed against each other. He dropped his face into Remy's shoulder, whispered, 'Move,' and lightly pressed his teeth into his bare skin, tasting salt.

Remy rocked his hips, again in that tentative, almost experimental way – and, of course, it was an experiment, for him. Another noise escaped him, deep in his throat. He rocked again, and again, and then faster, harder, thighs tightening around Feilan's hips, arms locking about his shoulders, clinging tight and chasing the friction of cock against cushioned cock. The small gasps escaping him began to increase in frequency and volume until they echoed off the walls. He was close. Feilan clamped harder on his arse and helped him, jerking him against his own length in time with the urgent thrust of his hips.

When Remy spent in a gush of warmth against Feilan's groin, he groaned and pulled Feilan's hair in spasmodic rhythm, and then all at once let go so his upper body fell back into the water. His legs were still locked about Feilan's waist, however, and Feilan slid his hand under his back to support him.

'Did you faint?' he asked, amused.

Remy tipped his head back into the water so only his face was visible. His braided hair was darkened to near-black. His eyes were closed.

'No, really, did you faint?' Feilan said, prodding him. 'It was just a mutual rub, you know, I can do better. A *shitload* better.'

'No, I'm... That was...' Remy opened his eyes and lifted his head so he could look properly at Feilan. 'I wasn't paying nearly enough attention, but *was* it mutual? At the, ah, end, I mean?'

Feilan shook his head.

'Tell me what you would like, then,' Remy said, with only a tremor of nerves, and a delightful squeeze of his thighs, still about Feilan's hips.

Feilan bit back a smile. What he would have liked would have been to drag Remy back over to those steps, order him to brace his hands on the top step and spread-eagle his knees on the bottom step, and then take him like a hammer on an anvil.

But that was what he would have done with someone like Torben. Not his flighty husband. So he ran one finger from Remy's belly button to his throat and said, 'I'll wait.'

Remy swallowed, making Feilan's finger bob where it rested against the tender bump in his throat. 'Why don't you lie back on the stairs, and I'll give sucking you a try?'

'Yep, we're doing that,' Feilan said, already striding, with difficulty, through the water, pushing Remy before him, Remy laughing and sputtering as salty water splashed his face, squeezing his legs around Feilan's waist, hands trailing through the water, dark eyes gleaming.

Feilan rested against the steps, shoulders out of the water, elbows back to prop himself against the top step so he had a good view of Remy kneeling between his spread legs, head lowered shyly. Feilan's cock was jutting proud from the water, and it twitched as Remy slowly licked his lips, bending over him like a worshipper before a Chalcadean altar, water up to his chest.'

Remy looked up, mouth just brushing the top of Feilan's eager cock, so close he'd be able to taste Feilan's need. It was a sight, the reddened and leaking tip teasing those plush lips, about to push in, and Feilan groaned, deep. 'Stop torturing me.'

'I will.' The words sent warm air and soft vibration over Feilan's cock and he threw his head back, hips hitching. 'But please don't hold my head.'

Feilan grimaced. He'd been on the cusp of doing exactly that, reaching down and putting a firm hand on the back of Remy's head to turn that tantalising brush of lips into a full-throated swallow of his full length, perhaps a tight fist about the neat braid to keep him there.

Remy had seen Torben use Feilan's mouth. Of course he'd be wary of being used the same way. And he should be. Feilan barely knew any other way to do it.

He said, 'I won't. I'm at your disposal. You are in control.'

Grimly vowing to stay entirely still, he tightened his grip on the edge of the step under him, and tilted his head to watch as Remy slowly parted his lips and made the first exploratory foray with his tongue, wet heat across engorged skin, and Feilan almost broke his vow on the instant.

Remy opened his mouth wider and began to slide down over Feilan's length and—

A voice bellowed from the tunnel. 'You done yet?'

Remy squeaked and recoiled backwards into the deeper water with a splash that drowned out Feilan's heartfelt profanity.

'Berguthi's balls, you're loud, Rufran,' Torben said, sauntering in, linens draped over his shoulder. 'Wanton little cocksucker under all that primness, right?'

Remy, very red, ducked back under the water, swimming away from Feilan. Feilan started to reach after him, trying for a bare ankle, but Torben tossed a rough cake of lye soap his way. He caught it and had to restrain himself from pitching it with prejudice back at his friend's head.

Torben laughed as he kicked off his boots. In Vaer, he said, 'I gave you a solid space of time past when Foxy quietened down, Little Wolf, it should've been plenty.'

'Why are you here?' Feilan grated.

Torben tossed aside his shirt. 'Same reason as you.' His trousers and braes followed. His cock was half-hard. He glanced down at it compla-cently. 'Well, not exactly the same reason, obviously. Unless you've rethought your stance on sharing, I'm here to bathe.'

'I mean, why *here*? How did you find this place?'

'Noura told me where to find it; she got it from a servant. She's on her way. So's the Incised. Crushed. Micah. Your personal orgy was about to be interrupted anyway.' He shrugged. 'Thought you might appreciate the warning.'

He jumped the stairs and landed with a mighty splash in the centre of the pool. He surfaced and pushed great handfuls of darkened blond locks from his face.

'Don't tell me you were trying to do something nice for me.'

'I can be nice, and as annoying as shit at the same time, can't I?' Torben asked him with his broad grin.

Feilan, shaking his head, paddled over to the other end of the pool to retrieve his embarrassed husband. Remy resisted being drawn from the shadowy recesses at that end, whispering, 'Please don't make me learn to do it while Torben is watching.'

'I wasn't going to,' Feilan said, a touch indignantly; Remy really did think he was a barbarian arsehole.

'Foxy could watch and learn,' Torben suggested idly as he swam over. He addressed Remy in his rough Midlands. 'What do you think, Rufran? Shall I show you exactly what he likes?'

He put a heavy hand on Feilan's stomach, watching Remy with his eyes bright in the lamplight. Feilan shut his own eyes. For a moment, he was overcome with rampaging lust – Torben breaching him roughly from behind, a fist in his hair to pull his head back so that Remy could shove his more circumspect cock down his throat, its slender length crammed all the way. Torben grunting with each deep thrust, Remy making those soft, uncontrolled sounds of pleasure—

'I'm not sharing either, Thunder Bear,' Remy said, in heavily accented but still intelligible Vaer. Carefully, but determinedly, he removed Torben's hand from Feilan's stomach.

'Ja.' Torben placidly paddled a circle. Then he swung around to face Remy and said, 'He's not yours.'

Remy cringed. Feilan, beyond startled, said, 'By Njorda's tits, who are you to try to claim me?'

'I didn't claim you're mine,' Torben said. 'But you're not his, either. Sham marriage. Could be over tonight. It's all over at next moon-gloam, regardless. And then *this*—' He thrust a finger at each of them in turn, before finishing grimly, '—is done with.'

'And why, exactly, is that any concern of yours, when you'll be off south raiding?'

'I didn't say it was my concern,' Torben said. He pointed the finger at Remy's face again. 'You get him for this handful of days. That's all. Don't get any serthing ideas.'

He pushed off the rocky floor, swimming away with short and powerful strokes.

'I think I'm going to go to the grotto now,' Remy said in a tiny voice. 'I will have people waiting soon.'

'Hold on.' Feilan waited till Torben had stopped his angry progression across the pool and the water had stopped lapping before he said, very clearly, 'Coward.'

Torben stood up in a great splash. 'Say it again.'

'You,' Feilan began, before conceding that the width of the pool and the weight of twenty-five years was not quite enough shield for repeating that intensity of insult, 'refuse to take me for yourself, and you think you can warn off my lovers?'

'Not all your lovers,' Torben said sulkily. 'Just your serthing husband.'

Feilan dropped both hands onto Remy's tense shoulders. 'My husband—'

'I do not want to be involved in this argument!' Remy interjected.

'You started the argument!'

Remy flailed away, dark eyes flashing sudden fury. 'Are you blaming *me* because *he's* jealous?'

'I'm not jealous!' Torben shouted, in defiance of all evidence to the contrary.

His voice was still bouncing off the walls when a loud whistle and a clatter announced the arrival of Noura, Micah by her side, onto the small shore of the cavern lake. They were openly askance as they eyed the triangle of dispute.

'Alliance off?' Noura demanded.

'No,' Feilan said, blatantly watching her as she stripped bare as if the men in the lake were mere buzzy gnats. 'One of us is just being a bigger dick than usual.'

'Bugger off, Little Wolf.'

Feilan made a rude gesture Torben's way as he dispassionately assessed Noura's injuries. She looked surprisingly well this morning.

She'd taken off all the bandaging already, and the stitched wounds were showing signs of healthy healing, under more glistening daubs of the green-tinged salve; Remy must have left her a jar of it. Her body wore the marks of many older battles, and, as suggested by the odd flattening under her clothes, she only had one breast, large and sagging. The other side was a mass of seamed scar tissue.

Micah was slowly removing his own silky layers, self-possessed under Torben's far less dispassionate gaze as he bared a slim but strong chest. 'We are here to discuss this alliance, yes?'

'Yes,' Feilan said, relieved to find Micah immediately amenable.

'Then you do not dismiss this nonsense' – he neatly inscribed an invisible line connecting Feilan, Torben and Remy as he spoke – 'with glibness. The word is that you are the only champion here under a marriage contract. I will not entertain an alliance with someone whose contract is about to be voided because he's playing about.'

'It's not.' Feilan, paradoxically encouraged by the implication of Micah's words, decided to risk a gesture of goodwill. He slapped the surface of the water until little waves were lapping the walls. Under the echoing cover, he said, 'The marriage itself is false, but our agreement isn't. I'm being paid in kind.'

As one, Noura and Micah turned and looked at Remy, who folded his arms over his unprepossessing chest and began to blush.

'And you find your payment...adequate?' Micah enquired.

'Yes, he's got a massive...'

Remy looked horrified and Micah sighed, 'I am dealing with children,' but Torben chortled, good humour restored, which was Feilan's aim.

'...trade network. I'm a merchant, friends. I get the western Riverlands once Queen Adeline's firmly seated on her throne.'

Noura, looking entirely unconvinced, eased into the water. She floated on her back, lazily backstroking, her one breast bobbing, indifferent to their curious stares.

After a time, during which Feilan scowled at Torben to try to make him shut up, Torben couldn't help himself. 'So. One tit. What's that about?'

Noura said, 'Sliced it off so I could use a bow better.'

Despite himself, this immediately drew Feilan in. 'That story's *true*?'

She roared with laughter. 'No, you pillock. Got a hard lump, my master let me consult a shaman of my people, and he said he had to cut it off or I'd die. Hurt like shit, but I'm alive.'

'Poor you,' said Micah silkily, paddling past like a very elegant dog, one of the long-snouted, long-haired, long-limbed skinny hounds favoured in the caliphates for hunting fast things. It probably soothed the coyly modest Remy greatly that the eunuch had kept his own smallclothes on, a wrap of cloth about his curving hips.

Noura waggled her immense surviving breast at him with both hands. 'You comparing the pain of squeezing your tiny pair to having to hack off one of these?'

'I'll thank you not to speculate on the size of my long-lost cockles, madam,' said Micah with a sniffiness that was at least partly for show, and they all four laughed, Remy too nervous to join in.

They lolled in the shallows by the stairs, passing the soap around and trading stories of battles. Feilan held his tongue and listened. Remy was keeping close beside him, also quiet, and wearing a pronounced frown.

Eventually, Feilan cleared his throat and caught the attention of the three warriors. 'Let's talk, then.'

'We were talking, baby wolf,' Micah said.

Feilan shot Torben a nasty look for that piece of translation work, and said, 'About alliance. Us against the regent's bloc.'

'Already told you, I have to win,' Noura said.

'As do I. I do not believe you did not mark us both as your worst enemies the moment we told you our stories.'

Feilan, realising he'd neglected to keep Remy informed, turned to his husband. 'Noura needs a freedom tattoo. Micah needs his little prince kept safe. Neither are motivated by money. It makes them both dreadfully dangerous to us.'

'I see,' Remy said. 'Then, why...'

'Indeed,' Micah said. 'I understand why you might desire to eliminate us as enemies by recruiting us as friends. But why do you think you can?'

'Noura Alikarmi, you want your daughter freed. Your price is her freedom tattoo. I can offer you that.'

She jeered so loudly it rang off the rocky ceiling. 'You can't fake the freedom mark.'

Feilan smiled. 'A *genuine* freedom tattoo. I guarantee it.' He paused, and took another risk, because he hadn't even written the letter yet. 'Freyja Anjasdottir of the golden name guarantees it.'

Both Micah and Noura, or her master, would almost certainly have coins stamped with Freyja's mark in their belt pouches right now. The name arrested their attention on the instant.

'Who are you to speak for Freyja Anjasdottir?' Noura said, tone modulating from hostile disbelief to curiosity. 'Some minor trader wouldn't dare throw her name about.'

He paused, then said, 'I didn't introduce myself properly, did I? I'm Aleifr Freyjasson.'

'Straight line to the merchant queen,' Torben said, actually being helpful for once.

'Her son?' Noura nodded, thoughtful.

'I've heard of you, in my line of work,' Micah murmured. 'Spymaster.'

'Don't be dramatic,' Feilan said with a grin, and not without a feeling of mingled flattery and no little concern, since Micah's line of work was apparently assassination.

He could see Remy gazing at him from the corner of his eye, perhaps with newfound respect; he couldn't deny it felt nice to have a certain notoriety that did not revolve around Vaer manhood.

'The catch,' he went on, 'is it won't be anytime soon. Before the next new moon, yes. But not today or tomorrow.'

Noura rolled her shoulders, expression collapsing back to unimpressed stone. 'I will not turn from my chance on these next few nights.'

'Understood,' Feilan said. 'And if I offer two genuine freedom tattoos?'

'Two?'

'Agree to risk the alliance now, and before the next turn of the moon, you will have freedom for both yourself and your Aminah.'

She paddled for a time, deep in thought. 'I won't risk my daughter's freedom for a selfish gamble on my own,' she said finally.

Feilan was ready for this. 'You're already gambling your daughter's freedom, working alone,' he pointed out. 'You saw what happened last night. You wouldn't have survived without our help.' She looked mulish. 'Just for *your* help, against the regent's bloc, against the monster, I'm guaranteeing your daughter's freedom. Whether you survive or not – and whether Adeline wins or not. But I need your agreement to ally, now.'

Noura vanished under the water, and came up spitting brine. 'Two genuine marks,' she said, 'if I live. And Aminah's, no matter what.' She jerked her chin at Torben. 'He going to be a problem?'

'Me?' Torben said, as if he'd never once been.

'Always,' Feilan said, and Torben flung a scoop of water accurately at his face. He wiped it off, smiling. 'In what regard?'

With a thump of her chest, she said, 'Woman warrior.'

Torben scoffed. 'Only weak men fear strong women.'

Noura seemed mollified by this succinct dismissal of the rampant misogyny of their world, but she still waited for Feilan's silent nod to verify Torben's sincerity – he was spouting a basic tenet of true Vaer manhood – before she offered him a large hand. 'Deal.'

Feilan shook on it. 'Deal.'

She smiled and her grip tightened. 'If you don't come through, I will rip your stones out through your throat.'

'Noted,' he said, extracting his fingers with a wince. 'Freyja's word is golden, you know it. We'll get the freedom tattoo on Aminah if we have to buy her ourselves to do it.'

'May your sky crack,' she said. 'No one ever gets to buy my girl.'

Feilan now floated himself about in the water to face Micah. 'My turn, I think,' the eunuch said, a hint of disdain in his cool voice.

'You're harder,' Feilan said bluntly. 'Remy, Prince Afzal's step-mother—'

'Lady Darya?'

'Yes. Her. Would Adeline help us get Afzal out from her reach, even for a few moments?'

'She will dispatch him the moment she suspects a ploy,' Micah said, shaking his head.

'In front of the queen she's trying to win regency over?'

'The rules of this contest neglect to define the suitability of the winning contender for his or her duties,' Micah said. 'Regardless, she has no chance of winning it without my cooperation, so she will have nothing to lose by exposing her ruthless side to the Nivardus.'

'Adeline would help,' Remy managed to put in. 'They're friends.'

'If your plan is to remove Afzal from Darya's side and then slaughter your way through her guard to get at her, it will not work and I will not countenance an alliance based off such poor plotting.'

'Credit me with more subtlety than that,' Feilan said, though he had not yet come up with anything other than the exact sort of brute force attack Micah was decrying. 'Tell me more about your situation.'

'You know what you need to know. She parleyed her marriage into guardianship of my sworn blood-brother's child, the prince of a minor realm, and now desires to parley *that* into the regency of both his realm, and Seven Hills. She has informed me that she will not hesitate to kill the boy, if I do not deliver the monster's head. You may think this drastic; I believe she has planned it all along, for if all else fails, his death at least delivers her a valuable consultation prize: rule of his realm, and a vital blow to me.'

'But then she's thrown away her shield, and you'll kill her,' Torben said.

Noura added, 'Surely that's what's kept him alive so far.'

'She has been slowly increasing the number of guards around her, to the cost of the prince's treasury, and eliminating those of the advisory council who show loyalty to his right of rule. She now believes she has enough men between her and me.' Micah tipped his head to one side, as if considering this belief from all sides. 'She is incorrect. Her head will never rest easy on her pillow again, should Afzal come to harm by her hand. But that does not matter, if she truly believes she is safe to act as she likes against him, yes? And even then. Even if she kills him, and I come for her. She will die with the satisfaction of knowing...' He looked briefly disconcerted, then swallowed hard and finished. 'Of knowing she cut out my heart, before I cut out hers. My vengeance will not restore the boy.'

For all his distancing – *I owed a debt to the child's father* – cool-eyed Micah Alexei loved his little ward. Darya knew it, and knew the advantage it gave her. That he had given it away to them now was surely a sign he was leaning towards some sort of alliance.

'Leave it with me,' Feilan said. 'The hunt will not be complete until the next moon. I will give you a solution by then.'

'For the next two nights, then, I will not turn on any of you,' Micah said. 'But I will not stay my blade if I have a chance to take the head of the monster.'

Feilan and Torben looked at each other.

'How nice,' Micah said. 'The Vaer warriors are reconciled and pretending they are not plotting my murder if victory falls within my grasp.'

'We weren't planning on *murdering* you,' Feilan said, smiling.

'Speak for yourself,' Torben said. 'I was.'

Feilan splashed water at him. 'Remy, I need you to ask Adeline to be very...' He tried to think of the right word. 'When a woman expects...' Remy was giving him a suspicious look. 'She has to send Prince Afzal to fetch things for her.'

'She has to...'

'Ask him to do little things for her. Many little things. Like she thinks he's wooing her.'

'They're too young—'

'Not real wooing. A child's idea of it. If he likes me, he'll summon that servant over for me. He'll fetch me a cup of herbed water. He'll run to my quarters, and find my shawl. That sort of thing.'

'Ah.' Micah was smiling oddly. 'Chivalry.'

Feilan snapped his fingers. 'That's the word. She must expect him to be very chivalrous towards her.'

'You want Darya to become used to Afzal running short errands on behalf of the princess she hopes to marry him off to. You want her to learn to relax for those few but frequent moments he is absent from her side.'

'Exactly. I imagine you can't get word to him?'

'I cannot come within sight of the boy or risk her knife, and I trust no one who attends him. But—'

'Then, Remy, you have to make sure Adeline knows what we're about, and that she lets Afzal in on it so he doesn't feel ill-treated, but she cannot let Darya hear.'

'Darya will never allow it.'

Feilan held up an admonitory finger to Micah, continuing to address Remy. 'She needs to keep it very minor at first. Not ever out of Darya's sight, until she learns to think it harmless. If she refuses all, Adeline needs to throw a tantrum and demand her little prince serve her. Remember, her relatives actually wish her well, in their own way, so even if Darya wins the regency, they will still hold power here, to insist on her consent to marry. Darya needs to see that consent washing away on a spoilt little girl's tears. Can we trust Adeline to get that done?'

'She can do it.' Remy was looking somewhat pale, but he sounded certain enough.

'That's a start, then.' Feilan looked to Micah, raising his eyebrows.

'You have failed to consider a basic fact,' Micah said. 'Afzal cannot walk.'

Feilan stared at him. 'I failed to consider it because I didn't know it. He cannot walk unaided?'

'He has no use of his legs whatsoever. The same incident that killed his father.' Micah smiled thinly. 'He rides very well, but must otherwise be carried. I am aware that in Vaeringa he would be exposed to the elements rather than left to live as a useless mouth.'

'Hoi!' Torben said. 'We don't do that to children.' Feilan flicked him a glance. He shrugged. 'We do it to babies. Sickly ones. Not small ones.'

He smirked at Feilan, who returned him a dirty look – his father had liked to remind him of the fate he'd narrowly avoided by dint of being both firstborn and male – while the other three shook their heads in blank disapproval.

'Everybody does it!' Torben said. 'We live in the land of ice, we can't afford to keep sickly babes alive. Any of your people would do the same, as soon as a drought came along.'

'We do not and will not,' Micah said.

'We don't,' Noura said. 'You can tie a baby to a horse and see if it comes good or crosses the skybridge of its own accord.' She thought for a moment, then added, 'Our elders, though. They can't keep up, they get left behind.'

'Barbaric,' Micah murmured. Remy, conspicuously keeping quiet, looked like he agreed.

'You had a blood relative who crushed your baby testicles so you wouldn't interfere with his line of succession,' Feilan pointed out, 'and pimped you off to assassin school, too.'

'At least he let me live.'

'If you call that living.' Torben might not have meant his mutter to be overheard, but Micah did.

'Excuse me?' he said coldly. 'Are you implying I am better off dead because I am not hindered by uncontrolled animal desire?'

Torben paused as if thinking about it.

'Most holy of the high,' Micah swore. 'You are impossible.'

'But you're curious, aren't you, gelding?'

Feilan held his palms up for peace, kicking Torben ineffectually under the water. 'I see now why you need a subtle approach. Give me time, please.'

'Perhaps,' Micah said, in a tone which indicated that was all the concession Feilan would win for now.

'And do still encourage their friendship,' he added to Remy.

By accord, they moved out of the water. The warriors emerged to dry themselves off without embarrassment, while the shyer Remy hesitated at the steps until Feilan held up a swath of linen for him to hide himself under.

Then Remy went to his cave, the warriors went to practice fighting in unison, and Feilan went to write a letter and collect another goat.

17

A T THE FEAST BEFORE THE SECOND night of hunting, Remy threw a fit.
'They should be in the stables,' he insisted. 'I don't want the champions of other contenders housed near me! Especially not *foreigners*.' He spat that last word with venom, scowling at Micah in particular.

The chaos of the first night had almost halved the number of warriors in the hunt, and thus the contenders. Bertrand's bloc of ten was down to eight. Adeline had her tiny bloc of three, perhaps four. There were another six who were loosely independent, though Feilan could guess bribes had made a small network among them, if not a formal alliance. He could also guess that most were going to do their best to sit out the rest of the hunt, and would take the field tonight merely to fulfil the terms of their mercenary contract. The bonus for bringing in the head was not worth fighting the two alliances over.

The exodus of disqualified contenders had begun that morning, leaving rooms vacant, while the surviving champions had demanded the same privilege Feilan and Torben possessed – an escape from the open bunks of the warrior stables into safe rooms with latching, defensible, doors. It was Uncle Bertrand's gracious capitulation to this unified demand that had prompted Remy's outburst.

For a moment, Feilan was puzzled. Remy had seemed committed to the newly-brokered alliance, which had quickly become common knowledge among the other surviving champions. He'd even already managed to have a quiet word to Adeline – or perhaps Prince Afzal's attendance at Remy and Adeline's afternoon visit earlier had been a mere happy coincidence, albeit one under the firm supervision of Micah's bane, Darya, and four of her ever-present bodyguards, dressed in light blue robes fastened with sashes, unsheathed swords hanging showily at their waists.

Feilan had stridden into the foyer after his daily errand, skirted past the tensing bodyguards, delivered a firm kiss to the top of his flustered husband's head and a polite demurral to an amused Adeline, and gone on to their room to keep out of the way.

Remy hadn't followed; he'd avoided Feilan since the pool that morning, in a way Feilan recognised this time as his habitual withdrawal while he was thinking things over. That was, he assumed, in response to Feilan accusing him of starting an argument with Torben he wasn't prepared to finish, which had been, in retrospect, and indeed in the very moment, unfair.

Therefore, when Remy acted the spoilt young royal just as Adeline was meant to if she couldn't get her way through empty-headed coquetry, Feilan at first assumed he was trying to make things difficult in a way that surprised him in its pettiness. Remy was prickly and awkward and lonely; he didn't seem petty.

Then he saw the undercurrents, and understood.

Within moments, Uncle Bertrand, with a good-natured chuckle at Remy's expense, offered Micah and Noura rooms in Third Hill East.

Darya, meanwhile, smiled to herself as she sipped her wine, Prince Afzal silently pushing limp green beans around his plate beside her, a different boy to the animated child chatting to Adeline that afternoon. Darya knew Micah had an alliance; she thought Remy, the contender overseeing it, was thoughtlessly sabotaging it with a blanket prejudice that would stop proud Micah seeking anything further from him. She would not, now, find Adeline's friendship with her ward as suspicious as she might have if Adeline's favourite uncle had been at all welcoming towards Micah.

Remy sat in suitably sullen silence, all dramatically thwarted pout, for the rest of the meal. Feilan, taking his leave to go out to the field, kissed his cheek and murmured, 'Well played, Uncle Remy,' in his ear.

Remy flushed, violently. Feilan smiled to himself. Remy's siblings were going to think he'd whispered something *filthy*.

He led his little gang of warriors to the same outcrop where he and Torben had waited the night before, moving slowly until their eyes adjusted to the dim skyglow. The mist was thicker tonight, and higher. Yestereve, they'd been above the white blanket smothering the great bowl of the hunting ground, but now it swirled about their feet and turned everything more than a few handspans away into shadow. Feilan, even ice-bred as he was, was glad for the warmth of the leather jerkin.

Once again, the occasional sound, even more muffled than the previous night, rose to their position – the call of livestock, yes, but also the ring of blade on blade, and the thuds and grunts of ambush. The uncle's bloc was on the hunt again, still not discriminating between monster and unlucky lone champion. It was, Feilan, mused, entirely unnecessary – those men were merely bored.

He wasn't concerned, however. The four of them together were unassailable, too risky even for all eight of the uncle's bloc to attack. Despite Micah declining to formally accept an alliance – yet – he had agreed he would not turn on any of them, and so they could all take turns to watch for an assault coming out of the mist without also having to watch their backs. It quickly became tedious, of course, and they slowly relaxed enough to address a few remarks to each other in a mix of Midlands and Vaer. Feilan filled in the blanks in the rumours they'd gathered about the local political situation, confirming Great-Uncle Bertrand's position as the enemy of Adeline and her favourite uncle.

'Why,' Micah enquired, and Feilan braced for a disdainful question about Remy, 'are you so certain nothing will come of this monster hunt until next moon?'

'Just a guess,' Feilan said, not trying very hard to not look *too* innocent.

Micah folded his arms, wearing an expression of great scepticism. 'I do suppose you have been told before that you are far too clever for your own good.'

'All the serthing time, Sveltlar,' Torben said. 'Always with the bright ideas, this one.'

The eunuch swept him with heavy-eyed contempt before turning back to Feilan. 'And you do have your mighty warrior under control?'

Feilan had to fight to keep from smiling at the accidental allusion to yet another Vaer kenning, but Torben crowed with boisterous laughter. It rang loud, but quickly fell as dead as the toll of a muffled bell in the blanketing mist. Noura, shaking her head, took a few steps away, alertness redoubled.

Torben grabbed his crotch. 'Sure do.'

'They are as children,' Micah called to Noura. 'Are you certain of your choice?'

'Have to be, now,' she said laconically over her shoulder, eyes raking their misty surrounds.

'If you are arguing,' Micah insisted, 'which of you wins? Which of you issues the orders, and which obeys?'

Torben folded his arms, biceps bulging, forearms corded. 'When it comes to the monster hunt, we all follow Feilan's instructions, hear?'

'Thanks, Thunder Bear,' Feilan murmured.

'That's logic, that is,' Torben said. 'If we're fighting the other champions, though, I'm in charge. Feilan doesn't know a cursed thing about that.'

'Knows all about fighting monsters, does he?' Noura called.

Torben shrugged. 'Probably not the actual fighting bit.'

'I was raised Vaer,' Feilan protested. 'I can fight.' To an outrageously dubious look from Torben, he added, 'I can swing a sword, jolterhead.'

'The fact you think it's just swinging a sword—'

'You must realise your incessant bickering does not inspire me with confidence in regards to the proffered alliance,' Micah informed them.

Feilan shot his friend a nasty look. Torben snorted. 'It's just flirting. Like you and me.'

'I am,' Micah said, 'appalled.'

'So you say.'

Micah so abandoned his cool-eyed facade as to look to Feilan for assistance. Feilan obliged. 'Torben, stop threatening the poor man with a good time. He's not interested.'

Torben merely looked smugly complacent to this rebuke, in a way that abruptly reminded Feilan of his attitude in bed and made him itch to punch him, for all the good it would do.

''Ware,' Noura called suddenly. 'Movement.'

Torben instantly turned to face the direction of Noura's point, hand to sword grip. 'Get behind me, Little Wolf.'

Feilan indulged himself, smacking his friend solidly across the back of the head. Torben sounded serious enough, but he was just digging in on the Little-Wolf-can't-fight jape. His chuckle confirmed it, even as he swung a meaty arm back and pushed Feilan off-balance far too easily.

The shadowy figures approaching out of the mist resolved into the uncle's bloc. They had the sweaty, blood-splattered look of men who'd been engaged in fierce fighting, but there were still eight of them.

Feilan expected them to turn when they realised they come up on the other major alliance, but their leader paused, and eyed them.

Flanked by Noura and Micah, Torben said, 'You can't take us. Don't mind if you try, though.'

'Don't have to kill all of you,' the leader said.

His gaze flicked to Feilan, just once, and that was enough to tell Feilan he had been very mistaken when he had assumed the eight wouldn't risk attacking the four. They would – if they could score the clever one's head.

He wasn't used to thinking of himself as a visible threat.

He fell back immediately, expecting the others to do the same so they could position themselves for the battle. He was taken by surprise by Torben's headlong charge into their midst. Noura lunged after him, protecting his offside as stoutly as any Vaer bersverdr. Micah sighed delicately and strolled up to his own first opponent, weapon not even visible yet.

Feilan followed them in, drawing his borrowed sword. As was his general experience, the fight was short and brutal. Torben might mock him for describing wielding an edged blade as merely swinging a sword, but it was apt enough in this instance. He just had to swing it harder and faster than the scarred mercenary facing him, while blocking or batting aside his attempts to do the same. He hadn't performed so well in his first raid; he'd been competent in defence of Freyja in the years since.

But it had been a while, and the mercenary was more than competent, as befitted a sellsword who'd survived long enough for grey hair. Luckily, he tended to give away his intentions by subtle cues of body and gaze an observant man could exploit, so Feilan held him at bay long enough for a roaring Torben to barrel into him and knock him down. Torben skewered him right between the shoulder blades, the longsword buried halfway into the soil by the force of the blow.

Feilan stepped to his back, ready to defend him while he tugged his sword loose, and assessed the current situation, twitching his head to clear the flood of blue from his eyes.

Noura kicked a bleeding mercenary aside and struck a wicked blow at her next opponent, who dodged and almost tripped over the body of the first man Torben had killed, the leader. Micah fought with his long knives, the blades narrow and almost triangular, weaving his way sinuously past the reaches of the two men he faced to sink the needle points home repeatedly; it must have felt like trying to strike a swarm of bees.

The final pair were sensibly hanging back. Even as Feilan stepped up to one of Micah's foes, the rest of them – leader lost, bersverdr on the rampage, his companions putting up a fierce fight – saw sense and rapidly withdrew into the fog. Torben, still bellowing, made to chase them, and Feilan grabbed him by the collar and dragged him to a stop.

Micah wiped his twin blades on the trailing end of his sash and vanished them under it. He was wearing his coolly impassive expression, so his quick step up into Torben's face took both Vaer by surprise.

'You rushed in because your lover was under threat.'

Only the fact that he had very conspicuously put his knives away saved him from Torben's full reaction. As it was, Torben, all a-bristle from the brief but ferocious fight, spread a large hand over Micah's throat, his freed sword lax in his other hand. He wasn't squeezing, not yet, and he didn't push Micah away. He stared down at him, silent. The battle-rage was still pumping too hard through his blood for him to remember words.

The Vaer called it the gift of the bear-god, His blessing. He was said to be working through the bear-warriors, flooding them with divine strength, sweeping them into battle against awful odds and washing them out the other side victorious. Feilan was surprised – shocked, almost – He'd come for such a minor skirmish.

Micah wrapped long fingers around the thick wrist of the hand at his throat and began to twist. 'Your impulsive behaviour put both my own self and Noura Alikarmi in more danger than necessary. This is unacceptable.'

The eunuch could not know the risk he was running; or perhaps he did, and chose to take it. Still, Torben merely stared, unaffected by the pressure Micah was asserting against his wrist. Then his grip on Micah's throat slowly began to tighten. Micah, swallowing against it, reached for his sash with his free hand.

Feilan kicked Torben in the ankle.

The big man turned, snarling, and backhanded him across the face, hard enough to knock him sideways. While Noura grabbed Micah by the shoulders and dragged him away, not without a suspiciously maternal shake, Feilan backed up, watching as Torben came shambling after him, sword hanging loosely in one hand, his other hand a fist.

'Come on, Thunder Bear,' he said softly. 'You didn't really go on the offensive so abruptly just because their boss-man looked at me once, did you?'

Torben spat to one side. His glazed, intent stare shifted, and he blinked a few times. His god was leaving him.

'You did not,' Feilan said, smiling, but keeping the same careful space between them. 'You were bored, you wanted a fight. You got a fight, and now you want a fuck. Right?'

Torben came to a stop. 'Yeah,' he said gruffly.

'Yes, you want a fuck.'

'Yes, I attacked that bugger for looking at you.'

'There you go, being surprisingly sweet again,' Feilan said. When Torben closed the space between them, he risked holding still, and earned himself a short and rib-creaking hug. 'I was fine, you jolter-head.'

'I could also use the fuck, if you're offering,' Torben said, pressing his face against the top of Feilan's head in what could almost be a kiss, if Torben had ever once kissed him with that sort of affection in twenty-five years.

The other two cautiously approached. Torben let Feilan go. 'Don't come at me when I'm still in the battle,' he told Micah.

'That was…' Micah narrowed his eyes at Feilan's warning shake of the head and finished anyway. 'Bear-Skin?' He thought for a moment, and came up with the Vaer term. 'Berserkr?'

'That's a very insulting word, No-Nuts,' Torben said flatly.

'I am of the opinion that an insulting word *should* apply to someone who came within a hair of throttling his ally.'

'I don't count you as brother till you clasp hands on Feilan's alliance.'

'I am unlikely to do so, if you are the quality of impulsive, bull-headed ally I can expect.'

Indifferent, Torben waved around at the two felled mercenaries. 'And how many did you kill, *assassin*?'

He examined his blood- and dirt-splattered blade before setting to thoroughly cleaning it with cloth torn from dead men, while Micah crossed his arms and looked – there was no other word for it – petulant.

'I wounded two of them,' he said.

'Not so easy when they're awake and armed and facing you, is it?'

'Torben,' Feilan said.

Torben ignored the warning. 'One hundred and seven ways, and all of them from behind.' He gave a leer, somewhat lacklustre.

'Oh, no, darling, I know more than a few face-to-face techniques.'

Micah stepped in close again, as he had so riskily done when Torben had been blessed by the bear-god. Torben smiled complacently at him, letting him push right up to his chest. Torben was holding the half-scrubbed longsword down and away; Micah was keeping his hands clear of his waist, where his dagger-spike weapons hid under his sash. Given that mutual care, it was nothing but a pissing contest.

For now.

'Truce, boys,' Feilan said, deliberately lilting the words as he put a hand on each chest and pushed them apart.

He earned a minor grimace of distaste from Torben, who pointedly strode off to finish polishing his sword, and a sweeping up-and-down look from Micah from beneath eyelashes that suddenly seemed outrageously long.

'You're as bad as each other,' Feilan said, if under his breath.

'They were after you,' Noura announced, having sensibly elected to stand aside from the entirety of the cock-swinging. 'Reason for that?'

'I was probably too obvious in what I think of their employer,' Feilan said. 'I told you about him.'

The hand behind the throne was now more than ready to give it a good hard shove to tip the queen off, and further, had apparently and personally greatly disliked the look of recognition and challenge Feilan had levelled his way at the feast.

'Too cracked smart,' Noura said, 'for your own good.'

'Yes, I know it,' Feilan said, smiling. 'Too many bright ideas.'

WHEN THEY WALKED in off the hunting ground, leaving the bodies, Remy once again greeted Feilan with a willing kiss and a fuss over the side of his face, which was swelling from Torben's blow. But he untucked himself from under Feilan's arm as soon as they were far enough down the arcade to be lost to the view of family, despite the risk of spies.

In their room, Remy, not meeting Feilan's eyes, made him sit and unplugged a jar of salve that he retrieved from the silver tray by the aquamanile. The little ceramic jar had a stopper of crystal and gold, very much unlike the wax Remy used to seal the jars and vials he sent home with his visitors – he did take some very small prerogative as a minor prince of this minor kingdom, then.

The contents were different to the green and sky-blue paste Remy put on open cuts. This one smelled more yellow, a jaundiced tinge that made Feilan twist his face away from it. Remy seized his chin in one slender hand, assertive enough to give Feilan a frisson. His fingers were cool as he daubed the side of Feilan's face with the salve.

Torben wasn't the only one left het up after battles. Feilan wanted to push his husband down from where he stood between Feilan's legs to tend him, push him down to his knees and make him tend to the part of him that was really aching. He touched his shoulder, half a caress, a question in it.

Remy pulled away. Quickly washing and changing into the linen shift he insisted on sleeping in, he subsided onto his side of the bed without a word.

Shaking his head, Feilan followed suit, prepared to wait the mood out, own mood not eased by the sounds of Torben getting his wished-for fuck from the room next door from some willing soul. He was too tired to lie awake long, however.

18

Sometime towards dawn, Feilan rolled over and flung out an arm, discovering bare thighs. He opened heavy eyes to find Remy half-sitting up in bed, back against the wall, gaze half-lidded and abstracted. His thin shift had ridden up enough to bare most of his lean legs.

Feilan should have rolled away. He tightened his hold and pressed his nose into Remy's flank. 'Hyndla?'

He was greeted with silence and peeked up to see Remy frowning, on the edge of offence. Scant knowledge was a dangerous thing: the literal meaning of the Vaer was 'little bitch', which Remy plainly knew. But it actually referred to the nippy thoughts that chased around in your head in the dark of the night.

'I'm asking if you're fretting,' he translated.

Remy said only, 'It's early. Go back to sleep.'

'Come down here and tell me what's wrong.'

'No.'

Feilan tugged. 'At my every whim, remember?'

Not without a put-upon huff, Remy slithered into his arms in a show of instant compliance that only served to push the hem of his shift higher.

'Oh, you *know* I don't mean it,' Feilan said chidingly as bare hips pressed into his.

Remy made a muffled noise, half against his shoulder, half into the pillow. His skin was cool under Feilan's fingers. He was used to Remy self-contained on the other side of the bed, or already up and gone, an early rising habit explained by nipping worries. He wanted to feel him close and warm and drowsy.

He set his thumbs to the nape of Remy's neck and rubbed the tense cords there and down into his shoulders, and felt him give an all-over shiver, limp relaxation following in its wake.

Remy sighed and snuggled closer. 'Feilan.'

'You're back,' Feilan said, unable to hide a note of fondness.

'From my sulk,' Remy said.

He pulled back so they could see each other's faces as the room began to lighten into an obscenely early morning. His hair was finally coming loose from the braid, a tangled mess not helped by the salt bath the day before.

'From thinking things over.' Feilan stroked his hair, then, to avoid tugging knots, stroked his back instead, smoothing rucked linen. 'What's the verdict? Am I a mouthy arsehole for blaming you for that argument?'

He felt Remy frown against his shoulder. 'What? Oh, that. Yes, probably. That wasn't what I was thinking about.'

'No?'

'It was what Micah said about his little prince. About his guardian's willingness to kill him, if she didn't get what she wanted.'

'Ah,' Feilan said, enlightened. 'Worried about Adeline?'

'I have decided,' Remy said cautiously, 'that my siblings wouldn't hurt her. Not even Hugo, who is, as it stands, her heir. They all love her too much. And...and they're a little unpleasant, I know, but they're not, none of us are, that ruthless, really.'

'I concur,' Feilan said, since Remy was looking at him in a way that made him think he wanted to know if he had assessed this right. 'Adeline is not in the same sort of danger as Afzal. She has too many uncles and aunts who genuinely wish her well, in their own way.'

'But...' Remy bit his lip, watching Feilan very closely.

'I am worried by Bertrand, yes,' Feilan said, not without some regret as Remy closed his eyes against the final shredding of his trust in his childhood guardian and substitute father. 'I can't predict how long well-wishing will hold him before his ambition takes over. He's had it his way for a very long time now.'

Remy swallowed heavily. It took a moment before that innate stubborn streak rose to the fore and let him speak. 'I shouldn't ask this of you...'

'Roll it on in to my marital duties, Rufran. I'll have a suitable plan to keep him at bay by the time the moon's at gloam again.'

The easiest thing would be the sword, but he already knew Remy wouldn't like that, and it was, politically and morally, an unpalatable start to Adeline's reign without more proof than his own intuition. He'd come up with something more appropriate, perhaps the same subtle move that would whisk Afzal safely from Darya's clutches. Whatever that would be.

Remy's smile to the bland promise was its own reward, but the shy kiss he pressed to the corner of Feilan's mouth didn't go astray. Feilan had to ruin it by adding, 'It's a selfish decision, Rufran. Last night was a fairly blatant attempt by your uncle to get me murdered.'

Remy gaped. 'What?'

Feilan had forgotten that the so-called spectators couldn't actually see any of what went on in the hunting grounds, and that Remy was not close enough to any of his siblings to have heard news of the attack from them. He explained quickly, lingering on the way the leader had looked at him, intent plain enough to set Torben off.

'I'm guessing he had orders,' Feilan said. 'Wasn't bright enough to have thought of it himself, given he wasn't bright enough to not provoke Torben.' He added, 'He's dead now.'

'Good,' Remy said, and flushed. 'I don't wish death on people, but...good.'

Feilan, smiling, pushed back a stray lock of tangled carnelian hair. 'Worried about me,' he murmured.

'Of course I am,' Remy said crossly.

'One more uneventful night, and then we're all safe till next new moon.'

'Why are you so sure the hunt won't end tonight?'

Feilan couldn't help a smug look. 'Can I tell you a secret?'

Before he could catch up with his own surprise – he didn't trust anyone but Freyja with his secrets – Remy had already nodded, all earnest goodwill.

Feilan met that dark, sincere gaze. 'The monster comes into the great valley at dark of moon to hunt, right? It takes your sheep. That's what your shepherds say.'

'Yes,' Remy said. 'It sleeps the rest of the time, we suppose, but we can't find its den. We haven't,' he added judiciously, 'looked very hard.'

'I don't think it does sleep,' Feilan said. 'I listened to all the stories around here, and a creature that big needs too much food to sleep most of the time.'

'Bears—'

'—eat their own bodyweight before they sleep. A few sheep aren't going to tide this creature over for a whole month, in torpor or not. I think it has a migratory circuit which puts it at Seven Hills at new moon. I've been tethering goats at the entrance to an abandoned salt mine just beyond the confines of the hunting ground, and a few days ago, something started taking them.'

Remy's velvety eyes were gratifyingly wide.

'I've got it trained,' Feilan said comfortably. 'It's not even bothering to enter the valley, because it's getting its food on a platter. And we're sitting at the only way to reach the mine from the hunting ground, so the other warriors can't come past us to get at it. We'll take the head at my convenience.'

His husband was apparently impressed enough to lay a hand over Feilan's cheek, though he then did say, 'You could just take it tonight and get this all over and done with?'

'Don't you like being married to me?' Feilan asked, putting a touch of injury into his voice.

Remy said, 'No! I mean, *yes*, it's... Oh, you're teasing.'

Holding him closer, Feilan said, 'I'm teasing. I don't underestimate my friend's ability, but no story I've heard suggests to me that even he can take this thing alone. We've got Noura now, and that'll help, but I don't have what I promised her yet.'

His mother had not answered either of his letters, aside from returning the coded beads that confirmed she'd safely received them. He wasn't letting himself be concerned about that, for now. She wouldn't reply, until she had an answer for him, and he couldn't expect that within a single sunrise of the request.

He went on, 'And I won't act until I have Micah's help secured, too. I certainly don't need that one hanging about near us waiting for me to make my move, which was almost surely his plan until I tempted him with an alliance. Even tonight, he'd still take the opportunity to win the head for himself. He's smarter than I'm used to having to plan around.'

'That must be unusual for you,' Remy said.

Feilan eyed him before accepting he wasn't being sarcastic. 'Right,' he said finally. He ran a hand over Remy's loosened hair. 'Are you going to let me fix your braid for you this time?'

'You truly want to do a servant's job?' He sounded very doubtful.

Swallowing the ingrained Vaer surge of pride that screamed he was no one's thrall, Feilan said, 'I'm here to serve you, aren't I, husband?'

He worked his fingers into Remy's hair, undoing the remnants of the braid, copious with his touch, feeling Remy's weight coming heavier onto him with every stroke. He was starting to sit up to fetch one of the silver combs off the tray on the sideboard when Remy put a hand on his chest, firm enough to convey a decision.

Feilan was already smiling when Remy shifted, sharply. He was suddenly straddling Feilan, thighs lightly bracing about Feilan's hips. He was naked under his linen shift, and Feilan could feel the rub of his husband's hard cock through his own braes.

Feilan set his hands gently at Remy's waist, warning himself to not move. 'If this is another attempt to pay what you think you owe, I did tell you I'm tackling your uncle on my own behalf.'

'No. But I *was* thinking about our argument at the salt pool, a little,' Remy said. 'I was thinking Torben warned me off.'

'I see you took it to heart,' Feilan said, fighting the urge to slide his hands down further, making himself hold still until Remy spelled out his full intentions.

'I did, actually. And then I realised that he didn't warn me off at all.'

Feilan raised his brows. 'You don't think so?'

'What he really did, if you think about it, was give you to me.' Remy squeezed his thighs tighter, cutting off Feilan's desire to quibble about this notion that Torben had any right to be giving him to anyone; his desire to quibble about anything, really. 'All the way until the next new moon. So...' Licking his lips, Remy put his hands to Feilan's shirt, pushing it slowly up to bare his stomach. 'I thought perhaps you could spend the time showing me the ins and outs' – and here he shot Feilan a glimmering look, fighting a tiny smile – 'of fucking. If that's an acceptable addition to our agree—'

Feilan hooked his hand about Remy's nape and dragged him down. Their mouths met, as frantic as the day before in the bathing pool at first, before Feilan let Remy gentle the biting kiss into something slower, calmer, but more assured.

If his husband had any qualms left about fucking a barbarian, he was hiding them well.

Remy undid Feilan's laces, and lifted his shirt off over his head. Taking tacit permission to touch, he ran the tips of his fingers over the muscles of Feilan's chest and into the thatched blond hair there. He followed a trail of hair down until his fingers snagged against Feilan's braes.

'Will you let me—'

'Yes.'

He could see the gratification on Remy's face, the shy pleasure at Feilan's unabashed desire. Together, they stripped off the braes, so that Feilan lay bare. But when Remy, straddling Feilan again, began to lift the hem of his own pale shift, Feilan caught his hands.

'Leave that. I like it.' To illustrate, he touched Remy's thighs, letting the movement of his hands up and down Remy's skin raise and lower the shift, giving them both glimpses of the treasures beyond.

Remy let out a barely audible puff of air. He ran his thumbs over Feilan's nipples, and began to draw his hands all the way down, back towards where he had stopped before. This time, however, his fingertips snagged over the patch of thick scar tissue laid across Feilan's side.

'This is where…'

'My first and only raiding season. Ended quick smart with a sword in my gut.'

'Torben saved you,' Remy said, face lowered to examine the scar. 'You said that, when he signed his contract. He said he owed you, and you said he didn't. Because of this?'

'Yes.'

Remy met his eye, and then glanced at the side of his face, where the skin was tender, and probably bruised, but not as swollen as usual after a punch in the face, presumably thanks to Remy's salve.

'He hit you.'

'It's more accurate to say the bear-god hit me, and Torben stopped Him doing worse.'

'That's the stupidest thing I've heard you say so far,' Remy said softly.

Feilan said, 'Are you sucking my cock, or what?'

Remy watched his face for another moment, and then slid down his body in a single graceful move. He ran a finger down Feilan's hard length, followed it with his tongue, and then put his lips about the tip. Feilan closed his eyes and enjoyed the irregular sensations as Remy tested the waters, adjusting his rhythm and angle repeatedly as he explored Feilan's cock and balls with his lips and tongue.

After a time, he found a method that agreed with him, and he began to steadily take Feilan deeper. But he soon choked, and came back off.

'Sorry,' he said, out of breath.

'All good, Rufran.' Feilan gave his cheek a quick, fond touch. 'Take your time. Use your hand instead, if you want. No fuss.'

He was regretting it even as he said it. Remy nodded, face set in a frown that read as determined rather than distressed, and lowered his head again, flattening his tongue to take Feilan deep. His head bobbed as he worked, hands spread over Feilan's thighs. Finding his pace now, he began to speed up, and moved one of those braced hands to caress Feilan's balls. Feilan grunted appreciatively, letting his head fall back and slitting his eyes in sheer pleasure. He was rocking his hips slightly but otherwise keeping himself still.

Then Remy decided to add in a little suction, and that did for Feilan so fast he wasn't able to get out a warning.

Remy choked as Feilan's spend filled his mouth; he'd climaxed so violently after days and days of abstinence and almost as long lusting after his husband that he'd bet his seed had hit the back of Remy's throat. Remy sat up, eyes wide, lips closed. Feilan jerked his chin towards the table with the aquamanile and its matching bowl, and Remy crawled off the bed to spit. He rinsed his mouth, looking at Feilan with an odd expression.

'Didn't enjoy that one too much?' Feilan asked. 'You're not going to like everything.'

'I don't know,' Remy said hesitantly. 'I feel like I did it wrong. It's not how... It wasn't what you did with Torben.'

Feilan recalled that Remy tended towards verbalising his uncertainties: now he knew him better, he knew he'd talked himself through their first time together back in Siftar, and he prosecuted ideas and possibilities aloud in his cave when presented cases with unusual symptoms. He'd probably have quite taken to Feilan murmuring helpful instructions during the proceedings a moment ago.

With that in mind, Feilan raised his brows and said, 'I'd go so far as to say that was an entirely different sex act, svasa. Look, I came and there were no unexpected teeth involved, you can't have gone far wrong.'

That made Remy both blush and smile. He returned to bed, cuddling against Feilan's side. Feilan was a little adrift, floating in the drowsy post-release haze. He caressed Remy's back with long, lazy strokes, and lowered his head to take a kiss, which Remy hesitated over.

Feilan could easily guess at the cause of that. 'It's the taste of my own seed, I won't complain.'

He caught Remy's face in both hands and kissed him deeply, licking between his lips to chase the acrid tinge and make the point. By the time he was done, Remy was back on top of him, lying full length, satisfyingly hard against his stomach, hips shifting insistently.

'I think you might want to fuck me, Rufran,' Feilan told him cheerily.

Remy stilled, looking mortified. 'Oh, no, no, that's fine, I had a turn yesterday. Um. Thank you?'

Here was a man who had been taught to never ask for too much, curse his uncle and every one of his brothers and sisters. Feilan said, 'It's not about turns. It's about sharing pleasure. It'd be my pleasure to take your cock, any way it'd be your pleasure to give it to me.'

'I see,' Remy said, very slowly. 'Doesn't...doesn't the smaller man...'

'No, go on, I'm interested to hear your theory,' Feilan told him, snickering.

'My theory is that men who take the piss don't get fucked in any way except the proverbial,' Remy said with endearingly spiky acerbity.

Feilan laughed outright. 'Apt enough. Whoever wants to take the cock, takes the cock, Rufran, and right now, I want to lie back here and take your cock. Want to give face-fucking a try?'

That stymied the cheeky little drit. 'I – what?'

'You heard.'

'It was very rough, when Torben did that to you.'

'I like rough,' Feilan reminded him.

'I...don't think I do. I don't think I can do that to you, Feilan.' He touched the highest point of Feilan's cheekbone, where the bruise from Torben's punch must be.

Feilan smiled. 'Then make it gentle, Remy.'

He adjusted himself into a half-recline with pillows, and then manoeuvred a cautiously compliant Remy into position, kneeling with most of his weight against Feilan's shoulders. Feilan pushed the linen shift up to reveal Remy's slender cock, engorged and leaking, right there, reddened and ripe for the taking. Didn't think he could do it to him, Njorda's *arse*.

'Come on, then,' he said. If Remy wanted the reassurance of instructions, he'd give him instructions. 'Gentle. Very gently choke me with your cock until you spurt half a vika down my throat.'

Remy spluttered into the shocked laugh that meant he was trying to be appalled but couldn't quite manage it.

'Come on,' Feilan repeated, hands on Remy's hips to hold the shift out of the way, adding the merest suggestion of a tug. He licked the tip of Remy's hot cock, and Remy jolted.

Remy sank both hands into Feilan's hair and Feilan allowed himself a grin of triumph before Remy eased his cock into his mouth, nudging his lips wider. Feilan immediately ran his hands around to grip Remy's tight arse under the shift, again applying just enough of a hint of pressure to make Remy slide his cock in deeper. Remy gasped and Feilan moaned approval around the weight on his tongue and against the roof of his mouth. His only regret was that the shift, so enticingly modest before, was now getting in the way; his forehead was brushing linen instead of Remy's bare stomach as Remy pushed his cock in to the very root, balls drawn tight and pressing into Feilan's chin, thighs bracketing his ears.

They paused there, Remy's breathing ragged over Feilan's head, his hands tight in his hair. Remy pulled out, and pushed back in, still slowly. He made that gasping sound of pleasure again. Feilan gave an encouraging squeeze, with a little jerk to it, indicating what he wanted.

Remy, obedient, thrust again, less hesitant this time, deeper. And then again. His small moans were getting louder. The fists in Feilan's hair clamped even tighter, and he tipped Feilan's head back, and then he wasn't shy at all anymore.

Feilan kept his eyes shut, his breathing shallow through his nose, his hands clamped around Remy's flexing arse, and his tongue flat, and revelled in the pump of Remy's cock in and out of his mouth and throat, the neediness of the sounds his husband was making, the assertive clutch of his hands.

Remy cried out something in that archaic Riverlander language, and Feilan coughed against the sudden flood of thick wet heat down his throat. His inadvertent protest made Remy pull out too soon, and the rest of his seed splattered over Feilan's face and chest.

Feilan opened his eyes to see Remy sitting back on Feilan's thighs, both hands clapped over his mouth, eyes wide with horror, linen shift fallen back down to cover his spent cock. He looked remarkably pure for a man who'd just enthusiastically fucked someone's throat and then spent on their face.

Feilan wiped the warm, sticky mess off his cheekbone with his knuckles, staring accusingly at his husband. Remy didn't seem to be breathing.

Unable to hold the facade of offence any longer, Feilan began to laugh.

'Oh!' Remy said, sagging in relief. 'Oh, but let me get a cloth—'

'No need.' Feilan groped about to find his discarded braes and wiped himself off. 'Njorda's tits, you know how to treat your men, don't you? Very well, I mean,' he hastened to add. 'Spurt on my face anytime.'

Remy was still hiding his own burning face in his hands when Feilan, grinning, crawled out of bed to fetch the comb he'd been so pleasantly diverted from, plus oil and a small bowl of water.

When he returned to bed, Remy had emerged and gone tense, eyes fixed on the comb. 'Don't...'

'I'll be careful of the knots,' Feilan assured him. 'I won't hurt you.'

'It's...' Remy swallowed hard, and Feilan abruptly recognised the look he was wearing. It was the same look he'd had when Torben had accidentally threatened to destroy Adeline's hair clasp.

'Was this Margalita's?' He tried to put the comb into Remy's hand, contrite. He'd been using it for days, just because it was on the tray and his were still at the bottom of his trunk.

'My mother's,' Remy said. He closed his hand about Feilan's in brief reassurance. 'You can use it. You can use it, Feilan.'

So Feilan had Remy lie back against his chest, between his thighs; he already knew he had a cuddler on his hands. He gently worked the comb through Remy's tangled and slightly salty hair, using oil on the fingers of his other hand to smooth and unknot it as he went.

'Going to take a while,' he muttered.

'It can't be much more of a mess than you left it that first night.'

Feilan remembered smugly wiping his sticky hand through Remy's hair. 'Yeah, I was being a barbarian arsehole.'

'You're still a bit of a barbarian arsehole,' Remy pointed out in his most sanctimonious tones.

Feilan snorted, lightly weaving fingers into Remy's locks. 'And you're still a provocative little shit.'

He nudged aside the loose neckline of the shift and put his mouth to Remy's bared shoulder, and used oily fingers to pull him close against his chest and torso, his quiescent cock pressing against Remy's taut arse.

'I am not,' Remy said, squirming in Feilan's lap with suspicious rhythm while he stroked his bitten-down nails over the meat of Feilan's thighs before pressing his thumbs in, 'provocative.'

Feilan wrapped Remy's hair around his fist and tugged, and heard Remy's breath hitch satisfyingly. His head came back against Feilan's shoulder, baring a long, vulnerable curve of throat. He'd closed his eyes.

Feilan tightened his hold until Remy's eyes blinked open and he shot a look of alarm up at him, body tensing. He eased off until Remy's spine melted against him again. 'Good?'

Remy made to nod, was pulled up short by Feilan's calibrated grip in his hair. His breath hitched again. Feilan pressed another kiss to his shoulder. He'd, if not quite *inflicted* his preferences on Remy, certainly failed to give Remy room to explore his own. He was hearing them now, he suspected. Experimentally, and still holding him captive by his hair, he lightly ran the teeth of the comb over Remy's nipples. They pebbled, hard nubs taut under the thin linen of the shift. Remy arched, and he dug his short nails hard into Feilan's thighs, biting off another soft gasp.

'Good,' Feilan confirmed, to both of them. 'Let's get the last of these knots out so I can put this oil to good use, yes?'

'And put the knots back in,' Remy murmured.

Feilan huffed a laugh, nuzzling against Remy's cheek. Lashes lowered, Remy wore that giveaway tilt on his lips, evidently pleased to have amused the barbarian arsehole.

The coy smile was drowned by a knock, more a thunderous hammering that gave away the identity of the visitor even before Torben flung open the door to brightly enquire, 'Rooms ain't soundproof, are they?'

'We're aware,' Feilan said, pointedly sliding the comb over Remy's hair, 'thanks very much to you.'

Torben paused, staring at them, cheerful expression darkening. Remy had already whipped his hands from their possessive hold on Feilan's thighs; Feilan kept his arm around him so he couldn't wriggle out from between his thighs as well. They weren't doing anything that needed shame or even embarrassment.

Torben said, 'I forget how much of an arsefucked you are sometimes, Little Wolf.'

Feilan pushed down the instinctive Vaer roar of outrage, and a sharper hurt: as much as Torben had stood by and let others do it, he himself had never actually called him a rassragr, the worst word, before.

'Oh, you braid each other's hair on raids all the serthing time, Tryggvi,' he said lightly, giving the comb a suggestive waggle.

It wasn't that Feilan was tending Remy's hair, he knew. It was their interrupted air of affection. Men didn't do that. Men fucked – everyone knew they fucked – but they didn't cuddle afterwards like they were actually fond of each other.

Switching to Midlands, Torben said, 'I told you he's not yours, Rufran.'

Remy pushed Feilan's hand aside and rose to kneeling, facing Torben. Diffuse rays of the morning sun fell through the high open slits, so useful for lighting and fresh air, so fatal to privacy, and bathed him like some sort of Chalcadean church iconography: the dark red hair, the pale skin of thighs and bared shoulder, the undyed linen shift, the pink cheeks, the wide, dark, innocent eyes.

By all the gods Feilan did not pray to, the man was a vision. He was a little too distracted by admiration to realise that Remy's stir out of his embrace had not been a retreat.

Remy said, 'He's made it clear he's not yours, either.'

By the time Feilan had recovered from the sheer astonishment of being fought over, Torben had crossed the room and seized Remy's shift in a bunched fist, snarling, 'Driti skroggr—'

Feilan tangled in the linens as he tried to lunge to get between them, but Remy merely flashed that black-eyed look that could only be inciting Torben further. 'Release me before I curse you.'

Torben loomed over him. 'You— You're not a witch.'

'Hit me, then,' Remy said, 'and when your cock falls off, you'll know I actually am.'

Torben didn't recoil, but he did hesitate long enough to slide a questioning glance towards Feilan.

'Go ahead and hit him, then we'll see if your cock falls off.' In hushed tones, and drooping his little finger illustratively, he added a dire warning. 'It's probably a kenning.'

Not without a stagy harrumph to convey ongoing scepticism, Torben let go. Marching back to the door, he spoke with all appearance of indifference. 'You done, futhflogar? Because, Aleifr "I can fight" Ulfrsson, you better come do some practice with this alliance you seem to think I need.'

'Freyjasson,' Feilan corrected him. He hadn't gone by the patronymic since the day he'd been exiled, but Torben's habits died hard.

'You can't change our entire naming system to suit yourself,' Torben said, the quibble a hint that he was still smarting from the fear-respect bucket of ice-water Remy had just so cleverly drenched him with.

'Funny thing about being a Cursed,' Feilan said in Vaer, 'I can do whatever I arsefucked buggering want.' The double-profanity appeared to effectively convey his own annoyance: Torben's chin dipped. 'I'll be along.'

Once Torben had gone out, not quite in defeat, closing the door firmly behind him, Feilan turned back to Remy, who said, in quite a remote way, 'What does skroggr mean?'

Feilan said, 'Fox,' with enough flippancy to give away that it was not quite so complimentary as Rufran. 'And a futhflogr is a man who runs away from cunnies, but that's just plain funny.'

It hadn't been funny when they'd been back in the village, of course. Like using serth, his very nature, as an obscenity, it was something he'd had to train himself not to flinch at. He'd gotten very good at not flinching.

'I wonder,' Remy said, still in those distant tones, 'if you are quite aware of how much energy you spend managing him?'

'He's my friend, Remy.'

'I should go to my grotto,' Remy said, rising with an impatient flick of his loose hair from his eyes. 'I'll have people waiting.'

They rapidly washed and dressed in a thick silence, Feilan unsure if he should apologise, and what he would be apologising *for*, exactly, if he did. They stepped out together to find Torben waiting in the hallway, face sternly impassive but fingers drumming on the embossed antler of his sword grip.

Feilan, still confused but unwilling to leave it, took Remy's face in his hands and gave him a rough kiss that made him close his eyes. 'See you this afternoon, svasa.' To Torben, he said, 'Come on, then, jolterhead.'

'Why does Foxy get to be called beloved and I get the insult?' Torben demanded as they went out towards the foyer.

'Because one of you is more of a dick than the other one.'

'Still holding a grudge, are we?'

'I've been holding *several* grudges, for *several* years,' Feilan said, smiling.

Torben grinned and smacked him firmly on the arse, and no more was said, as ever.

19

THE PRACTICE WENT AS WELL AS to be expected with four strangers using three different fighting styles and four different weapon types. Feilan had eventually excused himself for his daily errand – catching whichever mangy goat a local herder saw fit to sell him, circuitously leading it to the cave without being observed or followed, and tethering it there, leaving it bleating – and returned in time to join Remy and Adeline for their afternoon visit in the foyer of Third Hill East.

Little Prince Afzal was there, with Darya and two of her guards, and a third man, very large and vacant-eyed, who Feilan guessed carried the boy about, for he saw no wheeled wicker chair of the sort he'd encountered elsewhere. Such a contraption would give Afzal some measure of independence inside his own house of rule, no doubt a distasteful idea to his stepmother.

The two, or perhaps three, guards wouldn't have been enough to stop Micah, but they'd've slowed him just long enough for Darya to get a knife into Afzal's throat. She eyed Feilan, the champion with an alliance with her enemy, with a great deal of suspicion, which eased somewhat as he acted the besotted fool with Remy. That wasn't difficult.

The youngest of Remy's sisters was there, too: Lady Not-So-Bad, Rosmunda, and her husband, Conrad. They were only six months married themselves. It had been an arranged alliance like all the Nivardus siblings' marriages, including her childless first, but they seemed well-suited, and quietly fond of each other in a way that suggested the young widow's second marriage hadn't been *entirely* arranged.

The doting aunt cooed over how darling Adeline and Afzal were, helpfully advancing Feilan's plan. He couldn't tell if this was inadvertent or whether Remy had decided to trust his sister. He hoped he hadn't, though she was the only sibling to defend him at the suppers, and she'd been speaking up for him more and more. Feilan guessed this was because she had a large Vaer warrior on her side now, or at least someone who could be mistaken as one, if not compared too closely to Torben.

She smiled at Feilan with real warmth, and Feilan was amused to realise she approved of him, or, at least, very much approved of her baby brother's innocently blissful expression as he curled into Feilan's habitual arm over his shoulders. Feilan kissed the top of his head, and Remy snuggled closer.

Even putting aside the awkward end to their morning, this was remarkably sweet of him, since Feilan had gone straight from the practice session to chasing a goat about its pen. It was old and ornery, and needed wrestling to get the tether on. He had to reek of both old sweat and annoyed goat, the sort of perfume that would smell puce to him. Remy was doing a fine show of acting intoxicated by manly musk, however.

It was with decided regret that Feilan realised he didn't have time to either wash himself or pin his husband to their bed before the nightmeal.

And now he, Torben, Noura and Micah had taken the field for the third night, the final night of true moon-gloam before it began to grow big again, and thus the final night of the official contest for this month. Feilan was fairly sure, from the stories he'd gathered, that the monster lingered in the region longer, but it would openly break the rules to take its head after tonight.

That would give him a solid month to achieve his three aims: the promised freedom tattoos for Noura, the plan to safely extricate Afzal for Micah, and a method to neutralise any inconveniently bright ideas from Uncle Bertrand when he realised he was going to lose his authority over Adeline.

Feilan did still privately think that those two latter items had a single solution, which was the wholesale murder of both ill-intentioned guardians. But Micah would not trust the simplicity of it, and Remy would not countenance the brutality of it, and so Feilan needed to keep thinking on it.

He strongly suspected the answer to the questions he had asked his mother would help with leashing Uncle Bertrand. Freyja would reply soon, on that, and the tattoos.

As he mused, he rolled his shoulders, which were aching from the sparring that morning. His whole body was complaining, different muscles and joints more or less loudly. He was, in truth, a comfortable trader a long way from a youth spent with a sword and shield trying to earn the approval of his father and the bear-god.

Torben sniggered at him, while the other two, bored, strolled into the mist to do a short patrol of what all the other mercenaries – five survivors in Bertrand's bloc, since one of the men Micah had wounded hadn't taken the field tonight, and only three solo now – must know was their territory by now.

'Shut your mouth,' Feilan told him, managing a smile.

'Of all the things for you to get narky about,' Torben said. 'We've all known you can't fight since you had sixteen summers. Even before you almost died on your first raid.'

'Lots of bear-warriors die on their first raid,' Feilan said, folding his arms.

'Yeah, and they're dogshit fighters, too, Little Wolf.'

Feilan scowled. He wasn't sure why he was finding Torben's needling on this one subject so effective. His friend was right: he'd never been as good with a sword as the real bersverdar, the ones who heard the bear-god as a roar rather than a whisper.

But he'd been good enough to protect Freyja for years, until they were reliably earning enough money to hire guards, until other Cursed from all over the heartland began to gather around them.

Those had been hard years. They had been good years, too. In the village, the two of them had been Ulfr's victims, allied but ultimately each alone. He had supposed Freyja loved him, from the way she stood between him and his father. But when she rescued him, he had *known* it. And once she had the chance to finish raising him out from under Ulfr's dark shadow, their closeness had grown, their care for each other a precious, chosen, golden thing that made the only solid weight in his heart.

Meanwhile, his younger self gained in precious confidence every time his mere presence made an unscrupulous dealer think twice about trying to cheat Freyja Anjasdottir, every time he drew the bastard sword that had so aptly replaced his father's unwieldy longsword and scared off a robber band with sheer Vaer bravado, every time he'd actually had to use that blade.

He hadn't, he thought now, had to do that *often*. But he *had* had to, and he hadn't done it surrounded by stalwart comrades on every side, either.

'You'll want to shut your mouth,' he told Torben, putting a snap into his voice.

Torben laughed, perennially unoffended – the only thing that could really offend the man was inaccurately impugning his warrior courage... or accurately calling him a serthr. 'Do you know, I think Freyja picked me for the mercenary contract so you'd have to spend real time with me for the first time since we were sixteen and realise I'm not worth moping over.'

Feilan obligingly performed his usual brow raise out of respect for Torben's apparent acquiescence to the polite request to change the serthing subject. 'I've never in my life moped over you.'

'Sure,' Torben said. 'At least three men looked miserable when you left Siftar, and one of them was that Meik fellow, who I'm fairly sure is not even cursed.'

'Don't need to be a Cursed to enjoy shoving your cock in a man's mouth occasionally. You'd know.'

Torben ignored the bait. 'Yeah. You had your occasional fucks. Why did none of them ever turn into more?'

'Not because of you.' Feilan heard the defensive note and winced. He was lying: it was because of Torben.

'No?' Torben was smirking, radiating the usual arrogant complacency he took to bed with Feilan.

'Do you actually think I spend my whole year counting the days until summer rolls around and you sail in for a fly-by-night fuck?'

'Wouldn't surprise me.'

Feilan scoffed. 'And what, spent all the years before you started camping nearby pining over my long-lost first love? As if I wasn't travelling through entire lands with whole crops of men who don't have the backwards prejudice our people are stuck in.'

'Why did none of them become anything to you?'

'Who says they didn't?' Feilan said, struggling to recall the name of any who had.

Only his patient Ystheran, Helios Taurasi, came to mind, and they'd both gone into their handful of months together knowing one of them would leave Low village eventually and the other would never voluntarily leave.

'I do.'

'We were travelling.'

'For a dozen years. Haven't you been just as long at Siftar?'

'Longer,' Feilan had to admit. Twelve years establishing Freyja's reputation and her trade network, travelling to every corner of the great landmass of Enea and crossing the sea to the east as well. Thirteen years at Siftar, their spindly ash sapling now a full-grown tree. 'But we were busy establishing the trading post, the first few years. I didn't have time for anything more back then.'

'And then I showed up seven summers ago.'

'Doesn't mean anything.'

'Doesn't it?'

It meant, Feilan thought, biting his tongue on a bitter response to the incendiary smugness, that twenty-five years ago, he'd been badly betrayed by the boy he loved, who had turned out to value him only as a *you'll-do*, to be discarded the moment he became inconvenient.

Never, in all those years since, had he felt more than a passing desire to ever trust someone like that again, to ever let himself make someone precious who would not make him precious in return. He'd been glad to move on from town to town, notwithstanding the occasional brief pang, Helios the pangiest. He'd certainly been content to keep his Siftar lovers at arm's length.

He'd only noticed that habit in the last few years.

Well. Seven summers ago, to be precise.

But he didn't say that. Vaer men didn't say things like that to each other. He and Torben didn't say things like that to each other.

He could say it to Remy, and Remy would listen. Remy would look at him with that naive trust, so very open and unsullied that it would be too easy to trust him in return, if only because he was too innocent at playing his own game to conceive of ofundi krokr, the malicious trick – betrayal.

And Feilan *had* trusted him – he had told no one else about the goat ploy. That hinted of something he didn't need to examine yet. He would leave that stone unturned, just for now.

'Maybe Freyja did want me to remember how obnoxious you are,' he said at last. 'I didn't get my brains from my father, did I? But *you* found some brains somewhere, spotting one of her manoeuvres. Head not so jolted about, after all, Thunder Bear.'

'Always so mouthy.' Torben stepped in closer. 'But I never noticed how funny you think you are.'

'No, you knew that,' Feilan said, exasperated. 'You'd forgotten.'

Dropping his voice into its deepest rumble, Torben murmured, 'I don't think I appreciate you enough, do I?'

He reached a slow hand to brush Feilan's hair back. Feilan stared up at him in surprise. Torben didn't caress. Torben grabbed, and took.

'We've got a little time, before the other two circle back.' Torben's hand stroked over Feilan's hair to rest at his nape. 'Let me show you how much I appreciate you, Little Wolf.'

'This is just more jealousy, isn't it?' Feilan asked, holding still. 'You think Remy's wriggling on in to a space you can't fit.'

The hand on the back of his neck tightened. 'Isn't he?'

'It's just one more moon-turn. And then it's done.'

Torben's face twisted, then almost immediately smoothed over. He dropped his hand. 'He's such a scrawny little bugger,' he said, sounding almost wistful. 'What do you even see in him?'

Feilan opened his mouth and then decided Torben would never understand Remy's tart sweetness as anything other than weakness, his persistent courage on behalf of his niece as anything other than weakness, his open-hearted trust in the face of years of rejection as anything other than weakness.

He said, 'Yeah, that'd be the sex.'

'He can't be the sort of man you prefer in bed.'

'What would you know about what I prefer, in bed or anywhere?'

'My cock knows *all* about it,' Torben said, his broad grin suddenly ascendant.

It struck Feilan that Torben's grin in this moment served the very same purpose his own ever-ready smile so often did. 'Thunder Bear...'

'Never mind,' Torben said heartily. 'So what if you're choosing him for now? You'll come chasing a bit of this again, soon enough.' He slapped his chest.

'I'm not... This is... You're being...'

Feilan, so rarely at a loss for words, gave up the endeavour and shoved Torben, who swatted him fondly enough in return, if, as always, more firmly than he generally enjoyed. The world steadied back to their usual keel.

A goat ran past them, full tilt.

It was trailing its tether, much abbreviated. Feilan had a moment to note it: the woven hemp rope he'd tied around a narrow stony jut hadn't come loose, and its new short length ended cleanly, not frayed as if chewed through or abraded by rough rock.

Then the monster was upon them.

20

IT CAME AT A GROUND-EATING lope, intent on the prey Feilan had habituated it to.

Despite his acceptance that there was more to the local stories than a rogue bear, he'd still developed a bear-shaped idea in his head, somewhat taller than a man, covered in thick hair, clumsy but fierce.

He couldn't have been more wrong. It towered twice Torben's height, maybe five or six ells, and was pale and scaly, not hairy. It had two legs, jointed strangely, and four arms terminating in claws as long and thick as Feilan's forearm. Its head was elongated, and sleek as an otter's. It moved with terrifying grace.

He'd assessed it within a few heartbeats, hand instinctively locked around his other wrist, mother's talisman and husband's charm under his clammy palm. He even had time to debate letting it go on past in pursuit of the bolting goat. That would give the other warriors a chance at it, but he was suddenly not convinced that even the bigger bloc was going to be effective. He certainly didn't want Torben to face it with only him here to help.

Then the monster halted. It bent its neck as if peering down at them from its lofty height. It raised its narrow snout and sniffed the air. Strangely, it itself seemed to have no scent, or at least, not one strong enough to trigger colour.

It turned its head and looked along the invisible trail of the goat, long vanished back towards the familiar safety of the herd. A forked tongue flickered from its mouth, probing from between teeth as long and sharp as Micah's daggers.

It swung its head the other way, and looked at Feilan.

He smelled of sweat and goat. He'd gone from training to goat pen to afternoon visit to nightmeal without ever having a chance to wash. If he hadn't been inured to it already, his own stink might have left hazy hues in the corners of his eyes.

He smelled of goat, which he'd trained this thing to eat.

He took a step back, drawing his bastard sword.

'Bigger than I thought it'd be,' Torben said casually. 'Get behind me.'

It was the same phrase he'd used to tease Feilan yesterday. This time he was deadly serious.

'Wait,' Feilan said, but his voice wasn't working and it came out as the merest puff.

Torben strolled towards the monster, unsheathing his longsword.

Feilan heard a shout – Noura and Micah, running out of the mist. Torben had heard it too, and he'd even managed to grasp what it meant: Noura might be running to help them, but Micah wasn't bound into the alliance yet, and he would be trying to take the head for himself. He'd either be expecting the others to honour his win, or willing to kill them if they wouldn't.

Therefore Torben didn't wait for their assistance but kept on with his approach, raising the sword, head tilted. Feilan guessed he was examining its pale armour-like scales, planning his attack for the gaps at the joints.

The monster roared, uncurling all four arms, jointed and muscular. The pale scythe-like claws seemed to glint in the starlight before it brought them down on Torben as fast and jagged as a lightning strike.

It threw him aside as if he were a discarded doll, ripped open in three ragged lines, sheeting blood.

Feilan couldn't move for the shock of it, blinded by the bright coruscating blue that washed over his vision as the thick pungency of the blood hit him. It had been so fast. So easy. Torben hadn't even got a single blow in.

His vision cleared. The monster stalked towards him, deceptively slow. Feilan thought, incoherently, *Too fast*, and charged at it. A figure thundered past: Noura. She struck with all her strength at its flank with her curved blade as Feilan went in low and tried to hamstring it on the same side. It shrieked and flailed, flinging them both away.

Feilan lay dazed; it had been a short flight and a hard landing. Noura had bounced onto her recently-injured side and was also slow to get back up. The monster circled, listing, favouring the side on which they had coordinated their attack, but very much not incapacitated.

Then Micah was there, coming from behind to spring lithely up its back. He leapt higher one, two, three times, and each time he landed, Feilan heard the meaty thunk, thunk, thunk as his wicked blades sank home in the joints between the scaly plating, the last into the tender skin between the shoulder and neck scales.

The monster screamed. It threw itself onto its back like a dog trying to scratch an itch. Micah rolled clear and balanced on his toes, more knives already to hand. Noura pulled Feilan to his feet and they moved to form the three points of a triangle with Micah, the monster at its centre.

It sniffed the air again. Then with one mighty bound, it cleared Micah's head and cantered away into the mist.

They'd injured it, and made it easier for the uncle's bloc to take it. It didn't occur to Feilan that they had to follow it and finish the job. He dropped his sword and ran to Torben.

He couldn't pray – the gods turned Their backs to the Cursed – but he did anyway, to any god that would hear him.

Torben was alive. He wouldn't be for long. It was exactly as had happened to Remy's brother, exactly as Remy had described.

Torben gripped Feilan's wrist, so little strength in it that Feilan wanted to tear those calloused fingers from his skin so he wouldn't have to feel the weakness.

Voice wavering, Torben said, 'I have to tell you where my hoards are buried, Aleifr.'

Feilan said, '*You will not,*' and he was almost shouting.

Micah pushed him aside. 'Give me something to bind him with.'

Bind him, Feilan thought, *bind him, he can barely move, why bind him?*

Micah pulled a knife. Feilan *wasn't* thinking. Noura held him back while Micah used the knife to cut Torben's wrecked and bloody shirt free. She handed Micah her undershirt, and the injuries were so extensive that he simply folded it up and pressed it over all three gaping wounds. Feilan silently stripped off the leather jerkin and handed over his shirt, and Micah cut it into strips to hold the padding tight.

'That is as well as I can do until I have the equipment to sew him up,' Micah said. He rose and looked Feilan full in the face. 'Courage, my friend. He's not done yet. Let's get him to the witch.'

Noura crouched and put an arm around Torben's shoulders, getting ready to lift. 'It's going to hurt like shit,' she told him. 'But you might live. Ready?'

Torben made a grunt that might have been concurrence. Feilan, adrift in a situation he couldn't think his way out of, got his arm around Torben on the other side, and together he and Noura lifted him. He screamed, and Feilan almost dropped him, which made him shout again, shorter.

'Keep it together, Little Wolf,' he said hoarsely, and that was enough to steady Feilan so he could actually be helpful.

Later, the trek back towards First Hill would be nothing but murk in Feilan's memory, a nightmarishly endless slog, warm blood soaking his skin as the padding became sodden with it, Torben's weight slumping heavier and heavier onto his shoulders, Torben's feet moving ever slower, until Feilan and Noura were dragging him, their own strength flagging.

But Torben was still breathing. He was still breathing. He was barely conscious, his feet were dragging, he'd lost half his weight in blood, he was ashy from shock, he was still breathing. Feilan would not put him down until his breathing stopped.

Micah was saying something, and Feilan thought it was important, but he couldn't make sense of it.

Micah punched his shoulder. 'Listen!'

'I'm listening,' Feilan said dully.

'We cannot go in past the spectators,' Micah said, in tones that said he was repeating himself. 'He must walk in, or be disqualified, and he cannot walk unaided tonight. Can you take us somewhere safe, where no one will see?'

'Remy's cave,' Feilan said, and almost broke, because that felt almost as far as they'd already walked.

But walk it they did, step by agonising step, low across the sides of the hills to stay in the mist. Micah ranged about them, knives to hand, looking out for other warriors or the monster on the rampage, and if they'd met either of those, they'd have been done. As it was, Feilan could barely tell the difference between the occasional scream echoing out of the mist and the one long scream in the back of his head.

But at last they were dragging Torben's weight up the slope to the cave, Micah scouting ahead to be sure none of the handful of Seven Hills guards were patrolling this far down the arcade. Feilan and Noura used the very last dregs of their strength to lower Torben to the stony floor, while Micah lit a lamp and did a fast reconnoitre of the benches and shelves.

'No needles,' he said. He tossed them a bundle of clean linens from Remy's neat stores. 'Rebind him. I'll be back as fast as I can.'

Pulling the sodden, matted padding free made Torben groan but not stir. Working together, Feilan and Noura wadded fresh linen thickly over each of the three huge gashes, and held it firmly in place. Then silence reigned, a silence Feilan desperately wished to hear broken by running footsteps coming along the arcade above.

He closed his eyes, hands pressing down on the inadequate cloth trying to hold the last of Torben's life inside him. The smell of blood with its tang of heated iron was strong in the air, tainting Feilan's vision, even with eyes tight shut, with a haze of that unreal blue, purple-tinged, bone-white at the edges, the colour of the grip of Feilan's father's longsword.

'All right?' Noura asked.

'I always knew he'd die,' he said. 'I just never thought I'd have to see it.'

'Hurts like shit,' she said again.

'But I'll live,' he said, and he choked.

Like him, Noura couldn't spare a hand off trying to staunch the bleeding, but she shifted her weight so that her shoulder was touching his, a solid point of warmth that made him realise how cold and shaky he was.

He opened his eyes and looked at Torben's face. It was slack and grey.

After aeons, Remy was flinging himself down beside him. Feilan hadn't heard the footsteps after all. Micah knelt on Torben's far side, further from the injuries. With cool efficiency, he directed his helpers: Noura to hold the padding in place and inch it back from each gash, as Remy helped Micah sew it up.

That left Feilan, who knew Remy's cave almost as well as Remy did by now, to fetch and carry. He fetched a lamp. And another one. And a bowl of water from the spring at the rear. And another one. A large jar of paste under Remy's direction, that he put all over his and Micah's hands before rinsing them off in the first bowl. A bottle of some thick liquid, smelling a vivid chartreuse that burst sharply into the dim air as Remy uncorked it and poured it over the first wound before Micah started in with the needle. More clean cloths. He took soaked-red ones away. The water in the second bowl became bloody. He emptied it out onto the grass, looking at its pale pink colour under the light cast from the lamps, and refilled it, and brought it back over. Another bottle of the viscous medicine to be poured on the second wound. Another fresh bowl of water. A third bottle. A third bowl.

And at last Noura was stepping back, her job done, holding the last bloody wads that had kept a little of Torben's blood inside his broken body. And Micah sighed and sagged and sat back on his haunches, the hand holding the needle fallen to his side. His fingers were clamped so hard about the tiny sliver that he had to use his other hand to pry it free.

And Remy was sending Feilan for one last medicine, a small jar, a colour Feilan recognised: it was the same blue salve Remy had given Noura, for her comparatively minor injuries. Remy slavered the entire contents over a field of fresh stitches.

Torben hadn't stirred once.

Micah touched his temple, his lips, his chest, some sort of silent prayer. 'I will keep watch here. You and you' – he nodded to Feilan and Noura – 'go show yourselves, coming in off the hunting ground. Tell them the warrior and the eunuch are staying out there together. Let them assume what they will assume.'

'You have to walk in,' Noura said.

'There is no rule that says it must be before morning,' Micah said. 'You and Feilan must keep us from being disqualified by attesting to our good health and our...' He grimaced, and enunciated his next word with delicate distaste. 'Passion.'

'Darya...' Remy said, without looking up.

'Knows I am not given to such nonsense and further that my first loyalty will ever be to Afzal. She will assume I am ensnaring my closest rival, the better to pretend I am so enamoured as to allow him the win whilst in the meantime effecting that exact trap upon him.' He turned to Feilan, and then, sighing, to Noura. 'Confirm to them that we have not taken the monster's head, so that they are reassured we are not illicitly hunting it outside the time set by the competition.'

'They didn't see you when you summoned the witch?' Noura asked, when Feilan just stared at him limply.

'No one had to see me. He was already on his way.'

Remy flushed under their sudden attention. 'I wasn't,' he said. 'I was fetching something from Third Hill.' He touched his wrist absently – the protective talisman was missing. He'd forgotten to wear it.

Feilan took off his own, and tied it around Torben's wrist. He tried to murmur an invocation to Njorda but the words wouldn't come.

'You must wash up and go back now,' Micah said. 'And you two, get moving.'

Feilan was bare-chested and covered in blood. He dimly heard the others decide this needed to be rectified: if the uncle knew they had had an encounter with the monster, he might suspect the lie behind Torben and Micah's supposed interlude.

It might all be moot. They had injured it, and driven it into the hunting ground. The uncle's bloc could easily have taken it. The subterfuge that had delayed Torben's care could have all been for nothing.

Noura guided him to the spring, and helped him wash, while Remy ran to Third Hill East and came back with a fresh shirt, and a stack of extra blankets too, which he helped Micah spread over Torben until only his golden hair was visible.

Then Feilan and Noura plunged back into the mist and made their way across the curve of the hunting ground. They were both exhausted, and couldn't move much above a walk, alert all the time for figures coming at them out of the white vapour. The most they encountered was a panicking flock of sheep, fleeing full-pelt. They must have forced their way through their pen's fence, or battered it down, in their frenzy to escape the angry monster.

Noura, frowning, made Feilan sit in a sheltered hollow while she ran a brief errand, returning with the jerkin and sword he'd discarded by Torben's body.

Once she'd got him to wear both, she looked at him closely. 'You back with me? Or do I need to slap you?'

'I could use a brisk maternal slap,' Feilan said, which earned him a savage punch on the arm instead. 'Thanks.'

'Come on, you pillock. You'll have to do the talking. Slaves don't answer back.'

By the time they emerged onto the trodden grass before the barracks, the last of the surviving warriors to return, Feilan was calm enough to play the game. He was calm enough to think about that neatly sliced tether, too. He had known its implications the moment he'd seen it. It was time to think about them.

The spectators, the handful left of them, were long since bored of the lack of spectacle associated with the monster hunt. That they were still up there, listless, unimpressed when the two warriors came slowly out of the mist empty-handed, told Feilan immediately that no one had brought in the monster's head yet. Barring further excitement tonight, the contest was on again, next new moon.

Remy, having run back along the arcade to rejoin the spectators while

Feilan and Noura were inching their way tiredly across the hillsides, came quickly down the steps off the rooftop to greet Feilan with his usual kiss, exactly as per their established habit.

Then Feilan and Noura followed him back up. They separated at the top of the stairs, she to bend her knee to her master, he to explain Torben and Micah's absence to the uncle before he could disqualify them for being dead.

When Bertrand made the predictable fuss, Feilan obediently trotted out Micah's script: there was no rule that said they had to return before sunrise, they had no plan to hunt the monster, they had been overcome – this with a twist of a smile and a significant glance towards Adeline and Afzal to make it clear he couldn't specify the precise nature of the overcoming in front of the children – and were best left to it.

And then, because he was calm enough to play the game – and he would yet play the game for Adeline, despite the inevitable conclusion he could draw from the severed tether – he added, with disgust, 'That's not to say I approve,' so that Uncle Bertrand would think the alliance was fraying and so that the within-earshot Darya knew he wasn't friendly towards Micah, perhaps because he was too clever for Micah to fool with wiles like the warrior.

Remy tucked himself under Feilan's arm, own arm looped about his waist. 'They'll be back by morning, uncle,' he said; he was almost mimicking Adeline's usual sweet, obliging tone. 'That's all right, isn't it? The rules of the contest say they have to be capable of walking back in. It doesn't say when.'

Adeline said, 'Oh, yes, that's true, isn't it?' and Lady Rosmunda said, 'Yes, it is, darling.'

Bertrand flicked an evaluative glance among the siblings, recognised that most would back their niece, and said only, sourly, 'It best be by dawn, nephew.' He dismissed them with a nod.

Remy's hold about Feilan's waist became support as they descended the stairs. Feilan wanted to go straight back to watch over Torben, but he couldn't. Now the hunt was over for the night, the spectators would be filtering to their accommodations down each arcade, and so would be the network of spying servants. He couldn't lead them straight to Remy's cave. They had to do exactly as expected, and go to Remy's room.

He was flagging badly, but he was buoyed, not by Remy's support, but by a growing heat, flooding through him, stiffening his spine, imbuing his exhausted body with new energy.

In desperation over Torben's torn and bleeding body, he'd prayed to the Vaer gods, who would never answer one such as he, Cursed and cast from the light of Their blessings forever.

Except one god *had* answered.

Torben's god.

Feilan walked with Remy's arm around him all the way back to their room, and the gift of the bear-god fell heavy upon him.

21

REMY CLOSED THE DOOR OF THEIR room behind them and turned to Feilan. 'Are you all right? That was—'

Feilan picked him up by his tunic and slammed his back into the nearest wall.

Remy gave a startled yelp and put a hand over both of Feilan's. That was all he did to defend himself – he didn't try to pry Feilan's grip loose, or start struggling and kicking, or rake his short nails into Feilan's eyes. He merely hung there, one hand resting atop Feilan's clenched-white fists.

Weak, said the bear-god. Oddly, He sounded just like Ulfr Njallsson.

Remy stroked his hand over Feilan's hands and wrists. It was, part of Feilan still had the wherewithal to recognise, reflexive, an attempt to soothe the beast. Only the last shreds of Feilan's self-control stopped him from punching him.

Remy asked, softly, softly, 'What is it?'

'Who did you tell?' Feilan snarled.

'Tell what?'

'Did you cut a deal with Uncle? Is that why? Or did you just want Torben dead more than you wanted Adeline on the throne?'

Remy's other hand was creeping towards the sideboard where the aquamanile sat. Feilan dragged him across the wall the other way, out of reach of that weapon. His grip tightened, and he leaned all his weight against Remy, pressing him hard into the plaster.

Remy's breath shortened satisfyingly. 'I...don't...'

'Don't lie to me.'

'I don't,' Remy said again, fighting the pressure on his chest to get the words out loud and firm.

The bear-god roared in Feilan's head, demanding he relinquish all to Him so He could smash this treacherous, provocative little bug.

Underneath it, almost too quiet to be heard, came another voice.

You are Cursed, it said. *You may feel anger, but it is not from the bear-god. You are nothing to Him. This anger is human. You may feel it, but you may* not *inflict it on others. It is controllable.* Control. It.

Slowly, slowly, Feilan, concentrating on his mother's voice, lowered Remy until his feet could touch the ground. He lessened his grip by painstaking degrees. The bear-god's rage howled inside him, demanding the gratification of fist on flesh, and Freyja's calmly imperious voice battled it, reminding him, over and over, that the bear-god's gift was no excuse, Vaer pride was no excuse, Vaer temperament was no excuse, betrayal was no excuse, there was no excuse *ever* to lash out in anger.

Feilan lost the last of his air in one long gust as he finally managed to release Remy's tunic. He stumbled away, making sure his husband was outside of his own reach. As hoarsely as if he had been the one crushed against a wall, he said, 'Go.'

Eyes shut tight, he pushed the heel of his hand hard against his forehead, between his eyebrows, almost physically trying to shove the bear-god out of his head. He heard Remy's footsteps in retreat. It took him a moment to understand that he'd not heard them retreat beyond the door, nor had he heard the door close.

'Are you all right?' Remy asked him again, this time from the doorway and far more cautiously.

Feilan laughed, a sick sound. After a moment, he said, 'I'm not the one thrown into a wall by someone I trusted.'

He pressed his hand to his head again, because, figuratively, that was exactly what had happened.

No. Excuse. Little Wolf.

'Was that your bear-god? You stopped Him doing worse?'

'You said yourself, it's a jolterheaded way of thinking about it,' Feilan said. Every bone in his body was suddenly aching. He slumped onto the bed, lowering his head. 'I'm Cursed. No god touches me. How badly did I hurt you?'

'I'll feel it in the morning,' Remy said. 'Nothing broken.'

The trust between them was broken. Feilan didn't say that; it had been broken before his reprehensible behaviour had added to the damage.

'Who did you tell?' he asked again, staring down at his hands, big and worn, knuckles prominent. Twenty-five years of mercantile pursuits hadn't erased a childhood spent training to fight, a wooden sword pushed into his chubby fist the moment he could walk. 'I won't hurt you again, Remy. I just need to know who you told.'

'Told *what*?' Remy sounded far too bewildered.

'Stop it,' Feilan said, struggling to keep his tone even. 'There's no point pretending. You're the only person I trusted enough to let in on the ploy with the goat.'

'The goat?'

Feilan's head jerked up with the force of another alarming surge of rage. He ignored the pitch-perfect confusion and forced himself to keep talking – the bear-god did not trade in words. 'And then tonight, someone knew exactly where it was. They cut its tether and drove it down to us, setting the monster on us.'

'You think I did that?'

'Not personally, no,' Feilan said. 'Too ruthless for you. But you told someone. Your uncle?'

'But why would I destroy my own champion's efforts?' Remy shook his head. 'I don't think you're thinking straight yet, Faro. I think you're still in shock.'

That was *outrageous*; Feilan squashed the outrage down, breathed it out, clung to the shelter of Freyja's voice, making it loud enough to drown out the roar of the bear-god, who sounded so much like his father it made him shake with a child's fear. He fought to deafen himself to its demand that he prove himself a proper man, the true blood-and-flame bear-warrior he'd been raised to be before his dishonour.

Keeping his voice low, he said, 'Because that is how the game is played, Remy. You have your pieces, and you position them as best you can on the board. And maybe you see that their position is not as good as it could be. And maybe one of them directly threatened you, and scared you. And now you find you have another play to make – information your uncle would want. And you can use it to get a deal for Adeline, more freedom than she'd otherwise have under her inevitable regent.'

Remy had started shaking his head about halfway through this calm explanation. 'No,' he said. 'No, I would never betray Adeline like that.'

'It's not betraying her if it gets her more than she'd get when you lose outright.'

'No. That's not what she asked me for. I wouldn't go behind her back. And...' Remy bit his lip. He slowly drew up to his full, unimpressive height. 'And I wouldn't betray you like that, either, Feilan. I would never do you harm. I...I love you. I would *never* betray you.'

Everything went quiet in Feilan's head. 'You what?'

'I love you.'

'Remy,' Feilan said, on a puff of air. But here was an argument he was prepared to have; it only needed words, and words beat back the bear-god. '*Rufran*. You've known me less than a month. I just tried to put you through a wall. You do not love me.'

Remy's cheeks were staining pink, but he said, 'I do. You pointed it out yourself. You told me I loved Queen Margalita. And I feel the same way about you as I did about her.' He made the sort of gesture a lawspeaker might have made at the local Thing.

'Ah.' Feilan sagged back. He was mostly relieved. 'Yes. Did you know her well, Remy? Or was she nice to you when no one else was, and gave you unsuspected tingly feelings?'

Remy folded his arms, mouth setting. 'There's no need to be cruel.'

'I'm not trying to be,' Feilan said. 'Njorda's tits. Will you come over here? I won't hurt you.'

'I know you won't,' Remy said, coming to him.

'Can't know that,' Feilan muttered, but he put his arms around Remy as Remy sank unhesitatingly to straddle his lap and embrace him.

He stroked Remy's back. 'I should put something on this for you.'

'It doesn't hurt.'

'It will. You know it will. And when you feel that ache, you think really hard about what love is and is not, good?' He faltered over that habitual last word, crawlingly unseemly.

'I know what it is,' Remy said stubbornly. 'And I know you won't do it again.'

'I won't,' Feilan said. He pulled a face, because that set the bear-god off into an ugly muttered protest in the back of his head. The battle-fury hadn't had its usual outlet. It would take time to fully ebb. But he was in control now. 'I won't. Serthing *gods*, Freyja would be ashamed of me. But Remy, you did tell someone. Rosmunda? You told her about the plan with Adeline and Afzal. She's been helping it along. So you thought you could trust her about the goat, too.'

Remy slithered off his lap to sit by him, apparently so he could turn and properly look him in the eye with full earnestness. 'I've told her nothing. She genuinely finds their friendship sweet. And I didn't tell her about your goat, either. I promise. I didn't tell anyone at all. You said it was a secret. I kept it a secret.' He gestured up at the window slits. 'Someone could have heard from outside. We know sound carries.'

He winced – he'd probably realised the carelessness inherent in reminding Feilan of Torben even obliquely right now. Torben's parlous state was not exactly far from Feilan's thoughts already.

He said, 'We were speaking too quietly for that.'

'Air currents,' Remy said, quite vaguely.

Feilan hummed to acknowledge the suggestion without actually countenancing it. He touched Remy's shoulder lightly. 'Let me tend to you. Acting like a woman disgusts the bear-god. It'll make Him go away for good.'

He knew he was being superstitious. He'd even agreed with Remy – and Freyja – that it was beyond foolish to ascribe any responsibility for his own temper on a god who had turned His back on him like all the rest of the pantheon. And yet. That tell-tale pulse through his veins was obstinately slow to dissipate.

He seized on a bright idea. He'd remind the bear-god He was currently embodied within a cock-craving Cursed and needed to find a worthier vessel.

'Is caring for another womanly?' Remy asked, somewhere between innocent enquiry and his old acerbic scepticism regarding barbarian ways. The man spent his days caring for others, after all.

'In the heartland, it's women's work,' Feilan said, distracted. 'I'll get one of your salves. The one with the sky in it.'

'The...sky?'

'You know. The flash of blue. Sky-blue. You used it on Torben tonight, and on Noura, didn't you, and yourself, for that cut. It heals well, and fast. No, it'd have to the jaundiced one, wouldn't it? The one you gave me yesterday, after Torben hit me. Reduced the swelling substantially.' He ran his hands down Remy's back again.

Remy looked at him closely. 'Jaundiced?'

'Disgusting yellow smell.'

'That's the arnica and comfrey salve. It smells yellow?'

Noura appeared in the open doorway, then, holding a bottle. 'Ah. I was coming to see if you needed to have firewater poured down your throat, but it looks like your little witch has you in hand.'

Feilan thought it equally likely she'd heard him raise his voice. 'Bring it over.'

She sat on his other side, glancing without much interest around the sparse room. Remy's wouldn't be much different to her own guest chamber, Feilan supposed, remembering again how isolated Remy must have been before he invited two Vaer home with him.

No wonder he had it in his head he was in love with Feilan.

Feilan took the bottle and had a long pull. It was an unfamiliar clear grain-distillation, sharp, potent, stronger than the small ale common here. He pressed it on Remy, who took a few smaller sips before handing it back to Noura. They took it in turns like that until half the bottle was gone.

'Thanks,' Feilan said eventually, turning to Noura. 'You need to get back to Aminah?'

She cuffed his ear lightly. 'I sleep here. She sleeps at the foot of our master's bed.'

'I'm a jolterhead. Sorry.'

Noura shrugged in her usual brusque fashion, though Feilan guessed it was part of her method of holding her walls intact. 'Don't apologise. Get her out.'

He'd had enough of the bottle to ask. 'How did it happen?'

She'd had enough of the bottle to answer. 'Nothing unusual. Territory got invaded. We rode out to fight in our great horde, and fell beneath superior forces. Disciplined devil-creatures. They're coming this way, too, putting their dead-straight roads through more territory every year. You Vaer better get ready for them or they'll overrun all your favourite raiding haunts.'

Feilan nodded. His network had been whispering about the western expansion of an ever-evolving alliance of east-coast city-states for years. It was part of why Olvar, the baby emperor who had so disgusted Torben by permanently claiming entire townships, was intent on his own expansion.

Noura went on, tone even flatter, 'They gave our warriors honourable deaths, but when they realised I was a woman, they stopped treating me like a warrior and started treating me like a woman. When they were done, they sold me at the slave markets. Didn't fetch much,' she added with grim satisfaction. 'My master bought me cheap as a boast: look at me, daring to master the wild steppes woman.'

'Your daughter...'

She laughed harshly. 'Not his. He never tried it, weak as piss. No, I was already carrying her by the time I was on the auctioneer's block. An invader put her in me.' She looked at them both, then snarled, 'Don't you *dare* pity me. She's the joy of my life.'

Feilan held up his hands, discovered the bottle in one, and took a sip. 'Right,' he said. 'I'm sorry. I know this world isn't kind to women.'

Noura snatched the bottle. 'This world,' she grated, 'isn't kind to *anyone*. But it's especially not kind to those who are strong in ways it refuses to recognise as strength. You know that. You *both* know that.'

She gave a definitive nod and drained the bottle to its dregs. 'My joy,' she repeated, 'but also my tether. I have a long leash, because she's a short leash, chained by his side. The worst was watching him watch her. Waiting for her to *ripen*.' She spat on the floor and threw the bottle after it. It bounced across the rug and onto bare polished stone but didn't break. 'His men had to beat me bloody the first time he took her to his bed. She was not much older than your Adeline.'

Feilan shook his head slowly: Noura *had* to win a freedom tattoo for her daughter, and yet there was not a power across all the grand kingdoms and minor holdings of Enea that could make Feilan let her master win control of another little girl.

He wished Freyja would write back.

'Yeah, one more thing that hurts like shit,' Noura said, 'but whether I live or die next moon, Feilan—'

'I will get her out.' He would personally see to it, if Freyja failed to come through.

'I'll fly down from the Eternal Sky to twist your stones off if you don't, and my ancestors will spit on your descendants until it cracks open and ends us all.'

Having delivered this matter-of-fact curse, Noura rose, gave them both another brisk nod, and departed, kicking the bottle carelessly aside and closing the door behind her.

Feilan glanced over at Remy. His husband had been so quiet, he wouldn't have been surprised to find him dozing off amid alcohol fumes, but he was looking at the closed door with a frown.

'I can sleep in Torben's room,' Feilan said.

Remy blinked out of his fixation. 'No,' he said. 'I just— You will help her daughter?

'Both of them.'

Remy slid his arms around him and rested his head against his shoulder. 'I don't care what you say. You are kind.'

Feilan sighed. 'And now I'll get that salve to treat where I so-kindly hurt you, you trusting jolterheaded *fool*.'

He fetched the salve from the tray, picking it unerringly from the couple of other identical jars because of that unpleasant fragrant undertone of sickly yellow, apparent even in the dim room, and returned to the bed. Remy had trouble lifting one of his arms as Feilan helped him out of his tunic; his shoulders were beginning to stiffen up where Feilan had slammed him against the plaster.

See? he wanted to say, and didn't. Too much of that, and it sounded like he was demanding the sympathy and comfort that only one of them deserved right now.

He smoothed the thick salve over Remy's shoulders and upper back, and touched fingers lightly to the back of his head, exploring for a lump, trying to recall those rage-filled moments to know if he'd thrown him hard enough to make his head bounce into the wall, too. He couldn't.

'Did I get you here?'

'No.'

'Your chest? I'll have left bruises there.'

'No,' Remy said again, which was just pigheaded; Feilan was no bear-warrior, but he wasn't small and he'd been leaning his considerable weight onto Remy. That left its traces.

Feilan made Remy turn so he could look at his chest for himself, but Remy was correct – he bore no visible sign of the assault there. Feilan rubbed the remnants of the salve across his slender pectorals anyway. Remy's skin goosepimpled under the touch and Feilan silently held out his tunic to him. Remy bunched it up in both hands, looking uncertain.

'I am sorry,' Feilan said, because he hadn't said it – Vaer men didn't, and so it was another way to remind the bear-god he wasn't a Vaer man, and he owed it to Remy regardless.

'The man you love almost died and you think I did it,' Remy said. 'Circumstances were extenuating. Not to say I'll be as understanding next time. But, Feilan – at least grant yourself the same grace you grant Torben, or admit he doesn't deserve it either.'

'There won't be a next time,' Feilan said, judiciously ignoring the rest. 'And I believe you when you say you didn't tell anyone.' He grunted, more to himself than at Remy. 'And, look, I don't love Torben, not in the way you think. I can't, because...'

He'd imagined himself telling Remy about this, this very evening, before the monster attacked, when he'd suddenly realised he trusted Remy more deeply than he had anyone else except Freyja for years.

But it hadn't taken long for the bear-god's rage to persuade him otherwise, had it?

He'd had one of his bright ideas about that, before Noura's well-intended interruption.

'Let's just say betrayal's a touchy subject for me.' He curled his fingers against Remy's cheek. 'Would you fuck me? Or is that too much to ask?'

'I don't...' Remy looked down at himself, and then back at Feilan, his slight smile lingering at the edges of his mouth. 'I don't believe you've been driven into wild lust by the sight of my scrawny chest.'

'You're lovely,' Feilan assured him. 'But no, it's superstition. I need to thoroughly remind the bear-god I'm a Cursed. Don't complain, you get a fuck out of it.'

Remy was still looking amused in a confused sort of way. 'If you know it's superstition—'

'Remy!' Feilan said, louder but carefully not too loud. 'I've been to one side of Enea to the other many times over. I've met people with one god and people with twenty-five gods. I've met people who think their gods walk with them every day and people who believe the gods left them alone a long time ago, and people who have no gods and appease nature spirits instead. And I've met people who ascribe everything from losing their purse to the colours in the northern sky to the very rising of the sun to pure magic, and I've even met a bunch of vaettar, little elves, with abilities I couldn't begin to explain away *except* with magic. All of it very different to Vaer beliefs. I know we can't all be right. I know it's all just superstition of one kind or another. It doesn't mean I'm immune to it.'

He was still a little drunk, and not explaining himself as clearly as he'd like. It came down to this. 'Will you take me like you'd take a woman to scare the bear-god away for good, or not?'

'I'll do anything you want me to do,' Remy said, 'if that *is* what you want.'

He left unsaid the corollary: *because I love you.* Feilan heard it anyway, and had to bite his tongue. He said, 'You are beautiful, husband,' and spread his palms over Remy's bare and gleaming chest. 'Put your beautiful cock inside me.'

Remy followed him unhesitatingly as he lay down, lying atop him to kiss him for a long, dreamy while before breaking off to ask, 'Will you help me? You used your fingers, for me, and I don't know how to do that.'

'I don't want coddling,' Feilan said, and received such a severe look that he laughed. 'All right. Get some oil.'

He rapidly stripped himself, and Remy brought back a viscous and golden oil from the tray, expensive and perfumed. Feilan breathed in the strong but delicate scent when Remy tugged the stopper out and tipped the oil onto his fingers.

'What colour is this?' Remy asked as he rubbed his fingers together, spreading the oil.

'Golden yellow,' Feilan said, puzzled. Then, at Remy's lift of the bottle towards his nose, he understood. 'Oh, what colour does it smell? Pale green, like unripe olives.'

Remy closed his eyes, head tipped to the side; Feilan supposed he was trying to map whatever colour he smelled to the colour Feilan smelled. Helios had become interested in colour-matching as well during their affair on Ysthera, though Feilan suspected that was more to do with poking fun: Vaer had seven colour words, Ystheran twelve just to delineate the precise shade of sunlit greenery. That Feilan, until his Ystheran improved, had to describe the colour of smells with cobbled phrases such as 'mostly blue, but as if a storm was blowing up during spring' appeared to both amuse and bemuse him no end.

'Is it... Do beautiful smells have beautiful colours for you?'

'Sometimes,' Feilan said, working on easing the rest of Remy's clothes off. 'Not always. Reeky smells have murky colours, though. Except blood. Blood's the most astonishing blue you'll ever see: you could use it as a beacon.'

'I see.' Remy looked like he was thinking up more questions, which was suggestive of a delaying tactic.

Feilan ran his palms down his bared flanks. 'If you don't want to do this—'

'Oh, no, I *do*.' Immediately putting the little glass flask aside, Remy bent over Feilan, oiled hand sliding between his thighs. He was frowning.

Feilan touched the pronounced line between his eyes. Again, he said, 'Remy, if you don't want to...'

'I'm concentrating. Like this?'

Feilan made a mild sound of agreement as Remy probed into his hole, revelling in the stretch. 'And then, if you can— Yes, like that.' He jolted at the burst of sensation. 'Add another.'

'We,' Remy said, in his witchiest voice, 'will proceed at *my* pace, not yours.'

Feilan made a mocking noise at the stern tone, which transformed partway through to a rather appreciative one, because Remy had just crooked his finger without altering his stern expression, and Feilan suddenly didn't think he'd be able to observe him bossing his clients about his cave with any sort of equanimity ever again.

Remy did eventually add a second finger, and then a third, and then, frown more pronounced, oiled his cock, which Feilan watched with heavy-lidded eyes. He'd been exhausted, physically and emotionally, and tipsy, and merely trying to quieten his own mind with a sacrilegious act, but now he felt the familiar energy of desire.

He thought, given how fiercely Remy was frowning, that if he stroked Remy right now like he dearly wanted to, he might be enjoyably spattered with copious seed again, but he wouldn't get the fucking, the literal serthing, he needed.

'Do we have to do it on hands and knees?' Remy asked. 'I'd prefer to be able to kiss you.'

'Come on, then,' Feilan said roughly, half-drunk again on pleasure.

He hooked a leg up, and Remy came between his spread thighs, intent and looking like he'd want to be talking himself through the process if he hadn't presumed Feilan would mock him for it. He felt Remy's steady push into his tightness, filling his body with vital warmth and emptying his head of every thought. Then Remy was deep inside and his mouth was on his, and they were slowly rocking together, Feilan moaning and Remy gasping into his mouth.

Feilan dug his fingers into Remy's hips and urged him on harder. '*Take* me.'

Remy obeyed, his fists gripped commandingly into Feilan's hair, thrusting with a rising urgency that quite displaced their comparatively languid previous pace. Feilan fell back and arched into it, and Remy cried out and reared up over him, hips bucking. Feilan shut his eyes and exulted in the pulse inside him as Remy climaxed.

Remy slid out of Feilan, and then slid down his body, and his mouth engulfed Feilan's cock to the root in one open-throated swoop. Feilan felt him swallow around his cock, throat rippling, and he cursed, spending with helpless, almost violent, jerks of his hips that had to be challenging Remy.

But Remy swallowed again, and came up looking very pleased with himself. Feilan dragged him down for a kiss, licking his own spend off his lips.

'Good,' he pronounced, rolled Remy off him, and wrapped his arms and legs around him. He was asleep before he had time to remember to worry about Torben.

22

REMY, DRESSED AND DISCONCERTINGLY ALERT, ROUSED Feilan in the dark, too early. Feilan, full of hazed pleasure, pulled him down into bed for a long kiss. Then he woke up enough to remember what he was dreading.

'He's alive,' Remy told him immediately, propped against his chest where Feilan had dragged him. 'Sleeping. Micah, too, now Noura's keeping watch.'

Feilan pressed his forehead against Remy's. 'Thank you.'

'Don't thank me. You're the one who has to wake him up and get him on his feet.'

'Take the thanks. I said I wouldn't make you cope with blood again, and then I did, and you did so well. I didn't exactly show my gratitude for that last night.'

Remy bit back a smile. 'Ah, I think you rather *did*, eventually.'

Planting a kiss to the corner of that tiny, pleased smile, Feilan murmured, 'Enjoy it?'

'Very much so.' He declined further kisses, however, wriggling off Feilan to let him up. He was moving well, no sign of pain in his back and shoulders. 'And I can't claim to enjoy wading through blood, but if there's one thing the last few nights have proven, it's that Margalita and Geroald weren't my fault.' He swallowed. Carefully, eyes lowered, he said, 'No matter what some people might like to imply, if they could have been saved, I would have saved them.'

Feilan would have liked to jump on this admission to make Remy renounce his uncle entirely, but he wasn't a *complete* jolterhead, and wrapped his arms around him instead. He heard him catch his breath.

'It's quite healing, actually, to know that,' Remy said, notwithstanding that he sounded like he was trying not to cry. He pulled free, wiping at his eyes. 'I'll fetch some clean clothes for Torben.'

Noura was sitting at the mouth of the cave, looking out at the shadowy view in the indistinct gloam before dawn. Feilan thanked her, too, and was glad to receive only one of her brusque shrugs rather than a sudden emotional intimacy he wasn't entirely capable of appreciating. She wanted her pair of tattoos and keeping Torben alive was key, regardless of any feelings around violent bloody death she might have accumulated.

Torben was asleep on his back in the nest of blankets. He didn't look like he'd moved at all, and Feilan felt a chill, a hobgoblin cavorting among the dry bones of his gravemound. He shook it off. He had lagged behind events badly last night; he couldn't let himself fall victim to his shock and fear again today.

The exhausted Micah had collapsed on a scrap of blanket next to Torben, curled like a cat into Torben's uninjured side. Feilan nudged Micah's shoulder with one foot and then leapt backwards. You never knew, not with warriors, and not with assassins, or whatever Micah was. The lithe eunuch came up fast, but not aggressively, though he did distinctly relax when he saw it was just Feilan.

'Dawn's coming.' Feilan stepped past him, and pressed the toe of his boot into Torben's ribs, announcing himself with steady pressure instead of a kick. 'Wake up, Thunder Bear.'

Torben didn't stir for just long enough that Feilan had to push away that chill again, but then his bright blue eyes blinked open. He stared up at Feilan.

'Did I tell you where my hoards are buried?' he asked eventually, voice rasping.

'No, and you're not going to.'

'Berguthi's balls, I'm not going to,' Torben agreed. 'Those are *mine*.'

Feilan made the sudden weakness in his knees look like a deliberate choice to kneel. He bent to kiss Torben's forehead, and clasped his hand, palm to palm, thumb to thumb. He knew the message this would send Remy, and the others, and for the moment he didn't care – Torben believed he'd missed finding his death, and that was tantamount to making it true.

Torben made a grizzle of complaint, but didn't untangle himself. He used his free hand to push blankets aside, and eyed off the bandaging. His chest, his whole body, was roped with old scars: this injury, too, would become merely another scrawled line in the liturgy of the luck and skill of survival.

'Do I want to look?' he asked.

'Nope,' Feilan said, finally letting go. 'You were never very handsome, and this hasn't improved things.'

It was standard warrior cant; Torben snorted. 'Who did this? Skinny Shanks and Foxy, I suppose?'

'You could thank them.'

While Torben frowned in blank confusion, Remy approached and handed Feilan a clay cup. It was the drink he'd been giving him in the mornings, but Feilan could see extra colours in it, cool shades of blue and green whirling within the bright zings of lemon-yellow. He looked up at Remy questioningly.

'This will get him moving,' Remy said. 'But it's dangerous. Energy and pain relief, when he should be lying still. He needs to go straight to bed once he's performed for my uncle.'

Torben accepted the drink from Feilan's hand, and let Feilan and Micah slowly lever him into a sitting position, Micah resting one hand on the bandaging as if he could sense the state of the stitches at the movement. Torben was enough in command of himself to not audibly groan, but he did breathe out in a gust.

'What's going on?' he demanded as he alternated between sips and grimacing at the taste of the sips like a bratty child.

'We have to get you on your feet,' Feilan told him. 'You and Micah are due to walk in off the hunting ground under the eye of Uncle Bertrand, or be disqualified.'

'We are all going to carefully help him rise so he does not pull his stitches,' Micah told them.

With Remy and Feilan on one side, and Noura and Micah on the other, they worked together to set Torben on his feet. He stood swaying. Grumbling deep in his chest, he tried to walk, and both Feilan and Micah had to catch him, taking his weight against a shoulder each. Noura and Remy worked around them to get a replacement shirt on him, unbloodied and unrent. Noura had rubbed it in the dirt first to make it plausibly stained.

'We have to get him all the way across the hunting ground,' Feilan said, tired by the very thought, and very much doubting Torben's ability to walk up the last slope to the spectator's field by himself.

Torben waved him off. 'I'm fine.'

He shrugged off their support, and strolled towards the cave mouth. Feilan looked at that, and then looked at Remy. Between the salve that had healed Remy's cut almost overnight and dramatically accelerated the healing of Noura's – and now Torben's? – wounds, and the salve that had taken away the damage to his own face and apparently Remy's back almost as effectively, he began to suspect that Remy's consistent denial of witchcraft was the one lie his husband was telling.

'He's not magically healed,' Remy said to that look. 'I did warn you. It won't last, and he's doing himself more damage while it does.'

'I will contain him.' Micah hurried after Torben. Feilan heard him say, 'Do you understand the plan? We walk in off the field as if we spent the night as lovers. You have my permission to be smug.'

Torben grunted in acknowledgement, then added something that Feilan couldn't quite hear but did not have to. This was followed by another grunt, this one of well-deserved pain.

In a bid to keep their usual routine so as not to rouse the attention of their spies, Feilan had to stay with Remy in the witch-cave as visitors began to arrive for the daily consultations. Noura would meet Torben as Micah walked him back to his room.

Remy gave her a flask of some liquid he said would counteract both the energising drink and the blood loss. 'You'll probably have to make him drink it.'

Noura gave one of her unflappable shrugs and marched away.

Hours later, Feilan knocked on Torben's door. Micah answered, bodily blocking the ajar space. When he saw it was Feilan, he allowed the door to open a little more, lounging against the door frame. He looked tired, but he'd washed and discarded his bloodied clothing.

He was now shirtless, and wearing thin gold chains dangling from both nipples and looped about his shapely biceps. His navel was pierced with gold, too. The effect of the gold against his dark, smooth skin was striking. Gauzy trousers hung low on his hips, the fine weave clinging to the muscles of his thighs and calves.

'Ah...'

'If you are done with your ogling,' Micah said icily, 'I will report he is safely abed and sleeping well.'

Feilan managed to tear his gaze away and peek past. Torben was out cold on his back atop the linens, swathed in fresh bandaging that told Feilan he'd probably bled after his exertions. But his colour was good, the movement of his chest steady.

He wanted to touch him, to feel his breathing, to check for fever. 'I can watch over him for a time.'

'You understand the ploy you have committed us both to? Your friend cannot be confined to bed due to severe injury. He is instead merely closeted with his new lover, who is *enthralling*.'

Micah waved at himself, his bare chest, the sheer and clinging trousers, the gold links decorating his lickable skin. Feilan followed the motion, and couldn't disagree.

'So enthralling he won't let him out of his bed. His new lover is also very jealous, and is as a guard dog at the door to the lovers' chamber to chase off rivals. I shall have to keep up your ridiculous pretence until we put about a better story to explain his further confinement.'

His tone was delicately aggrieved. Feilan opened his mouth to point out that *Micah* had come up with this particular ploy, not him. He watched the eunuch tug a blanket over Torben's sleeping form, and suddenly realised how slow he was being.

Micah had risked getting himself disqualified for the sake of saving a member of an alliance he hadn't yet agreed to join. That had to mean he'd known, the moment he'd seen the monster, he'd never take it alone. All Feilan had to do now was come through on the plan to save Afzal. That was simultaneously reassuring and concerning.

He said, 'Thank you.'

'I suggest you thank your husband,' Micah said. 'This man should be dying, if not dead, and we all know it.'

Feilan nodded blindly, guiltily. He'd thanked Remy by throwing him into the wall.

He heard a step down the hallway, and turned to see Adeline, fidgeting with a fold of her kirtle, expression sombre. She was early, if here for the usual afternoon visit with her uncle. Micah shook his head warningly and closed the door.

'Heilsa, Lina,' Feilan said. 'Remy's still out on his village rounds.'

'I'm here to see Torben,' she said. 'He didn't come to First Hill today. And...' She hesitated. 'He came in very late? Is he...'

Feilan debated with himself. Adeline plainly suspected something had happened the night before, beyond the scraps she'd been allowed to know. It didn't mean Bertrand or Darya would be equally suspicious, since they'd been fed the story about Micah's irresistible charms, and half-naked Micah had likely answered several knocks before Feilan's own, to keep the tale hot for retelling. That didn't mean they *wouldn't* be suspicious, and it'd be easier if Adeline was not in a position to give anything away.

Worse, telling the truth would risk the idealistic, upright queen deciding she would not be a party to cheating, even if it cost her an independent throne.

But Remy didn't lie to his niece. Feilan would have to risk the truth.

He walked with Adeline to the foyer and waited until she'd thanked and dismissed the attendant laying out trays of seedcakes and herbal tea. Once they were alone in the very centre of the open space, he quietly said, 'He's hurt. He's alive, but he's hurt. Best not to tell anyone.'

Adeline was silent. She took a long sip of her tea. Her cup was one of the heavy-bottomed pottery mugs common locally, thickly cast and naturally glazed by salts and minerals when the clay was kiln-fired. The Nivardus royal line hadn't yet succumbed to the passion for the delicate, beautiful, expensive Ystheran ceramics.

'He did walk in unaided,' he added, overlooking the fact that his entire alliance had secretly departed the arena to make that happen, indisputably violating the rules.

'I felt sorry for the monster,' Adeline said. 'It was killing our sheep, so my father and Uncle Hugo set out to hunt it, and I felt sorry for it, because it's not its fault it needs to eat. And it killed him, and that was never worth the sheep we might have saved.'

Before Feilan could muster a response, she set her cup down with a firm click. 'And it's hurt Torben. And it's killed most of the other champions. And I am so angry at it.' Her dark eyes grew wet. 'I hate it, and I hate this contest, and those men are dying on my behalf, they're dying *for me,* and is that worth the crown?'

Feilan said, 'They're dying for *coin,* the same way mercenaries have died for hundreds of years.'

What else were battle-bold men good for, except battle? But the blunt correction did not seem to assuage Adeline's guilt. She wiped at her eyes, mouth downturned, and picked at a crack in the glaze of her mug, avoiding his gaze.

Feilan started to pick up his own cup of tea, before sitting back abruptly. 'Adeline, *you* didn't set this contest. This contest didn't have to happen at all. If Bertrand hadn't—'

'The monster needs dealing with,' she said, head lowered. 'It'll just keep coming back, otherwise. We have more people living in its way these days, we can't allow relics of a savage age to range freely in these modern times. It's our responsibility.'

Her tone was one of dismal recitation: those were Great-Uncle Bertrand's words, and of course, they were true words, because the family patriarch was so very good at slithering his manipulations in under the shelter of truth. Something *did* have to be done. All those stories Feilan had collected about the monster from the townsfolk, and especially the villagers, hadn't just given him clues as to its habits and territory. Couched in the usual folktale rubrics of just deserts, the stories told of men and women being cut down, children being taken, when they went out at night against injunction. That huge beast was a predator to its core and it did not differentiate animal flesh from human flesh. The River-lands allies had probably agreed with alacrity to Bertrand's suggestion, because they'd also be subject to the inevitable juxtaposition of over-spilling populations and a timeworn hunting ground. The human hold on the resource-rich river valleys could no longer be paid for by irregular sacrifice to an ancient, solitary creature of talons and teeth.

It galled him to agree with a single thing Bertrand said.

'It *is* your responsibility,' he admitted, eventually. 'Every ruler sends men to die for them, Adeline. Every good ruler weighs the cost of their crown. If the weight is too heavy for you, withdraw Torben and let your regent, and then the husband he gives you, take the burden from you.'

Adeline lifted her chin, face set in stern lines. He hadn't meant to be harsh, but he was comforted to see that his blunt words had provoked Remy's stubborn streak to rear up in his niece. 'No. It's my responsibility, Uncle Faro. I was raised to serve my people as best I could. That doesn't mean being a squeamish baby about what must be done.'

She wrinkled her nose, suddenly more child than queen again; there was nothing, Feilan supposed, more annoying to a child than being thought a slightly younger child.

'Right,' he said. 'For what it's worth, you're not wrong to regret deaths in your name. You're not even wrong to feel sorry for the monster. Compassion is an undervalued part of making hard decisions.' Even he, who had to fight ingrained Vaer conditioning to accept that kindness wasn't weakness, knew that. 'It just can't be the *only* part.'

Adeline smiled and patted his hand. He might have said more, might have tried again to gently point out some of Bertrand's games, but just then young Prince Afzal came in, carried in the arms of the large, blank-eyed man Feilan had seen with him before. Afzal, with or without his carrier's help, had worked out a position which meant he was carried upright upon the man's thick forearms, rather than cradled like a baby, but he still looked much happier once settled into a chair by Adeline, carefully pulling a woven blanket over his spindly legs.

She brightened considerably, greeting him with genuine fondness and offering him tea, cake and cushions in quick succession.

Feilan rose to leave. Afzal was, as usual, accompanied by Darya, and he instinctively wanted to avoid her, and her large guardsmen.

'Oh, stay, do,' Adeline said, catching his hand. 'Uncle Remy will be here soon.'

Uncle Remy was arriving now, in fact, with Rosmunda and Conrad on his heels, looking so shyly pleased to see him with Adeline that Feilan had no recourse but to acquiesce.

23

Feilan had assumed he would travel back to Siftar while the moon waxed, to put his fingers back into his network and to make sure his plan for the freedom tattoos was proceeding. Perhaps he'd bring Remy with him too, to give the man some distance from his family and maintain their fiction of a marriage.

The other champions, however, were not leaving and, further, were treating Seven Hills as a paid sojourn. Though only Torben had been the recipient of the monster's attentions, a couple more mercenaries hadn't made it through the final night due to pure human intervention. Bertrand's bloc was down to four, the proxies, conveniently, for Bertrand, Hughard, Lambert and Odila. The married-out siblings, the twins, extended their visit; their families returned home.

Feilan's careful observations told him the bloc had folded the last two surviving independent warriors into their alliance to bring their numbers back up – not with the approval of the contenders those two were contracted to, of course, but merely for their own greater chance of surviving with an extra handful of gold. Bertrand had more money for bribes now he'd lost half his champions and the fee they would have tried to claim next month.

Bertrand reiterated to Remy that champions were not actually even allowed to leave. This suggested to Feilan, quite strongly, that Bertrand was intercepting, and possibly even deciphering, letters from Siftar, but, barred from visiting, there was little he could do about it. Instead, he once again wrote in the beggar's script, including the beads they used to pass codes, and once again warning the messenger that if he did not receive back the correct bead to indicate safe arrival of his letter, the messenger would find out about it.

Torben spent days asleep. This was only partly the natural sleep of a very injured man; Remy passed daily flasks to Feilan, all of which had the same underlying herbal smell, always shades of green with various other colours as Remy mixed in different chopped herbs and oily pastes. Every time Torben stirred, Feilan or Micah or Noura would pour a cup of marrow broth and a cup of that day's medicine down his throat, and he would sleep again. After some debate with the others, Feilan let slip to one of Remy's attendants that Torben had fallen ill with fever following his chilly night cavorting with Micah in the mist. He and the others took it in turns to watch the hallway, to be sure no one would come knocking and get a glimpse of the heavy bandaging.

By the time the moon waxed to glare, Feilan had safely received a reassuring jade bead from Siftar, and Torben was waking more often, and beginning to complain. Micah once again camped in his room, undertaking to simultaneously keep him in bed and his hopeful lovers at bay and provide a plausibly scandalous reason why a man of Torben's constitution was not emerging to join the carousing of the other warriors. Darya, he said tersely, was pleased with his tactics.

Over the nights of the moon-glare, the Nivardus family attended their shrine. This was regular worship owed to their goddess and their ancestors, source of the opportunity Remy and Adeline had taken to slip away the previous month. Bertrand had the visiting temple priest cast some sort of divination, and he returned triumphant, Remy downcast, for the omens foretold the ascendance of the lion, which they both clearly thought referred only to the head of the family, notwithstanding the lion was the symbol for the entire Nivardus family.

Remy also went out to attend a different grave-marker, and nervously invited Feilan along. 'She taught me so much,' he said, kneeling by the long, low mound. 'She has no family to remember her.'

He must have feared the same, not very long ago. He anointed the grass, kept short by the grazing sheep, with a herbal concoction wafting the usual notes of blue and green, murmuring a prayer for the spirit of the last witch of Seven Hills. Feilan, touched Remy had wanted him here, took a bead from Freyja's bracelet and laid it by the small stone marker in silent thanks to a woman whose name only Remy now remembered.

But it was a sunny day, the weather warming now even here in the high downs, and mercifully free of the fleas and gnats which plagued Siftar's floodplain in summer. Feilan curled his arms about Remy and lay with him in the sunshine on the soft grass, and listened while he talked about her, his predecessor, his mentor and surrogate mother and only friend until Queen Margalita had come to Seven Hills. Unlike his thoughts of his mother and his sister-in-law, his memories of Achima had not been tainted by Bertrand's drip-feed of poison into his ear, so Remy was teary but smiling as he talked, and he kissed Feilan with deep gratitude before they walked back to Third Hill East.

As the moon began to relentlessly wane towards its gloam, Micah finally let Torben out of bed and allowed him to slowly work his underused muscles. They all worked on a strategy to fight a beast that stood twice Torben's height, that could leap at least three times his height, that was armoured enough that even Micah's precise blades hadn't pierced its shell properly, that bore claws and teeth longer and sharper than any sword, that was inhumanly fast.

Feilan joined Remy and Adeline every day at their afternoon visit, along with Afzal, always with Darya, and Rosmunda, usually with Conrad. As ever, he kept his hands busy and his presence nonthreatening with his nailbinders, alternating between dolls and striped stockings and doling them out indiscriminately. Adeline received both, to her delight. Afzal looked wistful, but Feilan meanly held out until Adeline requested them on his behalf, another little droplet to add to Darya's assumptions about her ward's friendship with the Seven Hills queen.

Rosmunda contrived to speak with him privately, one day when they'd lingered long enough to walk to First Hill for the nightmeal together. She tugged on his elbow and drew him back behind the rest.

'I wanted to thank you,' she said, displaying the same disconcerting sincerity as her younger brother, 'for what you're doing for Remy. I've never seen him so happy.'

Feilan acknowledged this with a grunt that had layers to it.

'Yes. It's obvious you think we have not done well by him.' Her smile was tight, but when her husband, Conrad, glanced back, she waved him off.

'And here I thought I was being subtle,' Feilan said.

She laughed, a low honeyed sound. 'Like Uncle Bertrand?'

'Ah.' Feilan relaxed the set of his shoulders, which made Conrad finally stop turning around to check on the well-being of the wife walking beside the barbarian. 'So you *have* noticed it.'

'I do now. But not before I went away. I was,' she added, 'thirteen when I was sent away into marriage.'

Feilan did a rough calculation. Rosmunda was enough years older than Remy that he could make an obvious surmise. 'You must have only just lost your mother. Your father, too.'

'Three months from funerals to wedding,' she said, the lightest undertone of bitterness coming through. 'My sisters, too, within the year, as soon as their greater matches were made.'

'That's one way to deal with the guardianship of seven grieving children, I suppose,' he murmured.

'I know you think we're all fools,' she said. 'But you must understand. Our father, the king... He fell to pieces when Mother did not come home. And we were all just children, even Geroald. We needed him, and he did not—' She cleared her throat, swallowing what must have felt like a chunk of bile. 'But Uncle Bertrand did not fail us. He was always there. He took care of us, and held the kingdom in perfect trust for his brother, and for Geroald soon after. He held us when we cried. He assured us girls marriage would keep us safe. He told us it wasn't anyone's fault.' She stopped in the middle of the arcade, hand on his forearm. 'Especially not our father's. Especially not Remy's. You see it, yes?'

'Yes,' he said, swallowing fury. Bertrand must have seen the golden chance to split the siblings into factions by sacrificing the little boy whose quiet defiant streak might even then have niggled at him.

He couldn't help but think that Adeline, also a grieving child with Bertrand ever supportive at her side, had managed to hold firm by Remy, when none of his siblings had. But Bertrand had been typically crafty: he'd separated the siblings, holding close the three eldest, the three who were perhaps the most compliant, making the young and defenceless Remy into their inconvenient redheaded burden.

Rosmunda began to walk again. 'Yes. And off I went into a marriage which, contrary to all the comforting words my uncle had for me as he sent me away, was *not* in name only until I was older. My body was not ready to carry the baby; she died and my womb was too torn to ever carry another.'

Feilan closed his eyes briefly. He said, 'I'm sorry.'

She shook her head, her mouth set in a stubborn line he recognised. 'No. This is merely to tell you I would have been amenable to any wild idea Remy had to keep Adeline from the control of a regent who sees no harm in child brides. And I entirely see why he did not deign to trust me.'

'Are you claiming he can trust you now?'

'I'll earn it, I hope. Because I didn't speak for him, when I first came home, after remarrying.' She smiled absently towards her husband's back, where he chatted cheerfully to, or at, Remy. 'At first, I was confused. We all adored Remy, you see. He was the baby of the family. We girls *doted* on him. Even the three boys treated him like our personal dolly. And then I came home, and... Well, you know.' She gestured vaguely. 'It's easier to see, when you've not been here for years. It's easier to see when your husband recognises it as strange. It's easier to see, when he doesn't dare do it when the Vaer barbarian is there, standing by Remy.'

Again she stopped, turning to him to deploy the same wide-eyed earnestness that felled him whenever Remy did it. 'So, no, I'm not trying to claim I've won Remy's trust back yet. But I am telling you I will stand by him, just like you.'

'Right,' Feilan said, and gave her a brisk nod of approval.

'Goodness, you are surprisingly reassuring.'

Feilan took a moment to be sure this wasn't sarcasm, and then said with a smile, 'Thanks, what every man longs to hear.'

'Excuse me!' Conrad swooped back down the arcade. He was a tall man, beardless, light brown hair combed back into a tight bun, dark blue eyes and mirthful, youthful grin – he was a good deal younger than both Feilan and Rosmunda. 'I'll beg you not to flirt with my wife.'

Since he was plainly teasing, Feilan smiled at him, too. 'She should be more worried about me flirting with *you*.'

'Excuse me, don't flirt with my husband,' Remy said to his sister and brother-in-law, and looked pleased in that shy way when he earned laughs from both of them. Feilan hooked his arm about him and they went into the nightmeal.

Amongst all this – through Torben's increasingly-querulous convalescence and his carefully-monitored release, and the other warriors' increasingly-expensive carousing, and Uncle Bertrand's machinations, and Adeline's and Afzal's developing friendship that looked like childish courtship to Darya, and Remy and Rosmunda's growing rapprochement, and Micah's pretence that he was working his wiles on Torben to his own advantage, and Feilan's pacing as he waited to hear from Siftar and came up with various bright ideas to save the prince and leash the uncle – Feilan and Remy discovered, together, the extent of Remy's preferences.

He knew how to say no, though Feilan didn't hear that much. It was working out what turned a simple yes into a frantic *yes, yes, yes* that exercised Feilan most over the month. He bent over Remy's willing form with the myriad techniques of tongue and lips, hands and fingers, waiting for the telltale signs, the hitch in the breath, the widening of the eyes, the cries he couldn't stifle.

When he finally realised the denominator of Remy's responses, he could have kicked himself for his complacency from years coasting along in Siftar. Remy liked the most commonplace of things: he wanted to feel greatly desired, but also utterly safe.

So he protested Feilan sinking to his knees in the cave with a villager halfway up the hill, but when Feilan pushed him to the dim alcove by the spring without a person in sight in any direction, he undid his ties and slid his cock into Feilan's mouth without any hesitation or coy demurral at all. Feilan would have enjoyed it more if the cat hadn't been twining around his legs as he worked Remy with tongue and throat, but Remy returned the favour the very next day, digging his fingers into Feilan's flanks as Feilan lavished him with praise for his rapidly improving technique.

Remy didn't want to be shoved against the wall – no surprises there, and Feilan didn't particularly want to cast that shadow again anyway – but he did respond meltingly to being pinned there, big hands locked around fine-boned wrists. He took being ordered to his knees with obedience but mild disdain, but took being begged for his mouth with quiet satisfaction, eyes dark.

And he took Feilan's cock too, bent over the bed or a bench with his fingers clenched tight against linen or wood, spine arched, voice ragged as he demanded more. He didn't much like having Feilan that way, though, preferring instead to be face to face when he played the active part, drinking in kisses and instruction and praise all in equal measure. Sometimes, he straddled Feilan and rode his cock with such great enthusiasm that a frustrated Torben thumped the wall between his bed and theirs and shouted, 'I'm frigging myself to this, you know!'

Remy blushed but he also glowed. He wasn't, after all, *much* of a voyeur. He didn't want to take advantage of sunrise at Torben's pavilion, nor take part in any public display along the arcade where they might be seen – but he was gratifyingly quick to let Feilan lay him on the small beach of the bathing pool and kiss and lick the salt from every last patch of skin while using his fingers to good effect, or prod him down the side of Third Hill East, any place out of sight yet where they might be overheard.

In fact, when Feilan pulled Remy's hand away as he tried to smother his own gasps and whimpers and growled, 'Let them all hear how your husband pleases you,' he spent with such a loud cry that Micah's voice floated out, dry and precise, to announce, 'I think near everyone was frigging themselves to that. And some of us are trying to *sleep.*'

In between, there was the kissing, enough to leave Remy's mouth swollen from the rub of Feilan's beard, enough to leave visible marks on his neck and collarbones, enough to leave him pleading to be taken back to their room even under the judgemental eyes of his family. Remy, it seemed, loved kissing even more than Feilan did, and Feilan would deny the man nothing.

Wanted, and safe: the two things Renart Nivardus probably had not felt since his mother did not come home from her ransoming.

Because he thought he was merely doing as Remy had asked, and showing his once-innocent husband the pleasures of fucking, it did not occur to Feilan that he was being cruel.

Not until one late night as the moon-gloam grew imminent, when Remy, lying sprawled and panting atop him after riding him hard and climaxing all over his chest at the barest slide of fingers, asked him to stay after the completion of the monster hunt.

'I can't stay,' Feilan said, puzzled. 'Freyja needs me in Siftar.'

'I see,' Remy said.

He rolled off Feilan, wincing a little as Feilan's spent cock slid out of him. Artlessly nude, he padded over to the aquamanile to wash. His hair was tangled; he never wore it other than loose and uncovered these days.

Feilan watched his slender back while he poured water from aquamanile to bowl, confused and slightly annoyed. Remy normally kissed him after sex, long, slow, luxurious kisses that left Feilan floating, just as lovely as the urgent, demanding kisses before sex and the needy, desperate kisses during sex.

But now Remy was keeping his back turned resolutely to the bed where Feilan had been surprised out of luxuriating in his post-sex haze. Feilan couldn't see his face at all.

Remy hadn't mentioned ever again that he thought he was in love.

Guilt struck Feilan, then, and a niggle of something he guessed was regret. He said, 'You could come to Siftar?' without even knowing if he was offering something permanent, or a mere visit.

Turning, Remy smiled at him, a little tremulous. 'Queen Adeline will need me here, whether we win or lose.'

'Ah.' He *did* know he was being cruel when he shrugged and said, 'Plenty of people about to fuck, Rufran, now you know what you're about.'

Remy proved himself braver than him when he answered. 'I only want you, Faro.'

Feilan held out his hand, and Remy came to his arms, ducking his face to bury it into Feilan's shoulder. 'It's less than a half-day ride away.' Feilan briefly pressed his lips against Remy's carnelian hair. 'Maybe quicker by the river-road. There'll be plenty of back and forth once we get the trade route open.'

Remy nodded against his shoulder. Feilan ran his hands up and down Remy's back. He'd quickly discovered that Remy was starved for touch: it fell upon him like the first rains on parched ground, sinking endlessly under his skin as if he could never be satisfied.

Sometimes Feilan wanted to set First Hill on fire.

Instead he stroked Remy's bare skin, the roughened pads of his fingers on the way down his spine, his neatly-tended nails on the way back up. Remy shivered, arching his spine for more. Feilan shifted and kissed down Remy's taut spine, rubbing with his beard. He took one of Remy's calves in both hands, and Remy groaned as Feilan's thumbs rubbed along the tight muscles there.

Having fondled his husband into pliancy, Feilan said, as gently as he could, 'Remember I was just a you'll-do, Remy. You needed someone for a specific job and I was the first suitable person you saw. You'll find other suitable people once I'm gone.'

He switched to the other calf, but Remy rolled over, twitching himself loose. 'Is that what you think? That I picked you because you were the first man I came across?'

'Yes? That's what you said.'

'No, I said— Oh. I said I chose you because I knew you wouldn't hurt me. That's not the same.'

'Remy, your thinking is clouded.' He ran his thumbs down Remy's calf to remind him why. 'You're misremembering how much you disliked me at first.'

'I was terrified in Siftar,' Remy said. 'I'd kidnapped the queen of Seven Hills, and run off from my family. I had to negotiate with the people who stole my mother. I was very alone. I did not behave well towards you.'

'You were obnoxiously rude,' Feilan agreed.

'And you were still kind to me.'

'Not kind,' Feilan murmured, but Remy was already going on.

'You went out of your way to help me and make sure I was safe. You have such a reassuring presence. And...' He sat up to touch Feilan's cheek.

'You don't think I would have come up with the idea of trapping you into a marriage contract if I wasn't having thoughts about you?' He turned the ring on his finger, making it gleam as it caught glimmers of the dim light falling through the window slits. 'I didn't choose you because you were the first person I thought safe enough to try to trick. I chose you because you were the *only* person I could imagine letting touch me. I chose you because I *chose* you.'

He looked at Feilan, who had gone very still. 'And *then* I decided to trick you into marrying me. Sorry.'

'Regretting your choice of husband again?'

'You know I'm not.'

Feilan let out a breath. He pressed his palms to Remy's skin again, fingers spread wide, and slid them up his thighs, his stomach, his chest, Remy giving way under the firm touch until Feilan was propped over him and could kiss him. Remy drank it in, parched earth soaking up the rain, body responding, curving into Feilan's.

'Sorry,' Remy breathed again. 'I know I'm needy. And not...not how you like it. I'm sure I've been quite dull for you this month.'

'Svasa, you've been perfect.' He kissed him again, tasting that willing mouth. 'Look, let's get this monster hunt over and done. Then we'll talk about all this again, good?'

'Yes, please,' Remy said.

The man deserved a reward for his courage, doughty as any warrior. Feilan lowered his head, brushing kisses over Remy's collarbone and into the hollow of his throat. A press of teeth on nipples that stiffened into nubs begging to be tugged at. Lips on shivering skin, following the curve of stomach and hipbone. Tongue teasing straining cock, swirling about its head with delicate licks.

Feilan took Remy in, moving his head in deliberately unhurried bobs, working his length with languid indolence the way he knew his husband liked it best. If he'd shown Remy the joys of fucking, he realised, then Remy had shown him the indulgence of lovemaking.

The startling thought made his grip on Remy's hips tighten. He almost resorted to merciless technique to force the climax out of him. Instead, he slowed his movements even further and loosened his hold, his own pleasure mounting inexorably as Remy dissolved under him, too lost in the leisurely decadence of Feilan's mouth to do more than loll in languid bliss. He spent, eventually, in relaxed undulations in perfect sympathy with Feilan's dawdling pace.

Feilan licked up the last of the seed, and crawled back up the bed. He cuddled up behind a sleepy, sated Remy, who twisted one arm back to pull him even closer.

He supposed he'd just made everything worse for his husband.

24

FEILAN HAD TO ADMIT TO BEING slightly worried when he still hadn't heard back from Freyja, the moon had waned to almost full gloam, and Noura's suspicious looks had become outright glaring. She didn't bother demanding to know where the freedom tattoos were, or threaten to cut his stones off or sabotage their alliance. She didn't have to. He was almost out of time.

He was sitting by Torben in the pavilion on their last free evening before the monster hunt would begin again. He had parchment on the bench beside him, his latest letter to Freyja inked with only a few runes of the beggar's script before he'd stopped to think.

He rolled the collection of beads he'd had back from Siftar between the fingers of one hand, ivory and jade and various agates, different every time to match the beads Feilan had sent so that the questionably-reliable messenger couldn't make substitutions. The beads confirmed Freyja had safely received his prior messages; she'd acknowledged his requests, and her lack of further reply implied she was working on them.

Torben was not quite at full strength, but he had made a truly miraculous recovery under the constant administration of Remy's herbal salves and potions. Micah had picked out his stitches a few days before, the same service he'd performed for Noura, his steady hands tick-ticking down the stitched silk with a sharp scalpel.

The warrior rucked up his shirt and touched the reddened seams of the brutal injury that had almost killed him, stroking his fingers along his newest scars almost reverentially. 'Gave a blood sacrifice to that thing, didn't I?'

'Its turn, tomorrow night.'

Torben said nothing for a moment, his attention fixed on his torso. Finally, he said, softly, 'Might not beat it, Little Wolf.'

'You will,' Feilan replied automatically, then bit his tongue. He'd never heard Torben express doubt: it was Vaer kneejerk to try to silence it. 'It was bigger than we expected,' he ventured.

'Faster. Nothing that big has any right to move that fast. And that armour...' Torben dropped his hand and straightened. 'I'll bring out my spear, it's got a bit more reach on it. You might have to take the head, though.'

He meant he might be so damaged in the killing of it that Feilan would have to be the one to ward Micah off and carry its decapitated head in to claim the prize. Feilan debated, then said, 'Thunder Bear, if you're done in by it, Adeline's done in.'

'I'd be cursed sorry about that,' Torben said. 'I like the kid.'

A scuff alerted Feilan to a presence behind them; he turned to see Remy hesitating at the entrance to the pavilion. He was wearing an odd expression. Feilan hoped he hadn't overheard them – his Vaer was good enough that he'd have been thoroughly discouraged.

'Getting dragged off to bed again, are we?' Torben said acerbically.

Micah had been sternly blocking Torben's potential partners from his room, on the grounds that it would be beyond foolish to ruin the effect of their tedious mutual sequestering when Darya was thoroughly convinced Micah had Torben's cock wrapped round his little finger – rather wince-inducing imagery – and was thus in more control of him than Feilan was.

The logic didn't make Torben any happier about being denied bedplay now he was strong enough to manage it, especially because Micah's usual attire – or at least the attire he chose to wear while pretending to a torrid affair – featured tight leather vests that not only showed off his muscular arms and shoulders and sleekly narrow waist, but which laced, not at front or the sides as was typical, but crisscross right up his long, lithe spine. Even Remy looked twice, and Torben was left, in what Feilan firmly believed was subtle vengeance well-earned and well-served, somewhat surly about it.

Remy said, 'Feilan, you have a visitor, and Uncle is trying very hard to turn her away.'

'Njorda's tits.' Feilan leapt up, snatching the fruitless letter to fold away into his belt-pouch. 'Stay here,' he ordered Torben. 'You're still resting.'

Torben, scowling, banged the stone bench with a loose fist, because he was constantly being told, by Feilan, by Micah, by Noura, that he wasn't allowed to do things, and there was only so long a Vaer warrior could take that. And truly, he had healed. Micah was merely being cautious, strangely fussy for such a cool-tempered man.

'Walk back to Third Hill,' Feilan amended. 'We'll meet you there.' He slipped back into Vaer. 'Thunder Bear—'

'Bugger off with the rallying cry, Little Wolf, it'll be fine.'

Feilan raised his palms in defeat and strode off with Remy.

'I sent Rosa for Adeline, too,' Remy told him as they hurried up the arcade. 'In case we need the queen's authority.'

'Do you know who it is?' Feilan said. 'Not Freyja.'

'Your tall friend, she stood sentry on the gate? You spilled ale on her.'

'Gytha,' Feilan said.

In the wide forecourt before First Hill, Gytha was facing a surprising number of the liveried Seven Hills guardsmen, a solid proportion of the sixteen usually on duty at any one time, their stone-faced captain, and even a few muscular stable hands who must have been called over for show.

Uncle Bertrand, a glowering Hughard at his shoulder, was explaining that strange lone Vaer were not welcome at Seven Hills, for reasons he was sure she would understand, and they would not be extending guest right. She was giving him her best blank look, but she lit up when she saw Feilan arrive.

'Brother!' she said.

'Little sister,' Feilan said immediately and, with a delight that was not at all feigned, opened his arms wide.

She obligingly came in for the fake brotherly hug. She topped him by a solid few inches; she wasn't much shorter than Torben. He had to reach up to demonstratively tug at one of her braids.

She muttered, 'You think you're hilarious.'

'Tell me you've brought what I need.'

'Yes,' she said, and grunted when he squeezed her even tighter. He hadn't quite let himself notice how worried he'd been growing. 'But I also have news I need to tell you privately.'

He nodded, and turned with a cheerful smile to Remy. 'You remember my sister from Siftar.'

Remy looked between the two of them and then said, 'Of course,' and suffered a boisterous hug from his husband's reputed younger sister.

'I must be mistaken, I thought you were Freyja Anjasdottir's only child.' Uncle Bertrand's doubt slithered behind his jolly smile, just present enough to make Hughard and the guard captain bristle further, perhaps without even understanding why.

'Only *son*,' Feilan said, while Gytha said, 'Half-sister.'

'Both,' Feilan said mildly. 'Remy?'

'I am very pleased to extend you guest right, Gytha,' Prince Renart of Seven Hills said, clasping Gytha's forearm and offering a formal bow over it.

Bertrand looked mildly distraught. 'Oh, dear! Why did you not say who she was before, Renart, instead of scurrying off to fetch your husband and leaving us to embarrass ourselves by being rude?'

'I knew he would be so happy to see a familiar face. I couldn't wait a single moment to delay his pleasure.'

Feilan looked happy.

'Careless,' Hughard adjudged. 'And as thoughtless as ever, to us and to your husband's guest.'

It had been some time since his family's scathing judgements had held power over Remy. He merely affected a polite expression of contrition, and otherwise ignored his uncle and brother.

Adeline arrived then, and professed herself delighted to meet Feilan's sister, which made Bertrand narrow his eyes – he was obviously wondering why she'd not had the honour of being introduced to her new uncle's sister back in Siftar. Feilan linked an arm with Gytha, and the other with Remy, and whisked them away.

At Third Hill East, Torben was waiting on his bed with the door open. He nodded to Gytha, who he knew only by sight, since she was of eastern Vaer fishing village stock. Feilan expected no trouble there; ironically enough, Vaer were much more understanding about women like Gytha, who owned their womanliness, than men like Feilan, who refused to.

Torben stood as if to follow them to Remy's room. He was moving well, Feilan noted, even after walking about for much of the day, and he'd stopped touching his side.

'In here,' he said, waving Torben back from his door and leading the others in. He hadn't forgotten he and Remy had been overheard talking about the goat in Remy's room.

He lowered the covers on the high narrow window slits, blocking the light, immediately increasing the stuffiness of the small room, but hopefully cutting off any eavesdroppers. He still wasn't convinced someone standing outside the wall could hear quiet conversations even with the slits uncovered.

Satisfied, he asked, 'Where's the tattooist?'

'Under guard in the town.'

Feilan raised his brows. 'A prisoner? He won't ink the freedom tattoos correctly if he's being forced.'

'*She* is well paid and willing. I left her with Eirikr and Helle, safely out of the way until I knew the lie of the land here.'

He was reminded, by the meaningful look she attached to her words, and the very fact that she had brought two more of Freyja's contracted guards with her, that she warned him she had private news. Without overt reaction, he turned to Torben and Remy.

'Go find Micah,' he told the former, 'and go together to the cave. Remy, you'll need to get the message to Noura that she's to bring Aminah as soon as she can slip her out from their master's claws.'

Torben turned to leave immediately, but Remy hesitated; it was plain he realised both errands were easily accomplished by one. But, at Feilan's reassuring smile, he nodded and left, firmly closing the door behind him so the latch caught properly.

Feilan got Gytha to scoot up the bed with him, so they were both resting their backs against the carved headboard, as far from both the slits and the door as possible. The servant-summoning rope with its gilt braid hung by Feilan's face, and he tucked it behind the headboard, quashing a memory of doing the same as Remy gripped the posts on their matching bed, spine taut, head thrown back.

Gytha handed him three beads.

Polished and carved iron: *trust the bearer*. He didn't have time to be surprised by the need for that code, because of the other two messages.

Amber set within lacy silver: *I am safe.*

Jet riven with a white flaw: *stay away.*

He looked up, brows raised high. 'What's going on?'

'Olvar has come to Siftar.'

Olvar Korisson. Torben's Snorri Snorrisson. The baby emperor with six towns already under his rule, and looking to expand.

'Takeover or alliance?' He braced for the answer.

Gytha rocked her hand back and forth, screwing up her freckled nose eloquently. 'He came in with his escort unarmed, just like anyone else, but he also has half an army camped in the field outside the overlander gate.'

'May fleas infest them,' Feilan swore.

'Apparently,' she said, 'there's an invasion threatening from the east.'

Feilan said, 'Not imminently,' quite grudgingly, because he saw Olvar's wisdom in preparing for its inevitable arrival, particularly after Noura's stubbornly offhand account. *Disciplined devil-creatures.* That made them the categorical opposite of Vaer bersverdar – except for rare instances like the men under Olvar's iron command. That didn't mean he had to like the thought of Siftar overrun.

'He wants the connections and resources – the silver – Freyja's trading network will give him, and her reputation and influence yoked to his, and he's no longer allowing an alliance to be optional.'

'There's a word for not taking a no.'

Gytha shook her head. 'She said to tell you she must have the River-lands trade opened. That connection tips the balance. She'll still... Well, he's too strong, Feilan, she'll still marry the man, but add that pebble to her stack of stones, and she holds the balance of power when they sign their marriage pact. If he is an emperor, she will be in truth his empress. But she *must* have word from you by the end of the moon-gloam that you have secured the Riverlands for her.'

Feilan held silent. He knew Freyja, and he knew the message in the words Gytha had faithfully relayed. If he did not know for rock-hard sure that he could win the monster hunt for Adeline, Freyja was telling him to ally to Bertrand instead. His gratitude for Vaer help should make access to the Riverlands beyond the Seven Hills bottleneck not only guaranteed, but only lightly tithed.

In fact, she likely expected him to change allegiances regardless of his chances of winning, given they'd both suspected from the very start that Bertrand would not truly give up his power over Adeline. Feilan *knew* he wouldn't, actually, now he'd seen how habituated Bertrand was to manipulating the person on the throne.

For Freyja to break a golden promise, to go back on her almost-wistful desire to support the little queen: she was in the tightest of corners back in Siftar. If she must surrender her position as merchant queen, she at least wanted to do it for no less of a trade than an imperial crown.

He looked again at the beads he was rolling about his palm: *I am safe but do not come home.* He clenched his fist closed.

Gytha took a folded packet of parchment from her leather pouch, and handed it over. 'She said you can use this to force his hand.'

Feilan unfolded it. Coming straight from Gytha's hand – *trust the bearer* – it wasn't ciphered. Freyja had done as he had asked, and found one of the crewmen involved in Queen Leonore's kidnapping all those years ago. People vanished and died and got lost. His offsiders must have worked the network to its limits to find the last man alive who had seen the queen step from his clinker to Bertrand's riverboat at the rendezvous.

Feilan had been right. The Vaer traders had accepted the ransom, and safely returned the queen untouched and well-fed. It was on the riverboat back to Seven Hill's port that the treachery had occurred.

The second lot of parchment enclosed within the first was so convenient as to seem falsified, if Feilan hadn't trusted Freyja and the width and breadth of his own information network and the ability of his people to thrum its web and bring forth its little spiders. The testimony was in a monk's hand, the ink faded, but clearly signed and stamped by the abbot of a southern monastery.

Years before, the abbot's clerk had recorded the rambling words of a child who'd been crew on that little riverboat. He'd only been eight or so, only a little older than young Prince Renart. He had seen a play of events he did not understand, but was only too glad to spill out to the man who had given him refuge, half frightened confession, half traumatised narration.

He had seen the man in charge of the expedition approach the woman with the kind eyes and the rich red cloak, in the aft of the riverboat, away from all eyes, except his, because he had crawled behind the water barrels to retrieve a fallen hook, and the man and the woman didn't know he was there.

The man had spoken in a low voice, hand around the woman's elbow. She had tried to pull away. His grip had tightened. His voice had risen. He had said, *Why so much pride? They all had you. What's one more?*

He put his other hand to her waist, tugging. She slapped him and said, *The barbarians had more honour than you. I will tell your brother you did this.* His eyes turned cold and flat like the stare of a dead fish and he put his hands around her throat to stop her threats. She struggled and fought and clawed, to no avail.

It had ended with Bertrand's face bruised and scratched and his brother's wife's body tipped overboard, sinking into the deepest waters with weighty chains about her ankles and barely a splash to mark her passing. It had ended with a riverboat burning, and a small family crew brutally set upon by mercenary guards, and a young boy leaping overboard, almost drowning, and fleeing to foreign sanctuary before more soldiers could come searching for him.

Feilan read the sickening contents, understanding that Freyja intended for him to use this, not to obtain years-late justice for a murdered queen, a murdered crew, an orphaned boy, and orphaned royal siblings, but to cosy up with two-faced, scheming Uncle Bertrand, make him grateful for not just Vaer help but Vaer silence, and force him into the supplicant position for a serthing trade deal.

He snarled an obscenity – rassragi serthi *serth* – roughly translatable as 'Arsefucked double-buggering *fuck*,' and thumped the back of his head into the wall.

Gytha was wisely silent, though she did lay her upturned palm on her knee. He absently took her hand, deep in thought.

Finally, he bowed his head.

When he'd first written to Freyja, he hadn't known any better: he'd thought uncovering evidence about the suspicious loss of Leonore would be enough to dislodge Bertrand. He had had no idea how deep he'd worked his slimy tentacles into the minds of the Nivardus siblings. These incriminating but circumstantial and too-convenient letters would never be enough to pry him loose, this persuasive man used to submission from the rest of the family, used to holding the reins and having everything his own way, used to being listened to and trusted and believed.

Freyja was correct to assume Feilan would have to use them for blackmail, not justice.

Even then, they'd only go so far in corralling him. Bertrand wouldn't want to entertain a new, forced, alliance when he knew his bloc had a better than even chance of winning in its own right. He might deign to make a trade deal once he was regent, but not on terms favourable to the barbarians who'd made locking down his regency more difficult than it had to be.

But if Feilan's alliance won, he'd have the carrot of Remy's regency – he'd have to make himself, not Torben, the winner to earn that juicy carrot – as well as the stick of this blackmail to obtain the best possible trade conditions for Freyja. Each piece might not work on its own: together, they were *golden*.

And so, Feilan's best ploy was to continue along the same path he was already on, with an added little twist to the plan.

He supposed he should take the two letters to the uncle and make the bargain that his win tomorrow night would seal. For now, he went next door and folded the thick packet of parchment into the false bottom of his trunk, where Vaer like him would normally hide gemstones and hacksilver.

The others would gather in the cave soon. He would deal with that first.

25

Evenings lingered now, the lengthening light falling mellow across the hills and burnishing the pink-stoned arches of the arcade, though Feilan noted that the mist had risen as usual in the hollows and dips lower down. It was thinner than it had been at the last new moon, but it should still be enough.

Gytha had taken the back path, running along past the skeps, quiet now in the dimming, cooling air, until she was the barest blot in the distance before curving out of sight towards the town. She'd gone to fetch up the tattooist.

Feilan sat in the last of the sunshine at the edge of the little flat area before the cave's overhang, where he'd once broken fast with Adeline and Remy. He stared out at the golden view, musing. He turned the letter he'd started writing to Freyja over and over in his hands. The few runes he'd written earlier were moot now. He needed to start it over.

He soon found instead that he was playing with the ring, his own ring, that he had gifted to himself, on Remy's behalf, and worn all this time, on Remy's behalf. He held it up so the dull metal caught a last glint from the westering sun, rays angling in from behind the overhang. It flashed gold back at him.

A warrior's honour was measured out in hacksilver, but a trader's reputation was worth solid gold. Freyja was bartering it away for an empress's diadem, and the fact that Olvar had left her no choice did not take the bitter taste from her son's mouth.

He heard overhead the telltale footsteps – one set loud and unfaltering, accompanied by the whisper of the second – and Torben and Micah came down the narrow path off the arcade. He tucked the abortive letter away. He hadn't thought of any words yet.

'You didn't come for the nightmeal,' Torben pointlessly informed him. 'Told 'em you were too busy talking to your sister.'

He handed over a mug of the small ale they drank here, and a hunk of dark bread. Feilan picked at it until Noura arrived, Aminah looking shy and heartbreakingly hopeful beside her.

'I told him it was women's troubles, that always makes that weak turd turn a funny colour.' Noura looked about. 'Where's our freedom marks?'

Feilan pointed down the hill. It was nothing but shadows now, but the shadows were moving, Gytha leading her little troop up towards them.

He'd been so looking forward to this, the fulfilled promise to Noura, the gift for Micah, laying out his clever plan to the admiration of his husband, though admittedly the quibbling of the others. Now it was all in the service of someone else's victory.

He hissed through his teeth. 'Where's Remy?'

He needed him here, because he had an important role to play tomorrow night, but he didn't want him here. The guilt would try to overwhelm him if he was subjected to his husband's trusting, loving gaze.

'Trapped talking to his uncle,' Torben said.

That meant being browbeaten. Feilan grimaced. He couldn't help him now.

The tattooist, it transpired, was of the advanced age which usually waited for Remy to come calling rather than climb the hill. Gytha and her two fellow Siftar sentries were working together to push her up the grassy slope in a wheeled chair. This proved too much long before they'd approached the overhang, so Torben and Noura went down the hill to help carry both old woman and chair over the uneven tufts and tussocks.

Entering into Remy's cave usually flashed blue and green across Feilan's vision when the mingled scents of his potions and salves and drying bundles of herbs first struck him. This evening, a pungent, acrid odour greeted him, along with a burst of strong but dull yellow the shade of mustard seeds. He shook his head to clear the reek from nose and eyes. Remy must have been mixing up something new this morning, before he'd ridden out on his usual rounds, some remedy powerful enough for its scent to have lingered in the still, cool air of the cave.

Since he still hadn't come, it was left to Micah to rummage through Remy's neat arrangements and fetch clean cloths and bowls of water to the main workbench. Feilan shifted lamps closer and lit them from their strikers, making sure the tattooist would have no complaints about visibility when she did her delicate, essential work.

Gytha's group arrived at the cave mouth. All three Siftar sentries were visibly red-faced, even though Torben and Noura had taken the burdens halfway up the last slope; Siftar was very flat. Torben cheerily slung the old woman from his back into the chair, a move that should have made her swear at him and instead made her give a shout of delight, and Noura pushed her over. Gytha put a satchel of equipment on the bench, and went to loiter with the other two sentries.

The tattooist was deeply wrinkled and almost bald under a southern cap, and probably the oldest woman Feilan could remember meeting, which gave him some concern until he watched her lay out her needles and ink and saw that her hands were as steady as Micah's.

Her age was their advantage. The few tattooists versed in the secrets of the freedom tattoos were generally not allowed to leave the job, just as the artisans on Ysthera were wedded to their own secretive work to keep those innovative techniques, or perhaps even magic, from common knowledge.

But this woman, introduced as Tyra-of-Tyr, must have been allowed to retire, because her advanced age, and probably her womanhood, meant her masters had assumed she was no longer capable of sharing the technique with forgers. They obviously had not expected her to turn to forgery herself.

'How long since you stopped work?' he asked, using Midlands.

'Eight years,' she said, her voice low and peaty. Then she grinned and made her hands quiver and her voice quaver. 'Too old for it, dearie. Barely in my right mind.'

Noura had already directed Aminah onto a low stool set before Tyra's chair, but she paused at that news. The designs of the freedom tattoos changed both by year and location. 'Then the freedom mark will be eight years out of date.'

Feilan, also aware of this, gave Gytha a sharp look in lieu of Freyja and his clerks who should have known better.

'And my stamp of authority will reflect that: you will have been free for eight years. In fact, you will wear the design of ten years ago, for that is when I was last in the north.'

'But the tattoos won't look ten years old,' Feilan said.

She glared. 'Scrog-for-brains, do I look like I was born yesterday?'

'You look like you were born five hundred years ago,' Torben said cheerfully, provoking her big, gummy smile again.

Noura slapped the workbench for their attention. 'My master will attest he did not free us ten years ago.'

'My sweet child,' the old woman said. 'You have been a slave too long. He will not be your master, and he can say as he likes, and you will have an unforgeable freedom mark and the matching unforgeable stamp which both aver you were freed ten years ago in Aldhelm. And if someone bothers to check that, they will discover that the tattooist providing said marks and stamps was indeed in Aldhelm ten years ago, freeing an entire clutch of slaves who helped take the town for Olvar the Bold.'

The name made Feilan flinch. He glanced over at the cave entrance. It was dusk out there now, a soft settling into the long summer evening. Remy should have finished up the interminable family supper, and come.

Tyra's peaty voice went on. 'It will be indisputable. You may, in fact, threaten to turn a case on him for attempting to enslave two freewomen with impeccable papers, yes? And I might further suggest that you do not in fact have to stay about and wait for him to make his protests. *You will be free.* You may walk down the hill with me and my escort this very night, and never look back.'

Feilan held up a finger, opening his mouth. He closed it again.

'Aminah will do that,' Noura said. 'I will wait.'

Torben cast Feilan a look which was probably meant to be subtle, to Micah's quiet amusement. Feilan shook his head to the silent, surprisingly canny, suggestion. He wanted Noura's willing assistance tomorrow night. That meant he had to risk letting her receive her prize tonight.

Noura snorted at their silent interchange. She leaned on the workbench by her daughter. 'Hold my hand, sweetheart,' she said. 'Squeeze when it hurts, but do not move.'

Tyra shifted the lamps about, and began to stir pinches and spoons of this and that powder from her pouch into her inkpots. Feilan eyed her procedure with some interest. It seemed the technique was in the ink, not the needle, for the set of silver implements looked normal. Tyra glared at him until he backed off. The secret would stay intact.

He joined Gytha and surveyed the evening. A low-wicked glow was cast overhead by the lamps of the arcade, a sparse trail once it passed Fourth Hill East, the furthermost arc of the Seven Hill guard patrol.

'Where's Remy?' he asked again, looking about the cave as if he thought his husband might be skulking in the dark alcove to the rear.

'Off in a snit because he's finally realised you fully intend to fuck him for a month and then sertha af back to Siftar without even a glance over your shoulder,' Torben suggested.

'Bugger off, Thunder Bear.' Feilan looked from the smirking Torben to the – it had to be said – rather judgemental faces of Noura and Micah, and switched back to Midlands. 'It's what he asked me to do. What? I told him I'd visit if he wanted.'

Now not only did his three regular companions look sceptical, but so did Tyra, and the three Siftar sentries, attention snared at the prospect of gossip. The only one who didn't was Aminah, and that was probably because she'd been told not to move her face while the needles danced by her eye.

Feilan waved a hand in lieu of words. He could hardly explain he was about to betray Remy and his husband wouldn't ever want to see him again.

'That man thinks the sun shines out of your veritable arse,' Torben told him.

'How veritably poetic of you.'

'Oh, Feilan,' Gytha said reproachfully. 'Learn to recognise when someone's in love with you, would you?'

'Remy's just infatu—' Feilan stopped. 'Ah. Gytha…'

'Not me, you jolterhead, Meik!'

Feilan, relieved, scoffed. 'I think you're being girly about a casual bedmates situation.'

'I think you're being a Vaer man about an emotional connection situation.'

'I'm not a Vaer man.'

'What's wrong with being a Vaer man?' Torben abruptly demanded.

As an effective distraction, Torben could have done worse. Feilan smiled and said, 'Since we don't have an entire moon-turn in which to answer that question—'

'No, I'm asking. What's so wrong about it?' Torben said. 'What's wrong with valuing strength, and having a code of honour, and wanting to protect your family?'

'Because you only value one kind of strength, defined so precisely that most Vaer men end up feeling weak and pretending otherwise, which is dangerous for *everyone*, and your code of honour is so rigid it ostracises everyone outside of a very narrow mould even as it traps you in there, and protecting your family – who you barely know – comes at the cost of other people's families?'

Torben seemed taken aback by how fast Feilan had trotted out his answer. He looked about and saw no disagreement on anyone else's face.

'Whatever. None of you are real men anyway. Rufran does a girl's job, you literally don't have the balls for it' – directed to Micah, of course – 'and you're...*you.*'

Abruptly very tired, Feilan said, 'Just call me rassragr, Tryggvi, you know you want to.'

Torben checked, grimaced, then turned his shoulder to nod to Noura. 'You do all right.'

'Not a compliment,' she said.

Feilan threw up his hands. 'Drop it, Torben. I'll tell you three the plan, and tell it to Remy later. We four go into the field as at last new moon. This time, we hunt the monster. It won't come till after full dark, but if it does, we merely drive it away from the uncle's bloc. As soon as the mist is thick enough to thoroughly disguise our movements, you, Micah, will circle to First Hill, slither your way past the holes in the guardsmen's patrols, and hide yourself within the warrior stables, which is empty since all the champions insisted on secure quarters. You will be underneath the spectators. Meanwhile, under Remy's instruction, Adeline will present a gift to Prince Afzal.'

Feilan pointed to the wicker chair Tyra sat in to perform her artistry, indicating in turn its large iron wheels, that could be propelled by hands, and its handles, that could be propelled by a willing helper.

'It's too big for him, I know,' he said. 'It's more the concept of it, than this particular form. The point is, Adeline will want to show it to Afzal straight away, so he will have to be brought down the stairs. And then Adeline will want to see him enjoy it, so they'll wheel off down the arcade, at great and heedless speed, as children delight in doing. And Lady Darya must allow it, because Remy and Rosa will be there too, to coo over this lovely, special friendship and the alliance it is inevitably leading to.'

'And you think she will assume I am out on the hunting ground,' Micah said, slowly. 'She will have seen me depart with her own eyes, after watching me supposedly manipulate this one—' He tipped his head at Torben. '—from new moon to new moon. She believes my entire plan revolves around using him to win, not this risky, reckless, foolishness.'

Feilan paused. He was now in a bind, were he to admit it to the others: the plan as it stood relied very much on Darya believing the alliance a sham, Micah working to his own ends, ultimately hers. Yet Feilan now also had to convince Uncle Bertrand the very same alliance was so solid that he was better off yielding to the carrot-and-stick of Freyja's offer rather than brazening it out and risking all on his own bloc and his family's blind faith.

He shook his head. 'Hear me out before you start badgering me. She may come down with Afzal, to see the gift with her own eyes. That makes it easier for you. She will certainly come down when her man tells her the children have been gone too long. She may or may not keep her bodyguards to hand, but Afzal's throat will *not* be to hand.'

And, since the additional part of the plan was that Remy would slip away to take custody of the children and hide them away safely – not in his cave or his room – it would have the benefit of keeping Adeline away from Bertrand in the fraught moment that he saw her champion carrying in the monster's head, granting her the blessing of their goddess for sole rule in her own right.

That had been the bright idea, anyway. Now, of course, Feilan would have sought Bertrand out before then, eyewitness testimonies in one hand, strong champions' alliance in the other, a golden offer on his perfidious lips. He couldn't keep the wince off his face.

'And so I step out of the warrior quarters and end her.'

'Yes,' Feilan said. 'However you like. And then you run back around past the cave and find us out on the field in the mist, because that thing is going to be serthing hard to kill and we have to get it done right then.'

'Not so hard that the three of you could not have already done it without me,' Micah pointed out.

'Or all three of us are already dead,' Noura called helpfully from by her daughter. 'And the other alliance has it.'

'And who is to say this wild plan with an obscene reliance on luck and impeccable timing is not *at all* for my benefit, but to remove the risk of me taking the head by simply removing me from the hunt?'

Feilan shrugged. 'Who's to say *you* are not *actually* manipulating my friend, and all of us, into thinking you're on our side when you do fully intend to hand that head to Darya?'

'He'd be coming through on our supposed passion if he really wanted to manipulate me,' Torben said, half a complaint.

'I'm going to leave the glaring fact that you just defended your faithful nurse lying there before us in all its obviousness,' Feilan said, not without a smile. 'There's other ways than sex to manipulate people.' Micah was looking both proud and put upon. 'Micah, you're either committing to this alliance or you're not. Now is the time to choose. Both ways are a risk. You know what you're up against if you go it alone, both us and the uncle's bloc. Do you really think your chance of winning alone, merely to keep Afzal in his prison, is higher than your chance of freeing him my way?'

'I know my abilities,' Micah said haughtily. 'I have never been the one who needed this alliance.'

'Finished,' Tyra called out. She brushed a gentle hand over Aminah's forehead. 'It will be red for a time. That's the only giveaway.'

They gathered to admire Aminah's new freedom. The unblinking eye of the slave tattoo had been rendered closed via abstract and ornate lines of a peculiar silver hue, reminiscent of old stretch marks or of the smell of lavender.

While Aminah and Noura exchanged places, Feilan looked longingly at Remy's jars and bottles, the glass aglint in the lamplight. He was positive one of the salves on those shelves would take the redness away without damaging new ink. He wished again Remy was there, and again was relieved he wasn't – and slightly puzzled.

He glanced towards the mouth of the cave. The nightmeal had to be long over.

Noura turned her face aside just as Tyra was about to press the first needle in. 'Wait,' she said. 'I can explain Aminah's absence with more of the women's troubles horseshit. But I can't do that with a freedom mark on my face. I should wait till after tomorrow night.'

Tyra tutted disapprovingly. 'I haven't been paid well enough to hang about at your convenience.'

Feilan suspected she'd been paid well enough to hang about anywhere she liked for the remainder of her days. Further, it was the perfect excuse to hold Noura obliged to him until he had what he needed from her.

He said, 'I have an idea about that. Get the tattoo.'

Noura held herself stiffly, staring at him. Then she nodded, and tilted her cheek back towards Tyra.

Feilan looked to the mouth of the cave again and found Aminah standing by his side, waiting for his attention, as if, disturbingly, he were her master.

It would take her a little time, he thought, to fully embrace her new condition.

'I want to thank you,' she said. 'This is very kind of you.'

'I'm not kind,' he said, 'just practical. It works better if we don't need to get Tyra back up here.'

She ignored him. 'Mama always told me she would find a way to free me. I don't think she ever once planned to free herself, too.'

'She might die tomorrow night,' Feilan said bluntly. 'That's the payment.'

Aminah nodded, unperturbed. 'We both know the cost. If she must die, she'd rather die free, knowing I'm free and safe, than any other outcome.' She started away, then turned back and said, quietly, 'She'll go after our former master.'

Feilan felt not a whit of surprise, and only one concern. 'Before or after the hunt?'

'After. If she lives through that, she'll see him dead before she joins me in the town.'

'You seem sure, but...'

'She could never kill him while she was his slave. You know what they do to slaves – the entire household of slaves – when a master is murdered. But now she's free. It's just one private citizen killing another.' Aminah looked up at him. 'He's the closest thing to a father I ever had.'

Feilan blinked. 'Are you asking me to save him?'

'No,' she said, and spat on the floor. 'I'm telling you why he deserves to die. And I'm telling you to help her get away after, or I'll cut your stones off.'

'Thanks, I appreciate a warning.' He gave a short bow. 'At your disposal.'

They exchanged smiles before he turned away. This time it was Micah who startled him by a sudden appearance at his side. He could only console himself that the assassin could have already killed him, if that had been the intention.

'I have chosen,' Micah said. He held out his hand, cool and steady, and they gripped forearms in the formal clasp. 'Although there is an outrageous amount of running involved in this plan.'

'Only for you,' Feilan said. 'You can't do it?'

'Do not presume to tell me what I am or am not capable of,' Micah said, though without his usual ice. 'I take it I do not have to warn you what I will do to you and your testicles should this go wrong.'

'Mother and daughter already have claim on mine,' Feilan said. 'You can have Torben's.'

'Hoi!' bellowed Torben, almost endangering the neat outline of Noura's tattoo. Then he grinned. 'They're all yours, Sveltlar.'

'What,' Micah enquired, ice now in full glacial flourish, 'would I want with your testicles, Vaer man?'

'Dunno,' Torben said. 'Suck on 'em?'

'Thunder Bear, *do not* bugger up my alliance!' Feilan hissed in village-Vaer.

'I am telling you, he *likes* it, Little Wolf.' He wiggled his fingers, and Micah sighed.

Before he walked away, though, Feilan had one more thing to say, flat and serious. 'Micah, you need to understand me on something. If you don't manage to kill Darya—'

'That can only happen if *your* plan fails.'

'—you still don't get to take the monster. If I see you try for it, I'll order Torben to kill you and he will not hesitate for a single heartbeat, no matter how enthralled you think you've got him.'

'The wolf cub has a bite, does he?' Micah purred, easing close, and closer, till Feilan was hard-pressed not to give ground. Into his ear, lithe body leaning against his, Micah purred, 'Perhaps I shall merely kill you first, then.'

'Right. Is this whole thing—' Feilan made a general wave of his hand over the silky invasion of proximity, carefully not letting his hand so much as brush Micah's shoulder. '—revenge for questioning the honour of your word?'

'Yes, you, as Noura would have it, *pillock,*' Micah said, smoothly pulling away. 'I said I am in, and I am in. I know my risks. You look to yours.'

Feilan sensibly refrained from pointing out that Micah remained one of the risks he was looking to.

By the time Tyra finished with Noura, the freedom tattoo's silver briefly gleaming bright like oil under the lamps before she added the final ink to age it, it was full dark. The moon, almost at gloam, was not due to rise until near dawn.

The old tattooist was clearly exhausted from squinting in the low light and keeping her hands rock-steady. With the chair left for Afzal, Eirikr and Helle would take it in turns to carry her back down the long curving path to the town.

Gytha took Aminah's arm with a confident nod to Noura. Aminah offered her a nod, too. Mother and daughter had not yet learned they were free to be as affectionate with each other as they liked, without it being turned into a weapon by the ugly-souled man who had owned them. Or perhaps they did not want to tempt the ever-jealous fates by celebrating until after tomorrow night.

Feilan made his way tiredly along the arcade, ignoring Torben and Micah jibing at each other and the quiet hum of Noura's purpose. She planned to go to her master in the morning, when he would have missed Aminah, to lay her daughter's alibi.

'But don't kill him then,' Feilan warned.

She'd loosened her plaited hair, and played with it as they walked, letting a coarse lock fall over the new tattoo. It wasn't enough to obscure it. 'About your idea?'

'Yes.' He sighed. 'Punch me.' He looked over his shoulder. 'You two do some shouting and swearing, too. Exchange a few blows. *Don't* hurt each other.'

He turned back to Noura, who raised her hands in bewilderment. He *had* just freed her daughter, he supposed. He poked her in the eye. She yelled and smacked him across the side of the head.

Hand clapped over her eye, she shouted, 'Why did you do that, you cracked pillock?'

He had his own hand against his ringing ear, but he used his other hand to touch the high point of his own cheekbone. 'So Micah can bandage it up, and not incidentally cover your cheek while he does it.'

'You— Oh. Might've warned me. Wouldn't have hit you so hard.'

'We needed it to look good.' He indicated over her shoulder, and she turned to see a servant trotting off up the arcade, no doubt running straight to First Hill. 'The uncle's going to think our alliance is falling apart.'

And that was when he knew he wasn't going to make a deal with Bertrand.

He turned to make sure Torben and Micah hadn't become too enthusiastic about their own fight, though they were so quiet that he wasn't overly concerned. Indeed, they were both standing stock still, facing him, the full paved width of the arcade between them. Torben had a surprised look on his face; Micah had his arms folded, looking icy.

'Did...did you have a bit of a wrestle to sell our falling-out?' Feilan asked, looking between the two. He hoped one had not accidentally hurt the other too badly. He was too tired for this.

'Yep,' Torben said.

'Shut up,' Micah said with a startling abandonment of eloquence, and stalked off ahead into Third Hill East.

'Get him to tend your eye,' Feilan told Noura. 'Doesn't have to be too dramatic. The fact that you're still willing to go into the hunting ground is going to allay your former master's suspicions considerably, if he'd even bestir himself to have any. I don't think he's going to demand to see a tattoo he knows can't be altered.'

'If he does, I'll kill him on the spot,' she said. 'But no, I don't either.' She went after Micah.

Feilan gave Torben a long look. 'I don't want to know,' he said at last. 'Just don't bugger up my alliance.'

He took himself off to bed. Remy was already there, curled up, pillow over his head, unmoving. He smelled faintly of the same pungent scent that had lingered about the cave. He might or might not have been asleep. He was either as exhausted as Feilan, or thinking hard about something.

Feilan felt an overwhelming urge to shake his shoulder and demand, at the very least, a cuddle, if not more. But then he might be compelled to spill out his reason for needing the physical comfort, his guilt for almost betraying Remy, his guilt for risking Freyja's future.

He let his husband be. They'd talk in the morning.

26

IT WAS INEVITABLE, FEILAN REFLECTED, THAT eventually Torben was going to talk Micah into a fuck – or that Micah was going to make a show of giving in to it for his own purposes – but they could have kept it to Torben's room instead of once again occupying the pavilion at the end of the arcade. He had some sympathy for his husband now he was the one having to walk past near sunrise, the gauzy curtains obscuring proceedings, but not nearly enough, and not dimming any of the sounds.

He should have gone straight on past to Remy's cave to finally uncover his early-rising husband, or turned and retraced his steps, but he was struck by the look on Micah's face.

They were both still mostly dressed, clothing pushed aside just enough. Micah had his arms wrapped around one of the pillars of the alcove as Torben took him with brutal strokes from behind, one hand tight on the narrow waist, the fingers of the other tangled into the laces crisscrossing Micah's lithe spine. Micah's sculptured chest was pressed into the smooth pillar before him, the side of his face against its side, whole body jolting with every thrust from the massive body behind him. His eyes were closed, and he wore the blissed-out expression that came with willingly receiving one of these mighty fucks from Torben, an expression Feilan knew he himself had worn on many an occasion.

Even as Feilan watched, amusement and jealousy equally mingled, Torben transferred his grip to wrap his big hands around the pillar above Micah's head, and used the leverage to sink himself even deeper. Micah, eyes still tight shut, swore at him shakily, and then reared, giving up an arm from around the pillar to hook it around Torben's neck. He wrestled Torben's head down as he himself tipped his own head back, and locked his mouth to Torben's.

Torben groaned. His body picked up the pounding pace. He kissed Micah back, messy, passionate, wild...and on the mouth.

Feilan, suddenly, abruptly, shockingly, furious, gave a Vaer exclamation, sakra sertha, that in polite translation meant, accurately enough, 'For buggery's sake!'

The two men broke apart, or their upper bodies did. Torben was still buried inside Micah, and looked merely puzzled to be interrupted, making no move to undock himself. Micah just looked impatient, as if he might start drumming his fingers on the pillar at any moment.

'You're kissing him,' Feilan said.

'We're fucking,' Torben said, still merely confused.

'*We* fucked! You never kissed me on the mouth. Never.'

'I don't kiss men.'

'Excuse me?' Micah jerked, twisting agilely, and Torben stumbled back.

Sighing extravagantly, he tucked himself away and did up his ties, mimicking Micah's own hasty return to dignity. 'You're practically a woman, so it's all right to kiss you,' he explained, with a remarkable lack of self-preservation even for him.

'I don't believe this,' Feilan seethed, while Micah very precisely enunciated, '*What* did you just say to me?'

'Come on, I can't manage two arguments at once!'

'I shall leave you to it, then,' Micah said frostily, and he stalked off, skirting past Feilan.

'Well done on ruining a perfectly spectacular fuck, Little Wolf,' Torben said, watching him go. 'He's got a spine like a snake.'

Feilan spread his palms at him in silent, yet steaming, indignation.

Torben had just enough self-awareness to look uncomfortable. 'You've got a beard. It'd be weird, kissing a man with a beard.' He tried on his most engaging smile. 'But, Berguthi's balls, did you and Remy make kissing a man without a beard look *fun*.'

'Thanks, lovely you had a chance to try it, then.'

'What do you want me to say?' Torben said, dropping the bonhomie. 'I can't go about things as blatantly as you can. I'm not a Cursed, and I don't want to be.'

'Fate worse than death, is it?' Feilan snapped.

'Yeah, it is. It's meant to be. You know that. But you've forgotten, because it all worked out for you.' He waved his hand in lazy punctuation. 'Well. Eventually, anyway.'

'That's right. Yes, that's right.' Feilan paced, trying to imbue his words with the staccato urgency of his footsteps. 'Getting cursed was the best thing that ever happened to me, *eventually*. It was finally out in the open. I didn't have to hide this huge part of myself anymore. Didn't have to face marrying a woman I could only end up disappointing, or shaming.' His ire, unanticipated, mounted yet higher. 'Didn't have to sneak around dirty storehouses so the so-called friend who led the other boys in tormenting me could get his cock sucked on the regular.'

Torben looked indignant. 'That's not fair, I was trying to protect you from worse.'

'You did a gods-awful job of it.'

'I did my best,' Torben said sulkily. 'What else was I supposed to do, let them beat you? At least I kept it to just words.'

'You know what else was just words?' *I was the one with Feilan last night.* Feilan winced and said instead, deepening his voice to mock Torben's tones, '"I'm the same as Feilan".'

'What?' Torben pulled a face. 'Don't be stupid, I'd never say that.'

'If more men told the truth, then everyone would know it's not some shameful thing for the weak-minded, the forsaken, the *wrong*. That it's not even unusual. That it's not something you do when women aren't around, *only if you take the man's part*' – that came out particularly viciously – 'but something you *want* and should be allowed to want. You can't tell me you don't look around the young bear-warriors back in the village and know exactly which ones are like us and need your help.'

'Like *you*.' It was very cold. Torben turned away, shoulders stiff. 'I'm not arsefucked. I'm *not* the same as you.'

'You *are*,' Feilan shouted. 'And if you admitted it, things might change. For every Cursed, man or woman, who escapes and makes a better, freer, life, there's those that die. Who don't survive the exile. Whose fathers beat them to death, whose mothers turn them out to freeze. Who kill themselves for the shame. Who live their whole life twisted up. You could help change that. For them and for yourself.'

Torben was shaking his head, such a short and continuous motion that it was more like a tremor engulfing his whole skull. 'You don't know what it's like.' He hit his chest. 'A warrior. A devotee of the bear-god. And *that*.'

'You want me to *pity* you?'

Torben reared up in reflexive anger. But then it faded, like the slow dropping of a shield at the end of a long and exhausting battle. 'I sometimes have to think about you.'

'You have to…' Feilan drew a blank. 'What?'

'With Ingunn. Other women, too. I have to think about you. To be able to, you know, perform.' He grimaced. 'Sometimes I have to roll Ingunn onto her stomach and have her from behind, so I can pretend I'm looking at *your* back.'

Feilan tried to mockingly point out the differences between himself and a big-hipped Vaer woman, and couldn't. 'Tryggvi, that's *awful*.'

'I know it's awful!' Torben said.

'I meant for her.'

'So did I.' He shifted his substantial weight. 'And for me. It's awful for me, too.'

That was outrageous. 'But it never had to be like that. You chose that life.'

'Chose it?'

'That you even have to ask. You jolterhead, you could have chosen different. You could have faced the cursing and exile back then.' He faltered before he could say, *with me*.

'No,' Torben said immediately. 'I'm a warrior. My life is for Berguthi. I would die if I was sundered from Him.'

'I didn't.'

'You're different.'

'Right,' Feilan said. 'Fine. You know what? Forget it. You're having your fun with Micah, and all the rest of them, and then you'll go back to the village and close it all off, and never know how much better your entire life could have been.'

Torben caught his arm. 'You act like it would have been as easy for me as it was for you.'

'You think it was *easy*?' Feilan yanked his arm away, tearing himself loose, and something inside himself, a canker that had been growing unheeded for twenty-five years, tore loose too. 'You coward! You complete and utter piece-of-shit *coward*.'

The warrior instantly bristled. 'You dare—'

'Do you know how many years it took me to shake off the shame our people crammed down my throat?' Feilan was snarling, unable to hold back the words even as the much bigger man loomed over him, tending towards wrath. 'How long before I could go to bed with a man and not hate myself for it? Do you not understand how much work I had to do, for you to stand there and tell me it was *easy*?'

Torben scoffed. 'You also just said it was the best thing that ev—'

'*You left me to die*,' Feilan howled, the accusation torn from the bottom of his soul. 'I loved you and you ran away and left me to face them alone and *you would have let me die for you*.'

Torben stopped as if frozen by the bitter wind of Feilan's unleashed rage.

To Feilan's further fury, tears started to his eyes. He wiped at them, almost striking his own face to dash them away. 'Oh, double-bugger it!'

'Little Wolf.'

Torben was trying to take him in his arms, and Feilan batted at him. 'Bugger off. You can bugger right off. I'm going to personally take the monster's head tonight and then Remy will be the queen's regent and I will make him make her banish the shit out of you, see if I don't.'

'No,' Torben was saying throughout, like a man stubbornly wading through mud that had reached his knees. 'No, no, no, I'm not having this.'

He finally managed to engulf Feilan, and dragged him into a tight hug. He dropped his head to Feilan's shoulder. 'It was the worst thing I ever did,' he said, raising his voice to be heard over Feilan's continued outrage. 'I've been ashamed of myself ever since. There wasn't a day I didn't think of you.'

'Shut up, shut up.' Feilan tried to escape the tight clasp, which only became tighter, endangering his ribs. 'It doesn't help.'

'I asked after you every summer, I was so happy to hear you and Freyja were doing well.'

'It's not helping,' Feilan repeated, though he was now failing to sustain his struggles.

'I'm so glad you had Freyja.' Torben's voice shook as he added, 'I'm so glad you got away from him.'

'I don't care.'

'I knew you'd settled at the Siftar post years and years ago. I couldn't bring myself to go to you.'

Feilan said nothing, because he was no longer so incensed that he could recklessly call his friend a coward again. Exhaustion was overwhelming him instead, washing through his body in a wave starting from his chest in the wake of the enormous release of bottled emotion. He sagged, and felt Torben take his weight.

'Then the commander was looking for a new staging camp and I said to do it near Freyja's trading post.'

'*You*— No, I refuse to care,' Feilan mumbled into his chest.

'That moment when I walked into the outpost seven summers ago and saw you again for the first time in... Berguthi's balls, how long?'

In a tiny, almost frightened voice, Feilan said, 'Near on eighteen summers, I think.'

'A lifetime, Little Wolf.'

His hold, impossibly, tightened. Low and sorrowful, still never lifting his head from where he'd hidden his face against Feilan's shoulder, Torben said, 'Gods, it was like the first sunrise after winter.'

'Oh, you ass,' Feilan said, somewhere between laughing and crying. 'You *donkey*.'

'I know. Believe me, I know.'

Torben finally raised his head and let Feilan go. They both stood, still too close, Torben looking like he might want to fold his arms across his chest or at least go stab something, Feilan shaky and oddly cold.

'I once longed to hear you say something like that.' Feilan took one last heaving breath, exhaling out the remnants of the maelstrom that had taken him. 'Now it just makes me want to punch you, you jolterhead.'

'I know.'

'Right,' Feilan said. 'Right, good.' He pressed the heels of his hands into his wet eyes and then made a shaking, shrugging off gesture, wiping away the last few moments. He couldn't deny he felt better – lighter – but this also wasn't the time. 'Forget all that hogshit. Let's just—'

'No.'

'No?'

'Since I might die tonight—'

'You're not dying tonight, jolterhead.'

Torben lifted his gaze, swore under his breath, and, touching his amulet, strode back into battle. Apparently it *was* the time, because, very gruffly, he said, 'I *would* die for you, Aleifr, you know that.'

'I do know it,' Feilan said softly, and because Torben had finally hoisted his courage like a flag, so did he. 'I just wish you could have brought yourself to live for me, Tryggvi. To be with me.'

'You'll never know how sorry I am that I can't. Or at least, that it's going to take me so long that I won't ask you to wait. Especially not now.'

'Probably about as sorry as I am,' Feilan said. '...Why especially not now?'

Torben made a raised-brow face that Feilan took a moment to recognise as a mimicry of himself, but before he could begin to feel insulted, Torben used one firm hand to lift his chin.

He kissed his mouth.

'I,' Feilan said, after he'd sunk deep into the sensation of Torben's mouth moving over his for the first time, feeling his heart pound and his body melt, 'can't believe I waited twenty-five years for that.'

'And?'

'And it was a terrible letdown.'

Torben roared with laughter. 'You only say that because you're in love with Foxy now. Can't say I understand it, can't say I like it, but you are.'

'Am I?' Feilan said, both eyebrows at his hairline, notwithstanding Torben had just made fun of him for exactly that expression.

'Yeah,' Torben said. 'You are.' He freed Feilan from his second, gentler, embrace. '*And* you're being a bigger arsehole than me about it, too.'

'I couldn't *possibly* be.'

'Little Wolf. I will literally burn down a town before I'll examine my own feelings and you're not any less of a Vaer man than me.'

Feilan said, 'I'm not...less of a... *What?*'

He felt he was justified in his bewilderment; being labelled as less of a man than real Vaer men was the *whole serthing point and punishment* of getting cursed.

'Oh, you can pretend you're so sophisticated with your travel and your languages and your ability to count and whatnot—'

'You can *count.*' Not beyond the silver reckoning, to be fair. 'You mean you can't read.'

Torben simultaneously flicked his ear and continued on as if he hadn't spoken. '—but the way you're stringing along a man who worships the ground you walk on...' He tutted and shook his head with dramatic disapproval. 'Do you not think you might be doing to him something cursed close to what I did to you?'

The point struck home, deep and true. He groaned, a sound more of sheer dismay than of dawning realisation, because he couldn't fool himself anymore that he hadn't realised it days ago. 'Oh, no.'

'So you better go do some grovelling, because he walked by while I was kissing you and I bet he's in a right pet now.'

Feilan gaped. He smacked Torben's solid chest, and then ruefully shook the sting out of his hand.

'All right,' Torben said, smirking. 'At least your husband only knows a few poisony ways to kill you. I have to go grovel to Micah and he knows one hundred and eleven.'

'I thought it was one hundred and seven.'

'He keeps adding more, Little Wolf.'

'Just for you.'

'Just for me. Nice and slow.'

'As you like,' Feilan said. 'But don't bugger up my alliance.'

Torben gave his lazy grin. 'I won't. And…we can be friends now, right? Foxy gets you, but I get to be your friend. That's what I was jealous about, you know. Mostly.'

Feilan made himself sound mockingly pained. 'I thought we already were friends.'

Torben struck his temple with the palm of one callused hand. 'I really am a jolterhead.'

'I've been saying,' Feilan said, 'for *some* time now.'

Torben grinned, and Feilan slouched onto one leg to smile back at him contentedly, with the distinct and happy sense of something falling into place.

He left Torben and went to Remy's cave.

27

Briskly sorting jars and rearranging pestles, Remy didn't look up when Feilan came in, but Feilan could tell from the way his shoulders stiffened that he knew he was there. The chair on wheels had been pushed to one side, out of the way of the workbenches, so Remy could stalk back and forth in fretful dudgeon, all the smooth grace and competence he usually exhibited in his domain left to rot by the wayside.

Feilan considered inflicting Torben's technique and simply walking over to forcibly hug him tight until all the venom squeezed out of him. It had worked before, after all. But given the jerky way he was moving and his refusal to even glance over, any Vaer presumption in this moment would more than likely spiral him even more into defensive anger.

He should probably leave him here, in the place where he felt safest, to work off his temper until he was ready to talk about seeing Feilan swallowed up in a passionate kiss from the man he'd described as the itch he couldn't help scratching.

Feilan weighed up that tactic.

Or he could probably explain himself *right serthing now*. 'It was—'

'The marriage isn't real,' Remy said.

'Which one?' Feilan was far gone enough to enquire. 'Oh, ours?'

'I got the words wrong. We used your byname instead of your real name. So it's not valid. It was never valid. You may go home.'

'I know,' Feilan said, waving it away. 'You made such a fuss about my byname, it was obvious you thought you'd botched it. No matter. We'll just do it again, if it bothers you. We do quite a nice handfast ceremony, actually, if you can stand a Vaer ritual.'

Remy turned around and stared at him, the same flat look he'd worn constantly in the first days of their marriage. 'I informed my uncle.

Guards are coming to remove you from Seven Hills.'

'Guards – what?' As if conjured, he heard the coordinated tramp of feet overhead, growing louder. 'This is precipitous. You need me for the monster hunt.'

Remy took off the gold ring he'd worn since the morning after their supposed wedding night. He set it on the bench. 'I need you for nothing.'

The utter contempt in voice and face forced Feilan to swallow a responding anger like a gulp of burning poison. 'I'm sorry I upset you,' he said. 'I will make amends as soon as you let me. But don't ruin Adeline's chances out of momentary ire.'

Remy turned his back. 'I am *protecting* her chances.'

The rejoinder made him frown but before he could query it, the Seven Hills guards marched into the cave. There were eight of them, half the on-duty guards. It would have been flattering, if he hadn't been busy battling his rising alarm and anger.

'Escort him out of Seven Hills,' Remy commanded, assuming the silken authority of the princeling he was. 'He may not delay to collect his belongings; they will be sent on. He may speak to no one, not Queen Adeline, not Lord Bertrand, not his friends. He must depart immediately.'

The guardsmen uncertainly moved to surround Feilan, unprofessionally pausing when he held up a palm to them as if he were their captain.

He said, 'Remy, svasa, this is not necessary. It was a *goodbye kiss*, that's all.' The volume of his voice had risen despite himself.

'Be careful,' Remy told the guards, taking an ostentatiously sidling step away with his hands raised and look of fear on his face that read to Feilan as pure mockery. 'He lashes out when he's angry.'

Feilan gave a short huff, narrowing his eyes at Remy, who said, flatly, 'Please don't let the barbarian hurt me.'

That finally tipped Feilan from the thin edge of his calm. 'Oh, sertha thu!' Remy smiled and Feilan discovered a Seven Hill curse on his tongue. 'Slough off and gout!'

In that moment of Feilan's flash of temper and Remy's satisfied acceptance of it, Torben appeared behind the soldiers and threw Feilan's sheathed sword to him over their heads, an assured and practised gesture. He was carrying his own longsword. He must have passed the guards as they marched along the arcade, and immediately gone to Third Hill East for the weapons.

Feilan caught the tossed blade with an equal confidence born from his bersverdr upbringing, no matter how reluctant it had been. The moment his hands closed around the tooled sheath, he felt the hypnotic pull of it: a bared blade in his hand, a countryman at his back, battle-rage in his soul: together, they could kill these guards, easily. A full rampage might even score them the entirety of Seven Hills, as spread out and under-prepared as it was. They could summon up the three Siftar sentries, to help load their pillage onto riverboats, to send on to Freyja.

This blood-and-flame desire passed through Feilan long enough for Torben to meet his eyes and silently ask the question.

But Feilan was past his initial shock now and understood what must have happened. Remy couldn't have summoned those guardsmen in response to seeing him kissing Torben: he'd gone straight on to his cave upon witnessing it. Even if the cave had the same bell-pulley system their room did – it didn't – they'd come too fast; unless they had already been alerted and assembled, it made the timing impossible.

And so. Bertrand had got to Remy last night during the family supper, when Feilan wasn't there to shield him. He'd played on the doubts that Feilan had been too honest to completely dismiss. He'd repeatedly warned him he couldn't guarantee the win. Remy had surely overheard Torben's brief waver, too, in the pavilion. It had perhaps struck him just as hard as it had Feilan, and what shitty, shitty timing for Torben to have a momentary glimpse of his own mortality!

Remy would have sat at that supper, wondering where his husband had gone, with Bertrand smiling and cooing and washing the sand out from beneath his feet.

His uncle must have made an offer he couldn't resist, some deal that would likely see them share the regency equally. That was why Remy had been in bed last night with his pillow over his head. He'd been thinking it over, deciding whether or not to betray his husband for the short-term benefit of his niece.

Then, this morning, before ever seeing the kiss, he'd gone to Bertrand with his decision, and here was the result. It would have only crystallised his decision if he'd heard talk of the falling-out among his allied champions last night.

The treachery was especially infuriating since Feilan had faced the same decision – his husband or the short-term benefit of his mother – and chosen his husband. He'd had to think about it, but he'd made the choice.

He had been as thoroughly betrayed as it was possible to be: no matter any incidental benefit to Freyja, he was here *solely* because of Remy, and Remy had turned on him.

Feilan lowered his sword, still sheathed.

'Right,' he said, and his note of sudden decision made Remy's gaze snap to his.

He smiled at his husband and strode out past the clustered guards.

They had to hurry in order to escort him, and not one dared stop Torben from cheerily pacing along beside him, saying, 'What's the plan, Little Wolf?'

That was plainly Remy's concern also. He called from behind, 'They may not speak. Torben, your contract is with Adeline. You are not to take instruction from this man.'

That little reminder must decidedly be because Remy knew Adeline would instruct her champion however her beloved uncle dictated: to win, to stand aside, to render assistance to the bloc, whatever his own uncle demanded of him.

Outrage crested in Feilan again: that conniving little *shit*, using Adeline's unwavering loyalty against her to take control of her alliance in such a cynical, underhanded way!

His brain chose that moment to haunt him with his own words: *It's not betraying her if it gets her more than she'd get when you lose outright.*

He turned to Torben and said, in rapid village-Vaer, 'Your contract is with *the bear-god*, you're contracted to *win*. Nothing changes that.'

'I know,' Torben said, bewildered.

'Stop talking to him!' Remy demanded, 'or I'll have the guardsmen—'

Feilan stopped dead. 'Ja, what?' Hands on hips, which made the sword he still carried stick out prominently, he surveyed the young uniformed soldiers until they quailed. 'I,' he said loudly, 'am helping my friend with his talisman for tonight's hunt.'

Torben had worn Feilan's talisman since Feilan had tied it about his wrist when he'd lain dying in the cave and the witch of Seven Hills had saved him. Shaking his head in suppressed outrage and hurt, Feilan caught Torben's thick wrist and raised it so they could both see the talisman.

He murmured, 'Listen carefully, Freyja did the beads wrong.'

'She did not!' Torben, scandalised, reached for his necklace amulet in superstitious dread.

'She did,' Feilan said.

He shifted his body to block the view of the Seven Hills watchers as far as he was able. 'You need to switch the position of these two beads.' He touched the last jasper bead and the single tiger-eye bead. 'Understand?'

Torben was silent as Feilan released his wrist and stepped back.

'Swap the beads,' Feilan repeated, 'before the hunt, or it won't work properly. Micah's quick. He'll help, if you tell him what I said to do. Stay here now, Thunder Bear, and don't provoke anything that loses you access to the hunt tonight. We are still going to win for Adeline, good?'

He said this last with a look at the hovering Remy. Remy said, 'Torben, you made your contract by swearing to the bear-god, you're beholden to Adeline and only Adeline. You work for her, not him.'

'I serthing know!' Torben said again, sounding even more bewildered, all the way to the edge of angry now. 'That's what I'm doing. That's what we've all been doing, this whole time.'

Ah. Just like Feilan, Remy must need the queen's alliance to win to make his deal with Bertrand more advantageous. It was galling to realise Remy planned to use Torben and the others to betray Adeline under the guise of helping her, and it only made it more insufferable that Feilan himself had briefly intended to do much the same thing.

Under that outrage, he was almost as bewildered as Torben. Perhaps Remy had finally seen the same thing Feilan had guessed from the start – Bertrand would never truly allow Adeline to rule in her own right, no matter the outcome of the contest or the watching eyes of the other Riverlands rulers.

If *Remy* were to win, a buffer between Bertrand and the queen... A different contender might have unnerved Bertrand, but not his cowed youngest nephew. That said nephew had been showing more and more of the spine he'd previously kept well-hidden would have just made Uncle Bertrand more determined to bring him back under the thumb. By that logic, both Nivardus men would want to negotiate while their respective positions were strong, but whatever Bertrand had offered Remy last night had probably had some stick to it, as well as carrot.

It was so exactly how Feilan had intended to tackle Bertrand that it burned like acid to know he'd got there first.

'Goodbye, Torben,' he said firmly. 'Go find Micah.'

Leaving Torben to his bemusement, and keeping his own emotions firmly leashed, Feilan set off again, letting the stoic guardsmen walk with him towards the First Hill forecourt and the road down to the town. He supposed he was meant to find his own way home, with whatever resources he happened to be carrying.

He touched his belt-pouch. He had no intention of departing for Siftar.

Bertrand was waiting in the forecourt, smirking. Remy made a noise under his breath. Did he think Feilan wouldn't have understood he was now working with his uncle? Adeline was there too, hands wringing together in a gesture of nerves Feilan hadn't seen since Siftar, and Rosmunda had her arm around her niece's sturdy and currently rigid shoulders.

They both looked alarmed, and very confused. Remy was indeed working behind the queen's back, then, and his sister's.

Remy went to stand by his uncle, a voluntary move that merely cemented his guilt. He even half-stepped in front of the older man when Feilan turned towards them, as if protecting him, shielding him from Feilan's anger.

'You may not speak to him,' Remy said, voice shaky, but all his stubborn defiance at the fore.

Feilan had intended to take the thick packet of parchments to Uncle Bertrand and make a different deal to the safer one Freyja had implicitly desired, a riskier arrangement requiring the patriarch to gracefully give way when Adeline's champion won tonight, in exchange for Feilan's silence – and his peaceable ongoing restraint. He didn't have that opportunity now.

But he did have an audience.

One hand still gripping the sheathed sword, the leather warm in his tight fist, he pulled parchment from his pouch and held it up with the other hand.

'Bertrand killed your mother,' he said, looking at Remy and at Rosmunda. 'She was safe, and he decided to have his way with her on the way home, and he killed her when she resisted. Might have been an accident. Suited him anyway.'

'What bitter, vicious lies!' Bertrand said, turning to his niece and nephew with an authentic look of grief and horror. 'Oh, my dear children, how can you stand to even *listen* to this?'

By all the fierce gods of the sacred heroes' halls, Feilan thought, staring at Bertrand with something very close to hatred, *Torben's method is such an easy solution*.

Cutting down Uncle Bertrand in bloody splendour would solve his immediate problem, and a few future problems as well. He'd never promised Remy any better. He didn't *owe* Remy any better, even if he had.

And it would confirm everything these people had ever thought about barbarians. It would traumatise the little girl, and her aunt and uncle as well. It would let the other siblings blame Remy for bringing a barbarian into their midst. It would irreparably destroy Remy's relationship with Rosmunda, and probably with his sweet and loyal niece as well. He would never again be held in affection by anyone.

Feilan loosened his grip on the sword, which only drew everyone's attention to it. The guardsmen shifted.

'Or maybe he always planned to murder her, to destroy your father,' he said, stepping away from them, closer to the clustered Nivardus family. They drew in towards each other. 'I don't have proof of that. I do have proof of the attempted assault and its outcome.'

And he held out the parchment to Remy, eyes steady on his husband's ashen face.

To his *immense* relief, Bertrand snatched the parchment. He wrestled with it, struggling almost comically to rip it. Eventually he managed it, and for a few moments, the rough rasp of him tearing strips was the only sound, loud in the early morning emptiness of the forecourt.

Feilan watched this performance with a display of mild interest. Only when Bertrand was done, scattering shreds at his feet, did he say, 'That wasn't the proof.'

Bertrand froze.

'But do feel free to tell us: why did you feel the need to work *very hard* to destroy it, if you didn't fear the contents?'

He looked over at his audience. Remy's face was blank, Adeline looked frightened, but Rosmunda wore an aghast expression that told him his logic had struck true with her.

'This is vile nonsense,' Bertrand said. 'Guards, send him away. Children, come with me.'

He turned and swept off, expecting, as always, immediate obedience.

Remy had put his face in his hands. He dropped them now. He looked at Feilan, eyes wide and dark, and over his shoulder at his departing uncle. His face was pinched and wan, bleak as a heartland winter landscape.

'Come on, Remy,' Feilan said. 'You must see it. You know you can't trust him.'

'I can't trust *you*,' he said.

'It was just a kiss!' Feilan swallowed the bubbling temper and a good mouthful of profanity. 'Look. Come with me, please. I'll—'

'I won't risk Adeline for your sake,' Remy said, and walked off after Bertrand.

Feilan ran his hands through his hair in muted frustration. 'Adeline? I need guest right. Please.'

Adeline paused. It was her turn to glance between Feilan and a departing relative. But this was the young girl who had lost her mother, heard her own father and all her relatives blame her youngest uncle, and still stubbornly clung to her bond with him, privileging her own knowledge of his true heart over the rumours and fulminations of others.

She trusted Remy, and she trusted him now. 'Sorry, Uncle Faro, I just can't,' she said, and followed her uncle into First Hill.

That left Rosmunda. She and Feilan stared at each other as the guardsmen finally moved to surround and seize him. Skin crawling, blood pounding, he nonetheless didn't resist as they began to drag him off the forecourt and onto the road, for all that would achieve; there was no gate, no walls. He could walk back into Seven Hills anytime he liked. He just needed guest right to be allowed to stay there rather than subject himself to an endless repeat of this half-arsed exile.

He stared at Rosmunda, silently pleading because if he tried to talk now he would shout like a true Vaer.

She said, 'I extend guest right.'

'Get your serthing hands off me, you lorti svinar!' Feilan indeed shouted.

The guards backed away with unbecoming haste. He scowled around at them with some venom; the humiliation of letting himself be man-handled off the premises had triggered that unsuspected Vaer pride, or perhaps it was just close enough to his last exiling – also Torben's fault! – to have awakened shameful memories.

'You have some real proof of your claim?' Rosmunda enquired in a shaking voice.

'Yes.' He glared pointedly at the guardsmen. 'Privately.'

Rosmunda held up a bejewelled hand, face set in thought. 'I will walk you down to town,' she said at last. 'You have that long to convince me.'

He couldn't mention the parchments hidden in his trunk – at least one of these guards would run straight to Uncle Bertrand to tell him. He said, 'Good, a copy of the proof is held by my friends down there,' and hoped he wasn't dooming Aminah and the Siftar sentries, or indeed the entire riverport, to an unpleasant afternoon.

'You are dismissed,' she told the guards.

The most senior of the guards spoke up. 'The barbarian, lady. He might harm you.'

She said, 'Send my husband here, he will accompany me.'

The guardsman eyed Feilan, openly wearing his doubt regarding a single escort. Feilan managed a complacent look about that piece of flattery.

'Stop it,' Rosmunda hissed at him, and to the guard, a more commanding, 'You, go!'

28

ROSMUNDA HAD NOT BEEN PLEASED WHEN Feilan had finally shared, halfway down the curving road, sightlines showing empty road in both directions, and only a few farmhands in the rolling fields to either side, that the proof was secured back in Seven Hills.

But she had listened, and Conrad had listened.

Feilan had, by necessity, had to trust both of them with at least enough details to engage them fully to his side and put the plan back on course. Remy had been meant to present the wheeled chair to Adeline and Afzal, and inveigle an immediate jaunt, but Feilan hadn't had the chance to tell him that. Rosmunda might have passed a message, except that Feilan was no longer sure Remy would play it true.

He *should*: the chair was the mechanism for fulfilling the alliance's promise to Micah. Break that promise, break the queen's alliance, thus delivering an easy win for Uncle Bertrand's bloc, to the fatal detriment of whatever deal Remy had bartered for. Now he'd taken control of the alliance with Feilan's expedient removal, he should want it to hold just as much as Feilan did.

But using Remy was too much of a risk now. Uncle Bertrand might very well order him to make sure Torben didn't win. Remy was naive enough to obey without ironclad assurances as to the fate of their deal if he did. And with Torben's god-sworn mercenary contract safely in Adeline's hands, destroying the alliance Feilan had mortared into place would be far easier than finding a way to disqualify the queen's champion under the canny eyes of the neutral witnesses.

And so Feilan turned the role over to Rosmunda, constraining her with a large shackle: she could not let Darya, Adeline, or Remy realise the gift was a continuation of the exiled-in-disgrace Feilan's plan, lest any of them baulk. Remy, in particular, had to be kept in the dark. Not that Remy would choose to deny the boy a gift that would give him freedom; he had a temper but wasn't spiteful. But, though he couldn't know the plan's particulars, he knew winning Micah a clean chance at Darya's throat was a central prong of it. It was a short step from noticing the wheeled chair in the cave that morning to guessing it had a role beyond a surprise gift from a doting aunt, and an even shorter step to understanding that it was the key to an alliance he may or may not wish to preserve.

Rosmunda would have to fetch the chair without arousing suspicion, give it to Adeline without alerting Remy, and then hope that both children would be excited enough to naturally want to take it for a ride along the lamplit arcade without the overt encouragement that might alert Darya.

'I'll want to see the proof before I help you,' she'd said firmly.

'I'll show it to you when I come back up tonight,' Feilan had countered, because he did not trust them so far as to tell them where it was hidden.

Conrad frowned at this, and put his hand on his wife's arm protect-ively. 'Why, exactly, did Remy have you thrown out?'

Feilan hesitated. Even now, he didn't want to condemn Remy by admitting it was because he'd accepted a deal with Bertrand and decided to stick with it even once he'd learned of his mother's fate at the man's hands. Even if he didn't outright believe Feilan, it was strange that the accusation and his uncle's blatant destruction of what he'd thought was its evidence hadn't given him the same pause it had given Rosmunda.

Perhaps that was what Remy was doing today, taking his usual time to think it over. Perhaps he would be waiting with contrite mien and open arms when Feilan returned that night.

And perhaps Feilan was engaging in wishful thinking as dangerous as surrendering to his simmering anger would be.

'Does Bertrand have some hold over him?' he asked at last.

His attempt at subtlety was wasted. Rosmunda's brows shot up. 'You think he allied himself to Uncle?' She began to shake her head. 'No. He didn't. He simply wouldn't.'

'Look, he loves Adeline,' Feilan said. 'If he thought he was doing his best by her—'

'Yes, he loves Adeline,' she said sharply. 'So he'd not betray her like that. He'd at least have asked her permission, and you saw her – she was as confused by all this as I was. And…' She raised her chin and met his eyes challengingly, as if she thought he'd argue. 'He loves you, too, Feilan. He'd not betray you, either.'

He *did* want to argue. Instead he bid them farewell. They would have the delicate task, in addition to their evening's activities, of implying to Uncle Bertrand that they'd rescinded Feilan's guest right, while making sure the guards knew that he was welcome when he walked back in tonight.

Feilan thought about her claim – *he loves you, he'd not betray you* – as he went down to the town. He was well aware that the first matter did not preclude the second. Every time he thought of it, the pressure, a roil of anger and hurt with just an undercurrent of self-pity, throbbed like a stab wound through him and the betrayal tried to close over his head and drown him.

Somewhere in the back of his mind, he knew he'd have already succumbed, if he and Torben hadn't had their exceedingly long-delayed conversation that very morning.

Instead, he took his outrage and turned it into defiance and a stubborn determination to do right by Adeline: Great-Uncle Bertrand and Uncle Remy did not get to win control of her modest throne tonight. That he still needed to parlay victory into a trade deal for Freyja was in his mind too, if distantly.

He found Gytha after discreet inquiry – Vaeringans in small foreign towns were always easy to find, their every move tracked – and updated her on his new exile. After some discussion, they elected to leave Eirikr and Helle watching over Tyra and Aminah. But Gytha would come back up to Seven Hills, taking the back path via Remy's cave once the murk and mist set in, ready to help out, unseen, on the hunting ground.

And now it was late evening and there was a new problem.

The mist was not rising.

It had been growing steadily thinner for the last month, but even the previous night, when Feilan had sat at the cave entrance and wrestled with his guilt, it had still been just thick enough to turn anyone within its extent into merest shadows, enough to plausibly deny any cheating movement on and off the hunting ground. Even with no moon, the summer twilight was long and the walkway was well lit – he'd been relying on the mist for the extra cover.

It wouldn't matter too much for the first part of the plan, provided Torben had passed on Feilan's message about swapping the beads, and provided Micah or Noura had understood that swapping the jasper, Feilan's eye colour, and the tiger-eye, Micah's eye colour, meant swapping their roles tonight.

And provided Micah only wanted Afzal free of Darya rather than the pleasure of sinking one of his needle blades into her throat himself.

That was a fairly big ask, Feilan realised. It was almost helpful that the lack of mist would prevent Micah from making the attempt...provided it didn't provoke him into taking the monster's head so he could have a chance at her some other time. Feilan could only predict that the man's cool head would prevail over his hot heart.

The main problem was that, provided all other provisions came to pass, the lack of mist would hinder Feilan and Gytha in joining the others. The monster was armoured, fast, and could clear their heads in one bound – it would need more than the three queen's warriors officially allowed out there to take it.

At this rate, Gytha wouldn't even be able to get past the Seven Hills guards, uncharacteristically posted in pairs within sight of each other all the way along the walkway as far as Feilan could see. He couldn't imagine the sentry line wouldn't extend all the way to Torben's pavilion.

For himself, he merely walked up the road to the forecourt as soon as he saw the first stars emerge.

'You're not allowed here,' a guard blurted when he strolled in.

'I am Lady Rosmunda's guest,' he said.

It took a little argument, and a message run to the spectators and back, but he was allowed in, still armed with the bastard sword Torben had fetched for him that morning, only to be escorted straight to the old barracks by no less than four guardsmen. No matter; it was where he wanted to be.

He was taken up the stairs to the roof, and to Bertrand, who stood with arms akimbo, affably annoyed and enjoying his advantage. Feilan couldn't help looking down at Remy, who huddled miserably on his cushion, set between Uncle Bertrand and Hughard. Remy wouldn't raise his gaze.

Feilan nudged his cushion with a booted foot. *Look at me, you treacherous shit.* Remy mutely shook his head.

'Rosmunda, what is the meaning of extending guest right to the barbarian?' Uncle Bertrand demanded. 'Oh. Where's she gone now?'

Handling the wheeled chair ploy, if Feilan's luck was holding and she wasn't refusing to begin her part until he showed her the testimonies.

'She had to help Adeline with something,' Conrad called. 'Um. You know.' He made the vaguest of vague gestures upwards, as if towards an entirely absent moon.

This either confused the male spectators, made them stroke their chins knowingly, or lost their already slight interest entirely. Darya, meanwhile, one of the few women left on the rooftop, rolled her eyes.

Really, so-called women's troubles were the best serthing excuse Feilan had ever come across for not explaining secretive movements to men. No wonder the women of his information network performed so ably. Well. Aside from intelligence, competence and an almost appalling level of steely-eyed ruthlessness, of course.

He nudged Remy's cushion again, Remy's last warning before he started nudging his ribs instead. *Look at me. Look me in the eye.*

'Hyndla,' he said, his tone making it clear he *very much* meant the literal meaning this time. 'Come on, you've shown me your spine often enough.'

Remy unfolded himself and stood. His hair was tightly bound, his face stark and set. He still wore the protective talisman from Freyja, but a leather thong hung about his neck now, too, and Feilan caught another whiff of that new pungent odour from the cave, not nearly as pretty as the bracelet beads.

'It's too late,' he told Feilan with the same stiff offence with which he'd confronted everything in Siftar. It was infuriating to be subject to it, when Feilan was the one who had the right to offence. 'They're already on the field. You can't change their instructions now.'

Feilan glanced down to the arena before the stables, lit in a clash of flickering gold and orange torchlight. He was really here, openly, to show himself to the others, especially Micah. He couldn't do anything so crass as to nod meaningfully, but he could let his casual gaze wander over his for the briefest of brief moments.

Micah was standing close to Torben, who waved his spear at Feilan in insouciant salute. Noura was distant from them, arms folded, head bandaged. Njorda's tits, Feilan hoped that was just them maintaining the fiction of the alliance's failure. The last two independent warriors also stood alone, though Feilan thought their secret alliance to Bertrand's four-man-strong bloc was in force.

'I don't need to change their instructions,' he said. 'They already know what they need to do.'

'I'm not going to let you win,' Remy whispered.

'Right back at you, Rufran,' Feilan answered, just as quietly.

Remy shook his head, glancing at his uncle fearfully. Bertrand, smiling benignly, dropped an uplifted hand, and the champions turned out into the hunting ground. It was different without the mist. The skyglow was enough to make the figures dimly visible even as they descended down the hill into the great bowl, but they soon vanished into the depths of the moonless night.

Feilan watched his alliance descend until not even indistinct shadows could be made out. Noura, a new taste of freedom in her mouth, might yet hold herself back from the fight. Torben, his mortality a real concept for him now, might yet flinch. Micah, ever reliant only upon himself, might yet choose his own plan over Feilan's disintegrating one.

But Remy was correct on that point: Feilan could do nothing but trust them and their united resolve now.

He nodded and moved on to the next step, securing Lady Rosmunda's continued assistance. 'I'm here to collect my things. I don't trust you svinar to send it on.'

'We searched your room,' Bertrand told him. 'We confiscated your valuables. Consider it your penalty for playing my nephew false.'

Feilan flicked a glance towards Conrad, who returned him a bland, uninformative smile. But this news could mean – *must* mean – Rosmunda was proceeding without expecting to see the evidence, for Bertrand had either found and secretly destroyed it, or genuinely turned up nothing. Both results signally failed to support Feilan's accusation, and yet Rosmunda was not on the roof.

He breathed out. Next step. 'Escort me,' he ordered Remy. 'I'll take what's left.'

This gambit was mostly to remove Remy before Adeline came to whisk Afzal out from under Darya's control, since Feilan couldn't be sure what his intentions were towards the queen's alliance. He might still need Torben to win, but he also might be acting in obedience to Bertrand, and either way, he now seemed so antipathetic towards Feilan that he might stymie the plan on spleeny reflex.

But Feilan couldn't deny he'd give an arm to get Remy alone, regardless. Perhaps then he could persuade him to confess the combination of promise and threat Uncle Bertrand had deployed to change his allegiance. He could shake the treacherous shit until his teeth rattled.

He could say, *I know I kept saying we might not win, but we* will. He could say, *I'll stay and help you keep Bertrand at bay so Adeline can rule.*

He could say, *Remy, it was one kiss, and I'm sorry.*

Even as Remy went ashy with obvious fear at the idea of accompanying the barbarian anywhere, his niece came bouncing up the stairs, calling out excitedly. Like Remy, she, too, now wore a necklace.

'You must come down, Afzal!' she cried. 'You have to see what my aunt has given us.' She turned pleading eyes on Darya. 'Oh, please, let him come see it. It's wonderful!'

Feilan smoothly reversed strategy; now the aim was to keep Remy on the rooftop, so he wouldn't see the chair and put the ploy together. 'One good thing,' he announced. 'At least I don't have to cater to the whims of a spoilt little girl anymore.'

Adeline flashed a look of confused hurt before shaking it off as part of the strange argument her uncle and his husband were having, or perhaps even accepting it as part of a plan she had lost the threads of. Remy's mettle was aroused on her behalf, however. His hands went to his hips, eyes spitting fury.

He glared at Feilan and his expression felt familiar: anger and defiance, and under that, the same deep hurt Feilan was trying to ignore.

Feilan didn't have time to unravel it. He had to keep Remy embroiled for long enough that Adeline successfully escaped off the roof with Afzal without Remy taking it into his head to follow them down to see what the fuss was about. Darya could do that; Feilan couldn't risk Remy doing so and blurting out a fatal warning.

He took Remy's arm, curving fingers tight around his bicep, expecting him to try to edge around him, either to join Adeline or to avoid the brewing argument, or both.

But Remy stood his ground, obstinately between Feilan and Bertrand, who was threatening to call the guards, but not actually doing so. He'd be enjoying his nephew's well-deserved discomfort, and probably also allowing Remy to be thoroughly reminded that it was better to deal with the villain he knew than the barbarian he did not.

Feilan had been intending to say something insulting, something distracting. Remy trembled under his touch, rendering him speechless with resentment and shame.

Beyond their tableau, Darya was so taken with the pretty pleading from the queen, and so smug about the alliance tearing itself into pieces before her, that she gave the most gracious of nods. The silent giant tasked with carrying Afzal scooped him up, a gentle movement at odds with the ugly sternness of his face. He followed Adeline down the stairs, Afzal in his arms.

A moment later, the boy gave a yelp, and then a pair of childish voices were raised in a babble of excitement, followed by a strange sound, something like the ringing of a bell mixed with a teeth-tingling scrape – the big iron wheels of the chair running across the stone paving of the arcade, rapidly quietening as it grew more distant.

Darya sat up, frowning, looking over at Feilan, who made sure to be scowling at Remy without regard for anything happening in his vicinity. By the time she had started for the stairs, her man had come back up. He respectfully bowed his head and murmured something to her, and she looked severely annoyed before returning to her cushion.

Feilan eyed off the big man with interest. He wondered if Micah had been entirely correct to presume that Afzal had no other ally but him.

Right. Next step, a simple one: he had to now storm off down the stairs as if departing Seven Hills in disgrace. He would secrete himself within the empty barracks below, wait for Darya to come down in pursuit of her ward and shield, and murder her for Micah.

Having held his Vaer impulses in check all day, he was rather looking forward to it. He even hoped she'd bring enough of her bodyguards to make it a challenge.

He let Remy go with a dramatic fling, shoving him into his uncle's arms with enough force to almost bowl both of them over.

'I'm leaving.' He spat at Remy's feet. 'Flari lortr.'

Remy, outrageously, became wholly indignant at this accusation. '*I'm the treacherous turd? Me?*'

Remy, Feilan realised, was wearing the mirror of his own betrayed expression. He stopped. 'You—'

Shouts rang out across the field, echoed by more on the rooftop itself.

The monster was coming.

It was even bigger than Feilan remembered, its insectoid speed preternatural on an armoured creature of that size. It tore up the slope towards Seven Hills. Behind it came the warriors, not just the alliance Feilan wanted to see, but Bertrand's bloc as well. The nine champions were in dogged pursuit, but it was easily gaining ground, its multiple limbs almost seeming to pull it along.

The distinctive sound of its claws ripping into the turf as it closed in shook Feilan awake.

'Go make sure Adeline's under cover,' he told Remy.

Remy stood frozen beside Bertrand, staring in shock at the fluid grace and speed of the thing that had killed his brother. Feilan arrived at a depressing conclusion about the monster's trajectory and ran for the stairs himself.

Then he had a sudden flash of memory – still half-blinded by the horrendous bright blue of the smithy smell of Torben's blood, watching in cold shock as the cornered monster leapt high to escape.

He spun. Spectators were crowding to the edge for a better view. Feilan roared, '*Get off the roof!*'

He was answered only by the sudden unison of shrieks from the front row of spectators as the monster landed with a rattling crash in the centre of the rooftop.

It reared there, poised, then scythed out with its claws, spilling blood. The crowded and panicking occupants of the front row were almost safe, since they were behind it, but Conrad had to roll away in great haste, clutching at his shoulder. The fatal blue flashed across Feilan's vision as more screams rang out.

The roof creaked ominously. The monster lashed its tail, knocking Hughard into his other siblings. Remy crouched by his uncle, face blank in terror.

Feilan drew his sword. Micah had warned them that if his blades could not pierce the armour, theirs would not. But he had also said, should they dare to get in close, they'd find seams between the pale and scaly armour plates.

He whistled, and the monster turned its sleek head his way, the beams underfoot giving another tortured groan. Saliva dripped from its long teeth. Its legs coiled, ready to spring.

'Come on, then,' Feilan whispered, raising the sword.

The roof collapsed.

29

Tʜᴇ ᴍᴏɴsᴛᴇʀ ᴘʟᴜᴍᴍᴇᴛᴇᴅ. Sᴏ ᴅɪᴅ most of the people in the front row — including Remy.

After a single calibrating glance, Feilan jumped from the jagged rim of the massive hole in the crumbling roof.

He landed on the monster's back, gripping hard on the edge of the armour plate by its neck, seeking to plunge his sword into the seam there between shoulder plate and neck plate. Its length was awkward. He wished, distantly, for a seax like Vaer men habitually carried.

The creature wasn't as stunned as he'd hoped; it shook itself like a wet hound and whipped tail and tongue at him. He ducked the muscular swipe of the tail but the sharp barbs of the tongue grazed his neck, leaving a trail of fire in their wake. He swore and stabbed downwards with all his might. The sword felt ridiculously inadequate, but the blade fit through the narrow gap between plates.

The monster shrieked, the sound drilling into Feilan's skull. Between that and its wild bucking and thrashing, he couldn't keep his hold and was flung wide. He hit the wall and, gasping with pain, fell hard by Remy.

Feilan grabbed his limp body with both hands, shoving him behind his own body, not thinking about whether there was any point.

But they were lucky, then. The monster, Feilan's sword sticking obscenely from its neck, charged for the open door, a paler rectangle in the gloom with the tempting scent of fresh night air beyond. Too big, it smashed its way through, taking half the wooden wall with it. Renewed screams started up; the spectators had been running down the stairs to escape the collapsing roof and now regretted that decision as the monster crashed through them.

Feilan spun on his knees. Remy's eyes were open and the relief took Feilan like a fist and left him shaking in its aftermath. 'Good?' He looked for blood, bright red on Remy's body, blue in his eyes. 'Svasa, are you unharmed? Answer!'

Remy clutched at him. 'Are *you*? Slubs and neps, you *jumped,* you *jolterhead.*'

Feilan dragged him outside, the need to keep him undercover warring with the justified fear that the whole structure would soon fold in on itself. He was vaguely aware Bertrand was following them out, amid others who had survived the fall, Remy's siblings among them.

It would have been too much to wish for, Feilan supposed, for the monster to have taken care of Uncle Bertrand and Hughard.

The wretched body of Noura's former master, on the other hand, was lying on the ground, split almost in half, blood pooling garishly dark under the flickering torchlight, the wash of blue across Feilan's eyes as brightly fantastical as ever.

It was probably a blow from a wild creature desperate to escape. It might have been a blow from a curved blade swung with years of impotent rage behind it.

Feilan kissed Remy roughly, a hard, defiant press of lips, near-savage with relief and fear. 'Stay safe,' he said. 'I'm going to get Adeline.'

'Adeline!' Remy said, in the horrified tones of one who had forgotten the larger context of the danger.

Feilan was already loping off along the walkway, following a trail of dead and dying Seven Hills guards – they'd seen the monster galloping in the direction their queen had gone and done their duty, to no avail. He raced onwards, jumping dismembered body parts and splashes and puddles of blood, the blue never leaving his vision now, barely aware of his own dread, a weight not just in his chest but in every limb, as he ran alone to find the children somewhere on the very arcade the monster was fleeing along.

Suddenly Torben was thundering by his side, and Noura, blade bare and bloodied, and Micah.

'The children,' Feilan shouted, pointing ahead. He forgotten to scavenge a sword from one of the dead guards, but it was too late to turn back.

Micah put on a burst of speed, outpacing them with those long, strong legs.

From up ahead, screams, high and terrified. It might not, Feilan told himself, be a child.

They came to Torben's pavilion, and the overturned chair, one iron wheel buckled.

Drag marks, and deep gouges atop those, the scouring of claws.

They plunged off the path after the vanishing form of Micah.

Partway down the slope, the monster loomed over Adeline, who, face a rictus of terror, eating knife in one shaking hand, stood over her sobbing friend and shrieked defiance into its wide, dripping maw.

Micah shouted and threw himself towards them. He would be too late.

Adeline sliced the leather thong about her neck, pulled free a stoppered vial, and threw it right at the monster's gaping mouth. It smashed against its teeth, releasing pungent odour and a flash of mustard-seed-yellow. The monster squealed, high-pitched and ear-piercing, rearing up to paw at its mouth like a dog with a noseful of spice.

And now there came a strange sound, like the soft explosion of an egg bursting, and a rising hum. The monster recoiled again, and both children cried out and slapped at themselves.

And again. The hum became an urgent, furious buzz. Adeline threw her cloak over herself and Afzal, both of them curling into entwined balls under it as the monster thrashed and flailed, bucking across the slope away from them.

Gytha, who had been patiently waiting to join the hunt as per Feilan's instructions, was among the skeps, heedless of stings. She picked up a third skep and hurled it at the monster to keep driving it back from the children. She'd saved their lives, but left them in the middle of swarms of angry bees.

The monster was shaking its head and plunging this way and that, its claw lashing the darkness. Many of the bees had followed it, but not enough.

Now, as Torben and Micah and Noura flung themselves helterskelter into the fight, Feilan ran to the huddled children. He was immediately stung, on his hands, his arms, his face. He picked up Afzal, and Gytha picked up Adeline, and they ran for Remy's cave.

Remy had come down the path.

'I said to—'

'I know what you said! Ow!' Remy slapped at his own face; the enraged bees were still chasing them.

Feilan pushed Afzal into Remy's arm and felt him stagger under the weight before his wiry strength caught the strain. 'I need— Either get them away, or get them into your cave and use something to repel the bees. Gytha, protect them.'

He ran for the fight, even as the uncle's bloc, the hired four and the secret two, came charging along the flank of the hill to join in. A few of them checked as they ran into the irate bees thronging the monster. Most were already taken by that strange and wild exhilaration that drove Torben and the others.

Feilan was feeling it too, because otherwise he would have been feeling the ache of his hip and shoulder and ankle where he'd hit the wall and floor, and the throb of the copious bee stings, and, increasingly, a thin line of heat where the monster's tongue had lacerated his neck. He certainly would have been somewhat slower to fling himself right into the midst of the chaos and rip his sword free from the monster's neck.

He wasn't quite taken by battle-rage, that had never been his fate, and the bear-god wouldn't bless him like that anyway, but the next thumb's measure of time was a blur, nothing but chaotic movement and frenetic shouts and shrieks, and striated flashes of blue pulsing in the corners of his eyes, washing across his vision every time fresh blood splashed or spouted.

The monster's blood smelled just like a human's as it went down under a surfeit of blades like a great boar worried by the hunting hounds.

Torben was fully in the grip of his god, roaring and battering away with his immense sword, his spear already embedded deep between two scales, his body taking itself out of the way of the slashing claws and ripping teeth with the unerring propulsion of divine instinct. Feilan, Noura and Micah were reduced to protecting his flanks, darting and stabbing, spinning and parrying, fighting both the cornered and weakening monster and their rival champions, who also fought both monster and humans, and all of them under incessant attack by the enraged bees.

Feilan's head only cleared when he heard his name screamed. He shook his head, swatting away more bees. The monster was laid out on the ground before them, Torben crouched over it and hacking away at its neck, gouts of blood from every blow. Noura and Micah stood guard, but only two of the other champions were yet living, and they were backing away.

The monster was diminished in death, its long limbs contracting, the lustre of its scales only apparent now it was fading. He had a moment to feel pity – Adeline had been right, it had never been this creature's fault that it had to fall afoul of civilisation – before he heard his name again, still in that frantic tone.

Upslope, more men. He recognised the light robes of Darya's bodyguards more by the sound the soft fabric made as they descended than by making out their figures in the dim light this far from the last torches of the arcade.

Beyond the onrushing men, at the mouth of the cave, Gytha wrestled with another, keeping him from reaching Afzal, desperately calling for help as she almost tripped over the body of one she'd already killed. The cave mouth was too wide for one person to effectively guard – it *was* really more of a grotto – and Darya was trying to slip past, holding something low in her hand. It was too dark for it to glint, but Feilan knew what it was: a knife, intended for a prince.

She would have seen for herself Micah standing by and allowing Torben to claim the prize, bringing down on his head her promised punishment. Once she got past the beleaguered Gytha, only the terrified Remy and Adeline would be between her and her terrible vengeance upon her dead husband's last friend.

'Micah!' Feilan shouted, and he bolted up the hill.

More chaos and flashes of blue as Feilan ran through the bodyguards, laying all about with his sword with the brutal Vaer efficiency he'd learned at his father's knee. He saw Gytha falling, clutching her stomach. He fell upon the bodyguard she'd been grappling with, then bent over her.

She had both hands pressed to a wound which flashed the stink and hue of hot blood at him, but she gasped, 'Go!'

Feilan straightened, and the lick of heat across his neck burst into flame at the motion. Dizzy, he stumbled onwards. Micah shot past him, but he was chased by someone else – the giant whose sole duty was to carry the prince, lumbering at the assassin's heels.

The cave was ripe with some woody scent, drifting smoky-grey. That would be Remy's defence against the bees. Afzal was all the way at the back of the cave, on the floor where the witch's domain narrowed into the private alcove by the spring. Feilan supposed Remy had hidden the children back there, from bees and monsters both. Afzal's legs were twisted behind him. The boy must have crawled his way out again, perhaps in a panic. He was crying in great wrenching sobs that sounded torn from his chest.

As his guardian bore down on him with bared blade, Feilan staggered after Micah and the giant, willing Remy to have enough courage to spring out of the alcove and whisk the boy back, giving Micah the extra few heartbeats he needed in this awful race for jugulars.

The giant lunged, his long reach advantaging him over all of them – but he didn't lunge for Micah. He grabbed Darya around the waist as she made to slash the prince's throat, and hauled her off her feet as readily as he picked up his prince.

She screamed at him to release her, thrashing and striking the knife into his meaty arms. With a great air of deliberation, he set her before Micah, who did not hesitate, not even to take a scant moment to revel. He knocked her knife aside, and his own blade was in and out of her throat as fast as his darting needle when he sewed up wounds, with decidedly opposite effect. He didn't move as he was splattered with her life's blood.

Feilan couldn't see his expression, but it was the last thing Darya saw.

The giant let the body drop, and turned and scooped up the prince, holding him tight in bleeding arms. The boy sobbed against his shoulder. Micah quickly wiped his face so he could approach the boy without scaring him with a dripping crimson mask. Feilan wondered how long it had been since he'd been able to safely be so much as within sight of the prince.

Then Afzal reached for his father's friend, choking out, 'Adeline! He took her,' and he had no room for wondering anything else.

He knew Afzal could not possibly be talking about Remy, who would never voluntarily take Adeline from the one place he felt safest, nor leave the other vulnerable child alone in such distress.

One quick check of the alcove confirmed it was empty. His head spun, and he shook it clear again, and ran from the cave, finding Gytha slowly wadding a torn strip of robe from one of the dead bodyguards against her wound.

'Did you see Bertrand?'

'No,' she said, breath coming in pained hisses. 'But they set on me so suddenly and I knew they'd kill that boy. Herd of walruses could have got past while I was trying to stop them.'

Micah was behind him. He started, but Micah said calmly, 'I will come with you.'

Feilan glanced upwards, towards the arcade. 'Help Gytha.'

'No,' she said through gritted teeth.

Feilan looked downslope now. Noura, strong as iron, was dripping blood but on her feet, years of arena fighting standing her in good stead.

She stood by Torben, who was hugging the great severed head in both arms even as he slowly knelt, the blessing of his god ebbing away, leaving only exhaustion and no doubt a new intimacy with the gashes and bone-deep bruises and strain along his new seam that he'd just earned himself.

He turned back to Micah, and notwithstanding that the eunuch had to be just as exhausted as the rest of them, said, 'Help everyone.'

Without waiting for argument – for there was none to be made, unless Micah was willing to leave his allies to bleed out – Feilan loped up the beaten path to the arcade.

It was deserted, eerily still and quiet. Some of the torches had guttered, and the rest flickered in the slightest of breezes, sending shadows skittering across his path.

He felt hazy and slow, as if under a seithr curse that fogged his thoughts and sapped his will. He reached for Freyja's talisman, finding his wrist bare.

Where would Bertrand have taken his hostages? Was he still wearing his affable smile, or had he shown his teeth at last? Had he marched them to First Hill, even now forcing Adeline to sign away her fairly-won freedom while Feilan dithered?

He began up the arcade, trying to hurry even as he heard the doubling echo of his own uneven footsteps. The throb in his neck overwhelmed all his other aches and pangs now. He passed the bodies of guardsmen, the scent of blood still fresh enough to make hazy clouds of fading blue wherever he looked.

He was so inured to the iron tang that he'd gone past Fourth Hill East before his faltering brain managed to alert him that his eyes had experienced the bright coruscating flash of freshest blood as he'd passed the walkway that led to the foyer.

Bright enough to be a beacon.

He ran, stumbling.

Down the walkway, through the empty foyer, down the passageway to the guest accommodations, looking for more twinkles of giveaway bright blue. He saw instead the dull yellow of mustard seed, along with a gust of that acrid smell that had marked whatever Remy had concocted as a weapon against the monster.

Adeline had used hers to hold back the creature for the vital few moments that had saved her and Afzal's life – Remy must have cracked his own vial now, the reek coming from one of the bedchambers up ahead.

He heard Bertrand, raising his voice for the first time. 'Is this *poison*? All I've done for you, and you've thrown poison in my face?'

'Let Adeline go, and I'll take you to the antidote.' Remy sounded tremulous but no less determined for all that.

Feilan staggered down the hall and slumped into the doorway, unable to make the dramatic entrance the situation called for. He could make out the figures inside by the faint glow coming through the usual high narrow window slits. Bertrand had Remy by the arm, digging his fingers in as he slowly wiped his splattered cheeks with a square of pale linen, a relatively bright patch in the dim room. The same hand that held the cloth also held a blade. His back was mostly to the doorway, Remy mostly facing it.

Remy's wide and frightened gaze met Feilan's for the briefest of moments, but his expression didn't alter. He was, perhaps, not filled with confidence by Feilan's sagging aspect. Fair: the room performed a lazy spin before he blinked his eyes clear again. His throat felt hot and it was hard to swallow.

'Antidote? You missed my mouth, you little fool, I didn't swallow any,' Bertrand sneered.

'Neither did the monster,' Remy said. 'It's still dead. Absorbs through the skin, Uncle. Acid in the blood. Pure witchcraft.'

His uncle cursed and backhanded him with surprising force for a small man. Remy fell, or at least let himself fall: that put him beside Adeline, the true queen of Seven Hills, a terrified little girl huddled on the floor of a dusty bedroom at the back end of her kingdom.

Remy slung an arm around Adeline's shoulders, the one Bertrand had been twisting. The sleeve of his other arm, Feilan noted, was soaked red. He whispered something to her, hugging her tight.

Bertrand loomed over them both. 'Very well. You will fetch the antidote, Renart. And you will authorise my regency, Adeline. No. You'll recognise the nonsense of a little girl on the throne and you'll abdicate in my favour.'

'Or?' Remy said, black eyes flashing defiance, daring his uncle to threaten him. 'You'll do what you did to my mother?'

Bertrand's hands clenched. 'Curse the Vaer and his proof. Swarf it, if it comes out, the throne will shield me.' He jerked his chin towards Remy's injured arm. 'Meanwhile, I won't miss your throat again, and I shall take great pleasure having your husband executed for your murder.'

'Feilan is the best man I know! No one will believe that,' Remy said, hotly enough that Feilan felt warmed through even in his muzzy state, though that was doused when Remy corrected himself. 'Rosa and Conrad will never believe that!'

'The rest will,' Bertrand said. 'They'll all sleep easier, with me on the throne where I have always belonged, and him gone, back to barbarian land or to the noose.' His tone sweetened, but with all subtlety stripped away, laying bare the threat. 'It's your choice whether all of you live or not, Renart. Or persist in your ridiculous defiance and die knowing you've doomed your queen and your husband both.'

Remy nodded, once. 'That's clear enough,' he said, very quietly.

Bertrand's shoulders relaxed. Feilan closed his eyes, fighting the dizziness. He had to—

Remy said, 'An openly treasonous plot, Your Majesty, and three witnesses to it.'

'Yes, I agree, Chief Adviser,' Adeline said, and she straightened from her huddle until she looked like she was sitting on a throne whose seat happened to be the floor.

'Three?' Bertrand turned his head to see Feilan leaning against the doorway.

'Uncle Faro said every good ruler weighs the cost of their crown,' she said, staring up at Bertrand with dark eyes and severe mien, nothing of the child in her. 'And I've weighed mine, and it weighs less than the cost of letting someone like you have it, Great-Uncle. And I can have Feilan arrest you—'

Feilan, who had only just managed to straighten up from his dazed slump, strongly doubted he had the stamina left to drag a struggling man all the way to First Hill, but he was willing to try.

'—and we can have a trial, and it will take months, and the outcome will be the same.' She smiled, thinly. 'If I must face it then, I can face it now. So I may as well pronounce the inevitable sentence here, with the other witnesses to hold me to account.'

Bertrand, with an armed barbarian a handspan from him, threw aside the knife and raised his hands. 'Adeline, dear,' he began in his old cloying tones. 'Little girls shouldn't—'

She slowly rose to her feet, Remy rising with her, though he was very pale now and blood was dripping from his fingers. 'Death to the traitor. Death to the man who threatened Seven Hills.' She squeezed Remy's unbloodied hand. 'Death to the man who murdered my grandmother. Death to the man who hurt my family over and over.'

'*I'm* your family!' he cried. 'I was protecting all of you.'

'You were using all of us,' she said matter-of-factly. 'And if you couldn't use us, you discarded us. Feilan, you may carry out the sentence.'

Thanks, he thought, barely cognisant enough for sarcasm, but all told, it was easier than arrest.

It was just pulling a gibbering man into the hallway, pushing him to his knees, raising a sword high over his vulnerable nape as he shamefully allowed his last words to be begging for his life, and nodding to Remy that it was time to swing the door shut and cover Adeline's ears so she wouldn't need to bear witness to the deserved end of the other monster of Seven Hills. It was a queen's burden in a brutal world; it didn't need to be a girl's nightmare.

Feilan let the blade fall.

Then he fell, into a cloud of blue.

30

Feilan woke up and found Freyja sitting by the bed, her stitching abandoned in her lap. She wore silver-threaded silk, and her braided hair was gathered at her nape. Her gaze was thoughtful, abstracted; it was a moment before she saw that his eyes had opened.

She smiled, fond and relieved. He smiled back, not yet moved to speak.

He looked about. It wasn't the room he'd shared with Remy, though his trunk was here. Both bed and room were smaller. He didn't think he was even in Third Hill East – but he must be in Seven Hills, because this room had the row of high window slits, and it had one of their thick mugs, which his mother picked up and offered to him.

Well. Not really an offer. She tried to hold it to his mouth when he didn't immediately lift a hand to take it.

He pushed it away and checked the window slits. The light suggested mid-morning, if he was on the same side of a Seven Hills hallway as his previous room. 'Have I slept late?'

'Very,' she said. 'It's the first day after the final night of the moon-gloam. I arrived two days ago.' She held out the mug again.

Feilan was indignant, and tugged down the blankets covering him. 'Has Remy been keeping me asleep?' he demanded. 'I wasn't even as badly injured as poor Gytha.' He caught his breath. 'Is she…'

'She's fine – that witch of yours is a gem, and so's the eunuch. *You* were poisoned, jolterhead. Its tongue, apparently.'

She touched her neck, and he mirrored the motion and discovered the line of a scab. It twinged under his fingers and he dropped his hand, remembering the heat spreading out, his confusion and dizziness, his weakness at the end. When Freyja offered the cup a third time, he took it, and, at a narrow-eyed look, sipped.

It was, of course, one of the witch's brews.

He was wearing a new talisman, protective beads pretty about his wrist and clinking quietly against each other as he drank.

'I'm going to apologise,' she said. 'I shouldn't have interfered. You knew what you were about.'

'Did I?'

She looked at him with her wry smile. 'You must have, my boy. Queen Adeline sits the throne in her own right, beloved uncle her chief adviser, and we have a most generous offer of trade access to the Riverlands.'

'Golden Freyja,' he said. 'You didn't take advantage of a traumatised little girl, did you?'

'They practically threw it at me.' She grimaced to his frown. 'They didn't even want to take a tithe for passage past the riverport, let alone a cut of the profits. I had to insist on it. I... Thanks to you, I do still have a golden reputation for fair dealing to maintain.'

He nodded. After a few more sips, he asked, 'Do I have an Imperial stepfather?'

A cloud passed over her face, and she held up her other hand, showing off extra rings. 'Yes.'

'You're not staying in Siftar, then.'

'I'll be going south to Aldhelm. I have an Imperial crown waiting for me. It's nothing I asked for, mind you, but once I take it up, I'll need the Imperial protection that comes along with it.'

She'd always had a queenly bearing. She didn't need to change one whit now she was an empress. But she couldn't sit about in a little trading town, not even one she had founded herself. The influence and wealth she had quietly wielded across Enea had become far too public, far too political, for that.

Feilan asked the only important question. 'Is he awful?'

'He's not,' she said. 'Not all Vaer men are like your father, Little Wolf. He is quite a bit older than me, however. And he has two sons. Do you understand what I'm telling you?'

Feilan thought of two beads, silver-caged amber and white-dashed jet. *I am safe but do not come home.* He swallowed. 'I can't go south with you.'

'I dare not risk you,' she said. 'I simply won't. Those two heirs to an empire will see you only as a rival. I must keep you tucked away so their thoughts don't turn your way.' She smiled suddenly. 'They're likely to kill each other, though. That might leave only one possible heir.'

The poison, or Remy's remedies, had made him slow. It took five long beats before he said, 'Don't...don't make that happen, though, Mother.'

She laughed outright. 'But wouldn't that be quite the kick in the balls for the men who exiled you? The second emperor of the new Vaer empire, the boy they cursed all those years ago?'

'I don't think I care,' Feilan said. 'I haven't given a buggering fuck what men like that think of me for years.'

She touched his cheek. 'That's my boy.'

'It's thanks to you,' he said. She looked, momentarily, taken aback, laying her hand fully against the side of his face. He picked at a thread in the blanket. 'Will you charge me with Siftar, then?'

Freyja raised her brows, his own manner. 'Do you know,' she said thoughtfully, 'I have had a long and generally happy life.'

'Ah, where is this going, because I'm the one languishing in the sickbed.'

He said it lightly, but he also put the cup aside and began to push himself up the pillows to a more upright position, watching her face. It was not like Freyja to be this sombre this long; he couldn't help suspect more bad news.

'I'm hale and hearty, my boy, and looking to continue so for as long as Njorda grants me. But I do have one small regret from my time in this world.'

'Ulfr,' said Feilan flatly.

Freyja set her hands in her lap, discovered her neglected embroidery, and gathered it up. Quietly, straightening the cloth, she said, 'Aleifr, if I hadn't had him, I wouldn't have you. So, no, I do not regret him for a single moment.'

Feilan blinked. He started to jest that he must be dying to receive such an emotional outburst from her, and then considered how uncharacteristically grim she was, and that she was in the very middle of empire-building and had still dropped it all and rushed to his bedside, and that Remy had felt obliged to keep him in deep sleep, the same way he'd treated Torben to increase his chances of survival.

He didn't much think his mother would appreciate the joke.

'My regret,' she said, 'is departing Ysthera when we did.'

This was even more unexpected than her last remark. 'Ysthera?' he said. 'But we made the connections we needed. We still have an excellent trade relationship even though they're on the other side of the city-state coalition. What's to regret?'

'We made trade connections there, yes, but *you* were making a real connection. A personal connection. And I didn't pay nearly enough attention, and I took you away from him.'

'We both knew our liaison would be temporary.'

Freyja ignored him. 'Remind me of his name.'

'Helios,' Feilan said after a moment. 'Look, I liked him well enough, but we did both know—'

She cut him off with a raised hand as she slowly sat back. 'Name one other man, in all these years, who you think of as fondly as Helios.' He opened his mouth. '*Except Tryggvi.*'

He shut his mouth, fighting not to smile. Freyja's patience was not as legendary as her reputation; she shortly said, 'Go on. Do I have to spell it out as if you've seen but five summers?'

Surrendering to the badgering with good grace, he admitted, 'Prince Renart of Seven Hills.'

'Remy. Your husband.'

'Who isn't waiting by my bedside,' he pointed out. 'Who exiled me from Seven Hills, and double-crossed me to make a deal with his uncle. Who isn't my husband, actually, as it turns out.'

'And?'

Feilan gave in. 'And I suppose I'd like to stay in the general vicinity.'

'Why not stay right here? Njorda knows these fools need someone hard-nosed behind the throne.'

With some force, almost snarling it out of deep reflex, he said, 'They need *no one* behind the throne.'

It was Freyja's turn to concede. She soothed him with a hand to his shoulder. 'Fair. Duly appointed adviser, then.'

'There's a reason it's my mother waiting for me by my sickbed, not my husband.'

Freyja gave him another fond look. 'You do have people waiting to see you, actually.'

She stood, and looked down at him. He could see behind her pale eyes the grief of their incipient parting, and the deep love that made it inevitable.

'I'll come say goodbye before I go,' she told him. 'But do have a think. You have been by my side for twenty-five years, the most loyal and steadfast aide I could have asked for – the best son I could ever have desired.'

'Tell me the truth,' Feilan said earnestly. 'One of us is dying, right?'

'I'm glad to see you still find yourself funny,' Freyja said. 'I know I don't say it often enough – old Vaer women are just as bad as Vaer men for dancing around the softer things.' She bestowed upon him her rarest of smiles, an openly doting one. 'My boy. I'll charge you with Siftar if you want it. But trading was never your true forte. Information-gathering is. You can go back and do that in Siftar, but there's a riverport right here that now has just as much access to traders and their gossip as Siftar ever did, and an easy route to send it south. Think about what you really want.'

He knew what he wanted.

But his next visitor was Torben, bandaged up and covered in bee sting welts, though substantially faded, as if the witch of Seven Hills had cooked up a salve. He was otherwise as bluffly hale as usual.

'Nice work, Thunder Bear,' Feilan told him, after he'd kissed Feilan's forehead like Freyja had.

'We did it the hard way,' Torben complained. He was awkward with sickness, and fidgeted by the bedside.

Feilan took pity. 'When are you heading south to join your raiding party?'

'Tomorrow,' Torben said, looking relieved to seize on logistics chat. Then he said, 'I'll be telling them to head to Aldhelm.'

'You're signing on with Olvar the Bold?' Feilan asked in surprise.

'I've been talking too much to Noura.'

'She's not gone?'

'She's going south to Aldhelm, too, with Aminah. Freyja wants her talking to the emperor the way she's been talking to me.'

Enlightened, Feilan said, 'About those disciplined easterners heading this way?'

He had to smile: Freyja didn't want him in the Riverlands as her old spymaster, or not only that. She wanted him here so he could help Queen Adeline prod the rest of the council of Riverlands rulers into helping the new Vaer empire stand against the eastern invaders. The wealthy, safe Riverlands owed Enea a tithe of service. It would mean change, but the whole world was changing: it always was.

Torben nodded. After a long pause, he said, 'Micah's going south, too. I'm escorting him and Afzal home before I find my boys.'

Feilan found he had to look away before he could say, 'That should be an interesting interlude.'

'One hundred and eleven interesting interludes,' Torben said. He paused. 'Might not see you again.'

'Don't be—'

'Might not see you again,' Torben repeated. 'Don't need one hundred and eleven when it only takes one, and those city-state soldiers know how to do it.' He looked Feilan in the eye and said gruffly, 'Love you, Aleifr. You.' He stopped and then rolled his eyes and said, 'You might as well know: you've always had part of my heart.'

'No, really. Am I dying?' Torben snorted, and Feilan grabbed his wrist, where he still sported Freyja's talisman. 'Love you too, jolterhead, always will.'

Torben kissed him, properly this time. He stood over Feilan, one hand still clasped around the side of his face, gazing down at him in silence for what felt like a full thumb's measure before he shook his head and stepped away.

He departed without a backwards look, already anticipating his next adventure.

Both Noura and Micah, bearing faded stings and clean bandages much as Torben had, came in separately to say their own farewells; they were part of the general exodus leaving Seven Hills for southern climes on the morrow. Noura embraced him, or at least locked an elbow roughly about his neck with genuine fondness, stinging the inflamed graze; Micah merely lowered his long eyelashes and wished him well in his coolest tones.

Feilan sulked at the feeling that everyone was leaving him. Visits from a reassuringly lively Gytha, and then from Adeline, Rosmunda and Conrad, helped. He managed to be gracious about the fact that they were not who he wanted to come through his door, especially because he could plainly see that, though they were appropriately grateful, they were also only just beginning the full reckoning of the harm Bertrand had inflicted on them, cuts small and large across many years, all suddenly bleeding.

But he was finally alone, only to discover that trying to get out of bed made him as sick and dizzy as when he'd had to drink with the traders back in the early days of Freyja's empire. He fought through it, struggled into trousers and a shirt, and made his way from the room, which turned out to be practically where he'd fallen, in Fourth Hill East. There'd been a bed right there, he supposed, and it was close to Remy's remedies.

He walked slowly along the arcade to Remy's grotto. All the patches of blood between his room and the pavilion had already been scrubbed away.

A last handful of clients was still waiting. Feilan sat down at the end of the queue, closing his eyes in the warm sunshine. The bees downslope had recovered their million-body equanimity after last night's travails, though the broken skeps scattered about the flattened and dying patch of grass where the monster had met its end made for busy traffic as the residents of the other skeps scavenged. The hum was soothing, the lingering smell of broken honeycomb pale amber behind his closed eyelids. It was soon counterpointed by the purr of Breone, who came to curl up in his lap and accept his stroking, a far cry from her first hissing flight from his outstretched hand.

When he opened his eyes again, everyone else was gone but Remy was standing in front of him, injured arm bandaged from wrist to elbow, face and hands lightly marred with a few telltale swellings from those angry bees. His carnelian hair fell loose to his shoulders. He was beautiful.

'Why are you here?' he demanded the moment Feilan met his eye.

'Oh, am I still exiled from Seven Hills?' Feilan asked with lifted brows.

This produced the instant contrition he'd been hoping for. Remy dropped to his knees before him, startling shy Breone from his lap. 'I meant, why are you out of bed?'

'Because my husband wasn't in it,' Feilan said, then further informed him, 'Freyja says you're a shit negotiator.'

He surprised a laugh out of Remy, and won a longing look, enough to risk opening his arms. Remy shuffled into them, nestling between Feilan's spread thighs.

'How's your arm?' he asked, gently lifting the offended limb. 'When I said you could use blood as a beacon, it wasn't an instruction.'

'It wasn't quite on purpose,' Remy said.

'What happened?'

'I suppose you've gathered Bertrand was sticking close to Darya's bodyguards for fear of the monster? He might have been dismayed they were heading right for it, but he must have seen us flee into the grotto, and I suppose he understood he had his last chance to hold onto power. He dragged Adeline out while Gytha was busy fighting. He was trying to take her to First Hill, I think, to force the regency, if not outright abdication. I broke her away from him and he chased us towards Fourth Hill East. He caught us at the walkway and went for my throat.' Remy looked down at his arm, taking a moment before he could speak again. 'He had a knife. I suppose he'd already decided how far he'd be willing to go. I used my forearm to block him. I should have known he's stronger than he looks. We tried to barricade ourselves in that room but he forced himself in. We were terrified.'

His fingers were running up and down the rough linen of his bandaged arm in compulsive strokes. Feilan caught his hand, and then drew him in, holding his slight frame tight against his body, feeling his warmth and his slight quiver.

'I know you kept trying to point out the games he was playing, but I don't think I could comprehend just how much of a mask he was wearing until he shoved his way in with that knife in his hand. I got between him and Adeline and smashed that vial of monster poison in his face. It didn't matter. He thought he had us. And then you were there.' He caught at Feilan's shirt. 'Swarf, I didn't think I could be more scared than I was when he came at us, and then you collapsed!'

He vaguely remembered it. He remembered making sure he fell away from the headless body with the blood still spraying from the stump of the neck. 'I was fairly sick, then?'

'You were poisoned, Faro. You had such a strong dose of poison from its tongue that you needed about five different medicinals and purgatives and still almost died.'

'Worried about me?' Remy merely sighed in exasperation to that, so Feilan said, 'Guess we can be grateful it was only its saliva and not its blood or claws or more of us would be laid up. Why didn't you come to me? Feeling guilty?'

Remy sucked in air and drew back. 'I tried very hard to sabotage you.'

'You thought I'd made a deal with Bertrand, didn't you?'

'No,' Remy said, surprising him. 'I knew you hadn't had a chance to, yet. But I knew you were planning on it. So I tried very hard to keep you from talking to him.'

'By throwing me off the premises.'

'Of course,' Remy said primly. 'It was the most straightforward method I could think of. I regret being so nasty about it, though. I didn't need to act how I did with the guards.'

Feilan shrugged. 'I was not pleasant on the roof. Well played, Uncle Remy.'

Remy made a noise under his breath which suggested that if he was anyone else, he'd have been muttering *Vaer!* like it was a curse word.

'Right. But when I set him up with destroying what he thought was evidence of the harm he did your mother? You must have realised then I didn't want to work with him.'

'Consider it from my point of view,' Remy said. 'I hadn't made a deal with Bertrand, and I thought you were trying to. So confronted with this new, *horrible* information...' His face crumpled as his attempt to remain factual faltered in the face of what Bertrand had committed against Queen Leonore. In a small voice, he said, 'What could I do? He was already my enemy. It just made him more so, still without any way of proving it to Hughard and the rest.'

'I don't know if he found the evidence, after,' Feilan said, 'but if not, I'll hand it over to the Nivardus family. But don't read it until you're ready, and don't read it alone, svasa.'

Remy began to weep then, face pressed to Feilan's chest. Feilan held him tight, letting the grief wash through him. All those bleeding cuts Bertrand had left behind him. He'd never been so savagely glad to have killed someone.

'Thank you,' Remy said at last, stirring and wiping his reddened eyes. 'Not least for making sure no one doubts the judgement Adeline passed that night, and that she need never regret it herself.'

'Starting her reign right,' Feilan said, in Freyja's dry tones.

He earned a huff of faint, pained, amusement. 'Anyway. I thought you *had* to work with him, whether you wanted to or not. So I assumed you'd waved the proof about to force him to talk to you privately, at least so he could see what you had. Or that you were hoping *I'd* want to know more, and invite you back in. Either way, you could get to him and make the offer your mother wanted you to make.'

Feilan nodded, satisfied to have his suspicions confirmed. 'You heard me talking to Gytha.'

'I heard you talking to Gytha. I didn't mean to,' Remy hastened to add. 'I remembered we'd been overheard talking about the goat in my room, so I went down to the backroom, to make sure the servants weren't lingering, somehow eavesdropping. And the bells at the ends of the rooms' bellpulls are there, of course.'

'You can't listen along *rope*,' Feilan said, even as he remembered the unusual gilt braid woven into the bellpulls.

'The pipe the rope runs along is a conductor, perhaps. The bell was a sort of amplifying cup. I think...' He began to blush. '...they were probably listening to us having sex, and listening in on Torben in the expectation of the same.'

In lieu of anything too mouthy, Feilan said merely, 'Good thing our surfeit covered his lack, then.'

Remy coughed lightly, still flushed. 'Your and Gytha's voices came through clear as – well, clear as a bell. I wasn't sure what I was hearing, until you swore about it. That's when I realised what Freyja expected of you.' Remy shifted back to look him in the eye. 'I'm so sorry I assumed you were going to betray me. I know how you feel about that sort of thing. I should have known you wouldn't.'

'Ah,' Feilan said, and paused long enough for Remy's dark, still-damp eyes to transform from soulfully guilty to indignant. 'I did have to think hard about it before I decided not to.'

Remy flopped against him, face pressed to his shoulder again. Feilan let him think, enjoying the feel of him in his arms, and the warm sunshine. At least he wasn't storming off.

Eventually Remy said, 'I suppose that's better.'

'I would love to hear the theory on this one,' Feilan said with a grin.

'It was an order from Freyja,' Remy explained. 'You've been hers for twenty-five years. It would have been strange if you hadn't had to think about it. *That* might have just been whim, or pride, or...' He frowned. 'Sex, I suppose. But this way, you...'

'This way, I chose you.'

'Yes.'

'Remy, I chose you all the way back when I realised I could get out of the fake marriage with a word, when I still thought you were just a little shit who desperately needed help.'

'And you chose to be kind, as much as you hate to admit it.' He eased out of Feilan's arms, looking very earnest. 'I expect you will head south with the others?'

'Do you,' Feilan said.

'I'm happy for you,' Remy said. 'I know I was in quite the temper that morning and I can't claim none of it was because of Torben, but—'

'Right, yes,' Feilan broke in. He rather thought Remy had had far *too* long to think, on this occasion, and was very much trying to get out a speech he did not need to make. 'You saw me arguing with Torben—'

'I most certainly did *not* see you arguing with Torben,' Remy said, wearing the merest ghost of a smile.

Feilan raised a corrective finger, smiling back, surging with relief because it wasn't much of a smile, but it *was* a smile. 'You saw the *end* of an argument with Torben. It was... I feel a lot lighter now. I was holding on to something I didn't need to hold on to anymore, and it was good to let it go.'

'Good,' Remy said. 'I really am pleased for you.' Then he leapt right into the speech Feilan had suspected he'd lined up. 'Listen, I know you don't want me telling you I love you.'

Feilan opened his mouth, but Remy was already rushing on, even rising so he could better deliver his oration. Feilan, mentally shrugging, leaned back on the little ledge and let him.

'So I won't. But I do have to say something. You have been wonderful. I cannot tell you how relieved I was when I saw you in the doorway that night. I knew right then that everything was going to turn out. I could not have chosen better, when I chose you. Thank you for making me feel loved. I know you don't!' he added in haste. 'But, just – thank you for making me feel like you do. I needed it. I didn't know how much I needed it. To feel...to feel chosen by someone. I just wanted you to know that, before you leave.'

Feilan looked down the grassy slope to the humming bees, the browning patch of grass, and beyond, to the sun-drenched view. He said, 'That's the third time you've told me you know I don't do something, and the third time you've been dead wrong.'

'What?' Remy said, sounding satisfyingly dazed.

Feilan smiled. He repeated, 'Every time you tell me you know I don't do something, you're wrong. I *do* kiss, I *do* want to hear that you love me, I *do* love *you*.' He held out his hand. 'I know *exactly* how special it is, to feel chosen by someone, Remy.'

Remy made no move to take his outstretched hand. 'Oh,' he said. 'I see.'

'Right.' He dropped his hand and considered Remy with his head on one side. 'Why does it make you frown like that? Are you angry? Could you do me a favour and go think it over for a while? As long as you need.'

'I'm not angry,' Remy said. 'I love you, too. But you did know that, I think.'

'Still frowning. I expected more enthusiasm than this.'

Remy flashed him a darkling look. 'I'm not sure I can give you what you need.'

'Enlighten me, what do I need?' He raised his brows. 'Is this about Torben?'

'It's not...*not* about Torben,' Remy admitted. 'But more than that, it's an entire life and lovers who aren't in Seven Hills. You can't stay here, and I can't leave, Feilan!' The words were suddenly falling out of him, urgent and agonised, and he paced the grass. 'Adeline needs me, and the townsfolk need me, and *I* need to be with my family while we come to terms with what Bertrand did to us, and I *can't* be selfish now, I just *can't.*'

Feilan half-closed his eyes. It was, in a way, a conversation he might have had years ago, with another man who couldn't leave somewhere Feilan couldn't stay. But it was different now. *He* was different now.

'Hoi!' he said, interrupting what appeared to be approaching a right state. 'Rufran. You know how you're at my every whim?'

'That doesn't apply anymore!' Remy said, still agitated. Then, with an endearing mix of reluctance and curiosity, 'Yes?'

'My whim, then, which isn't really a whim: I want to stay here, with you, for as long as you want me.'

'Oh.' Remy was smiling helplessly back at him, making his heart swell painfully in his chest. 'Forever, then?'

'Come here and kiss me, minn svasa,' Feilan said, 'and remind us both that we're no longer exiled.'

By the Author

THANKS FOR READING. If you enjoyed this book, find more titles and bonus material at wendypalmer.au.

Standalones
Fair Haven

Vaer World
Domesticated Magic
Little Wolf and the Witch

Artisans
The Uses of Illicit Art
The Use of Myriad Arts

Mosaic Virus duology
Bastard's Grace
Six Feet of Ridiculous
Mosaic Garden: Stories from Aspermonde

The Domain trilogy
Wild Imperative
Cursed Girls
Lost Child

If you liked *Little Wolf and the Witch*, you might like *Domesticated Magic*, set some 200 years after Olvar the Bold conquers the continent:

Mateo Taurasi and his family fled their island home when their people turned to sorcery. Mateo's own magic is tame but it's still banned in the Vaeringan Empire...and his family still use it every day in their cosy teahouse. The last thing they need is an Imperial barging in to catch them at it.

Luckily, Jonas just wants to offer them a trade deal too good to resist. As hard as he tries, Mateo begins to find the cheerfully charming Jonas too good to resist, too.

But an unfairly attractive Imperial is not Mateo's only problem. Rumours of sorcery loose in the city mean trouble for the Taurasi. With Jonas caught up in the mess, Mateo must investigate.

His family already lost their world once. Mateo can't let them lose again. Not even if it costs him the man he *really* wishes he didn't have feelings for.

Read on for Chapter 1...

CHAPTER 1

ATEO WAS UP WELL BEFORE THE sun to dress in the formal robes for the morning ritual, and he was not happy about it. There was a reason it had become the morning ritual rather than the dawn ritual during his tenure as Soul of Kindred Taurasi, and a reason he'd refused the full regalia even before Anika had sold most of it off.

But it was the first ritual since the news had reached the Imperial port city of Anceral that Ysthera, the Sunlit Isle, had sunk to the bottom of the sea, forever lost. Sometimes sops had to be thrown to a frightened and grieving people, no matter how much they tried to pretend to him that they were not frightened and grieving.

Anika herself had brought the silk robes over from storage, and she stayed to help Mateo dress in the layers, and painted his face with the kohl and powders, and styled his hair into an elaborate coiffure that involved a good hour, a great deal of paste, and a fair number of pinned and looped braids.

Then he did the same for her, because if the Soul had to do it, so did the Heart, except her costuming was, unfairly, very much less extravagant.

By the time they crossed the misty street to the teahouse, Mateo's bad hip was already aching from the unfamiliar stress of the dressing palaver and the unfamiliar weight that was this awful ritual costume and the unfamiliar chill of being awake and moving this wretchedly early.

It was fair to say Mattias Taurasi, Soul of Kindred Taurasi, was not in the best of moods.

Anika, on the other hand, was looking very fetching in her silks and cosmetics and was her usual buoyant self—or at least, that was the self she presented to her people, when her buoyancy was needed to keep some eighty refugees afloat.

Darius, Anika's uncle, had left the teahouse shutters closed but lit the porch lamps, a golden glow against the light mist, and lit the interior lamps, and lit the fires in the big kitchen stove and in the small ceramic stove in the near corner, which was where Mateo went to stand, angling his hip to the radiating warmth.

He didn't rub the hip. Too many of his people were already here, kneeling on their cushions, the woven fabrics making bright squares of patterned colour against the polished parquetry.

Penelope came in. She was a Taurasi elder, inky hair stranded with silver but spine ever straight. She had been Heart before Anika and before Charion, who had been lost on the day of the exile. Penelope was perfectly pleasant, a stickler for tradition, and had a way of reminding Anika and Mateo that they were both a good ten or fifteen or even twenty years too young for their roles.

'Oh, don't you look lovely,' she said to Mateo when she saw him in the regalia. 'Very ceremonial today, that makes a welcome change.'

This, of course, was to point out that he usually did not look ceremonial at all.

'You could be wearing the status markers,' she suggested, touching her throat and her earlobes to indicate the lack of jewellery in those places on Mateo.

He looked around at the others. 'They…know my status, Penelope.'

'Always in such a mood in the morning,' she said, walking off to find her cushion.

'Well, *now* I am,' he muttered, unjustly, which merely proved her point and further annoyed him.

Anika had gone behind the counter into the small kitchen workspace and was reading the esoteric marks carved into the mossy-green wax of a tabula, picked from the top of a short stack. The little boxwood-framed tablets were used for sending messages throughout the city, in preference to the far more expensive innovation of paper.

As not only their Heart but one of the few literate Taurasi, Anika dealt with the Imperials, and the Imperials had learnt to be thorough administrators. A steady stream of tablets issued from the governor's residence and its associated army of clerical scribes, as well as from friends, customers and associates of the Come-By-Chance Teahouse. Anika wielded an iron stylus to carve her own marks—acknowledgements, replies, counterpoints—and dutifully sent them back.

Shaking her head, Anika rubbed the wax clean with the flattened wedge end of the stylus and dropped the offending tabula close by the kitchen stove where she brewed her herbal teas. The wax would soften in the heat, melting away any last trace of whatever unpleasant message the surface had held. That message, it seemed, would not be receiving a response, dutiful or otherwise.

It was typical, thought Mateo in his morning gloom, that Imperials took something as beautiful as pure beeswax, golden and gently scented, and polluted it into mossy darkness with resins and soot just to make it more useful to their own narrow needs.

Eminently pragmatic, were Imperials, in language, in dress, in worship, in food, and in their longstanding overlordship across the entire landmass from Chalcadea in the west to the city-states here on the east coast.

Anika set aside the rest of the tabulae for later attention. She came around the counter to stand on the lowest step of the short flight of stairs that led up to the storage room and her own private quarters.

That lowest step acted as the metaphorical equivalent of the village dais back on Ysthera. Mateo paced over to join her. The layered robes made his walk slow and stately, which was, now he thought about it, probably half the point of the blighted things.

He looked about the young and old faces upturned attentively towards him. Almost all the adult Taurasi were here today, emerging from the traditionally prescribed three days of private mourning and the rituals that went along with that. It hardly seemed adequate to mark the passing of an entire island and its people; certainly, none of the sole surviving Ystheran Kindred could truly be finished mourning.

But they had mortgages, and children to feed. The teahouse had to re-open to customers. Kindred Taurasi had to find its strength and move on, as it had done before, Anika its steadfast guiding light and unfaltering bulwark both.

Most of the Taurasi were kneeling on their cushions now, in ragged rows. They stared silently up at Anika and Mateo, their Heart and Soul, the very last Heart and Soul in all the world. The air felt heavy, the moment too significant.

Timon wolf-whistled, then, and the anticipatory tension broke. Anika laughed and took Mateo's hand, and they bowed together to their people, and their people, kneeling, made the genuflection in return. Most did it in the moderate way that Mateo preferred, if it had to happen at all, but Penelope and her faction lowered their foreheads all the way to the floor as per the oldest tradition.

Anika sighed, seeing that. She raised her voice into oration. 'We have taken a heavy blow,' she said, and the Taurasi murmured in return. 'We have all lost family and friends, far more permanently than we ever expected. I think we all thought we would go home one day, didn't we?'

Again came the murmur of agreement.

'We suffered when we made the decision to leave the island, and we suffered on the day of the exile itself,' she went on.

The Taurasi response was louder this time, and Andrea, Timon's twin sister, called, 'Aniketa the Unconquerable!'

'Yes, yes, all right, settle down,' Anika said, waving a hand. 'We suffered then, and we suffer now. Our Sunlit Isle, gone beneath the waves well over a week ago, and none of us felt a thing.'

It felt pointed; it wasn't, of course. But Mateo bowed his head, feeling the sting all the same. He was a Soul, blessed of their sleeping goddess. Shouldn't he have felt something when Ysthera cracked and all the other Souls were lost, their web of interconnection sundered forever? Should not something in him have cried out as most of their people were crushed or drowned in cataclysm?

Anika lifted her voice now. 'Yet we are Taurasi. We are strong, and we are brave, and we are resilient, and, most importantly, we are together. We will prevail.' She raised a fist. 'Kindred Taurasi!'

'Kindred Taurasi!' came the chorus, a throbbing echo that rang through the teahouse.

'That said,' she went on, quieter. 'We suffer, but we need not suffer alone. If anyone finds themselves awake in the middle of the night, ruminating on these things, you are always welcome to talk to me. Or Mateo.' She smiled at him. 'Though not today. We all know how Teo copes with mornings.'

The grouchy face Mateo helpfully pulled, and the resultant ripple of laughter, effectively shifted the mood towards a more normal morning gathering.

'Right.' Anika clapped her hands, signalling the final switch from leader to administrator. 'We were discussing sending our children to the temple school at the bottom of the hill. Do we have more to say or are we ready to vote?'

Penelope immediately rose. 'We must vote no. Our children would be indoctrinated into Imperial customs and the Imperial language and the Imperial worship of a truly profligate number of gods.'

'Yes, that's why they strongly encourage us to send our children to the local school,' Anika said patiently. 'Please bear in mind, when I say they strongly encourage us, it is on the threshold of being a mandate. They are merely playing nice, for now.'

That was probably the waxen message she'd deliberately obliterated, then.

'One of their mandates is no magic,' Timon pointed out. 'We defy that one.'

'Not openly,' Anika said, with a glance towards the door as if an Imperial spy might be eavesdropping. 'Nevertheless, it will be our burden, to ensure we do not sacrifice our children's heritage, if we decide in favour.'

This merely triggered the Ystheran tendency to be overdramatic. 'This is how they destroy us,' Penelope declaimed, to scattered applause. 'Not with swords to our throats but with words forcibly inscribed into the impressionable clay of our children's minds!'

It was Helena's turn to stand up. She was a mother, with three children of her own and another two fostered under her care. She'd allied into Taurasi, to a man now lost, and was nervous to address the whole Kindred. She smoothed her sash as she cleared her throat. 'I'm concerned... *We're* concerned'—she waved her hand, indicating the people on the cushions around her, mostly other parents, blood and foster, a few with babes in arms—'our children will not have the skills and knowledge they need to make their way in our new world, if they don't attend a local school. If we try too hard to save our past, we may be sacrificing their future instead.'

'Why can't we teach them ourselves?' someone demanded from the crowd.

'It's not enough,' Anika said. 'If we have to do it at all, better to send them down the hill and do it properly.'

Timon, absently scratching the welter of scars on his face, said, 'We left Ysthera to preserve our way of life. This won't help.'

His sister, herself wearing a scar through her left eyebrow, said, 'There is no going back to Ysthera, Ti, not anymore, if there ever was. We must face reality.'

'I know that,' he snapped. Anika raised a soothing hand, and his hackles settled. 'Ask the children what they want.'

Lucius rose. He was an adolescent, only recently old enough to attend the morning ritual. Ystherans didn't tend towards facial or body hair but Lucius was making a try, somewhat patchy, at growing a moustache in one of the varied local fashions. Like Helena, he was uncertain about addressing the group.

Fidgeting, he said, 'It's been really difficult finding work down in the city, not having been to one of their schools. Not knowing the customs. Not being even basically literate. Numbers. We should at least know how to tell numbers.'

He sat down in a hurry, signalling the end of his contribution. Penelope, who had not sat down yet, said, 'That is why we should be trying harder to be sure all of us can be gainfully employed within the enclave itself. You could apprentice to my workshop, dear. Learn the clay.'

'Please don't call us an enclave,' Anika reminded her. 'It makes the governor twitchy.'

Andrea said, sharply, 'Some of us like working down in Anceral.'

Selia, who also worked down in the brewery, added, 'Some of us are thinking of *living* down in Anceral.'

This got some audible gasps, and the discussion rapidly became acrimonious; someone again suggested hiring local tutors rather than consigning the children to a school out of Taurasi oversight, someone else snapped that that would bring strangers too intimately into their lives, whereupon there was a chorus of pointing out that the whole teahouse did that, every afternoon, and an answering outcry that Anika was managing that well enough and how else, exactly, were they to live if they did not cater to the Ancerans?

Anika pulled a slight face at Mateo but she let the rivulets of the argument run in their diverse directions; squabbles meant the Taurasi were moving beyond the first deep bite of grief. Eventually she clapped her hands again, calling for silence.

'I am hearing that it is too soon to make the vote,' she said serenely. 'You have all made good points. I know this is contentious. I know the diverging path forwards feels momentous, given Ysthera's fate and the precariousness of our own. There is no need to rush to a decision.' She raised a finger. 'But a decision must be made.'

She nodded once, signalling the end of the morning meeting, and the start of the morning ritual.

Every Ystheran held within themselves a sacred receptacle, the *scaphosieros* in the most archaic of terminology, to hold the magic that was the last gift of their shattered goddess, transmitted by their Soul during the ritualised daily libation.

The Taurasi who had been standing knelt again. Mateo moved among them, the silk hems of his robes brushing the swept wooden floor in a soft sibilance that echoed the gentle hum of the magic rising in him like water from a wellspring. He felt the tendrils of his kith's call, a gentle tickle as if of thin roots growing through welcoming soil, seeking nourishment.

He did not need to touch them to pass on the gift, but today he did. They were tense, and fractious, and scared. Ysthera was lost, and their fate was yawning underneath them, a hungry mouth ready to swallow them into oblivion should they slip from the narrow bridge Anika led them over towards an unknown future. Mateo laid hands on bowed heads or shoulders, murmuring words that were not strictly necessary, but served a purpose nonetheless.

He was aglow with the magic, and as it flowed out to the others, the teahouse filled with delicate amber light, its hue slowly deepening, thickening, a bowl of the purest golden honey. It was a marvel that no one without Ystheran blood could perceive.

'Let's practice the shield, everyone,' Anika called.

Traditionally, only the Coterie, those few chosen to gird the Soul, formed the defensive shield, but after the day of the exile, even Penelope and her fellow conservatists saw the sense of every Taurasi having some skill at interweaving into a larger communal working. There was precedent for it, after all, back when Penelope had been Heart.

Mateo returned to Anika's side. She had already taken her fill of magic, as had the twins, the other members of the Coterie. Mateo had once supported four in his Coterie. It was taking a long time to identify a suitable Taurasi to take up the fourth place, and the fifth place that Mateo now felt able to support as well.

He pushed the magic out, the trickle becoming a gush. The Taurasi caught at it and let it flow through them. The honey aura rippled and a cascading thrum rose louder and louder as they lifted the magic shield overhead.

'Modulate,' Anika called. 'Take more if you feel you can.'

The draw on Mateo increased as the kith obeyed, and the shield thickened. Anika looked at him, and he nodded reassurance; he was fine. He would have turned off the metaphorical tap if he wasn't.

'Remember when our Soul is flooding us like this, it is up to *you* to recognise when it is too much for you.' She put a flat hand to her sternum and then squeezed it slowly closed. 'Learn what too much feels like. Your heart will stop if you get this wrong, kith of my Kindred.'

She walked among the Taurasi, watching each face, looking for signs of strain. She also nudged a few into opening themselves further to take more of the flow. Sometimes Ystherans with small receptacles—pockets, somewhat derogatorily—assumed their access to the flow was correspondingly narrow, but that was not necessarily true. Nor did a Coterie-worthy receptacle mean immunity to the dangers of overflow. That was another thing hammered into Taurasi hearts on the day they'd made it off the island.

'Look up, Kindred,' Anika called. 'Is our shield not a thing of beauty?' It was, smooth as glass, thick as honey, translucent as purest amber. 'Well done, everyone. Release.'

The shield dropped and the hum and glow of the magic faded as Mateo let it sink away, back into the endless reservoir pooled deep within him. The Taurasi were relaxed, chatting and laughing now, some already heaping up their cushions in the corner by the stove and rolling out the tables and chairs for the afternoon customers, others lingering over their bowls.

They'd be moving towards their chores or their projects or their jobs soon, soothed by the magic and by the familiar ritual that furnished it to them. Anika had been right about wearing the robes, of course. The Taurasi had begun the slow process of healing from yet another cataclysm.

Mateo had served his people well today; he had time for a burst of satisfaction about that as he offered Anika a bow and started for the door.

Then the door opened and an Imperial walked in.